DEFY THE STARS

CATHRINA CONSTANTINE

Copyright © 2022 by Cathrina Constantine

All rights reserved. This book or any portion thereof may not be reproduced or used in any manner whatsoever without the express written permission of the publisher except for the use of brief quotations in a book review.

Cover and Interior Design by The Illustrated Author Design Services

Edited by Melissa Levine: Red Pen Editing https://www.red-penediting.net/

Wickedly Series
Wickedly It Begins
Wickedly They Come
Wickedly They Dream

Tallas Series
Tallas
Snow On Cinders

Incense and Peppermints
Wings of Flesh and Bones
Marly In Pieces
The Upside Down of Nora Gaines
The Omen of Crows Nest

Dedicated to All Souls who Defy the Stars…

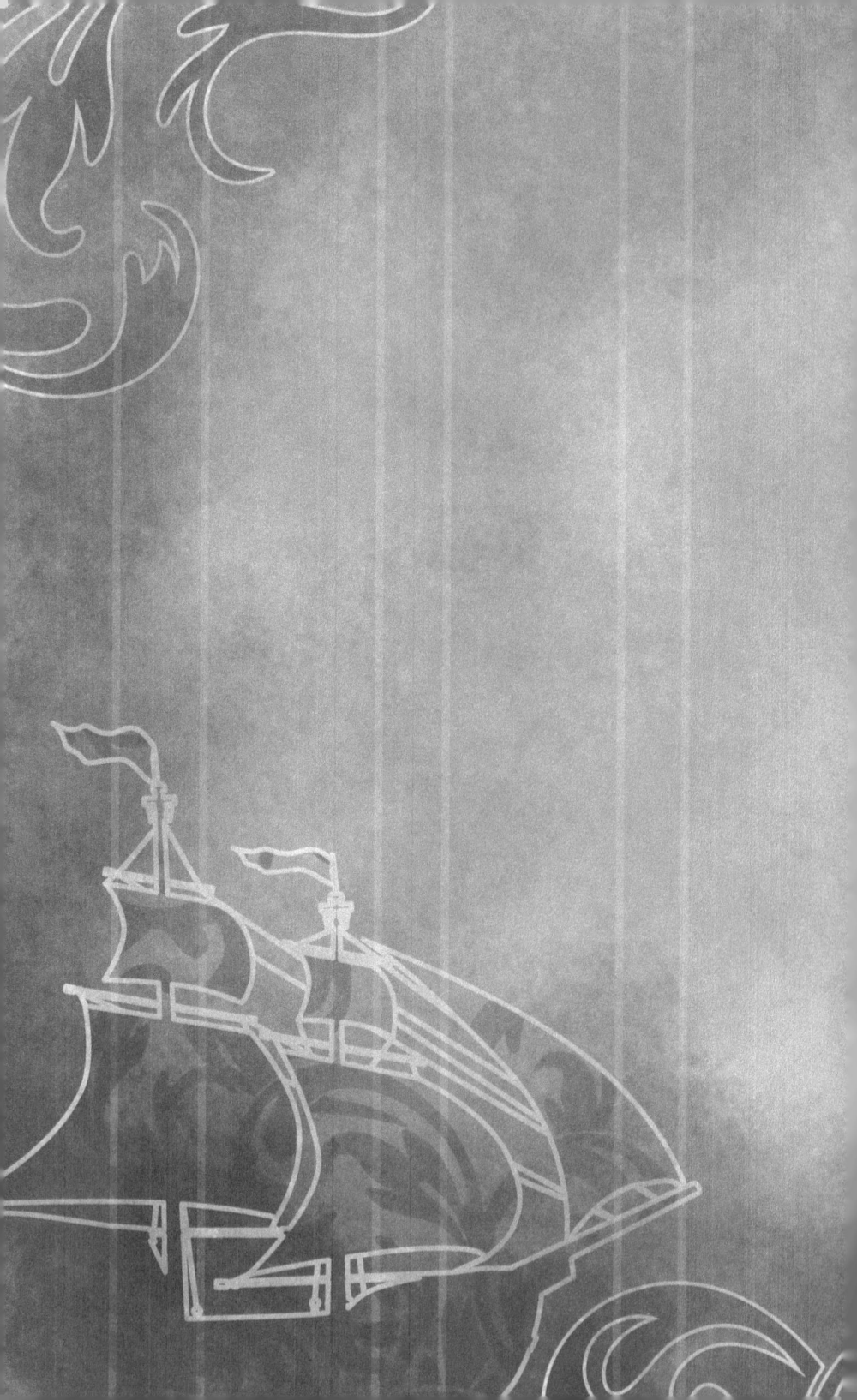

ONE
POLK

More than one will die tonight. Polk Asgard sensed it in his bones.

Polk slipped out his Derringer, a muzzle-loading caplock, single shot with a walnut stock. He pressed the barrel to his temple. Turning to his men, he said, "No snitches. One bullet."

"No snitches. One bullet," they mirrored.

Under sheets of darkness, Polk, Dirge, and Gavan prowled from the periphery of the woods to the Foundling Orphanage, which housed children of diversity. The bolted door was laughable. No contest for Polk's strength. Grating metal squealed like a stuck pig. Remaining motionless, they listened and lingered. If their entrance roused those in slumber, it would necessitate an alternative course of action. Which Polk would rather not implement. He hated destroying people as a whole, but it might become inevitable.

He'd been offered an exorbitant sum for one body. Preferably alive.

His benefactor provided vital information for his required specimens. One detail had literally been branded into his brain—never, on the penalty of a heinous death, snitch. The last person who made the grievous mistake of cooperating with the authorities had his skin sliced and peeled from his bones. His spine-chilling screams haunted Polk still.

If patrolling constables had the mettle to nab them, they may as well put a bullet into their own skulls. It'd be less painful and quick.

Apparently, their intrusion hadn't made a stir, and they crept into the building. He winced as stairs creaked underfoot. Coming to the upper level, Polk stalled to recalculate his bearings. At the end of the hallway was their goldmine.

He motioned for his men to stand guard as he stole into the room. A rocking chair sat near the window, a bookcase stacked with books and stuffed animals. Building blocks, toys, and a ragdoll. He peered over the railing into one of four cribs. There it was. His paycheck.

He fingered the vial of tonic in his pocket. *Can't have it wailing. One drip should do the trick.* He parted the baby's lips with the dropper and pressed the bulb.

The baby appeared ordinary. *What's so special about it?* Why would his benefactor want an infant and pay such an amount? It wasn't his business to question.

He grabbed the blanket hanging over the rocker. Gently, he tucked it around the chubby body. Lifting the baby, he clasped it to his chest. It cooed, and then settled into him. The tonic had kicked in.

Exiting the room, he shooed his men to lead the way. Regretfully, the headmaster, an ogre stepped out of the first room, blocking their route.

Dammit!

"What are you doing here?" the ogre said, clenching his words. Sighting the baby in Polk's arms, the ogre grew in stature, loosening a jangling growl. Using his arm like a battering ram, he clobbered Gavan in the nose. A cringe-worthy noise of cracking bones and splattering blood. Gavan fell. Dead by the looks of him. His boss never should have enlisted a mortal for this line of work. *Humans are easy kills.*

Before the ogre hazard a second lethal strike, Polk stuffed the baby into the arms of his partner, Dirge, and in doing so pushed them backward. Polk wasn't mortal like Gavan. His goliath frame was advantageous and challenging to overthrow.

In a fluid motion, Polk gripped the pommel of his dagger that was attached to his belt. Devoid of thought, he sliced through the ogre's jugular. A harkening scream came from the bedroom. The ogre's partner. He had wanted to avoid a calamitous situation and loathed when things went wrong. *Shit happens.* Lacking recourse Polk pivoted on point and flit his dagger. His aim true. Silencing her screams. Hurrying in, he ripped the blade from her heart and swung toward the dormitory across the hall. Some of the orphans might have awakened. He went in.

The job took longer than projected. After digging a grave by a shed and depositing a small corpse, they fled under the deepening shroud of twilight. Dirge had the baby secured in his arms, while Polk carried a young boy.

Once they made it to the hidden cove where they'd anchored their boat, Dirge opened his mouth. "I never seen you make a blunder like this." His gaze directed to the drugged boy who lay beside the infant on the deck of a sailing craft.

"Aye. When I went into the dormitory, the kid was awake. He wasn't afraid. Didn't cry, even when he saw the dagger stained with blood. His eyes…" Polk said breathily, recalling the child's expression.

"What about 'em." Dirge clutched the oars and put his bulk into rowing. Surrounded by blackness, their source of light were drizzling moonbeams. His rowing agitated peaceful waters, creating a rippling effect milling to the shore. "He a freak of nature or something? Maybe bossman has the wrong kid."

"Beats me."

Throwing the child overboard drilled into Polk's cranium like a vexing ice pick, and the best solution. Why *did* he take the boy?

Recollecting the scene in the dormitory, he'd swung the dagger toward the boy's throat. And he hadn't flinched. *His eyes!* In the murkiness, he could have sworn the boy's gaze brightened like hot embers. At that precise moment, he needed the boy to live, like he needed oxygen to breathe.

He was brought back by the wind stinging his cheeks. *I must have imagined it—picturing my own death.* A quiver grazed down Polk's spine as he scrubbed the sight from his eyes.

"Maybe I'm softening in my old age," Polk said. "The kid's a stray, nobody will care or look for him. And he's young, 'bout three or four. Can use him like one of our crew. Don't you think?" Polk didn't expect empathy from his cohort and didn't receive any.

"I don't like it," Dirge groused while hoisting the sails. "You should've gutted 'im like the others."

Polk instructed, "Set your sight to the northeast."

"Not that forsaken ice land?" Dirge bemoaned. A hulking troll, his hairless head pitched from shoulder to shoulder. "Without Gavan, it'll be rough when we slam into those choppy waters. This kettle will be thrashing."

"Just handle the rudder. I'll man the oars." Polk squinted into the coal-like night. Fortunately, scudding clouds unlocked a span of stars hanging across the sky, making it simpler to navigate.

Dirge manned the rudder and the craft glided over glassy water, heading for their destination. "Are you gonna tell him about the boy?"

Polk paused a beat, and said, "Not if I like breathing."

TWO
CREW

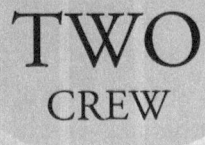

sixteen years later

Crew cranked the window letting out the suffocating smell of death.

"Why are you telling me this?" He bracketed his arms on the casement that overlooked Thistle Commons. A slate-gray fog had rolled in, wreathing evergreens and a network of trees. He stretched his shoulders to relieve his building fury.

Enslaving magicals and creatures into the mortal slave trade had been outlawed after the signed accords. And now, Polk informed him of a subversive brewing cauldron leaking underground, and he was, or had been, a main supplier.

"Polk, answer me." Crew turned from the morning view and fixed his sight on the big man, now shriveling by the hour.

"Don't look at me like that," Polk said, and coughed up phlegm. "I thought you should know for some dadgum reason. When conflicts between mortals and magicals intensified, the territories were apportioned with magical wards. The tollhouses made it difficult but not impossible to conduct business." Polk bit down on his lip. "I'm dying, Crew. There's nothing left of me. I'm a bag of rotting bones. This malignancy is devouring me from the inside out."

For months, Crew had been by Polk's side as he underwent treatment, but to little avail.

Polk's agony was coming to an end. He never was a moral father figure, nevertheless, Crew loved him. Watching the big guy wasting away, and rather than crumbling into a blubbering fool, Crew had manned-up by hardening his heart, not against Polk, against the disease.

Crew softened his stance and stepped to his bedside. "What do you want me to say?" Biting back a litany of expletives, he strived to calm his nerves which were like strings of a lute ready to snap. He pocketed his hands, discouraging them from ringing Polk's neck and finishing the job before the cancer did.

"You're a body snatcher for profit. You spared me and I'm supposed to be grateful?" he ground out and hated himself for being so brutal on the big guy. "What makes you think that baby you handed off to your benefactor is my brother?"

A grimacing frown settled on Polk's face. "We were granted an excessive commission for the tyke. When my benefactor cornered me and Dirge, he was livid because we couldn't deliver the answers he wanted. So, he traveled to the Foundling Orphanage and contacted the new, ummm…" Polk dabbed moisture forming above his mouth, "headmistress. The prior caretakers had been…er, murdered." Clearing his throat, he went on, "The headmistress had retained a ledger, and a report of two boys, brothers, had been abandoned on the orphanage's porch. And it was those two boys that had been taken."

Crew felt stricken. Once upon a time, he'd been part of a family. Why did his parents leave them at the orphanage? What kind of people would throw their kids away? How different his life might have been?

"Wait a second." Crew tugged on his earlobe. "This guy you call your benefactor must have deduced you took two boys. Does he think it's a coincidence when I suddenly cropped up as your son. He can't be that daft."

Polk shut his eyes. His hands trembled, clutching his blanket. "Polk? Are you all right?"

"They found the older brother," his words slurred together, "buried in a shallow grave on the Foundling property."

Confused, Crew said, "*What?*"

"I hope the gods forgive me and Dirge for what we did." Polk's eyes welled. "We went into the orphan's graveyard and dug up a boy that just died of influenza. We buried him where they'd find the grave. He looked sorta like you. I had to make it look good, aye, so I twisted his neck like we killed him. Crew, he was already dead. I didn't hurt him any. We had to do it, to protect you."

"You mean to protect *you* and Dirge." Seconds passed into minutes as Crew deliberated. Polk's story was crazy. No one would believe it.

"I have a *brother*—somewhere out there." Perplexed, he turned back to the window, his pulse quickening. *A brother. I have a brother.* Feeling a sense of urgency, he said, "I have to find him."

"He might be dead." Polk was quick to remark. "I wouldn't go off half-cocked searching for him."

"What makes you think he's dead? You said he was a few years younger, maybe sixteen, seventeen by now."

Lethargy and sickness had carved deep into Polk's body and his heavy breathing embodied the room. "My benefactor... he's a scientist. A wizard, a doctor that...that... experiments."

"Like a barbaric Doctor Frankenstein?" Thoughts of his little brother living with such a man had turned the eggs and bacon into a brick that he'd eaten earlier. "Sounds like a sick maniac."

"He's a genius. Someday that sick maniac will find a cure for what ails me." Polk passed a hand across his chapped lips, which were ebbing of pigment like the rest of his skin that had been stripped of color. "My team and I go into the magical territories and beyond. Scouting for anybody that resembles a specimen the wizard might be interested in. There's instances when he tells us who and where we need to go. Like when—"

"Like when you found me?" Crew prompted.

Polk lowered his gaze. "That was during the discriminating feuds and before those nonsensical accords. The treaties didn't reduce the slave trade. They enriched it. More coin to be had."

Crew drew in a breath and exhaled before saying, "Your benefactor is a slave trader, aye? And you were neck deep into this shit? Taking faeries, pucks, elves, pixies, sprites, goblins—"

"Egads, not goblins. Never goblins."

"Creatures. Nonmagical and magical," he went on despite Polk's interference. "And you're a giant. Isn't that ironic? Marketing creatures to become indentured servants to mortals." Crew's heart was racing, what if Polk was right about his brother? And he was already enslaved or dead. "Your benefactor thinks we're all expendable." His lancing gaze struck the big man. "What does he do to them? I mean, *before* these creatures voyage across the sea to be sold?"

"What the hell, Crew." Squeezing his eyes, Polk massaged his brow. "I'm neither a doctor nor his assistant. He pays well. You haven't complained, living affluently whenever the Faire is on hiatus." Polk pulled on the collar of his nightshirt as if it were strangling him. "Hey, don't get your shorts in a knot; most creatures capitulate. Those that the doc feels aren't marketable, they end up working for—"

"The Circus Faire," Crew uttered. "What about the creatures who aren't marketable and *don't* capitulate?"

"It's wiser and healthier to yield." Polk picked imaginary lint from his blanket.

Crew should've figured it out sooner, much sooner. Not necessarily equating that Polk and his cronies were body snatchers.

When Polk brought him into the fold, Crew felt like an outcast. Little had he realized that he'd remain an outcast because of Polk. While working the Faire he'd sensed inklings of nefarious undercurrents. Rumors had been circulating behind the trappings of the performances, though, he'd remained aloof to whatever was taking place. It took years of hard labor, working alongside them before they'd begun to trust him.

"It's not all bad," Polk reasoned. "They make a decent wage and travel places where they'd be ostracized. They *are* freaks of humankind."

Crew scraped his nails across the nape of his neck, digging into his skin. "Like you. Like me! Freaks."

"You're different. You look mortal. You do your job, kid, and you do it well. Nobody would be the wiser, and why I never told a soul where you came from. Dirge knows, but he'd never snitch—never." Polk rested his head against the pillow, each physical effort strenuous. "The wizard thinks you're my son. I swore to him, you knew nothing about the business. Nothing. If he heard differently you and I would be six feet under." Polk fidgeted, propping himself up and groped with shaky fingers for the water glass on the nightstand.

Crew assisted him by positioning the glass in his hand. And, citing the Circus Faire's Ringmaster, said, "Is Dyke in on the action?" He watched, as the once well-known strongest man in the world feebly brought the rim to his parched lips.

After wetting his throat, Polk replied, "Not exactly. Dyke knows better than to ask questions. He does what he's told. Keeps the wheels oiled, so to say. Hey, if it makes you feel any better." He patted his chest. "I'm a freak, just like the rest of 'em. Under these bones house a bloodline of misfits. My father was a giant and my mam a troll. They died when I was in breeches, and I was raised as a foundling like you. The headmaster was an abusive demon. But it made me stronger. Bet you didn't expect to hear that." His mouth pursed into a lipless grin.

"Aye, you're jumping on the freak wagon?"

"My benefactor, he's seen you. Working at the Faire. He wants to set up a meeting."

"For what?" Crew took the empty glass from Polk's hand and set it on the nightstand, and flicking his finger, the empty glass refilled with water. It unnerved him to think a wizard had been keeping sights on him.

"To take over where I left off." Drawing his brow, Polk's fingers rounded his neck. He'd been suffering from cankers in his throat.

The notion of becoming a wizard's lackey felt bitter on Crew's tongue. Moreover, murder and kidnapping weren't in him. Polk shifted on the mattress and his face contorted. How much time did the big guy have? A week? By the appearance of his hollowed eyes and parchment-like skin stretching over his bones, he figured the grim reaper would be making a visit very soon.

"I know you can't stomach the thought," he squeaked out, the malignancy robbing him of his voice. "It could be an opportunity to find out about your brother. See if he's alive. You have the power to get into the benefactor's head."

When Crew woke this morning, he hadn't expected Polk's final confession. Affirming that he wasn't his biological father, that was and wasn't a shocker. He never acted like one. Polk cared for him, and Crew believed the big guy loved him too. "Things are changing, aren't they?"

"I left a will. You'll be provided for. At least for a while. It won't last forever, though."

"I might have a brother out there—somewhere. Alive or dead," Crew said. "I have to find out what happened to him." Musingly, he chewed on the tender skin of his cheek. His eyes flared, peering at Polk. "I won't kill anybody." The thought stiffened his body.

Polk wiggled a loose wrist, ridding it of numbness. "Just meet with him. Listen to what he has to say. Then, I'll croak knowing you'll be taken care of."

"How much does he know about me?" Crew didn't like to dwell on the big guy's passing and pressed the burdening emotion from his brow.

With each breath, Polk's wheezing lungs sounded like an out of tune jukebox. "You might recognize him; he comes often to the Faire."

"Go on." Crew knew he was being hard on him. Polk was a lying scoundrel, a cheat, a murderer, and if Crew dug into his background, he'd unearth plenty of filth. He was angry because Polk was leaving him, alone, again. But this time, he wouldn't be coming back.

"I didn't tell him where you came from, honest."

"Aye, because he would've gotten rid of me and you years ago."

Polk didn't have a witty comeback. "I told him your mother left you on my doorstep with a note saying you was my kid."

"He believed that?"

Polk grunted. "He didn't question. Why else would he want to meet you?"

"If he's seen me, then he knows we look nothing alike."

"You're tall and big like me; that's enough, ain't it?"

Crew returned to the window. Linking his arms behind him, he watched a horse and buggy trundling through Thistle Commons. Since Polk's diagnosis, he'd been pondering his future. Age wasn't a factor, nor money at the moment. His gig at the Circus Faire provided him with shelter and amusement and they paid traveling expenses. What kind of deplorable mess would he be getting himself into with this wizard? Would he be able to locate his brother? What if the doctor had already used him for one of his noxious experiments, and his brother were dead, what then? *I don't have the killer instinct—or do I.*

"By the way, the Faire is setting up in Alderwood," Polk rasped, breaking into Crew's pondering. "I remember when we was there. It was the first time you ever talked to me about a certain girl."

Sage. He remembered. *It's been a while.* He'd been young and she was even younger. Classical fae, no matter what skin color, were too impeccable for his tastes and often hid their emotions. Nevertheless, he'd been attracted to Sage and her sweet innocence. She hadn't gotten into his face or tempted him with her charms like the others. Besides, he was the charmer. Spellbinding people with his eyes and then pitching his voice to compel them to do his bidding. With Sage it had backfired, and she'd charmed him without trying.

"She's not fae," Polk stated. "Hard to judge sometimes." His gaze sought Crew, seeking a response, but the boy kept his backside to him. "She lives in a district consisting of low fae, interspersing with pucks and whatnot. Like a carnival of misfits. An ideal setting to take someone where the authorities turn a blind eye. She doesn't resemble her siblings. Not with that hair and skin tone."

"You investigated her?" Crew spoke into the pane of glass, his consonants bouncing back at him. He spun from the view of the park. Polk had sunk into the mattress and was bringing the blanket to his chin.

"I had to. The doc wanted information about her lineage. And the funny thing was I kept coming up short."

"What about it?"

"The wizard has an interest in her. Has for years. Perhaps he saw something in her that fascinated him. I knew you had a soft spot for the girl, so back then, I turned his attention elsewhere. Now that the Circus Faire is in Alderwood again, he won't have me to dissuade him. If you play your cards right, you might be able to use your persuasive talents to find your brother *and* save the girl."

THREE
SAGE

A far-off cry caught Sage's ear. She made her way outside of *Galdoons* to investigate. Others had also paused on the walkways, hearing the heralding voice.

"The Circus Faire is coming! The Circus Faire is coming!" trumpeted Darney Galdoon. He was flying low, parallel to the ground, clawed toes scoring the dirt lane and flagging a pamphlet that was showering sparks.

"The Circus Faire is coming!" Over and over, broadcasting his refrain until he flew past Sage and banked into an immense hollowed redwood with an attached sign that read: *Galdoons*. Sage followed him. Darney furled his gossamer wings and sailed onto a toadstool. He panted an excited toothy smile that reached his ochre eyes, and his hands shook as he handed the pamphlet to his father standing behind the counter.

The sprites keenness was contagious as Sage reclaimed her seat, holding onto her own a smile.

"I spotted it being tossed about in the sky and sparks were shooting out of it," Darney said, squiggling like a jitterbug.

His father stared at the pamphlet. A circus tent began to blossom from the pliant canvas in a kaleidoscope of colors and shooting multicolored fireworks.

"Well, looky here," Fergan Galdoon said, captivated by the pamphlet. Setting it on the counter for all to marvel, he twisted the tips of his green handlebar mustache. Short and plump in stature, his ochre eyes matched his son's. "Darney, you was but a wee babe of three when the Circus Faire made its last appearance. I hope you aren't believing all those fantastical tales. Those have a habit of growing out of proportion like granny's pumpkin patch."

"Sage, look!" Darney swiped the pamphlet from the counter and swiveled on the toadstool toward the girl sitting next to him. She was attired like a hunter: breeches, doeskin moccasins, a sheathed dagger hung from a belt, and a bow strung over her shoulder. The girl tossed a thick braid, the color of saffron, over her shoulder, and violet eyes twinkled in her olive-skinned face. She graced young Darney with a smile. "Did you see this?"

"I did, Darney," Sage admitted, peering at the sprite with spikes of scarlet hair. When the news had reached her, butterflies had developed a fondness for attacking her stomach. The sparkling watermelon soda she'd been sipping prior to his interruption had lost its appeal. "I hope you're doubling up on your chores; you'll need lots of coin to play games."

"And the rides!" he said enthusiastically, and then addressed his father, "Can I sweep the floor for an extra copper?"

Fergan sent a conspiratorial wink to Sage. "Sure, Darney. Then you can haul water from the spring and bring it to mama." Fergan reached behind him to a counter displayed with decadent cookies. Wrapping two in brown paper, he said, "Here, Sage, a sweet treat for your little sister and one for you. And the rabbits are much appreciated. Stop by and see the misses when you get a chance and stay for supper. She simmers a hearty hasenpfeffer stew."

"How many in your brood now?"

Fergan positioned an index finger on his bottom lip and raised his eyes toward the barked dome of *Galdoons* before saying, "Six. The seventh anticipated any day now."

"A lively home, I imagine."

"It's the bestest," Darney declared, hopping off the toadstool.

"Thank you, Fergan." She slid her cup of watermelon juice on the counter. "I'd best be getting home. Bye, Darney."

"See you at the Circus Faire!" Darney said as he worked the broom's bristles over the planked floor.

Sage made her way through the main square of Alderwood. A woodlands valley village settled on the fringe of the Saarnak Mountain range, and due to the imminent attractions of the Faire, it was pulsating with energy. Dozens of pamphlets had arrived within the past few days. News had spread into the harbor township of Foundling and beyond, where pamphlets had also been distributed. The grand event had tongues wagging. Even the oppressive taxes recently issued by the king's regent had been swept under the rugs.

On this sunny afternoon, faeries and pixies skirted above, more fae and creatures than usual wandered through the rural village. Sage's friend, Marne hailed from the coachmen carriage wheeling by. Wagons lined the side of the road near Apostle's Mercantile, the only merchant for miles. And a line was forming on the walk leading into Morgana's. With the Circus Faire pending, Alderwood's seamstress would be swamped with rush orders.

Farmers had penned in sows, chickens, and other livestock, and crates abounding with the first harvest of tomatoes, beans, potatoes, and onions. The resident hedge witch, Urian, had a booth hosting a hodgepodge of herbal remedies and tonics. Men and boys took their leisure around the Smoke Shop, toking pipes and tobacco and drinking bubbly birch beer. Sage recognized Chevil, a mage physician, driving a phaeton carriage and heading past the square into the low valley.

Since the announcement of the Circus, Sage's heart had been aflutter with thoughts of Crew. Their first kiss and the ones that followed had filled her dreams. She licked her lips as if tasting him still. That happened three years ago when she was fourteen and naïve. Back then, Crew had promised, and literally crossed his heart, to return. She'd pined after him like a lovesick dolt, and at fourteen her hormones had been irrepressible.

Months after the Faire's departure, she'd scoured the Chronicle Edition for an article of the enigmatic carnival. In the entertainment segment, an editorial regarding the Circus Faire's voyage across the Sea of Tears. As months rolled into years, her dreams of ever seeing him again had dwindled.

Crew had taken a piece of her heart. She frequently ruminated about those magical weeks and still felt deeply connected to him, a connection that transcended time. *Did he ever think of me? Of course, he does.* Because she'd stolen a piece of his heart too, and it beats fervently with hers.

"Sage," called Gart, a neighbor from down the lane.

Earlier, Sage had opened the top half of the door to let in the mornings essence of jasmine. A gangly faun with a friendly disposition leaned on the Steele's white-washed door. He fingered his starched high neck collar of his shirt and then tugged on his linen waistcoat, visibly uncomfortable. "I heard the Faire arrived sometime during the night. Setting up in Planker's clearing. I'm heading there now, want to come?" His dark-brown complexion gleamed in the morning light, adorning his scrolled horns on the sides of his head.

"I can't." She removed a spray of shrunken daisies from a fruit jar and went toward Gart. "I'm watching Eadith. Marne and I are heading there this afternoon."

"It'll be mobbed by then." His nose tweaked, catching a scent. "Want me to get rid of those flowers for you?"

"Um, no. I'll put them in the mulcher."

He tapped his knuckle on the doorpost as if his work there were done. Hurrying off, his feet left cloven prints in the clay-laden lane.

Her chat with Gart pulled on her nerves. The entire village would beat her there while she was trapped at home. Her brother Parry had no intention of going to the Faire this day. Mama knew how excited she'd been and should have asked *him* to watch Eadith.

Retrieving a canning jar, she added fresh water and inserted the stems of the dead daisies. The bouquet wilted along the rim like limp tassels. She fiddled with the arrangement until satisfied, then spread her hands over them. Each stem sucked up the water and stiffened upright. Withered petals unfurled and whitened, blooming to new life.

She dusted her hands on her apron and carried the jar to the table and groaned. A note from her parents was front and centered: *Make sure Eadith eats breakfast. Edras promised to pick her up by ten. Have fun at the Faire.* An addendum, she recognized Papa's printing: *Make sure your brother trims.* Ugh!

"Hey, dung breath." Sage's good morning to Parry. Her brother dashed for the door, clinching a scuttleball under his arm. "Papa says you have to trim." Parry lolled his head around his shoulders with an animated eye roll his as if she'd asked him to slaughter a hog for dinner. "Just do it," she said.

"I'll pay you to do it for me." His sharp teeth showed through his coaxing grin. Parry had inherited Mama's dark brown skin and fine puce hair, a Gwain trait. His shorn mane exposed minor points to his ears. An inaptness believed the fae, whose beauty was proven to be unrivaled. High-bred fae vaunted exquisite, pointed ears. Parry's ears also sported a tuft of puce hair which made up for his lack of curvature.

In retrospect, not all fae had the orthodox points to their ears. Mama was born across the sea, now strictly human territory. The Gwain clan had relations with mortals. Over a span of decades, their offspring had reduced their well-formed ears.

Fae relations with mortals, while offensive, was decreed unpunishable. Mortals hadn't any magic to speak of and considered weak. On the opposite spectrum, relations with magical interspecies was forbidden. Activating an imbalance of power and punishable by imprisonment or execution as proclaimed by King Vektor of the High Court of Hawkswing.

Parry expected her to bite the hook he dangled because he knew her too well. Coins. She'd need plenty if she planned on spending every day and night at the circus. "How much?"

"Two."

"Not worth it." She dismissed his offer with a brush of her wrist and bent to get the grill out of the cabinet.

Parry's furry tail swished as he moseyed around the kitchen. Angling his body over the table, he beat his fingers on the surface while reading the note. His ears twitched. "Four, then."

"Nope." She retrieved homemade waffles from the icebox and popped two onto the grill to toast.

He repositioned the ball beneath his other arm. "Hey, Pops doesn't say anything about pulling weeds, so it's a cinch job."

"Six and you got a deal," she bartered.

"Cripes, Sage, you drive a mean bargain. Would you pull weeds too, or else he'll make me do that tomorrow."

She was about to say sure, but then thought of another two or three coppers she could shake out of him to rid the weeds. "I won't have time. After Edras picks up Eadith, I'm going to the Faire."

"It's not even open yet."

"There's no law against watching," she said, growing impatient with this banter.

"I heard rumors the village council wasn't issuing them a permit."

"When has a permit ever stopped the Circus Faire?" said Tegan, their eldest brother walked into their conversation. Similar to Parry, he had a short tail, but unlike his brother, Tegan kept it concealed. Tegan resembled Papa with waves of caramel-shaded hair that branched over two nubby horns that rode on either side of his forehead, which Parry coveted for himself. He'd said on occasion, *They make Tegan look badass.* Built sturdier than Parry, his broad shoulders pulled at the seams of his shirt owing to hard labor in the copper mines.

His toffee-colored eyes, went from Sage to Parry. "It comes and goes like ghosts in the night. Popping up wherever and hoist their tents. That's the legend of the Circus Faire. People crave the distractions, and they employ some of the village kids." He pinched a waffle from the grill. "Sage, he won't be there."

"Hey, those aren't for you." She lunged, but not quick enough to snatch it out of his hands. He slathered honey on the fluffy goodness, and not bothering with utensils, rolled the waffle like a cigar and jammed it into his mouth.

"Who are you talking about?" she said, as heat crept into her cheeks.

Tegan spoke around a mouthful. "That guy you've been talking about as if he were the best thing since mama's acorn dessert. I worked with him, remember? Crew said he was scraping the *shi*…manure off his boots." His head turned toward Eadith, their youngest sister, coloring in a book on the couch.

Tegan had been hired the last time the Circus Faire had astounded them, by Dyke, the head honcho and Ringmaster. He'd assigned tasks to the youngsters seeking work, such as mucking animal cages, sweeping, and trash removal. Menial chores.

"He grew up in the circus. Where would he go?" Sage's heart flipped with thoughts of never seeing him again. "He'll be there." Her voice was laced with tenuous conviction.

"He said something about a university in the Unified Territory."

"He mentioned it, but I didn't think he was serious." She plated a waffle and cut it in sections and poured maple syrup overtop. "Crew said the circus was in his blood and liked traveling. See's things we'll never see. I heard stories of modern conveyances and things of wonder in the Unified Territory." Sage often dreamt of traversing beyond the wards. "He loves it."

"I warned you," Tegan washed his fingers under the waterspout, "to stay away from him. Carnie's are full of unabashed promises."

"Evidently the council gave them a permit." Parry backtracked their discussion. "There would be nothing to look forward to in this godforsaken village."

"The folks around here want the Faire," Tegan reasoned. "Kids get paid for drawing in crowds from neighboring hamlets, and they have a blast. I remember the council threatening Dyke; I was there when—"

"It's because of those missing persons," Sage barged in.

"You better give that waffle to Eadith before it gets cold," Tegan said. "Hey, Eadith, come and eat." Her tiny wings unraveled and she soared off the couch to the table. "Didn't Mama scold you for doing that?" He nipped her freckled nose with the knuckle of his finger. "Not in the house."

As if moving to a musical beat that were all hers, she shimmied her petite shoulders. In a sing-song voice, she said, "Yeah…yeahh…yeahhh…" Lengthening her syllables she cast them a childish beam, which always had the result of turning frowns into smiles. Eadith turned her sights to her waffle.

Parry juggled the scuttleball from hand to hand. "I have to admit, weird things happened after the Faire left without warning. Didn't Conklin Biggs go missing and Apostles Mercantile was robbed?"

"Good riddance to Conklin, that smelly ogre." Sage held a dishrag to clean sticky syrup from Eadith's face and fingers. She rinsed the dishrag under the waterspout, and as an afterthought said, "It could have been an outsider that robbed Apostles. Anybody can cross the boundaries easy enough."

"The tollhouses and the accords are a joke," Parry agreed. "People are saying the wards have been weakening, a glitch in fae magic—I think not."

"Come on, Par," Tegan's mocking chuckle vibrated his chest. "Don't be daft. High fae are crossing to see what's to be had in the Unified Territory. The restrictions don't apply to them only to us peons. If there's a glitch, it's there for a reason."

"Sounds like espionage to me." Parry twerked one of his eyebrows. "Aren't militia patrolling the boundaries?"

Sage confirmed, "High fae can handle them."

"There's been a few incidences, but…" Tegan didn't elaborate and forked his fingers into waves of caramel hair which parted over his pointed ears. He continued, "Debating about the wards, tollhouses, and the accords has been a font of contention. Rumors of racketeering mortals sneaking into the territories have folk on edge. And reports of abductions are on the rise again."

"Why would the council allow that to happen?" Sage asked.

"Money is always the root of all evil. Or a favor-for-a-favor-type deal. Who knows?" Tegan pulled on the cuffs of his long sleeves.

"Hey, I'm late." Parry vamoosed before the tide changed against him, to play or whatever he did with his friends, letting the door slam behind him.

Tegan yelled, "Don't let the door hit you in the ass."

Eadith giggled and Sage tutted.

"Edras won't be here for a while, and I promised to meet Marne at quarter past noon. Can you keep an eye on Eadith while I trim?"

"You got suckered in again." Tegan's cocky grin sat on his comely face. "I'll give you half an hour. I have to be at the mine soon. Hurry it up."

Pesky gnomes had an affinity for raiding their gardens to stock their larders. The weeds camouflaged the thieving rascals, and why Papa insisted on trimming, and the worst part, he wouldn't let them use magic.

With her chore accomplished, Sage trudged into the back hollow of the cottage. Her sister, Edras was in the throes of hustling Eadith out the front door. Edras turned toward her, and Sage marveled at her sister's flawless beauty and emerald-green eyes. Her auburn hair, twisted into a bun, rode the nape of her neck. Even in a plain black-and-white-gingham dress and a muslin apron overtop, she out bested all the females in Alderwood.

"Parry did it again, I see." Edras gave Sage's perspiring face a once over and the corner of her mouth quirked. "What did you trade for. Coins?"

Sage shrugged, pressing her lips together. "Papa wanted Parry to do it because he's a loafer and lacks responsibility."

"Franse still won't let you use your talents?"

"Sometimes, but you know how he is," Sage said.

"Franse is a true believer that hard work molds character."

To her sister, Franse and Isla Steele had simply been their caretakers. Good and decent fae who took them in, nothing more. When Edras had reached her seventeenth season, she'd moved into a cabin in the woods, not far from the Steeles or her sister, Sage.

"I could have shrunk the grassy weeds with a simple nose twitch." Sage brushed the weedy clippings from her apron. "As easy, and as fast as taking a breath."

Edras's mouth flattened into a stern line. "Don't blow it, Sage." She lowered her voice. "If you get caught, you're not only jeopardizing yourself, but the entire family—those people you call Mama and Papa."

"Just magic, right?" Sage nonchalantly twitched her shoulder. "That's what fae would see and think. Why do we have to hide—"

"*Just magic?* The Steels aren't…" Edras disrupted her own tirade. "Eadith." She looked down at the faery munchkin.

"Wait for me outdoors." Their little sister skipped outside, and Sage knew she was in store for one of Edras's tongue lashings.

Sage crossed her arms and willed herself into a mask of neutrality, underneath she was peeved. Her sister was a real stickler. Forever telling her what to do and what not to do.

Edras pushed her face within a nose length of Sage, her scowl too close for comfort. "You know the danger. These fae are inferior, with *limited* magic." She paused and withdrew a few inches. Her ire presented itself in her hot-pepper cheeks. "I've trained you better than this. Our *magic*, that you call it, doesn't entail spells or incantations, you know this. The power is within us." She thumped her hand to her chest. "It's a mere thought that can activate our energy, our power. I suppose we can fool people some of the time, but not all of the time. We can't have them getting suspicious of us. Keep it intact for when there's a real crisis."

"A *crisis*? Why have these talents and not use them?"

Edras squeezed her eyes, taking in a profound breath. "Dolorans are still being hunted. Mortals and magicals are fearful."

"Why are they afraid? The fae have their magic."

"It's not the same. They believe we're inherently evil." Her gaze moved around the room making sure no one was home. "Dolorans did terrible things during the conflicts. Tales of eviscerating bodies, those who wouldn't conform, or bow down to their usurpers. Dolorans suppressed magicals *and* mortals, taking territories by force."

"*Pfft.* That's ancient history. We are not monstrous assassins," Sage said imprudently, deeming herself with a moral code of ethics. "I'd never hurt anybody. Not on purpose anyway."

Edras' task was to teach Sage their Doloran talents, and its potential of producing both good and bad energy. Her sister's unyielding monologue was constant: Never—even under duress—speak of their lineage. That admonition included the

Steele family. However, Sage had the proclivity of bending her rules.

"Fae and mortals say otherwise." Edras scoffed. "History has a way of repeating itself. Let's catalogue a couple of *your* misadventures. That boy didn't trip and tumble into that thorn bush because he thought it'd be a hoot."

"You mean, Cal." Sage rubbed her rueful brow. "He's a pathetic bully. Beating up kids. I gave him what he deserved."

In an accusing tone, Edras said, "What about when Eadith inadvertently flew into a vendor's stall. Instead of havoc and shattered pottery, every object was undisturbed as if nothing happened. You stopped time, didn't you?"

"It was my fault. So, I righted everything," she justified. "I'm not vindictive."

"If Mage Orv were alive, he'd be pensive of your ripening talents." Mage Orv was legendary. And Edras liked to tell Sage stories of his exploits. A formidable magesmith and a Doloran, who died with their parents during the genocide. Edras meditatively passed the back of her fingers under her chin. "Sister, be careful—please."

"I wish you still lived with us, here, with the Steeles."

Edras' strict features softened. "I like my cozy cabin in the woods, thank you very much. Besides, they don't need another mouth to feed, and I could never bring myself to call them Mama and Papa. You were only a baby when they took us in."

Eadith banged through the door. "When are we going?"

"Hey, munchkin." Sage tousled her fingers into the girls curly head of hair. "Be good for Edras."

Holding onto Eadith's hand, Edras said, "At least you have the infamous Faire. To while away your days and nights for a few weeks."

"*Infamous?*" she said, shedding a questionable look. "That's a peculiar description."

A wicked grin slipped onto her sister's face. "Sage, how old are you? Seventeen, going on eighteen, now?"

"You know I'll be eighteen during the next harvest."

"You've come of age beautifully." She absently smoothed her hand over Eadith's russet curlicues. "I predict this summer you'll reach new heights. May I suggest visiting Madam Rouge, the oracle's tent." She threw her a smug wink.

FOUR
CREW

Polk was in pain. Morphine might alleviate his misery. Crew pulled his tweed newsboy cap over his forehead and hustled to the apothecary by going through Thistle Commons toward Finnick Row, where a person could purchase just about anything and everything—for a price.

Despite obtaining treatment across the border in the Unified Territory, Polk wanted to die on the non-mortal side of the boundaries, where restrictions were lax. Polk once proclaimed mortal doctors weren't as considerate as mage physicians or an herbalist witch, and desired to expire on his own terms.

Polk's malady had waylaid Crew's plans. He'd enrolled at the University of Frenburg and had been accepted, only to withdraw to nurse the big guy. They'd travelled with the Circus until Polk's weakening body wasn't fit or able to appease the spectators. Or aid in assembling and dissembling props and whatnot, which made him obsolete.

Dyke had said, "Polk, it's time to take that long-awaited vacation. Rest my friend." He'd clapped Polk on the back as if he were a thoroughbred horse, sending him out to pasture.

Presently, stringing between vendors' stalls full of sought-after goods on Finnick Row, Crew enjoyed the chaos. Demons huddled around a gaming booth and brownies trudged underfoot. The eye-catching fauns, also known as pucks, intrigued him with their horns and hooved feet. Winged faeries, sprites, and pixies floated above, which he'd been accustomed and often left him wishing he could fly. How resourceful his life would be if he could take to the skies.

However, those pintsized creatures were not to be compared to the daunting fae. Most of them resided in the Saarnak Territory, with migratory fae sprinkled throughout the land. Their sovereign, King Vektor, as folklore proclaimed, could shapeshift into a hawk. Hence naming his kingdom Hawkswing. Crew had encountered both honorable and conniving fae during his stays in the High Court of Hawkswing.

"Hey, stop that filthy, thieving puck!" thundered a fishmonger. "Stop him!"

A rush of wind, combined with the smell of cod, passed Crew as a youthful faun trotted by. His scruffy clothes whipping like kite tails, hung on his willowy body. The faun weaved between people, causing a ruckus. A shrill whistle added to the commotion as a constable ran after the thief.

The panicking faun tumbled over a basket of new tomatoes, upsetting them into the road. The constable was almost upon him. Crew flicked his fingers, inducing rolling tomatoes to bungle the constables footing. The faun was able to flee down the alley.

Crew smirked.

As if it were a daily occurrence, folk went about their business while providing the bellyaching constable, splattered in tomatoes, a wide berth.

Akin to the carnies at the Faire, vendors in Finnick Row coaxed onlookers to purchase goods. Crew, like everybody, was tempted by their wares, particularly the squat stacks of silver coins being peddled by Demelda, a skilled witch. Lovely in every sense of the word, it was her shock of cerise hair waterfalling down her back that drew people's gazes. And ever since he'd been knee-high in the weeds, he had the pleasure of her acquaintance.

She was in the throes of luring a captivated customer.

Crew chuckled discreetly as the man emptied his pocket of coins, and then she handed him a vial with a cloudy substance.

"Take it all, in one gulp," she advised him.

Crew browsed over the stacks of silver that had been imbued with miscellaneous spells. Temptation. Compulsion. Subservience. He stroked his fingertip over the embossed snowflake of one coin.

Delaying wasn't an option, but he was held fast by the striking Demelda taking him in. "Did you forge these coins?" he inquired.

"Ahh, Creeww," she elongated his name. "It's been too long. You've grown into a fetching young man, I must say. So—the rumors are true. You are not returning to the Circus Faire."

"Demelda, you heed rumors now?"

She angled her head, fixing her gaze on him. "Each silver coin is different, like—"

"A snowflake," he deduced.

"Their influence depends on the person handling them." Compressing an indulgent grin, she wittingly thwarted their eye-to-eye contact. "I sense you are a worthy judge of magic." In haste she snatched his hand, "Here," and fixed a snowflake coin on his palm and folded his fingers over it.

An inscrutable zing traveled through him, and the lively din of Finnick Row had diminished. He allowed her bewitched silver to penetrate him like a soothing balm, if only temporarily, to relinquish his anxieties which had been eating at him. Shuttering his eyes, he drew an open-mouthed breath and slowly exhaled, allowing the spell to relax his body.

Opening his eyes, he was compelled by her aura. And, seduced by her beauty, he leaned in, wanting to take her there, on the spot. Although, he hadn't the drive, or the time, and he wasn't fooled. He pushed back the incantation.

"For you, my handsome, boy, I will yield payment by sealing our lips with a kiss." Puckering her mouth, she drew near. He inhaled a rich scent that he'd been familiar with. Her mouth was inches from his, and glossy from a charmed fusion sought after by men and women alike. A charm that had the sway to weaken a person's willpower.

Crew plucked the silver from his palm and held it between his fingers, breaking the spell. "You are tempting, Demelda. I've tasted your wares when I was a kid. Back then, what you didn't know, I was *never* under your spell," he said smartly.

"And grown into a shrewd young man," said the beguiling witch who tempted fate and men. "Crew, how do you it? You can't be Polk's son. *What* are you?"

A mischievous curl peaked his lips. "Since you're here on Finnick Row, I'm assuming you haven't decided to return to the Faire either," he said, not supplying her with the answer she was seeking.

"Dyke offered me a contract that I'd be a fool to pass up," she said. "I'm leaving within the week for... Wait a minute. Are *you* going back? I'll be lonesome without you."

"I very much doubt that." He deposited the snowflake coin in the temptation pile. "Polk is dying."

Sighing sadness winded from her mouth. "I'd heard as much."

"I'm dawdling." An urgent need to rush came over him. "Perhaps we'll meet again." He swerved toward Beadie's Apothecary, a building on the corner.

"Wait—" Demelda bade him to linger. "Take this."

Crew glanced back over his shoulder. Her arm extended, fingers closed into a downward fist. She wiggled her hand, wishing to present him with something.

"It won't bite. Take it." She moved around her stall of amulets, talisman, dragon's tears, and charms, closing the short distance between them. "A trinket to ease your grief and Polk's."

Crew said, "The apothecary has what he needs." He squinted at her hand, not trusting the witch and her free offering.

"That brute was my favorite. Liked to hide his compassionate nature under that obstinate scowl of his." Her voice thickened, and eyes glistened. "Tell him—I'll miss his gentleness."

Confident her offering wasn't contaminated, he held his hand beneath her closed fist. Budding open her fingers, she let go of the trinket.

"It is rare, sought by many."

He studied the tarnished ring. "Looks ancient. Handcrafted. An engraved crescent moon and star. A relic?"

"Looks are deceiving, are they not." She fastened her hand over his that was holding the ring. "Best not to flaunt it. I swear this thing has a homing beacon." Removing her hand, and like before, she folded his fingers over it. "Ever since it came into my possession, I've had strange visitors foraging through my wares. Asking for rings."

"Where did you happen upon such a thing?"

Demelda pinched the sleeve of his town coat and, walking backward, drew him behind her stall. Prior to saying a word, her head veered from right to left, guarded. "Marek, an old mage, I hadn't seen in years. He claimed to have unearthed it from the Plateau in Saarnak."

"Elvish or high fae land?" Crew questioned. "The Court of Hawkswing is in Saarnak."

She hiked up her shoulders.

"This ring frightens you, aye? I can see it in your eyes. Who seeks it? The Crown?"

Again, her gaze darted to those milling around the vendors' stalls. "When Mage Marek left on his journey to Foundling, he was lighter, as if a yoke had been lifted from his shoulders. Last week, the butcher drove his buckboard to my door. In the back of the wagon was Marek's body, torn inside out. They even cut his eyes out of his head." A low whine emanated from

Demelda. Expressively taut, her mouth quivered. "Whoever killed him was searching for something."

"This?" Crew was about to hold up the ring, but she clutched his hand. "Then why give it to me, and how will it help Polk?"

"It won't cure him, if that's what you're hoping." She paused as people roamed to her stall and began picking through her wares. Wrapping her fingers around Crew's wrist, she towed him out of ear range and into a narrow alley. "I can't claim to know its merits. But once, I saw Marek tighten his fingers on the ring. He went into a trance, and said, 'Misbegotten prodigy, come to my kingdom of despair and ruins'."

"Keep it," Crew said, and attempted to force it back into her hand. "I don't need it. I don't want it."

"You have to take it. Mage Marek brought it for *you*."

Tapering his eyes, Crew said, "Make sense, Demelda."

"Right before he left, I promised the mage I'd give it to a certain boy." She gave a frivolous hand flip. "After Marek left, the boy he spoke of didn't show up. So, I figured it was mine. *All mine*. But then—when I saw Marek's body..." She rolled her lips into her mouth, shaking her head. "It's...it's cursed."

Crew jiggled the trinket in his hand. "Give it to one of your friends."

"I can't. I'm afraid the mage will haunt me." A slight tremor touched her shoulders as she ironed the palms of her hands on her dress. "Marek sought me out for a purpose. He saw me in one of his visions with the boy he'd been searching for. A boy whose eyes change colors, like a chameleon. You, Crew. *It's you*." Reaching up, she split her fingers through his hair that dangled in his eyes. "You know I'm right. And I don't think it's a coincidence that you happened by today. It's fate."

"No." He was uncomfortable with the conversation.

Crew hadn't been one to preen in mirrors. It had been Polk, when Crew was young, who kept squinting at him. "You look different today." Crew had thought it was a trick of the light, but it wasn't, and he hated looking at his reflection. Trying to hide his changeable irises had been challenging. Once he'd begun shaving and had to study the contours of his jawline, his eyes seldom startled him anymore. Polk had surmised his anomaly had something to do with his temperament. Or his special abilities. Whatever caused his incongruity, he'd learned to live with it.

"You're a foolish enchantress."

"You don't let people get too close, afraid they'll notice. I've seen how you charm mortals and Folk alike; it has to do with your eyes, doesn't it? Have you heard what people are saying," she whispered, "you're some kind of demon or a wicked sorcerer."

At this, Crew chuckled. "Indeed, I am no such thing. Here in faery, do you really think anybody cares what color my eyes are?"

"It's obvious that *you* do. I remember when Polk returned from one of his jobs with a newsboy cap that was three sizes too big for your head. You were always jerking down the brim of that dang thing to hide your pretty face. By the way, you've grown nicely into it." Her gaze slipped to the cap on his head.

"I can't stand here discussing this with you," he stated. She was wasting his time. "I have to get back to Polk." Providing Demelda with a brisk nod, he rammed the ring into his pocket and began to turn away, and then halted. "You put it on, didn't you?"

Her guilt-ridden mien said it all. She nibbled on her bottom lip.

"You're keeping secrets. What are you fearful of, besides those men who killed the mage?"

She lowered her gaze. "When Marek was still here, I put it on against his rambling nonsense of danger," she muttered. "It took me to a place I'd never seen in my life, and…and I became invisible." Demelda flicked her eyes to Crew's sardonic glower. "*It's true.* Cross my heart." She made the sign over her chest. "I felt empowered. Impregnable because of my invisibility. I realized, I could go anywhere, do anything with that ring on my fing"—her eyes glazed, remembering—"I saw Marek sitting at my table. He kept calling me. Cautioning that if I kept it on too long, I'd never come back. Then everything changed. I was in a land of gray ashes, and it was getting darker. This feeling came over me, like…I was going to die…I—"

"Hmph. We're all going to die, Demelda." He slid his hand into his pocket, the cool metal touched his fingers. "Why me?"

"He said it was your birthright." She sunk her hands into the wide pockets of her dress. "The mage was talking gibberish ever since he'd crossed my threshold, like he'd been in the sun too long."

"Birthright?"

Sounding agitated, she said, "That's all I know. You might want to show it to Polk…before…before… You know."

"Aye." Crew turned toward Beadie's Apothecary and stayed his course.

FIVE
SAGE

Sage would have to hurry if she were to meet Marne by half past twelve. Since nobody was in sight, and rather than wasting precious minutes by heating water in large stewing kettles for a bath, she poured water into the tub. Swirling her hands and creating a whirlpool, she called forth her power. Her hands grew hot and tingly. When it reached a temperature to her liking, she drizzled a liberal amount of oil that she'd concocted from their springtime flowers. Getting into the tub, the water skimmed over her body like refined satin, and she drank in the fragranced peonies.

Afterward, she wrapped a towel around herself and went into a room she shared with Eadith. Sage picked through her sparse wardrobe that needed updating. Two drawers of the bureau consisted of her brother's pants and hand-me-down shirts. Since Papa retired from the mine, his fur trading barely made ends meet. Mama sold fruit and vegetables from their gardens and combined with Tegan's wages from the mines had been adequate. But not enough for Sage to splurge for handcrafted clothing from Morgana's.

Nonetheless, she much preferred pants and hunting with Papa. When she'd reached a certain age, her mama's proclamation of decorum became bothersome. "A young lady does not wear breeches," she'd scolded. With Mama's guidance, a chagrined Sage had to learn how to thread a needle.

Today, she selected a high-collar, pin-striped blouse with puffy sleeves and cuffs, along with a dusty-peach skirt with a flaring hemline that brushed her ankles. She was somewhat enamored with her skirt that she'd spent a week, with mama's tutelage, embroidering whimsical vines and florets along the hemline.

She browsed herself in the looking glass, the reflection staring back had transformed in three years. If Crew were still with the Circus Faire, would he even recognize her?

The very last day she'd seen him, she dallied underneath the cool shade of an angel tree. Its encompassing branches and meandering root system had been Sage's fortress since she was a child. A place where she'd dwell and ponder for hours. As she scrabbled onto a low-lying limb and extending an arm to scale its cobbled bark, long fingers clasped her wrist.

She jumped in surprise. It was Crew. A mischievous grin played on his face, and she saw herself in the reflection of his eyes. "How did you know I'd be here?" It was his eyes that she had been riveted. Infatuated girls took turns defining them. Each a capricious portrayal: Robin's egg blue. Mossy green. Velvety grey.

"I've seen you here before. This angel tree hides loads of secrets," he'd drawled.

"How did you…?" she had wanted to ask many questions, but his eyes flashed, erasing her thoughts. Neither blue, green, or grey. Like the sweet nectar bathed in sunbeams his amber-honey irises glowed. Deliciously warm and mysterious with untold stories. Their radiance was emphasized by his inky-black hair spilling over his forehead.

Dismayed, Sage scoffed. *I'm setting myself up for a fall.*

Crew undoubtedly had girls waiting for him in every village. *Like me.* He'd been with all the girls, and perhaps, that season, Sage was his final conquest.

Finger picking the plumpest strawberries from a bowl, she popped them into her mouth, savoring the juicy sweetness.

She wandered outdoors, wiping berry juice from her lips. Standing under the blinding sun, she spied a sneaky gnome in the strawberry patch.

"Hey!" Squatting, Sage scooped a handful of stones and jogged toward the trespasser, throwing one at a time. "Shoo—you thieving varmint." On her next throw, she applied her talent. The stones trajectory sailed on course, knocking the hat off his head. He bolted into the overgrowth.

"Why do I even bother." She dropped the leftover stones and clapped dirt from her hands. *He'll be back.* She made a mental note to scavenge the patch when she returned, pick the berries before they were poached by morning.

Heading down the lane toward Shilow crossroads, she was thankful the rains had subsided a week prior or else she'd be wearing her boots. Her leather slippers, embellished with a silken bow, complimented her feet and it was as if she were walking on spongy moss. The supple shoes were a generous gift from her sister.

Thinking of Edras, it hurt to see how worrisome Mama and Papa had become whenever she'd whisk Sage away to her cabin in the woods. Their hushed conversations spoke words such as *risky* and *dangerous*. Putting her family in jeopardy, as Edras had mentioned, rubbed her raw. Recently, she'd confronted them. The opportunity arose while they were hoeing the fields for spring planting.

"Why does it bother you when Edras takes me to her house?" she'd asked point blank. Mama's hoe froze in mid-swing and Papa chopped his in the soil and he left it there, in a vertical stance.

"It's not that we don't care for Edras. We love her, like our own," Papa had clarified, and then lowered his voice. "We are low fae." He circled his finger, saying, "Provech." The hoe he'd grounded worked into the soil. Circling his finger in the opposite direction, the hoe stilled. "That's minor magic. It's Doloran powers that gets people killed."

"We don't use spells and incantations. It's what's inside of me." Sage had rapped her palm to her chest. "Those things need to be controlled or it gets bottled up like dew in a saltshaker." Immediately, guilt stung her. She'd broken her sister's cardinal rule, *never speak of their abilities*. A lack of discretion presented itself in Mama and Papa's sneers. She'd felt like an abhorred maggot which they'd unearthed.

"Come with me," Papa had ordered. Mama and Sage followed him out of the loamy fields. He stopped at the picnic table where earlier Mama had set a pitcher of sliced lemons in water. Pouring three glasses, he handed one to Mama and to Sage. "Sit."

"Papa, it's time." She sent him an encouraging smile. "Sage, for your ears alone. Don't tell Tegan because King Vektor is stirring up his armies. We don't want—"

"Enough, Mama." Papa hushed her and scratched the skin around his nubby horn on his forehead. He took a generous gulp of his lemon water, and after wiping his mouth, said, "We begin," he reached over the table and patted Sage's hand. "Mama and I owe our lives to Daria and Arth. Your real Papa and Mama. Daria is not Mama's sister as we told the council." His kind eyes stared into hers, and like Mama, fine lines stretched across his forehead. Even with age wearing heavy on them, both were classically beautiful on the inside and on the outside.

His declaration had not shocked her, Edras had been quite explicit, apprising Sage of their parents.

He'd licked his lips before continuing. "Mama and I were about your age when King Vektor's soldiers began rounding up those less privileged. Low fae to be his army of expendables. We have limited magical prowess, but together we can make a combustible unit. I refused to oblige in the king's folly. Owing to my stubbornness, I was led with others to be executed for my insubordination."

A subtle gasp fled from Sage's lips.

"Shhhh." Mama had placed a comforting hand on her arm. "I go on, Papa," she said, noticing the thickening gurgle in his throat. "Soldiers were taunting them, saying, if they made it past Endle's barn, they'd be spared. Men and women who stood their ground were immediately killed. Those who could fly were taken down as soon as their wings expanded. It was sport to those soldiers, that's all.

"Papa wasn't budging." She gave him an endearing glance. "I screamed for him to run. Soldiers were picking them off one by one. Papa was well past Endle's barn, and I thought he was saved. But no. I can still picture the arrows piercing him. The king's soldiers departed with a tally of Folk after they'd seen what their fate was if they didn't comply." She brought her glass to her lips to sip the lemon water.

"Papa was alive, barely, when we got him inside. He was dying and there was nothing I could do. A couple passing through Alderwood with a young girl knocked on our door. They'd seen the travesty from the ridge and wanted to help. I told them they were too late. They were worn from their travels, and while I didn't trust strangers, I let them in because of the child. I put a kettle on, and when I turned, they'd snuck into the bedroom. I found them leaning over Papa. Their hands hovering above, but not touching him. Even the child, as little as she was, was holding out her arms. Papa's chest expanded, taking a yawning breath. A miracle."

Papa had picked up where Mama left off. "Daria, Arth, and Edras were headed north to settle with their people. I knew the Bracken Passage would be almost impossible to get through at that time, so they remained with us until the thaw. Folk are suspicious, as you know, the conflicts were brutal back then. So, we told the villagers it was Mama's sister.

"Daria and Arth taught us about their culture and inbred powers. They admitted that some Dolorans had gone astray. That's why they were moving to form a new settlement, far from those instigating trouble." Papa had chased his fingers into his hair, once as caramelized as Tegan's, now streaked with gray.

"Discrimination and prejudice," Mama had interposed, smoothing the knuckles on her hand, "was gaining momentum in the territories. Mortals didn't trust magicals and vice versa. Years after Daria and Arth departed from us, we wondered if they'd been caught in the struggle. We knew nothing except hearsay until a young girl knocked on our door seeking refuge and cradling a baby in her arms."

SIX
CREW

Crew entered their suite, which bordered Thistle Commons, and smelled an intruder. Surveying their quarters, all was in order. A hacking cough propelled him into Polk's bedroom. He stopped short. Polk was upright in the bed and a man was patting him on the back, holding a glass of water to Polk's mouth.

"Drink, Polk. Drink," the man encouraged. "Take it easy, buddy."

When Polk saw him, he said, "Where ya been?"—and eased back onto his pillow.

The man set the glass on the nightstand and breezed his hands into the pockets of his classy trousers and stepped away from Polk's bed. Rimmed spectacles were perched on the man's hooked nose, and brownish-oatmeal hair was styled in the latest fashion and sporting wiry sideburns.

"This is Doctor Aerestol," Polk introduced, and then cleared the croak in his throat. "He wanted to meet you."

"How do you do," said the doctor and removed his hand from his pocket and outstretched it in courtesy. "Crew?"

Slim framed, he was a weasel of a man who people would completely overlook. He gave the man's hand a pump, and then Crew wiped his palm on his town coat, erasing the man's touch.

"Sit. Sit." Polk rested his hands on his chest. A year prior it had bulged with muscular pectorals, now emaciated, and his head of coppery-red hair had turned sparse and sickly. "Doctor Aerestol has a proposition for ya, boy." A pink tinge shined through Polk's pasty-gray skin. Crew figured the big guy had a fever again.

Too antsy to take a seat, Crew shrugged out of his coat, flung it on the bedpost, and stepped to the window. He propped his backend on the casement and crossed his arms.

Doctor Aerestol was unperturbed by the dismal conditions and lowered into the cushioned chair stationed alongside the nightstand. The chair where Crew had been sleeping for the past week.

"How old are you, boy?" the doctor inquired.

As a child, he'd seen kids celebrating birthdays with Burpos, a gummy candy that made them roar like a dragon or cackle like a witch. A Licstick effected vocal cords, from squeaky soprano or baritone cadences. The popular Barfbag Peas, a surprise in every pea, magicking a unicorn horn, mermaid scales, or the sought-after dragon wings. He'd asked Polk when his birthday was. The big guy had scratched his head, looking to the clouds as if they held the answer.

"What's tomorrow?" he'd said.

"Tuesday. August tenth."

"Your birthday is August tenth. How's that suit ya?"

Back then, *before* Polk confessed that he'd stolen him from a foundling home, he'd approximated Crew was three or four when his mother had abandoned him on his door stoop.

"Nineteen," Crew replied without batting an eye.

"You look strong like your father." Doctor Aerestol tilted his head, judging him with a critical eye. "Can you handle a weapon like Polk?"

Crew reflexively traced a finger over the scar beneath his earlobe on his neck. He'd been a lucky bastard that night. It was after midnight when a sack of coins had fallen from his hand. As he bent to retrieve it, a boy took him by surprise. A razor-edged blade slit his throat. A half inch deeper, he would have been a goner.

Crew had snapped out his jackknife. Their scuffling attracted an audience; people fenced them in. Onlookers heckled directives, thinking it was a performance.

Polk taught him well at a young age how to handle a weapon. It would have been effortless to kill the kid.

He apprehended the boy's arm that had flaunted the blade, twisted it behind his back and thrust him face down into the ground. "Here's a couple coins for an excellent show," Crew growled in the kid's ear. "Get the hell out of here."

Polk's gruff snickering brought Crew back into his bedroom. "He's better than I ever was. But Crew won't tell you that. He's one of those humble sort of fellas."

"I like humble," the doctor said. "A person with tight lips. Polk, you know what I mean."

Polk charged in, "He can be trusted to hold his tongue."

"I'd like to hear what the boy has to say." The doctor shifted in the chair, his calculating gaze pinpointing Crew.

"What do you want from me?" Crew rolled his shoulders.

"What do you plan to do with your life once Polk…" he canted his head toward the bed, "dies."

Hesitating, owing to the man's blunt statement, he finally said, "I'll work the Circus Faire. Maybe reapply to the university or—"

"I've seen you at the Faire," the man butt in, and steepled his fingers against his chin. "Do you recognize me?"

He was nondescript in every way. "Sorry. No. I don't recall seeing you."

After delivering his answer, the doctor's thin lips tweaked, a shark with a secret. "Exactly. I blend in. People look past me as if I'm not there." He sniffed, presuming to be teaching the boy a valuable lesson. "What do you know about my association with your father?"

Crew was quick to say, "Polk never mentioned you, Mister… I mean, Doctor Aerestol." Polk's clenched hands and body relaxed, and then he sighed. "When he said you were a doctor, I thought you were here to check on his condition."

The doctor narrowed his eyes, weighing Crew's riposte, and gave a faint nod. "Since Polk's ailment has worsened, his colleague, Dirge, hasn't been as…ermm… How shall I put this…?" He tapped his knuckle on his chin, "As skilled as Polk. I require a man with a brain and expert skills, like your father, to lead a team of men for me. I need not say more unless you'd be worthy of the opportunity."

A deafening quiet condensed Polk's room, punctuated by the *tic-tic-tic* of the mantel clock in the drawing room, which seemed to grow in decibel. Crew ran a hand over his jaw in thought. Polk wanted him to commit, to compromise. He wanted to save Sage from whatever this wizard had in store for her and to find his long-lost brother. Polk had said something that stayed with him: "You have to be in league with the devil. Learn how he thinks, acts, and then you can outsmart the bastard."

SEVEN
SAGE

Shilow crossroads was less than a waltz away, and the whooshing overhead banished Sage's musings. Gamayuns, faeries, and sylphs drew her attention. She was acquainted with flying creatures, though today it looked like an air traffic jam.

Her friend, Marne came into view wearing a vivacious smile which reached her periwinkle eyes, vanquishing Sage's brooding thoughts and to the exciting day ahead.

A circlet of variegated yellow and purple pansies sat on Marne's head. Her exquisite dress hadn't been designed by the local seamstress. It screamed opulence. Silver-and-sapphire brocade and a form-fitting bodice were embellished with a pearled-princess neckline. The inlaid sapphire fabric paired well with her pale-blue complexion and lips.

"Love your dress."

"I never had an opportunity to wear it here. It's an everyday apparel for the high court," she said pretentiously. "And look at these." She raised the hem of her dress and poked a slippered foot from underneath. She twisted her foot for Sage to see all the angles. Filigreed in metallic gold and silver with woven ribbons that shaped a blooming silver and gold rose on her slippers. "These are elven-fashioned. After dancing all night during the New Moon Revel, they still look brand new. Not a scratch."

Sage scuffed the heel of her slippers in the soil, deferring to rave about her new shoes with a satin bow. Feeling inferior, her eyes kept locating Marne's dipping princess décolletage. Apparently, in Hawkswing, with their endless revels and nights of debauchery, anything goes. The girl had been blessed with eye-catching curves which Sage had once envied.

Sage recalled that first time attending the Circus Faire. She'd worn her brother's hand-me-down, baggy breeches and a shirt, which hid her figure. Flat-chested and skinny as a beanpole, as her papa liked to say, all skin and bones.

She fingered the waistband of her skirt that accentuated her slender waist. Reinserting the edging of her blouse that had wormed its way out, she was pleased her boyish figure had attained subtle curves.

Marne dampened Sage's spirits with her greeting. "I wish you had wings. We could be there in seconds." Either to verify her competent flying or to belittle her, Marne spread her pretty butterfly wings and sailed upward. Alighting a few yards ahead, her wings folded. "I wish your parents would permit you to come with my family to King Vektor's Court this fall for the Equinox Revel. We can drink, eat, and dance all night. No restrictions at Court." She winked.

"It's nothing like this dull provincial village. The fae at the High Court are stunning, and you meet intrigue around every bend. Boys in Alderwood are…um, okay, but they wear hunters gear and that junk." She gave an unfavorable flap of her wrist. "At Court—Oh, Sage, you have to come and see the extravagant finery. All prestigious and prosperous in leathers, velvets, shiny silks, and golden twills bordering all their garments. It's marvelous."

Her friend was born in the High Court of Hawkswing, and since moving into Alderwood, Marne relished showing and impressing upon anyone who'd listen that she was high fae. Sage had accepted Marne and all her haughtiness. Because she knew underneath Marne's conceited pride there beat a lonely heart.

"I'll ask my papa," Sage said, doubtful. "I wish I could fly, too. Just like you."

"Except, we'd be a mess and windblown." Marne refixed the crown of pansies which had fallen over her brow. "Sage, you should see Groverton Road. Advertisements are plastered on the shops, buildings, and fences. Isn't it fabulous?"

"Nobody speaks of anything else. It's like a contagion, infecting all of Alderwood." Marne's snub forgotten, Sage skipped the yards separating them and linked her arm around her friends. "When they were here before, it was like magic, wasn't it?"

"Of course, its magic, silly," Marne said. "This time we'll stay all night."

Sage drew in an excited breath. "We know it's magical, but the Faire travels beyond the borders where mortals live. Since the accords and all that's happened, I'm surprised they let them pass, let alone perform magic."

"Don't believe that tripe about mortals saying magic are works of the devil." She tittered. "How ignorant can they be."

"It scares them," Sage said, repeating her sister's words verbatim.

"It's enthralling." Marne eagerly wiggled her shoulders. "Takes my breath away."

Sage playfully nudged her elbow into Marne and, like conjoined knots, they walked on. "They are beguiled by the mastery of magic, yet their puritanical upbringing tells them anything out of the ordinary is sinful."

Marne pffted. "Sinful! How ludicrous."

"I can sympathize as to why mortals loathe magic." Sage tipped her head toward Marne. "Leggan Dnego."

"Ah, yes—the notorious Leggan." A slurpy noise passed Marne's lips as if his name stuck to her tongue. "An inglorious wizard who struck the match, setting the world on fire. Grimog has a quarterly lesson on his nefarious exploits."

"Our teacher delights in those studies and gets all hot and bothered over the man who created anarchy. Supposedly, he influenced Dolorans to join forces with him. I can't tell if she's awestruck or repulsed by him." For a second Sage forgot about her new slippers and kicked a rock in her path. Miffed at herself, she hoped it hadn't left a mark.

"Grimog does go on tangents about Leggan. Allegedly they say he was born a mortal."

"Leggan is *not* mortal. No human can utilize black magic like that." Sage jerked on Marne's arm for affect. "Leggan has to have magical blood or *something* where he acquires his abilities." The girls paused to observe a squadron of cawing red-tailed black birds winging above. As an afterthought, she ruminated, "I wonder if Leggan is still alive."

"People say he's been dead for decades or he went underground."

A breeze caught a skein of Marne's cobalt hair. Since their elbows were clasped, she used her other hand to tuck the strands behind her ears, exposing her pretty pointed tips. Marne had inserted three mini chains to decorate her ears. Dangling on each chain, white coral from the Sea of Tears swayed with each step, an attention grabber. The upper-class fae were all about being noticed.

Sage touched her own earlobe which she felt hadn't an ounce of distinction. Somewhat deficient of the severe point, but thankfully, not rounded like mortals. Smoothing the outer rim, she made sure Papa's trinkets, made of copper and engraved with a moon and a hanging star, were secure on her ear. Ornamental earbobs similar to those widely worn by fae.

Her movements caught Marne's interest. "I've always been jealous of those earbobs your father makes for you and Edras. Do you think he'd make a pair for me?"

Sage and her sister lacked the Steele's genetic fine points, so, Papa had designed the ear toppers, shaped to dainty points. Their purpose was to disguise the upper portion of their ears, to dissuade any scrutiny by Cabal, the king's regent, which happened to be Marne's father.

"I can ask." Bemused that her wealthy friend, who traversed to the Court of Hawkswing, and could purchase and had purchased exquisite jewelry, would want earbobs crafted by her papa, a fur trader.

Satisfied, Marne then revisited their prior topic. "Speaking of magic." She stopped in her tracks to face Sage. "I still can't figure out how you brought that dead squirrel back to life yesterday. Now that's a trick mortals would pay lots of coins for." Snugging their conjoined arms into her side, she peered into Sage's eyes waiting for her to relinquish some kind of incredible secret.

"I told you the poor thing wasn't dead. It…it was hurt," Sage supplied. "I rubbed life into its weaking body."

"It looked pretty stiff."

"Maybe close to dying. I had to get the poor things blood flowing," she insisted. "I should've let nature take its course. It's risky to interfere. There could be adverse effect somewhere down the road."

"For you, or the squirrel?"

"I'm not sure." Her friend was correct. The squirrel had breathed its last. Its body had been in the throes of calcifying. And it had cost her. Sage had spent the rest of that day and night in bed, sapped of strength. Edras had cautioned her about dabbling with the dead and the netherworld. As much as her sister cautioned her, it simply added fuel to her fire and her excessive urge to invoke her abilities.

"I asked because what you did was extremely impressive. I didn't realize the Steeles were overly powerful. My father said Alderwood housed only low fae, none of them practiced in magic like those at Hawkswing, I told my father what you di—" Marne was cut off by the trampling of hooves coming from the rear. "The Galdoons. They're going to beat us to the Faire." The girls shambled to the side of the road, out of the path of the carriage drawn by four warthogs.

An exuberant Darney was hanging out the window waving his arms. "You better hurry. There's a zillion people behind us. We'd give you a ride but there's no room." A vestige of "*Sorrrry*" drifted in the air.

Being swallowed by a cloud of dust, the girls returned his salutation. "See you there, Darney."

"That sprite is adorable," Sage said. "Hey, I know a shortcut. C'mon." Unhitching their elbows she headed into the forest.

"Darney is exaggerating." To avoid getting her dress dirty, Marne raised the hem, moving through the briars. "I'd like to look presentable, not covered in burrs and filth," she demurred.

"I betcha it's open to the public by now." As careful as realistically possible, Sage kept an eye on her foot placement, dodging mud. "I was hoping we'd get there to watch them set up." High-stepping on a downed maple tree, Sage leapt off, and then picked up the pace.

"You just want to find Crew before Delaney does."

Hearing Delaney's name added doggedness to her strides. Sage toe-stepped on rocks over a trickling brook and made it across without getting her feet wet. She then paused to recalculate their bearings. If the Faire was setting up in Planker's clearing, as Gart had mentioned, then it'd be past the thicket of Hemlocks ahead.

"Sheesh, slow down, Sage. I shouldn't have teased you about Delaney."

"It doesn't bother me." *Not anymore*, she thought, as she pushed through the evergreens.

Marne mumbled to herself, then said, "I think there was something off about Crew."

"Besides being hotter than hot." Sage plucked burrs from her skirt. "And all the girls swarming him like ants wanting to devour every morsel he had to offer."

"You know what I mean. Just one look into his eyes and I felt hooked, didn't you?"

"Hmm. Magnetic. Definitely," Sage agreed as Marne hustled by her. "We were sort of childish and giggly back then."

"I spent a fortune the last time. All the money I'd saved."

"Me too, but it was worth it, wasn't it?" Sage smiled.

Thrills and lively cries flirted through the forest inciting a tingling sensation throughout Sage's body. "Hear that? It's right past those trees," Sage said, moving toward the clearing. "Let's have tons of fun."

"Loads of wicked fun coming up."

Sage snickered.

"Hey, not to put a sour note to our wickedness," Marne said, turning to Sage. "Did you hear what happened in Bryncliff?"

"No. Recently?"

"I can't believe your family hadn't heard the news." A wide-eyed Marne drew out her speculation like a suspenseful tale. "It happened a month ago, before the spring planting. They found Bemus Prattleford in his fields." She crinkled her nose. "His mouth was packed with mud, and his hands were cut off at his wrists, and his body was sliced into piecemeal."

"Ugh. That's ghastly." Distraught, Sage ringed her fingers around her lower neck. "Why would anyone…" Her sentence left ended, picturing Bemus' horrifying death.

"They say, he hexed his neighbors' cows so they couldn't produce milk, and then he hexed their crops too, all because of an argument."

"How did they figure that out?"

"The looney old man admitted it himself. He claimed he was a Doloran. And swore, if he were so inclined, he could wipe out his neighbor with a mere thought."

EIGHT
CREW

Months after Polk's diagnosis, a disease committed to rushing matters, and when his legs hadn't been able to withstand the big guy, he became bedridden. Dirge would come and go, and then Crew took up the slack. They played card games and talked until Polk was drained and fell asleep.

"Crew, you are my son," Polk had likened to say, his voice an unravelling fiber. "You're smarter than I ever was. Maybe…" he garbled, suffering before he died, "leave the circus. Get far away from the wizard. Live your life. Don't lose your soul."

Crew knelt beside Polk's bed and held onto his hand. The hands that had raised a six-hundred-pound barbell. The hands that had stopped an elephant by tackling it to the ground, and once hailed as *the strongest man alive*.

"Polk, you did good. No worries. We'll meet again." As the singing whippoorwill alighted on the windowsill, Polk had gasped his final breath. A devastating pang took up residence in Crew's chest. "Love you, big guy." His voice cracked and fell to pieces. He meant to say it sooner, thinking, if he suppressed his sentiments, Polk wouldn't die.

What drove his thoughts in futile circles, was why, at this late stage, Polk had confessed to abducting him and his brother. And then, insisting on that meeting with his benefactor, Doctor Aerestol, and Polk's advice to join forces with him. It all could have been avoided. Unless—the doctor had something on him. Something that had motivated Polk to do exactly what his benefactor demanded.

Wallowing in defeat wasn't in Crew's nature, and Polk wouldn't want that. He had cast Crew in steel since day one. It was time to move on. Polk already did. The big guy's agony had ended.

Crew arrived at the Circus Faire after midnight. He went straight to Dyke's tent and breezed through the flaps to see him with a lady. Neither intimidated nor embarrassed, he stated, "Polk's dead."

Dyke shooed him out of the tent, and said, "Kid, we all expected the outcome."

"Follow me," Crew said. "I have to show you something." He was through being the grunt, a drudge, and a siren to charm people into spending money.

"Can't this wait? I…um…have company." Dyke glimpsed over his shoulder. "I'm sorry to hear Polk's dead but life goes on, kid," he complained, acting putout.

"You won't be disappointed." Crew tucked his long hair beneath the brim of his cap. As an incentive he said, "It'll add coin to your coffers."

Dyke scratched his neck. "Fine. I'll give you ten minutes— You can think of this as a favor to Polk—then I need to get back."

Making strides through the circus revelers, past the sounds and lights, Crew continued into the darkest region toward the ridge that overlooked Alderwood. "Stand back," he said to Dyke, who had a smoking cigar clenched in his teeth.

Standing on the precipice of the ridge, Crew created a stupendous pyrotechnics display.

Dyke's bored and groggy gaze magnified, and the cigar fell from his mouth. "Polk always said you were special, kid."

NINE
SAGE

Sage and Marne entered through the Circus gates and were in awe. The sights none of which they'd ever experienced. Grander and loftier than three years prior or else they'd forgotten its breathtaking marvels.

Splashes of luminous colors and boisterous noise had their heads spinning. Booth after booth of hobgoblins pandering to those wandering about to play their games of chance. Filing the fringes of the acreage were inconceivable structures. Each edifice had carnies barring minors from entering, which whetted their appetites for going in. She read a few of the signs, *Must be of age to enter,* and watched as the carnies made the discretion as to who may cross the threshold. Perhaps her and Marne had a chance this time, unlike three years ago.

The outer shells of these structures were, in themselves, spectacular. One was erected of glass, though, on closer inspection it appeared to be ice with two turrets and a drawbridge. What struck Sage as odd, nobody, not even Marne, mentioned or gestured to the amazing castle.

Another fashioned into an elaborate tree house, reminding Sage of her angel tree with its mushrooming branches and wrestling root system. Inset in its trunk was an arching wood door with sigils carved into its gothic framework.

As eager as they were to visit the splendid structures and to see what they had to offer, they'd deferred for the moment to browse the Faire in its entirety. Not to mention the expenditure of coins, bleeding them dry on day one.

"You can sense the magic, can't you?" said Marne, her cheeks flushed with excitement.

"Magicals are hard at work here." As soon as Sage had passed through the gate, there was a sprinkling on her lips like sweet and tart lemon drops. Magic. "You know what is astounding? That the Circus Faire crosses into the Unified Territories to entertain mortals. I thought they detested magic creatures."

"C'mon, Sage," Marne's tone filled with cynicism. "Humans love this stuff."

Sage responded, "If I'm not mistaken, mortals are employed here too. It's funny how I can spot them, can't you?"

"Hmm, not so much. I guess that's your thing."

"It doesn't explain the bloody conflicts between mortals and magicals. It sickened me when Grimog taught us about the carnage and slave trade before the accords."

Marne nodded. "Yes, frightening to think about. And I'm glad those conflicts are behind us. Nowadays the Unified Territories are clamoring for our kind of entertainment. You know that, Sage. Nevertheless, when the final curtain falls, the Circus is supposed to take their freaky magic with them. Then, the Unified militia patrols for unsavory creatures, leaving no stone unturned."

"How do you know all this?"

"My father, of course. He's King Vektor's confidant." Upturning her nose, Marne sashayed like a princess. "Perplexing to the Crown and to the Unified Territory are the Dolorans. They say those people can pass for Fae or humans and are difficult to weed out. Any one of them could be living in our midst."

Sage had vowed to her sister that she wouldn't, under any circumstances, divulge her lineage, especially to her bestest friend. Over the years as they'd grown closer, Sage had considered telling Marne. Listening now to her, she realized she'd dodged a bullet.

"I recently overheard my father speaking to the council. They're in agreement that Bemus Prattleford got what he deserved. Dolorans are treacherous and have to be eliminated."

The tiny hairs on Sage's arms spiked. "That's harsh, Marne." Marne's retort turned her stomach sour, like goats milk on a summer's day. She ceased ogling the sights, and halting, turned to her. "Are you aware of the underground slave trade that is *still* in existence. And another thing," Sage was getting steamed, "it was the magicals who originated the explosive fireball effect during the signing of the accords. Remember Whipple's Landing? Mortals wouldn't permit magicals aboard the ferry to cross the channel. Once the ferry was halfway across, it was winched into the air and then flipped upside down. Mortal bodies plummeted, peppering the water like shark bait, and then the boat crashed overtop of them. A girl, a Doloran, rescued many of them from drowning."

"*Some* say there was a girl, but she disappeared. Nobody knows who or what she was."

"Come on, Marne," Sage cajoled. "People saw her on seashore; her hands were in the air. She levitated the boat, and bodies floated to the surface. And then—"

"Mortals feel they have the power to do whatever they want to us," as if belittled, Marne scoffed, "and Whipple's Landing was a cry for retribution. Sage, you of all people know, I wouldn't harm a living soul, not on purpose." Hedging closer to her, she lowered her voice, "I think it's all poppycock, don't you? Fae and Dolorans, it's magic, right?"

I beg to differ, but I'll let my friend off the hook, for now.

"Okay. Okay." Sage's brow heightened, conceding. While Marne's diatribe was plausible, it sounded as if she were mimicking her father. "Let's not bicker. Governing politics isn't our thing. Let's forget about it and have fun." Instating a truce, Sage and Marne hooked elbows and walked on. Bruised by her friends remark she'd brushed it off. Yet, it still smarted.

The atmosphere was replete with new hay scuffing underfoot, roasting boar, fried onions and potatoes, frosty lemonade, and sweet marzipan delicacies, which the girls had been ingesting heartily.

"Look—" Marne pointed. "That kid hit the jackpot with dragon wings and the other has a unicorn horn. We have to find the vendor selling Barfbag Peas."

"Aren't we a little old for Barfbags and Burpos?"

"Not at all. It'll be a riot. Over there." She cut between a knot of children, each one cackling or spitting dragon fire. "Licsticks. C'mon."

"Hey, Sage. Marne!"

The girls stopped in their tracks and turned toward the person calling them.

"The Faire hired a *puck?*" Marne spat, disdain growing over her face. "How low can they go."

"Shhh, he'll hear you." Sage waved to Gart.

"Who cares if he does?" Marne wrinkled her nose as if smelling animal dung. "I am not going over there, are you?"

"Gart is a friend. Puck isn't an acceptable term anymore."

"Not a friend of *mine*. And a puck is a puck. In Hawkswing pucks are mainly servants."

"Well, we're not in the High Court. In Alderwood, they are our friends and neighbors. C'mon, be nice."

"Nice? To that puck? I'd rather—"

Sage left Marne in the dust and went to where Gart was handing a small bag of toasted nuts to a young elfin boy. The pale-skinned elf opened his mouth, full of scissor teeth, and popped in the unshelled nuts.

"Gart, this is better than mucking animal stalls." Sage drew open her reticule and retrieved a coin.

His mouth bunched to the side, and then jutted his chin toward Marne. "She detests me, doesn't she?"

Sage didn't have to see Marne in the background, probably looking anywhere but at the pushcart and Gart, the faun. "She can be…exhausting. May I have a bag? And," glimpsing the young elf, spitting gnashed crumbs of shell from his mouth, "can you remove the shells." She offered him the coin.

"Sure, and it's on me." He deshelled the nuts and mixed hot hazelnuts and chestnuts in warmed honey, and filling a bag proffered it to her.

"You must take the coin. Giving freebies to every friend isn't proper. And I wouldn't want to be the cause of getting you ousted on your first day."

He snorted. "Right. Thanks." She placed the coin on his palm and took the offered bag. "Working here isn't as cracked up as I thought it'd be."

She selected a chestnut and blew on it to cool and then popped it into her mouth. "Why not," she asked between chews.

"I'd rather be walking around, playing the games, and getting into those outer tents. The last time the circus was here, I was too young to get in."

Sage licked the warm honey from her fingertips before scrounging in the bag for another. "Me too. But you'll get breaks." She sucked the honey off the nut. "Mmmm, tasty. I'll see you later."

"Have fun."

She rejoined Marne, who was in the Emporium's Bootery, and knee deep in a pair of eel skin boots.

"What do you think?" Marne said, her voice piped like a teeny mouse.

"You bought a Licstick?" Her soprano-like giggling had Sage in stitches. "Did you get me one?"

"Of course. The booth with the Barfbag Peas is down the *Avenue of Spirits*." Marne opened her reticule and handed-off a green Licstick. "Now back to my boots. Look how the light catches the colors. Yay or nay?" She raised the hem of her dress and turned her leg for a better view. A burly orc tramping by whistled. "I guess that's a yay."

It was hard to take Marne seriously with that voice. Sucking on the Licstick, a baritone tweet ejected from Sage's mouth. "I sound like an ogre." Sage, with her deep-tones and Marne's high-pitched squeaking joined in laughter. "In this heat, I vote nay for the boots. Unless you plan on saving them for the winter months."

"You're right. Besides, I don't feel like lugging them."

Sage chucked the remainder of her Licstick in the trash and opted for a sweetened hazelnut instead.

"Aren't you going to offer me one?"

"I didn't think you'd want any."

"Of course, I do."

"Gart shelled and toasted them."

"That's his job. And don't lecture me," Marne said using her uppity tone as her natural voice was returning. Sage gave the small paper bag to her friend and she chose three of the meatiest chestnuts to feast on.

The Circus Faire hadn't erected exhibits, vendors booths, and gaming tents in a methodical pattern, it was a disorderly conglomeration, which had people gasping with each new discovery.

The girls meandered, tarrying now and then. They stalled by the Marquee of Teslan, a hedge witch, where a gaggle of young girls were jockeying into position.

"What is she peddling?" Sage asked to no one in particular.

"A potion. To make you beautiful in the eyes of your true love," said a pixie. Her cotton-candy hair sparkled, sprinkled with pixie dust. As Teslan handed a vial to a waif-like sluagh, she sarcastically added, "Homely Creke will need more than a potion."

Sage and Marne traded glances and chuckled. Continuing on, they procrastinated near a spriggan twanging a tuneful song on a lute.

His garnet eyes spanned those assembling and arrested on Sage. The tune stopped in mid-twang, still staring at Sage. She felt uncomfortable. His fingered talons changed the harmony, a melodic tune carried on the wisps of breaths. A song of longing, lost love, and lost souls. The emotive melody touched Sage's heart. For reasons unknown, she knew this was for her. Sensing the impassioned anguish, a tear leaked down her cheek.

"Hey, let's move on before we start bawling." Marne two-handedly took Sage by the elbow and dragged her from the hypnotizing music.

Meandering past an herbal and remedy vendor, the girls gasped, glimpsing a phenomenal sight. A dashing figure, towering above the people crushing the avenue. An enormous centaur sauntered through the thongs wearing a fleece of many colors over his hind quarters. He cut an imposing path, parading his regal majesty. Centaurs had been on the verge of extinction due to those besieged in captivity.

Sage tossed the excess of nuts in the trash and darted into the path of the centaur. "Sir." The centaur was bearing down on her slight frame, and she fretted he hadn't seen her. "Sir!" Raising her voice, she said, "Can I ask you something?" As his stalwart figure neared, she began crisscrossing her arms in the air to glean his attention.

He abruptly halted and pawed the grassy earth with his hoof, creating a divot of soil. He stationed his hands on his hips. "Hello, my beauty. You should be careful where you're walking. I would've been saddened to see you trampled."

Craning her neck to meet his gaze, the centaur's disarming grin took Sage by surprise. He was ruggedly fetching with whorls of dark hair, dripping over expansive shoulders. His torso was strapped in bands of black leather, but it didn't hide the appearance of his muscular build.

"Do you know a boy named Crew? He worked here three years ago." She felt Marne's presence at her shoulder.

"We haven't seen him," Marne added.

"You're not the first girls to ask that question," he responded with levity. "Crew's a popular guy." He gripped one of the straps that crossed his chest, eyes glistening at them, pondering what he should exchange. "His father died recently." He paused for effect and soberly nodded when the girls' mouths formed disturbed O's. "But don't worry, my lovely ladies. He might be around here somewhere." His youthful guise brightened. "Look for the fire."

"The fire?" they echoed.

"If you can't find him, come and see me." He bowed, accompanied by a flamboyant hand swish. "I'm Endar at your service."

Endar turned toward the main event pavilion and folks parted for him. Young Darney Galdoon was scampering after the centaur, the sprite's mouth hung open and his big moon eyes were chockfull of wonder.

"Centaurs are extremely rare," Sage said, her gaze tracking the half-man, half-horse.

"That's why the Circus is so freaking amazing."

"Speaking of freaky." Sage gestured to canvas billboards being pushed by the wind.

Painted on the canvas was larger than life depictions of people in diverse poses, and the billboards that would intermittently change scenes with each wind thrust. A sign indicated a person had to be sixteen to be admitted into the Freak Show. Intrigued, they doled out coins to investigate.

It was a longhouse pavilion crammed with jostling people. The girls went with the flow and stalled by the first stage. Unmanned instruments, a lyre, fiddle, flute, and a trombone set the vibe with an eerie tempo. In a bodysuit designed with snake scales, a woman magically appeared. She slinked to the rhythm of the music.

"Besides being a bad dancer," Marne said, "what's so special about her?"

While Marne had been speaking her mind, the dancing woman began to choke, and all whisperings deadened. Clutching her throat, her lips parted. A forked tongue lashed out, and gradually a yellow python slithered from her widening mouth. Folks gasped as the hissing creature twined the woman's neck, torso, and legs.

The girls were pushed back by the crowd, afraid the snake might attack. The python wrapped every section of the woman's body. Twisting and slithering, it reversed its route. Slinking over its own body until it coiled atop of the woman's head, hissing at the petrified audience. The woman murmured something, and in a blink of an eye, the python plunged into her mouth and disappeared.

As the audience clapped, the unmanned instruments played a merry ditty. Snake woman took a bow, flicked a forked tongue, and *poof,* she vanished.

At another stage, a man dressed as a Victorian gentleman was animatedly articulating an Elvarkian monologue. Sage believed it was from the theatrical show of Quintek, but it wasn't one-sided. The gentleman unbuttoned his waistcoat and his brother, growing like a tumor from his chest, chimed in.

"I have to leave." Sage grabbed Marne's hand and scurried to the exit. "That was freaky." She fanned her hands over her face to conquer her nauseating heat.

"Hey, butterhead, that's why they call if a Freak Show." Marne laughed and then took a deep breath. "I smell smoke, don't you?"

Together they noisily snuffled.

"And where there's smoke—there's fire." Sage faced Marne, tweaking her eyebrow. "There!" She gestured. "See the sparks over the pavilion?"

"Let's go."

Merry shrieks greeted them as they passed by a pendulum of perpetual motion, the Whirly Falcon. People lay prone on flatboard contraptions strung up with pulleys and chains, swinging in midair. There was a queue to enter the Hobgoblin Maze. In the upper levels of misshapen windows, running streaks of people were screeching by.

The ground quaked as a troll lumbered by juggling five boulders. The girls went down the midway of attractions, overwhelmed by the sights and magic. A man magically balanced a table overhead where a baby elephant was pirouetting. Riding an albino tiger, a lilac-skinned fae decorated in boas galloped by, throwing stardust that developed into glittering fireflies.

They turned into a clearing where people were corralling into an immense ring. A blast of sparks motivated the crowd to step backward. Sizzling fireworks had folks "Ooooing," and "Ahhing," breathy shouts of awe.

The girls wormed between bodies, this way and that, past faeries, wood nymphs, brownies, pixies, and crotchety goblins, who hadn't paid them any heed, since they were too absorbed in the performance. Not reaching the front lines, Sage was able to peer overtop of Darney Galdoon's head of spiky hair. The sprite clapped and hopped, and cupping his hands around his mouth, cheering for more.

There he was. Crew. Her Crew. He'd grown in three years. Taller, broader, and dastardly more attractive if that were possible. His inky-black hair had grown wild, branching over his broad shoulders as he played with fire. The last time she'd seen him, he was simply part of the crew, setting up, taking down, odd jobs, and drawing people into the Circus. When did he become a main attraction?

A fire wrangler.

Two orbs of lightning flared above the palms of his hands. He juggled the orbs, creating a fluent spectrum of sapphires, golds, and vermillion in dizzying motion and mesmerizingly fast. He slapped his hands together, creating a thunderous crack, extinguishing the orbs. The gasping audience applauded wildly.

Crew turned his body in a circle as fiery ropes snaked out of his fingers; cerulean and magenta sparks, resembling tails of a comet swirled around him. As if wielding multiple lassoes, he whipped them overhead, drawing all eyes skyward. Extending his arms up, within seconds, there was a finale of mind-blowing fireworks and booming explosions. Waterfalling flares rained down, not touching the spectators, but over Crew. He didn't move, instead, he uplifted his face toward the falling stars. Immersed in dazzling light, his body burst into flames.

The throngs screamed.

Sage and Marne screamed.

TEN
CREW

Crew hadn't been a main attraction—for good reason. Polk wanted him behind the scenes. Hidden from his benefactor, Doctor Aerestol. Polk had witnessed firsthand what Crew was capable of.

Crew had been a boy in breeches and cap when Polk said, "I gotta take you with me."

"Yippee, I won't have to stay with the witch."

"Demelda's been good to you kid. Don't you forget that. I have a last-minute job and I don't have time to bring you to her place."

"She's okay. Teaches me cool stuff," Crew admitted, and Polk grunted. "Where we going?"

"Got a new guy working with us. I don't like 'em. And I don't trust 'em. Just keep quiet," Polk said. "Better yet, pretend you're invisible."

Guided by a waxing moon, Polk, Dirge, a man named Beeker, and young Crew had navigated a boat across the strait to Jaqa Cove. Stowing the craft in an underwater cavity that smelled rank, the men had disembarked into the gloomy dampness. Polk turned and extended his arm to aid Crew over the side.

Dirge's voice had echoed in the cave. "No snitches. One bullet."

"What the frig does that mean?" Beeker asked.

"Figure it out, Beeker," Dirge replied as he hefted a rucksack from the stern.

"Leave the kid in the boat." Beeker scowled, showing teeth that glinted in the dark, and then twitched his head toward Crew. "I don't like kids."

"He won't get in the way," Dirge had countered.

"*I said*—the kid stays here or count me out." Beeker pulled a dagger and held it under Dirge's jaw. "He'll be a whimpering pest and get us killed." The tip of the knife broke skin and a thin line of blood trickled along Dirge's neck. "You're gonna need me for this job."

Rumbling had worked its way up Polk's throat. He left Crew in the boat and turned toward Beeker. "You got a problem? Take it up with me, asshole."

Beeker neither as tall nor as strong as Polk, though known as a roughhousing scrapper, had thrust Dirge into Polk. They stumbled to their knees. "That brat is the problem," jeered Beeker. "When we get back, I'm telling the doctor. You'll both get an acid bath—"

Before Beeker had a chance to say another word, a torch of shooting fire had Polk and Dirge lurching backward. Beeker was thrown off his feet. His body burst into flames, and Beeker's hellacious screams would infect Crew for years. Polk and Dirge spun toward the boat where Crew's fingers were smoking.

※ ☆ ※

Crew had seen Sage standing amidst the congregating folks straightaway. Her hair absorbed the light of the sun, turning fiery, and was hard to miss. In his years of absence, she'd ripened into a breathtaking beauty. That very first time they'd met, her eyes snared him. Pale lilac with splashes of silvery blue, and from his perspective, he'd never seen anything like them.

Throughout his performance he had to concentrate, however, she drove him to distraction. Turning away from her, it enabled him to call forth threads of fire. For his finale, setting himself ablaze had the outcome he'd predicted, diverting his audience. Ramming his hand into his pocket, he extracted the ring and wedged it onto his finger. His corporal body rapidly faded, a bizarre feeling, being siphoned out of existence into another realm. A realm of shadows. Demelda had cautioned him not to remain in the shadow realm longer than necessary.

As the glimmering sparks dispersed into specks on the ground, shrieking spectators gasped. "Where did he go?"

"The fire burned him."

"There's nothing left of him."

"That's impossible!"

The crowd moved about, searching the area for a piece of him, charred bones, blood, or teeth.

Crew, shielding a hand in front of his face, protected himself from the shadow realm's billowing ashes. He emerged into a world of grays and ash. Leaning into the squalling wind, he walked a fine line between two blurry dimensions. He'd sensed something lurking near him in the ashes, and speedily diverged toward Madam Rouge's marquee. Moving to the rear of her tent, he pried the ring from his finger. The shadowy realm faded as the earthly dimension sharpened. Drinking in a fresh breath, he was glad to be liberated from that netherworld, and hid the relic in his pocket.

If anyone inquired where he'd disappeared to, which he suspected he'd be bombarded with questions, he was prepared. *An illusionist never reveals his secrets.*

As they'd arranged last night, Dyke, wearing his top hat and velveteen attire of a ringmaster, strode into view. "Ladies and gentlemen and children! Come one! Come All," he intoned, sweeping his arms in a grand promenade, a true master when it came to stealing peoples' attention. "Do not be alarmed! Our newest and epic attraction, Crew the Fire Illusionist, wishes to invite one and all for another extravaganza." Expressions of confoundment were replaced with incredulity, and a boon of cheering and clapping spread among them.

"Tonight. At midnight. On the ridge. Come one! Come all!"

Crew yanked his cap, with the fraying rim, from his back pocket. Jamming it on his head, he stole into the rear of Madam Rouge's tent. There was a four-poster bed festooned with tasseled curtains, an armoire made of cedar with rune carvings, a dresser with a small oval mirror, which was for slathering face make-up, and in the corner, a full-length looking glass.

Presuming it was a result of his disappearing act, his vision blurred. He dipped his head into his hands and rubbed his eyes.

"What have we here," Madam Rouge, the oracle said coming into the room.

He jerked to attention, doffing his cap like a gentleman. "Excuse me for intruding, Madam." And gave a respectful bow of his head.

"No problem, Crew."

To find himself in the private quarters of the oracle was sinful. Ageless and beautiful since Polk had first introduced them when he'd been a young scamp. Her azure eyes, ringed in black, eyes that were acclaimed to see the past, present, and future, coasted over him.

A rush of heat found Crew's face. He instantly recollected a time when Polk was performing. His performance ordinarily went on without a hitch, but that night he hadn't finished and walked off stage. He'd been terribly twitchy afterward, not himself. Valleys of worry had whittled into Polk's face and the weary slope of his shoulders were becoming prevalent.

Concerned, Crew had searched for him throughout the evening, ultimately heading to the oracles. It was an hour before dawn when he'd skulked outside of her tent and listened to her and Polk. It wasn't his most dignified moment.

"You look unwell," the oracle said bringing Crew back from the memory. She'd looped her arms in front of her, holding her hands together. "Perhaps, those fireworks depleted you."

"You were watching?"

"Wasn't everybody." Her words coated with candor drew the strain from his face. "Truly remarkable. You never visited me in the past, and now I know why."

"I'm not into tea leaves and tarot cards. I prefer to let fate fall where it may." When he pocketed his hand, the oracle's regard left his face, skipping to where his right hand came in contact with the ring.

"You *are* full of surprises, aren't you, boy?"

She sensed the relic?

Crew seldom cared for what the future wrought. However, things had changed after Polk's admission about not being his son. And realized, all those years, why Polk had forbidden him to pay a visit to the oracle. He wanted to hide Crew's identity. If word had reached his benefactor of his deceit, all bets were off.

Madam Rouge, a dark woman with calculating eyes, focused on Crew. No bangles and baubles adorned her, and vivid flaxen streaks were woven into her blacker than black hair. Layers of sheer fabric, in every imaginable shade, poured over her shoulders.

"Surprises?" He pulled his hand from his pocket to hold his cap in both hands.

A modest smile tipped her lips. "I watched you grow. From a sprout to this towering specimen." She gestured her arms airily over her head. "You never came to see me. It's because Polk wouldn't allow it, am I right?"

"You and Polk were close, aye?"

Angling her head, a tic found her eye. "I believe so."

✯

Polk used to drag him on rounds to collect tithings for Dyke. The crown of Crew's head narrowly reached Polk's belted waist as they'd gone into the oracle's tent, smelling of suffocating incense.

"My, what a pretty boy," she'd said. "You should bring him more often. It would make my financial contribution less taxing."

Polk had clamped his large hand on Crew's shoulder. "Takes after his old man, don't he?"

Her slender fingers, nails painted in red lacquer and embossed with sigils, cupped Crew's chin. Tilting his head upward, he didn't have an option but to meet her eyes. Her analyzing gaze lanced into him, and he sensed she had an ancient soul.

"Polk," she'd said, curious. "He has the most unusual eyes."

Polk coughed. "Um, takes after his mother."

"I've seen these eyes before," her flustered voice was plain to read.

Polk blustered. "Madam, if this isn't a good time—"

"Come back later. We have unfinished business, don't we?" She tweaked Crew's nose, but she hadn't been looking at him. Her sights were on the big guy, and a grin clung to her mouth.

Ever since, Polk had been remiss to bring him to the oracles on tithing days.

✯

Can I trust Madam Rouge? Those who toiled and labored for Dyke were disgraceful scandalmongers. The circus had its own soap opera of pathetic drama. For the most part, Crew kept his head down and his ears open, until today.

Dyke loved Madam Rouge, for one reason: She drew in crowds like flies to a dung heap. People willingly gave coins for her expertise. Adept in divination, tarot cards, palm, and tea readings. People even purported she could read their minds. That was Crew's belief when he was younger.

"Crew, don't you want to know," she said like a placating mother, "where you came from, what you are?"

"You already know everything, aye?" Crew's jaw clenched. It riled him that Polk might have told this woman the sordid details of his life.

The oracle lifted a patronizing eyebrow.

"Does it matter?" he responded, and shoved locks of hair off his forehead. "It won't change anything."

"Ahh, young and invincible, I see." When he didn't have a comeback, Madam folded an arm across her waist, cupped her elbow onto her palm, and gripped her chin with her fingers. Her eyes drifted over him. "You're dressed like a pauper. A star attraction should exhibit theatrical glitz."

Crew wore his dingy shirt, pants, and his ragged cap, which he was holding in his hands. He'd been a grunt, so getting dirty was his thing.

Madam Rouge went to the armoire with its rune carvings. Swinging open one of the paneled doors, she stood there, staring into it. After a minute, she reached in with both hands and extracted garments on hangars. Spreading them on the bed, and looking them over, her head bobbed in approval. "These will do."

A fashionable frock overcoat; twill trousers; long-sleeve, white, button-down; and a double-breasted, gold-brocade waistcoat with interwoven fibers of maroon and gold. As if forgetting something, she spun back to the armoire. "This is perfect to top it off." She tossed a charcoal-grey bowler on the bed. It landed on the pillow.

"Where'd you get these?" The idea of getting into another man's clothes didn't suit him.

"Oh, don't fret. They've never been worn."

"You hoard men's clothes?"

She released an exasperated breath. "Can't you just receive a gift with gratitude when one is offered?"

"What is it?" Crew jerked his chin. "That armoire isn't ordinary, aye?"

"Very clever. Now take off those rags and put these on."

Crew picked up the trousers. "Kind of swanky. Don't care for the gold threads woven into these pants."

"Oh, for goodness sake, boy. You are incorrigible." She thumped the heel of her palm to her forehead. "It's distinguished, sophisticated, and a bit of flash. Unlike Polk whose body was all muscle, these clothes are seamless for your physique."

"Hello? Hello? Is Madam Rouge here?" a female's voice called from the interior of the marquee.

"I have customers." Madam signaled to the clothes and mouthed, "Put them on."

Once the oracle departed through the canvas curtain, Crew disrobed. The trousers and shirt were an impeccable fit, the waistcoat snug, but he'd never worn one before. He neglected the overcoat, since the weather had turned stifling warm. Retrieving his thoroughly worn pants which he'd thrown on the bed, he extricated the ringed trinket that Demelda had given him and put it into an inner cuffed pocket sewn into the waistcoat. Madam Rouge had assessed his body frame to perfection. He took the bowler and went to the full length looking glass stationed in the corner of the room.

Scarcely recognizing himself, he finger-combed his long hair behind his ears. He placed the hat on his head and smirked. "I look ridiculous." Readjusting it from side to side and back to front, he preferred it tilted to the left, the brim lowered over his brow.

Refracted in the glass behind him was the armoire. Turning, he went toward the wooden handles, which were plaited branches. Clasping each handle, he opened the two paneled doors. Bemused, he moved in to get a closer look.

Nothing. Empty.

The oracle had a flair for magic.

Indistinct voices were coming from the front area, where Madam Rouge had her readings and whatnot. It was best to make a hasty exit. Leaving by the way he came in, his reflection in the glass made him pause. The person standing there was a stranger.

Crew, come here, Madam's voice, and it came to him internally. There was a physical tug, and a conscious pull that was difficult to defy. He could resist—if he opted. *Please, Crew, come out front.*

Okay. She was coercive, and he'd play along. He flung the bowler hat on the bed and seized his worn-in newsboy cap. Crew pushed through the canvas flaps, and thought, *Where did the day go?* It was midnight black and gleaming stars. Flittering dots of light would come and go, either faery dust or fireflies, the oracle's magic at work. Acclimating himself to the dimness, he moved forward.

Piercing the dark was a shining glass globe centered on a table. Its glow cast shadows over Madam Rouge's face, touching upon her one imperfection, her front teeth were uneven. Two others were at the table with their backs to him. Girls, by the looks of their long hair carpeting their shoulders.

The oracle's eyes slashed to his face. "So nice of you to join us. Sit. Sit down," she demanded, and motioned to a vacant seat next to her.

"Aye. I don't believe I had a choice." He swung his arm behind him to stuff his cap into his rear pocket, and realized he wasn't wearing his baggy pants with his overly used pockets, but sophisticated, tailored trousers. It took effort, but he stuffed the cap in.

As he neared, the crystal globes luminosity sprayed over the girls. He recognized Sage's head of magnificent hair. This wasn't how he'd envisioned their initial meeting, but it would have to do.

As he pulled out the chair to take a seat, there was a startled intake of breath. Whether it came from Sage or her friend, whose name he'd forgotten, he didn't know. An awkward moment ensued as a sudden tenseness bristled in the atmosphere. His gaze briefly connected with Sage's. She averted her eyes, and her impossibly long lashes feathered over her cheeks.

"Hello, Sage. It's been a while." Crew, the first to deliver introductions. "Maybe you don't remember me."

Her eyelashes fluttered. "Hello." She stacked her hands on the table in front of her. "You look familiar." Her tone, a combination of propriety and sass, had him grinning.

Tolerating through an uncomfortable lull, Crew shifted on his seat as did the girls.

"Crew, you felt the pull? The mystical sphere called you here, to me," the oracle said. Before he had a chance to reply she went on, "I saw Sage and you, together, but then it…" The oracle swished her hands over the lucent globe several times as if clearing cobwebs. Madam Rouge narrowed her eyes, concentrating. "Since Crew arrived, the haze is lifting—wait… the both of you are dashing into a castle made of glass, or is it ice…?" she paused. Her squinty gaze went from the crystal ball to Sage and then to Crew.

An odd prickle slid across Crew's neck. Was she putting on a performance for the girls? Did she expect them to hand over more coins to continue? Madam Rouge rested her arms on the table, inclining toward the globe. She was entrenched in what was transpiring, which appeared to be for her eyes alone.

Observably, she wasn't waiting for coins, and said, "Its attraction is deceptive. Cold. Icy." Her shoulders shivered. "You can't find what you're searching for. It's…it's…" In a trance, she straightened. "You *must leave* this place at once. Death and danger are lurking at—"

"Am I in there?" Marne disrupted the flow and leaned in, gaping into the globe. "It looks like dancing dwarves, and—"

The oracle swiftly covered the globe with an indigo cloth and the room lightened, as if she'd turned on lightbulbs. "I'd like to do a reading for you," Madam quickened to say, her eyes targeting Sage. "Free of charge."

"Free?" A delighted smile spread across Marne's face and clapped her hands in glee. "Of course. Yes, definitely."

"I'd rather not." Sage rose from the table, her legs shoving back the chair. "That was intriguing, Madam Rouge, what you said earlier, about my family."

"Ah, but my dear," said the oracle, "the cards will have more to offer regarding your future." She picked up a deck of tarot cards and began shuffling them.

"Sit, Sage," Marne said. "It's free. And I'd like to—"

"Marne, you can stay. I need some air."

"If you don't mind," said Marne, her gaze pleading.

"Not at all. I'll be outside." Sage snagged her drawstring reticule that was full of coins from the table.

Madam Rouge prompted Crew by twitching her head toward the girl who was in the process of leaving.

"Um. I have to go." Crew lurched up, capsizing his chair. As was his habit, he wrenched his cap from his rear pocket and docked it onto his head.

Tracking Sage's footsteps, he found her standing alone, gazing at the attractions as folks strolled by. The oracle's divination disturbed him, and he could only imagine what Sage was thinking. "That sounded grim, aye?" The girl seemed dazed. Batting her lashes that emphasized her attractive eyes.

"Grim is a good word for it."

They gazed at one another for a couple beats.

"Three years," Crew said, breaking the stiffness.

They had shared precious moments in that angel tree. Moments which he'd found himself reminiscing. The Circus had voyaged far into the Unified Territory, and then Polk was in a battle that he'd never beat. He'd often thought of returning to Alderwood, to see her again, but it wasn't in the cards, as Madam Rouge would have predicted.

"Yes. A long time." She toyed with a metal button on the cuff of her sleeve. "How—"

"Sage! Sage!" shouted a squat sprite with a handlebar mustache hurrying into their space. "Have you seen Darney?"

She swerved from Crew to the sprite.

"No, Fergan. The last I saw of him was during the fireworks." Her eyes skirted between Crew and the sprite.

"We can't find him anywhere. Darney knew we were leaving," he said, worriedly. "We have a check-in rule with the kids. Every thirty minutes. He's too young to be alone in these crowds."

"He's probably playing the games," Crew offered. "He'll turn up."

Fergan gave them a forlorn nod. "If you see Darney, tell him to get his wee butt to the western gate."

ELEVEN
SAGE

"Oh dear," Sage said, eyeing the crowds. "It must be a fright to lose a child in this menagerie."

"It's not uncommon," Crew drawled. Sage had forgotten how low and raspy his voice could be. It had the same effect on her as it had three years ago. What he didn't have back then was a frightful scar on the side of his neck. "Truth is, by nightfall the workers are swamped with lost whimpering kids."

"How unfortunate."

Crew ran his fingers along the brim of his cap. "I think the parents get involved in these outer attractions. They lose track of time, days even."

"So, what you're really saying, it's the parents who are lost?"

"Uhhm. I've seen people stumbling through the midway, looking stupefied, and asking what day it is."

"When do you shut down, close the gates?" she asked. He peered down at her, and oddly, his eyes weren't the color of honey-amber as she'd remembered. More comparable to toasted buckwheat. *Strange?* Captivated by him and his plump black lashes, she evaded his gaze, putting an end to her staring.

"We don't. Once the Faire is opened. It never closes until we pack up and leave." A whirring noise drew his eyes away from her. He glanced over her head to a gazebo resembling an opulent birdhouse, complete with a copper cupola.

Sage followed his gaze to the miniature, mechanical flying objects. Copper and silver-toned birds were winging among rotating propeller planes, a cow that continuously jumped over a moon, a cat playing a fiddle, a dish holding a spoon, and a delightful variety of mechanical objects.

"I love magic," she said, and glanced up into his face. His dreamy eyes gazed down at her and there was a wry twist to his lips. He didn't respond, and it was difficult to maintain her poise with him looming above. She issued a quick reminder to herself; *I am not a giggly adolescent with stars in my eyes.* And proud of herself for not crumbling like a twittering loon. She retained her dignity and went on to furnish him with Darney's description.

"Let's walk, shall we?" Crew shored up her elbow, escorting her from the main thoroughfare. Remembering his touch, the years melted away. Heat flowed over her like tantalizing bathwater, she tossed her hair off her shoulder to cool her neck. After he'd steered them away from the masses, he let go of her elbow. Her sudden attack of heatstroke hadn't diffused as he remained close, his arm brushing hers every other step. "Besides the rides and the games," Crew said, "if I was a kid, I'd want to sneak into one of these." With a tweak of his chin, he indicated the extraordinary edifices.

Crew was right. Years ago, hadn't her and Marne been tempted to wile their way in. It was near to impossible, but Darney was little and clever.

A person couldn't miss the towering ice castle, yet people passed by without a glance. The sun was on a measured decline, and lingering sunbeams set it aglow. Nobody took notice of the frolicking light show.

"I'd love to go into the castle," Sage said, wistfully. Crew snorted a laugh. "What's so funny?"

"Madam Rouge's divination." He rearranged his cap to ride lower over his brow, cloaking his dynamic eyes, and then pocketed his hands. "She saw us dashing in, aye?"

"Wait—that reminds me," she said, and came to a standstill. "I forgot about Marne at the oracles. I have to go back and get her."

"Hey," Crew said, pointing. "Is that him?"

Swarming bodies obstructed her sight, and then she caught a scarlet streak running into the castle. "It might be. He's fast."

"C'mon." Crew seized her hand.

Threading amid bodies with their hands connected, he slowed when they came to the castle. Sage craned her head, peering up at the vaulted roofline that was stabbing the sky. The castle was narrow, although, outweighed by its towering height. Four gabled turrets. Two on either side of the façade and two in the rear. The turrets were plated with dragon scales. *Impossible*, she thought, *dragons are extinct, aren't they?*

The entrance resembled a yawning mouth with a drawbridge lowered like a tongue across a moat. The bridge was scarcely wide enough for two adults to walk abreast and the length of three or four wheelbarrows.

"Is it really made out of ice?" Sage asked, amazed at the sight.

Crew didn't answer. He peered at the booth where it was customary for a carnie to collect coins for admission. A scrawled sign read, *Closed for repair*. "That's peculiar," he said. "No wonder everyone is passing by."

"Up there!" Sage exclaimed. "I saw Darney in the turret window. *Oh no!* Look—the bridge is going up."

"Let's go." Crew gently urged her toward the rising bridge. "It's moving slow. Can you jump on?"

Her slippered feet stalled on the precipice of the moat. A chasm. The depth unknown, unseen, and dark. The drawbridge crackled, sounding like Lake Insmead during the thaw. "Why would they close it with people inside?"

Again, Crew didn't give a reply. Instead he hopped onto the bridge, now a foot off the ground. He angled over the edge, extending his arms. "Come on. I gotcha."

She hesitated, the moat giving her pause, and the thought of the slippery ice and falling into the abyss.

"Trust me, Sage. Don't look down. I won't let you fall."

She lifted her gaze from the chasm to Crew. His inky hair spilling over his face and his arms stretching for her, reminiscent of that day in the angel tree. Reaching for him, the bridge squealed upward, two more feet. He grabbed onto her forearm and effortlessly hauled her up.

The soles of her slippers balanced on the thickened edge before Crew hooked his arm around her waist. Not slippery as she'd imagined, but the rising gradient had them scooching toward the entrance of the castle. More runes were etched into the arching framework, just like the other structures she'd seen. The drawbridge continued its gradual ascent as they hustled into a vestibule. A grating thump resonated as the bridge closed off the access.

"There is a rear exit, isn't there?" She hinted for reassurance. "I can't believe they closed the castle with people in here." Crew had removed his arm from her waist, and she felt somewhat abandoned, an emptiness inside her. Wishing she'd worn practical pants, she righted her mussed skirt, and her reticule of coins hanging on her wrist, tinkled as she moved. "There's no one here. I don't hear any noise. Do you?"

Crew swung to her. "Me either. We both saw him, aye?"

She nodded while peering at a grand staircase, parading upward like an invitation to the second level. The interior shone as if made of starlight, and gothic archways led into the turrets that had spiraling stairs.

"Crew," she said, matching his gait toward the grand staircase. "What's the attraction here, besides it being made of ice and impressive?"

"I don't know." His booted feet thudded on the floor and stopped. "This is the first I'm seeing of it too. My father was sick, and I haven't been traveling with the Faire for a while. Maybe Dyke chooses who gets to perform here."

She finally remembered what Endar, the centaur, had told her and Marne. "I'm sorry to hear about your father."

"Polk knew it was inevitable." A tremor touched his hand as he brushed his hair away from his face, and he avoided meeting her eyes. "The hard part was watching the big guy turn into a skeleton. He never complained and I wanted it to be over—for his sake." His body wobbled, and he caught himself by clutching the newel post shaped like a glossy teardrop.

"Are you all right?"

"This place feels off." He wiped the sleeve of his shirt across his forehead.

Whether it was the cold confines of the castle or sensing Crew's guarded demeanor, a shiver chased down her tailbone. "Let's hurry. See if Darney is in here and get out."

"Wait here," Crew suggested. "I'll check up there and be right back." He started climbing the stairs.

The walls were comparable to mirrored glass. And wherever she turned, she saw herself reflected like a bad dream. What initially appeared remarkable had grown into a frozen, impenetrable cage.

"I'm coming with you." She finger-plucked her skirt, raising it above her ankles, and hastened to join him in the middle of the staircase. "Um, I don't like being left behind," she stammered.

He'd stopped mounting the stairs and turned to her. In the diminishing light, gilt flecks shone in his eyes, and she temporarily fell into them. His features were molded like the angels: Strong, fearless, and a heavy dose of humility. He'd grown into a man, and at that precise moment, she sensed his character hadn't changed since she'd been with him years ago.

A spark ignited in his eyes and a perplexing pucker of his brow gave her reason to believe *something was off*, as he'd mentioned.

He offered a brusque dip of his chin and, side by side, they walked to the second level. "There isn't anything or anyone here," he said.

The upper level was a basic rectangular space, fabricated with the attached gabled turrets and spiraling stairs.

"Was it an illusion? We saw him, didn't we?" She went to the window.

Crew said in a hushed voice, "We need to leave."

"Crew." Sage scraped her nails on the glass, chips of frost sprinkled her fingers. "These aren't windows."

"Come on." He grabbed her arm, whirling them toward the stairs. "Run."

"*Run?*" She dug her heels into the floor, but he yanked her forward. "Wha—"

"I can explain, but there isn't time." They took the stairs at a rapid pace. "We have to get out."

Nervously, she asked, "You're scaring me. Is it melting with us on the inside? Is that why they're not letting anyone in?"

"Shhh…" He put a finger to his lips. His gaze was directed toward the sealed drawbridge, and then he turned. "This way."

After he spun her around, she saw water gushing over the upper landing of the grand staircase.

"What the hell!" Crew swore.

"It *is* melting," Sage mumbled, dumbstruck.

He let go of her hand. "Stand back." He shoved her behind him and started rubbing the tips of his fingers together. "My hands are frozen." Chafing his palms on his waistcoat, faster and faster, sparks flared.

He's going to burn through the walls, she thought. Backpedaling, her slippered feet and the hem of her skirt were becoming saturated.

"I c-c-can't…he…he's…d-d-do…" His body turned rigid.

"Crew, what's wrong? What's happening?" Sage clutched his arm. He felt like an icicle, his face chalky and lips turning blue. "Crew?" His arms sagged to his sides as water splashed to her knees.

Cumbersome in her waterlogged skirt, she murmured, "This isn't normal." Slitting her eyes, she meditated. A staticky atmosphere developed as she flexed her fingers. Pressing her lips together, her exertion was plain to read. The roiling waters stilled, solidifying like a snapshot. To drain the swamp was an easy absorption into the fabricated castle.

"You shouldn't have," he breathed heavily, "done that."

A sudden outburst of maniacal laughter echoed.

"Sage," Crew expressed somberly, "I'm sorry."

TWELVE
CREW

"Well, well, well." Doctor Aerestol came into view on the upper landing, glaring through the lenses of his glasses down the stairs at them. "It appears Alderwood has been concealing secrets."

"Who are you?" Sage asked, puzzled.

Crew answered, "Doctor Aerestol." Sidestepping near her, his body wouldn't cooperate, shifting rigidly. Icy blood flowed in his veins, and he couldn't generate an ounce of warmth. Sage peered at him questioningly. "He w-wants y-you…" His teeth chattered, not able to complete his thought.

"Crew is correct." The doctor unhurriedly moved along the stairs. "I was informed of Polk's death and hadn't expected Crew to return to the Faire just yet. As soon as word reached me that he was here, I came quickly. I couldn't take a chance of the two of you getting too close. A woman's wiles can turn the heads of men in the most devious of ways."

"How dare you," Sage scathed. "Crew and I haven't seen each other in years. We—"

"Oh, but, my dear, you conceal your wickedness. I sense it. And that lovely sister of yours is just what the doctor ordered."

A serpentine grin crawled across his face. "Crew, three years ago, I knew Polk was steering me in another direction. I let him—because I'd been enamored with plenty of creatures to bide my days. I didn't mind waiting for this young thing to come into her own." His fingers groomed over new growth of whiskers below his nose, a mustache.

"I still remember the day I took a stroll through Alderwood, admiring its quaintness. I went past the village to a small cottage. I spied someone in breeches, if it wasn't for her hair, I would've thought it was a boy. She was in the fields throwing stones at gnomes. A precise hit each time, even though the stone had been quite off its mark. That didn't surprise me. Magical beings can make corrections. However, my dear, when two stones were speeding straight for the gnomes eyeballs, you stopped time. Not a blade of stalky weeds stirred in the wind. You ran through the field and snatched the motionless stones hanging in the air before they blinded the creature. And without uttering an incantation, the wind returned, and the gnome dashed out of sight. Very benevolent of you. I checked the records, the Alderwood council regards the Steeles with fallible magic." His eyes tapered. "I had you followed. You are not a genetic byproduct of the Steele's, are you?"

Sage snuggled into Crew, linking her arm around his. Her closeness and body heat aided in deicing his bones. As she melded into his side, he tried to restrain his shivering. He evaded meeting her eyes because—he'd screwed up. He hadn't anticipated this reversal. The script he'd been formulating was disintegrating. The doctor was taking matters into his own hands, when he should have been in his goddamn laboratory playing with his goddamn experiments. Crew had Dirge on the ready, *after* he'd enlightened his plot to Sage and, *after* she'd agreed to his obscene, bizarre scheme. A scheme that wasn't foolproof.

"Either you are working for me or working against me." Aerestol chuckled, not a mirthful sound. The weasel of a man removed his glasses, folded the arms, and slipped them into the breast pocket of his vest. "Boy, you have been harboring feelings for this girl. Do you plan on double-crossing me?"

"What is going on?" Sage detached her warm body from his side. "Crew, what is he talking about?"

"Don't move a muscle, young lady." Aerestol outstretched his fingers. "You'll be dead before you can conjure a thought." The doctor circled his hand similar to flinging a lasso. A bundle of steely rope appeared, twining Sage from her shoulders to her knees. She shrieked, wrestling with her restraints. "My dear, the more you struggle, the tighter they become. The cord is infused with silver elements that should hinder your power. I'm not certain," he said stroking his chin. "My findings are inconclusive. Rumors abound how Dolorans acquire divergent skills during their lifetime."

"Aerestol, this is barbaric," Crew spurted, as best as he could through his popsicle lips. Robotically, he embraced a fraught Sage to his chest. Why hadn't Polk mentioned that his benefactor wasn't solely a Frankenstein of a doctor, that he had a gamut of tricks up his sleeve? *A magician? A wizard?* "Let's be done with this." His teeth clacked.

Sage leaned her head back onto him, either depleted, or she was renewing her strength. Her body warmed him. The doctor had overlooked his chemistry, the silver components in the rope aided in transmitting additional heat, defrosting him. He thought of a solution. *But will it work?* He spread his fingers over the twines of rope. In gradual increments, he began singeing them, to loosen Sage's fetters. He lowered his head and whispered in her ear, "Do not move."

The doctor tsked. "I can't stomach a conman." He remained on the second stair, Crew guessed, to appear taller than he was. "In my profession, I can't afford disloyalty."

Polk's words came back to irk him— "My benefactor thinks you're my son. I swore to him, you knew nothing about the business. Nothing. If he heard differently you'd be six feet under." How had the doctor surmised his duplicity? Almost like he had a crystal ball, a diviner. Madam Rouge! Of course. She was working with the wizard.

"Crew, when Polk told me of Beeker's demise, he'd neglected a vital statistic. Your pyrotechnic talents tickle me," he said, cynically. "To smother that knack of yours, I fashioned this castle exclusively for you. Engineering a glacial substance to extinguish your fire, even the air you're breathing is hampering you." The doctor wrung his hands. "Together, we can build an empire. Don't give me your answer now." There was a deranged twinkle in the doctor's eyes. "One way or another, we'll work this out, eh boy?"

Crew wondered—*If I put the ring on, would it encase Sage within its range of power?* He couldn't take the chance of leaving her behind, not when he'd gotten her into this fiasco. He kept his sights on the doctor.

Aerestol bellowed. "Bring them out!"

Two motley-skinned orcs trooped out from behind the grand stairwell. One had an eye patch, and both had underbites that bared cambered tusks. They marched past Crew and Sage to stand behind them and crossed their arms over their chests, sentinels. Next, a brawny ogre walked into view, holding Darney. The sprite had been gagged, muffling his cries.

"Oh, no." Sage's shoulders sagged.

Then, two demons joined the party, detectable by the red ringing the irises of their eyes. Scars disfigured their faces, and their lips had been sewn together with black twine. They were dragging another muzzled man. A man who Crew had been familiar with his entire life. Dirge.

A wrought-iron collar rounded Dirge's throat; the skin around the collar was bloody and raw as well as his wrists and ankles shackled in chains. A sheen coated his bald head and beads of sweat ran down his face. Crew met his terrorized gaze. And then Dirge tried to wrest himself free from the men confining him.

"Face Dirge towards his friends, and make him kneel." Aerestol finally came down the step. "I thought we'd taken the fight out of him by now." He scoffed. The two men kicked Dirge in the back of his legs, causing him to drop to his knees.

"Leave him alone!" Crew shouted. "He has nothing to do with this."

"Ahhh, I beg to differ." The doctor withdrew a glinting dagger from his pocket. "Ungag him," he ordered his henchmen.

"Tell me, Dirge, is Crew going to betray me?" He aimed the dagger at Polk's old friend and accomplice.

Dirge's twitching gaze sought Crew. "Never."

"Are you loyal to me, Dirge?"

"Loyal."

"Truthful to the core, eh?"

Dirge's eyes twitched before grunting, "Always."

"What's our mantra?"

"No snitches. One bullet."

The doctor's nostrils flared, and gloating like a preening peacock, he puffed out his chest. Aerestol was a small man who drew vigor by demeaning and torturing others. It made Crew more determined than ever to locate his domain, where he performed his immoral experiments. Find his brother, and destroy Polk's benefactor.

"My loyal and trustworthy minion,"—he jabbed the point of the dagger into Dirge's shoulder and, with each prick of the blade, Dirge grimaced. "Is this boy standing before us,"—now brandishing the dagger toward Crew tainted in Dirge's blood—"Polk's son?"

Dirge hesitated. His gaze darted to Crew. Jaw quivering, veins throbbed in his temples. He kinked his head up, and where the collar met the raw skin of his neck, engorged veins stemmed up his throat.

Aerestol winked at Crew while cautioning Dirge. "You know what will happen if you to lie to me."

Crew schooled his twitchiness until the doctor turned back to Dirge, and then he dug into the cuffed pocket inside his waistcoat for the ring.

"H-he *is*...Polk's...son," Dirge sputtered.

Evidently, the doctor didn't believe him. Aerestol vertically slashed the dagger over Dirge's forehead, through his eye and cheek bone. Blood smeared his face as Dirge's hair-raising squeal encapsulated them. As if the doctor had choreographed the procedure, the man on his right, with his mouth sewn shut, offered his hand. Aerestol slapped the blade on his palm. And bending slightly, Aerestol squeezed his thumbs into Dirge's socket, plucking out his eye. He raised it like a trophy, pincered between his soiled fingers.

"Dirge, you should have taken the bullet." The doctor let go of the eye. It splatted on the floor. Aerestol lifted his leg and squashed it like a bug under the sole of his shoe. "Take them away. You know what to do," he commanded his men.

Dirge's howling was replaced by gulped gurgling. They dragged him behind the stairwell. The man imprisoning Darney had followed. Doctor Aerestol took a moment to regard his handiwork, the blood splattering the crystalline floor shimmered like rubies. Swerving to Crew and Sage, he brushed his stained hands on his waistcoat, expressing a job well done.

While Sage and the henchmen had been transfixed on the doctor's method of persecution, Crew had succeeded in charring and slackening her bonds. He'd been choppily breathing, biting back his own sorrow, as Sage's empathetic screams split the air for poor Dirge.

He dipped his head near her ear, in a quiet whisper, said, "Can you work your right hand from the rope?" She was frenetically sobbing. "Sage, listen to me. Wiggle your right hand between the rope." Her trembling fingers, one by one, budded from the silvery cord. "Listen, carefully." He had seconds to spare, as the doctor had finished brutalizing Dirge. "I'm going to put a ring on your finger. Don't be frightened because you will become invisible, and the rope will fall from your body. Don't make a sound. Not a peep. Take your shoes off, if you must, and tiptoe to the rear exit. Get out of here." Aerestol was turning toward them. It had to be now. "Go." He shoved the ring onto her finger.

"Boy, we have an understandin—" Aerestol faltered, and gave a stupefied blink. Loops of silvery rope plopped to the ground. "Where is she? Where did she go?" He rotated on the pads of his shoes, scouring the area. "What are you playing at, boy?" he jeered, face reddening. "Find her!" he roared to his orc sentinels who had been standing behind them.

The orc sentinels separated. Each racing into the anterior turrets. They were thumping up the spiral stairs and sprinting back down the rear turrets. "No sign of her," grunted the one-eyed orc wearing an eye patch. Clearly, the doctor had taught this sentry a lesson exactly as he taught Dirge. Yet, the guy was alive and breathing. What was going to become of Dirge, and why didn't the doctor believe him?

"She just vanished." Crew lifted his shoulders along with his arms. "You think she's Doloran? Aren't they known for—"

"Crew, find her," the doctor ordered. "Bring her to me."

"I will. Where should I bring her?" That information was crucial, and Crew had yet to attain it.

※ ✯ ※

It had been during that first meeting with Aerestol, in Polk's tomb of a bedroom, when he shook hands with the merciless man. Crew had been edgy. His objective wasn't to fill the big guys boots by working for his benefactor. But Polk had dangled an incentive, one that was hard pressed to dismiss. Like a dutiful apprentice, Crew listened to what the doctor had to say.

"It's preposterous to glaze over the core aspects of the job, and Polk knows this." The doctor had withdrawn a hankie from his trousers, and taking off his glasses, polished the lenses.

"Crew, what I am requesting of you is illegal. I won't pander to stoolies or blackmail, so don't try it. If you deign to comply, we have a verbal contract of intent, and adhere to the penalties of your actions. You and your team will be in jeopardy of being killed, imprisoned, or even sent to the gallows." He put his spectacles back on. "I command complete discretion. Dirge will be your wingman," he affirmed, "like he was with Polk. Once your task is accomplished, I will provide the details on a need-to-know basis. No more. No less. Polk what's our motto?"

Polk's voice was a rough burn. "No snitches. One bullet."

"Crew, do I need to clarify?" A crooked grin settled on his face. "Everything I say, and everything that you see, is confidential. If you get nabbed by the authorities or the king's regent, it would be to your benefit to put a bullet into your own skull if you rat me out." He then removed a piece of paper from his pocket. "Your first test. Let's see what you can do for me."

Crew had unfolded the paper.

Tuesday, the 21st noon,
bring Demelda to Foundling Square,
and leave her there.

"Now destroy it," the doctor stipulated. "No one sees it."

Later, when Polk hadn't been delirious, Crew inquired, "Where does your benefactor live?"

"He has an estate in the Unified Territory, Quillen for business, he hobnobs with prominent mortals," Polk stated. "But he experiments in Wintervine where the weather is ruthless. He doesn't get interference and can work undisturbed."

"Have you been to those places?" Crew kept interrogating him while shuffling a deck of cards, and then dealt them out. He'd been consumed with thoughts of a brother he never knew existed and the pretty girl in Alderwood. Why did the Frankenstein doctor want them?

Polk fisted his hands. "I shouldn't have snitched. He'll kill me for telling you."

"At this point, does it matter?" They'd glared into each other's eyes. "Polk, we both know how this is going to end."

"If he learns I divulged where he does those dadgum experiments, he'll rip you apart. Piece by screaming piece."

"At some point, he'll have to tell me where he lives. How else am I going to get his merchandise to him?" Crew had favored saying merchandise rather than people or creatures.

"Don't try tracking him. He has cutthroats guarding him. Besides, there are wards and boobytraps. No one can get through them. Not even you."

The doctor walked toward the ropey cords and nudged them with the toe of his shoe. His unbelief was restored by a flicker of approbation, as if he exhumed an unexpected gem.

Crew spotted where he'd burned through the fibrous cords. To distract the doctor's inspection of the rope, he raised his voice, "Where? Where should I bring her?"

Deflecting Crew's question, he stood like a statue listening for movement. His gaze surfing across the lower level of the castle. "She's here. I sense *something*. The girl didn't just vanish."

"By the looks of it, she did just that," he posed, irony in his tone.

If Crew wasn't mistaken, a transparent figure of the girl stood off to his left. *Sage?* Was he seeing things? Nobody else was aware of her presence. Crew had gleaned adequate warmth and power to liquefy the castle wall and escape. He couldn't do it. His brother's life and possibly Sage's, depended on him by being obedient to the devil.

"What's this?" Aerestol went down on one knee. *Dammit, he saw the burnt rope.* The doctor rummaged into the mound of coils and withdrew Sage's handbag. The reticule jingled with its coins inside. "A paltry pittance." He rose and stuffed it into his trouser pocket.

"Pilfering money, doc?"

"Not stealing if she left it behind," he said, tweaking his nose. "What a shame. Polk spoke highly of you." Aerestol snapped his fingers and the sentinels redeployed, penning Crew in. While Crew was a head taller, the goons were packing revolvers tucked into the waistbands of their pants. "In my line of work, I can't afford to trust anyone. Rumormongers are dealt with accordingly. My advice? Don't become one." He hooked his thumbs into his vest, and with his head down, turned toward the grand staircase.

"Now what?" Crew said. Was he done for? Were his goons going to take him out. Kill him?

Aerestol pivoted, and as if improvising a reply, his head slanted sideways. "So far, you haven't impressed me, boy. You should have handed over the girl. Instead, I walk away empty handed. I can't tolerate that." He ran his fingers beneath his chin. "Perhaps Polk *was* speaking with a straight tongue. He never failed me. I tell you what, for his sake alone, your obeisance is most welcome *if* you want into my lucrative business." His mouth spread. "If you make it out alive…you know how to reach me, through Dyke. Ingrain this into that thick skull of yours. No snitches. One bullet." He jutted his chin towards the one-eyed goon. "Do it."

The sentry pulled his revolver from his waistband and targeted Crew's chest.

"Hey!" Crew barked, anxious to get Aerestol to look at him. The doctor swerved and Crew straightaway connected with his dark eyes. *Gotcha!* "So this is how we're going to end our business arrangement, aye? A bullet to the heart?" he pitched his voice. Aerestol's pupils enlarged. "I'm the only one who can bring the girl to you. Don't waste me and my talents." Crew blinked, terminating his connection, and the doctor squeezed his eyes and shook his head.

"His thigh," ordered Aerestol. "It's unfortunate that I can't stay to watch how this performance ends."

The orc lowered his gun and pulled the trigger.

White light sliced through Crew. And a blinding explosion of stars as intense pain ripped through him. His knees buckled.

THIRTEEN
SAGE

Crew was groping, trying to push something onto her finger. *A ring.* Suddenly, she found herself elsewhere. Darks and grays, a windy wasteland of decimated buildings. Her constricting tethers fell from her body, a tangled lump gathered around her feet. She stepped over them. The despicable man who gouged out Dirge's eyeball blurred before her. He'd howled at the orcs to find her when she was right there the whole time.

Crew was looking at her from the corner of his eyes. She remembered what he'd said, about not making a sound. Careful and noiselessly, she slipped off her slippered shoes and tiptoed to the wall. Standing erect, motionless. She waited, for what? She didn't know.

Her head reeled with wild accusations. This doctor ordered Crew to bring her to him. *Is Crew working with this man?* She didn't want to believe it, and why did he want her? And Darney? *What are they going to do to him?* She covered her mouth, afraid they'd hear her breathing.

When the one-eyed orc aimed his gun at Crew's chest, she'd swallowed her scream. Her body shuddered along with the blast. Fastening her hand across her nose and mouth, curbing ragged breaths, she watched. Crew cried out, clutched his leg, and fell. Blood oozed between his fingers and bright red droplets speckled the ice. Devoid of concern for Crew, the doctor and his men departed behind the staircase.

Petrified, she was afraid to move.

She waited, watching a defeated Crew struggling to stand. He fell again, onto his butt, his face a mess of agony.

"I know you're here," he said, gnashing his teeth. Writhing in pain, his face broke out in a sweat. "Take it off before…" A rasping growl passed his lips as he again attempted to stand.

Apprehensive, she went to him. She knelt and touched his arm.

"Take…off…the…ring. I'll explain." His cap had fallen from his head, and his dark hair stuck to the moisture on his forehead and cheeks.

She slid the oversized ring from her finger, and the dark, grayish realm faded. Her vision cleared, encountering the sight of blood marinating the leg of his trousers.

"The bullet went clean through," she said, after peeling his hands from his leg and inspected the wound.

"Aye, I'm a lucky guy." He held out his hand, palm up. She dropped the ring on his hand painted in his own blood. He put the trinket inside his waistcoat. "Thanks. Any trouble there?" he said, taking deep shuddering breaths.

"Was strange. I was here…but, not here." She'd been holding her slippers in her hands, and now wedged them on her cold feet.

"Sounds like what I experienced. I haven't explored its…" He groaned through clenched teeth.

"Stay where you are." Sage hovered her hand over his injury.

"If you could spare some material from that pretty skirt, I can wrap it to stanch the blood." He shifted and moaned, trying to get to his knees.

"I said"—sounding stern, she pushed him down by his shoulder—"don't move."

Defy the Stars

"Sheesh, cranky, girl."

Showing emphasis with a pointed finger, she said, "Stay still. Don't talk." The force of his eyes unnerved her, a kettle of glimmering bullion. "And don't look at me like that." Crew had made a bargain with that horrid man to bring her to him. His single conciliation was, he'd saved her. At the cost of getting a bullet to his leg.

"Goodness, girl. I can't do a darn thing right. I'm bleeding out and you want to…to what? What are you doing?"

Her fingers curled into claws. "Please, stop." She scoffed. "Let me help you. I need to concentrate."

"It damn hurts, aye." He paled. Pain lanced across his face as he outstretched his leg with the bullet hole, and angling backward, he braced his arms on the floor behind him. "Go for it."

"Before I do, swear to me, you'll tell me everything." Her voice flinty and unyielding. "*Everything.*"

He leaned forward and clamped his hands on his thigh. "This sucker is throbbing. I swear, I'll explain. Do whatever you do. Or leave me to rot."

Squeezing her eyes, she brought her hands together, contemplating. She'd healed Tegan's broken ankle. Papa's arthritic fingers due to hard labor in the mines. Eadith's dislocated shoulder. Mama was cutting a ham hock and the carving knife slipped, slicing into her arm, all were healed, and many animals throughout the years.

Why was this different? Crew wasn't family. Just a good-looking outsider. He could go to the council and make a charge against her. Attesting she was a Doloran. Reviled. Scorned. What would happen to the Steeles for harboring a forbidden species? Edras had warned her, time and again, never to expose themselves.

"Sage, are you done warming your hands? The cold is leaching into every orifice of my body. I won't be able to move."

"Shush," she yipped. Against her better judgement, she couldn't leave him like this. She had the power to heal, and if things ever turned against her, would she have the ruthlessness to stop a person from breathing? Once, she had been forced to put a deer out of its misery. She hoped she'd never have to make that choice again.

He trembled, biting down on his teeth. She stationed her hands above his blood-soaked thigh.

Steady

Concentrate

Calling forth her power, it stirred in the marrow of her bones. She'd practiced this a thousand times. The skin of her palms tingled, filling with healing heat, as she'd named it.

Seconds

Minutes

She opened her eyes. His torn skin was reconnecting, the bullet hole was closing in on itself. His external skin was mending, although, puckered and ruddy and already bruising. On the inside, where the bullet might have caused significant damage, she didn't know. Time would tell.

"How does it feel?" she queried.

"You're a healer," he said subtly. "You stopped the flooding water by…what? Time lapse?" He released a plume of clouding air as he skimmed his fingers over the lumpy wound, a twinge pulled his brow. She perceived it hadn't healed properly, that would require more time. Exhaling another airy breath, he composed himself. "Aerestol said you are a Doloran. I thought they were annihilated."

Recalling her sisters' warnings, she redirected him by saying, "That…that brute of a man?" Anger boiled in her chest. "You're working for him?"

He gripped his leg. "Much better." Avoiding her inquiry, as she'd avoided his, he stated, "Let's get out of here." Moving to his side, Crew clumsily climbed to his feet. "It's getting dark in here; the hour is late. Follow me." He swiveled and searched the floor for something.

"You're limping," Sage said.

"It's fine. You did great." He found his cap, picked it up, and rather than stick it on his head, he crammed it into his rear pocket. "Sorry, I'm an ingrate. I forgot to say thank you."

"It's not an instant cure. If I were to guess, the bullet caused damage to the muscle, tendons, ligaments, whatever it went through, making the pain radiate. I suggest resting your leg."

"Hah, you talk like a medic."

Cracking had them spinning their heads toward the sound, and the crystal-like floor vibrated. There was a strident snap, like the solid ice on Lake Insmead when it was about to give way. A cranny opened the northern wall. Then a chunk of ice fell from above, missing Crew's head by inches, and smashing into diamondlike rubbles. Jagged fissures snaked through the floor, widening below their feet.

"We got to get out of here," Crew hollered over the ear-shattering noise. He snatched her wrist. And with a tangible limp, he pulled her along, rushing behind the grand staircase.

Sage yanked her arm from his hold. "There's no exit!" She went to the glistening wall and smoothed her hands over its coldness. "There has to be a trick door somewhere, how else did they get out?"

"Hey, can you stop this?" Crew shouted. "Slow it down from dismantling on our heads?"

"I...I'll try." She closed her eyes and taking in deep breaths she strived to expel her energy.

"Good, girl," he praised. "It's working. C'mon. This way."

"We can't go back," she panted, strength waning. "There's no way out." Crew dithered while assessing their dilemma. Descending boulders and flakes of ice had frozen in midair. "I can't hold it forever." The floor and walls were breaking apart in slow motion, boulders of ice sluggishly fracturing around them.

A jarring noise had them glancing upward. "The upper level is coming down," Crew yelled. Extensive cracks and splintering had compelled them to dash back to the main entrance, which was closed off by the drawbridge.

Crew flicked his arm, an airborne force sizzled through the air. The drawbridge toppled. Not rational, nor caring, Sage's thoughts of escaping pushed her onward, resulting in her time-lapse power to dwindle. The ice castle shook.

"Watch it!" he alerted from behind. "The bridge isn't stable."

The drawbridge seesawed and cocked sideways. Sage gasped, gliding helplessly to the ledge. Entrenched in heart pounding panic, she fell to her knees, clawing the ice for purchase. The abyss called to her, dismal in the darkness. Her mental strength spent, and now physically encumbered. She was going to die. Slipping, sliding, her feet, knees, and then her legs dangled off the edge. Frantically she scraped the ice with her fingernails.

Vise grips strapped her wrists, prying her nails from the bridge, and hauled her from the ledge.

"I got you." Crew scooped her into his arms. His gait unstable, he went to where the bridge should have been connected with the ground. The drawbridge had elevated yards from their saving grace. "Hold tight. We have to jump."

There was a bone-shaking avalanche. The sound had her looping her arms around Crew's neck. The castle was beginning to implode.

"Put me down. We won't make it like this." She met his distraught gaze. The Faire's gaslights flashed in his eyes. "Put me down," she said, her voice remarkably steady.

He receded a step and lowered her to the bridge. "You won't make it with this on." His nimble fingers worked on the waist of her skirt seeking the latch, and then ripped the material. The skirt plunged to her ankles. Clad in her cotton petticoat, Sage kicked her skirt aside. It slithered and fell into the chasm.

Crew said, "A running leap." She caught his whisper in the wind. They clamped their hands. "Together." He wore an encouraging smile.

"A leap of faith."

They ran until the soles of their feet touched the ridge of dense ice. The drawbridge shattered underfoot. Splinters of ice ignited like crystalized firecrackers. Crew and Sage soared across the challenging abyss, peddling their legs. Sage again sensed an unbidden energy, lifting her up.

Her feet met the ground, and she collapsed into a barreling roll. Face down, nose denting the tamped soil, Sage flopped onto her back. Yelps and grunts resounded, and people standing above cast peevish frowns at her.

"What in tarnation is wrong with you girl?" Someone balked. "You nearly took out my legs."

"Where did she come from?" exclaimed another voice.

"She fell from the sky."

"Oh my goodness. She's indecent."

"I bet she's a performer at the Ale House."

Sage propped herself up, inhaling an enveloping pong. Two portly trolls sneered down their globular noses at her, she knew where the stink was coming from.

She twisted on the spot, searching for Crew. Her mouth dropped open. The castle was gone, in its place a vacant lot. They could have been killed, a catastrophe that nobody heard nor witnessed. Folks gave her a wide berth as she stumbled to her feet. Women snubbed their noses at her indecency, while men quirked approving brows.

In the array of parading regalia and women's flouncing skirts, Crew was nowhere to be seen.

"My Lady," said a rough, familiar voice. "May I be of service?"

Sage swerved toward the greeting, though, spurned Crew's extended hand. "Are you seeing what I'm seeing?" She incredulously gaped at the vacant plot of land.

"If you are implying that we are not seeing the castle, then yes." He wore a taut grin. "Come with me."

Tentative, like waking from a bad dream, she hugged her arms around her waist. "I am *not* going anywhere with you. I have had more than my share of excitement for one day." Moreover, *No coins*.

While they had been locked within the castle, a dark night had invaded the avenues. It hadn't detracted from ushering in a multitude. Indeed, the Faire's revelry was beginning to heighten, vociferous ringing of bells and whistles, whirring rides in the midway. Sage's belly grumbled as she drank in the influx of blueberry and strawberry snitzes and blintzes, honey toasted hazelnuts, and simmering squid. Ale pavilions, which had been mediocre during the daylight hours, were bursting at the seams. Sounds of gaiety and bawdy ballads drew folks in to quench their thirst and their tastes with ambrosia delights. Twilight was in the throes of summoning every imaginable creature to engage in whatever the Faire had to offer.

"Sage, I think it's best if you come with me."

"I have to find Marne."

"Err," he said, gazing at her legs. "You should go skirtless more often. You have nice legs."

A good portion of her legs were exposed, draped in her thigh-length pantalette with its eyelet border. "Oh, dear."

FOURTEEN
CREW

Disregarding Sage's quip of not going anywhere with him, Crew hooked his arm around her. He hissed lowly when a sting ramped up his thigh and into his groin. The jump had acerbated his wound. Gritting down the ache, he navigated them between bodies being entertained by the circus' carnival of antics.

"Where are we going?" she asked woodenly.

"Let's see if we can get you something to wear." He knew where he had to start, the oracle. "You can't go home wearing just your undergarments, can you?"

"Ahh, probably not. If I can find Marne—"

"You won't, not in this jungle."

They traipsed by the Ebenezer Ale pavilion, an open shelter with an L-shaped bar that supplied refreshments. Padmae Ocoso, a voluptuous selkie, was belting out a scintillating love song. The stricture of clothing must have been an unfavorable parody for her performance. Flaunting herself in her natural skin of iridescent scales, which barely served in concealing her breasts, was stimulating the patrons. Dancing lithely between tables, the men's caterwauling inspired her seductive dance.

"Who is that?" Sage asked. "Her voice is hypnotically low and coarse like a man's."

"Padmae's performed with the Circus for a while." Crew spotted a cigar-toking Dyke elbowing the bar rail, a mug of dark honey ale in hand. Also recognizable was a table of four men in the corner. Older men he'd worked side by side with while traveling with Polk. At this stage of the evening, he couldn't chance being seen and tried hustling Sage by. He snatched his cap from his back pocket and clipped it on his head.

"You know her?" Sage craned her neck to look over her shoulder.

"Everybody knows Padmae."

"Hey, Crew!" shouted Harry Clippin.

Crap! Pretending not to hear him, Crew eased through a row of people waiting to enter the Tent of Wonders.

"Crew!" Harry's voice cut through the air.

Sage said, "Someone is calling you."

Crew put on the brakes, crunched his teeth, and turned. "Harry." He fingered the brim of his cap and bowed his head, addressing a man in greasy overhauls.

"I thought it was you walking by." Harry spoke with a lisp, missing a front tooth. "I'm sorry to hear 'bout Polk. Dyke won't ever find nobody like him. And Dirge hasn't shown his face in days. Losing good men, that's hard to come by." He ironed his hands over his overalls. "Come have a drink with the crew. Bring your lady friend." He beamed, staring down at Sage's bare legs, and licked his lips.

Sage nuzzled into Crew's side. "Can't tonight, Harry. I have to get ready for my show. Dyke said I had to be on the ridge by eleven-thirty."

Harry glimpsed the sky as if it could tell time. "Yeppers." He dropped him a wink. "I get it. See you later, maybe?"

"Sure thing." Crew limped as he turned.

"Hey, what happened to your leg." Harry indicated Crew's fraying, bloody trousers. "Looks like ya ruined swanky pants. Not what I'm used to seeing you wear, boy."

"It's nothing, a flesh wound," Crew said. Harry the stoolpigeon—what the crew nicknamed him, had his nose into everybody's business. Crew engineered an excuse for his blood-tattered trousers because Harry was infamous for inventing his own farfetched stories. "I was helping Rohan with his throwing act and got caught in the crossfire." Listening to his outlandish lie, Sage shifted beneath his affixing arm hold.

Harry cackled, lifting his leg and slapping his kneecap. "That dern Rohan's a wild one. Dyke already gave him an ultimatum: One more botched performance and he's sending 'im packing. Rohan's gonna git somebody kilt one of these days. You's lucky, boy. This will be our secret; don't want Dyke to git a whiff of it. See ya on the ridge. Break a leg, kid."

This time Crew didn't dawdle. He took off, limping, and veered Sage into a constricted isle between tents. "We have to get out of sight."

"Who is Rohan? And what did that fellow mean by *he gets it*—gets what?" Her tone indignant.

"Rohan and his Flying Blades. His collection of shuriken's is topnotch."

"Harry doesn't think he's any good at throwing knives?"

Crew chuckled dryly. "He's phenomenal. Uses magic to do… whatever. Except after he downs a quart of vodka." *Harry will give Dyke an earful. Not my problem now.*

Shades lengthened beyond the outer sections, behind the tents and pavilions. Even the ruckus was pleasantly subdued as they came to Madam Rouge's. Eons had passed, albeit hours, since he'd snuck in. He guided Sage into the rear ingress.

"Where are we?"

"Shh…" Crew adapted to the shadowy dark while fine tuning his hearing. Sounds of merriment came from outside, but the oracle's main room was silent. He drew back the bifold curtain and peeked in. Dark. No customers. No tarot or divination readings. Madam Rouge was taking a break.

A thought slid down his throat, and it burned. *Is she meeting Doctor Aerestol?* Their plight originated with the oracle's premonition. Interpreting what she'd seen in her divination globe, the two of them dashing into the castle. A conjured spell, perhaps? It occurred to him that it wouldn't have worked if Fergan Galdoon hadn't been searching for Darney. A coincidence—or a magical setup?

"Crew," Sage whispered, standing close behind him, "what are we doing here?"

"Let's get you something to wear." Flipping his hand, palm up, firelight bathed the oracle's private quarters.

"That's different." Sage stared at the flames springing from his hand.

He lifted a brow. "Don't sell yourself short, lady." Stepping to a lantern on the nightstand, he covered the top circumference with his hand. A spark shot down, lighting the wick.

"Ermm... I'm not stealing her clothes," she said.

Crew went to the armoire and lit up the runes. "Borrowing." He inserted the tip of his index finger into one of the carvings and traced the rune. Then the next and the next, memorizing them. "Intriguing," he said. "Describe your skirt."

"My skirt?"

"It was yellow, aye?"

"Pastel peach. A straight skirt with a flaring hemline. I embroidered ivy and flowers on it."

"Picture it in your mind."

"Um, *ookay.*"

"Good," he said barely audible. Gripping the handles of the armoire, he pulled. "Just what you described." He withdrew a faultless replica of her skirt. Sage gasped, taking the garment.

"Crew?" Crew and Sage jolted as the oracle swept in. "What happened to your leg?"

"You're the soothsayer," he said. "Don't you already know?"

"Don't be pompous, it's unbecoming." Madam Rouge's silks poured into the room with her. "Sit. Let me take a look."

"No need. Sage took care of it."

Madam's narrowing gaze fastened on the girl. "You're a healer?" she said, wary mixed with inquisitiveness. Sage hugged the skirt to her chest and gave a slight nod. "Why did you bring her here? To ransack my armoire?"

"I don't have lady things in my quarters."

"No leftovers from Demelda?" She cast him a naughty wink. "Polk said—"

"I would've raided Demelda's wares," he interrupted her, "but word is, she never showed." He averted his eyes from the oracle, worried she'd read him like her tea leaves. "Dyke found a replacement, though."

"Teslan. Not charismatic or as theatrical as Demelda." Madam sighed. "Crew, when was the last time you saw Demelda?"

Crew made a face. "Finnick Row," he lied, and absently pressed his hand over his waistcoat, feeling the circular shape of the ring. "Before Polk died. We talked." He left it at that.

"She's dead."

Crew's head shot up. "Huh? What do you mean she's dead?"

"They found her body on the rocks, in an inlet on the Sea of Tears. In Foundling."

"Nooo," he groaned, panic-stricken. Squeezing his eyes, a vision of Demelda's confident, snarky, smile hit him like a blast of dynamite. Feeling off-kilter, his body swayed.

"Crew, are you all right?" Sage touched his arm.

Endeavoring to regulate his thrumming heart, he refocused on the oracle's impassive expression. "How do you know it was her? Bodies wash up on the shore all the time."

Madame raised her angular chin. "Dyke received a telegram from Foundling. The authorities knew she was one of the attractions at the Faire. He was sent for to identify her, at least what was left of it. Her body was eviscerated, torn apart," she simplified, not varnishing her words.

"Auhhg…" Sage moaned, placing a hand on her stomach.

Demelda's description of Mage Marek came to mind. His body had been torn inside out. Demelda feared it was due to that damn ring. *Why?* His face was numb as was the rest of him.

"Why…why didn't Dyke tell me?" his tongue stumbled.

"Astute businessman. He'd always known about the relationship you and Polk had with her. He was afraid if he told you, you'd leave the Circus."

"Dyke got that right." His numbness was refueling with bold audacity. Veering back to the armoire and, reaching in, he obtained trousers to replace his sullied pair. "You don't mind, do you? I think you owe me."

"*I owe you?*" she said condescendingly.

Sage had climbed into her new skirt as he and the oracle were bantering.

"You don't strike me as dimwitted." With each inhale, Crew's vigor was returning. "I won't be tricked a second time."

"Boy, talk sense."

The oracle was getting prickly; he saw it in her sour-mouthed mien. What irked him, he'd been a little busy trying to stay alive in that godforsaken castle and hadn't formulated a plan. And now with her crude revelation of Demelda's demise, the cards were stacking up against her. Should he accuse Madam Rouge of collaborating with Aerestol, or play the game?

"Crew, I know what you did," the oracle said. "The runes on the armoire. How effortlessly you absorbed their significance."

"Madam, you give me too much credit. Any troll with half a brain could have figured it out."

"No, my boy. You sell yourself short. And I find myself extremely intrigued. How and why did Polk keep you under wraps?"

"Hey, I'm just a circus grunt. Nothing more."

"Is that so?" Madam's sourness had switched to cheeky mischief. "Let me tell you what I see. Come, allow me a reading."

Crew was an orphan. He didn't know, until Polk told him with the truth. All these years, he thought his mother left him with his father. He'd been speculating about his real parents. *What am I? Who am I?* Growing up under the unbreakable thumb of the big guy, and by a fluke incident, he'd found himself able to do strange things. Things he couldn't rationalize. When he demonstrated his fiery talent, resulting in Beeker's death, Polk turned wide-eyed and pasty. Then he cuffed him on his head with his pan-sized hand and made Crew promise not to show or tell a living soul.

After the incident with Beeker, the three of them had been relaxing under the stars basking in the warmth of a bonfire. When out of the blue Polk ground his teeth and thundered, "*Never* do that shit again!" His eyes flared like a demon. "Those whatchamacallits—that Elven magic crap, or whatever is percolating in that blood of yours, you'd better cap it."

Dirge took a long draw of his brew, and said, "I told ya, Polk. Taking in the boy would get us killed. If ya gut him now, nobody would be the wiser." Dirge threw Crew a wink.

Polk plucked on his thistly eyebrows. "Wait until…until it's the right time. Get what I'm saying, boy?"

Crew unfastened the button on the waistband of his trousers. "Ladies, be prepared," he shoved the trousers off his hips, "to see a pair of hairy legs."

As if insulted, Madam veered her head away while slinging a wrist to cover her eyes. "Us ladies will give you privacy to change." She swept her arm toward the exit into her divination chamber, signaling Sage to move ahead of her. "Crew, we'll be waiting for you."

Polk is probably rolling in his grave. He once told him, "Never let the oracle get into your head with her cards of fate. Best for your wellbeing, she doesn't figure you out, boy."

Polk had the inclination of reciting the phrase: "Fate is a mean fucker." On his death bed, it was a well-declared refrain. "Fate dealt me the death card," he'd uttered, lips twisting. "Damn her."

During Polk's failing health, Crew had awoken to see that Polk's cot hadn't been slept in, again. In the early hours before the advent of a new day, the Faire was at its serenest. Games and rides had ceased due to a low attendance of children, although, tipsy people staggered along the midway. On a typical morning when passing the ale pavilions, bodies were slouched over tables. The putrid stench of stale beer and vomit assaulted his nostrils as he passed.

The big guy had been making time with the lanky soothsayer, and coming to his destination, he snuck behind the oracles.

He heard Polk's voice, though muffled. "You cursed me, Kade. You've taken my soul and my body. I have nothing left to give."

"There is more," the oracle. A temporary lull in their conversation had Crew hunkering to his haunches. "Bring me the boy. After you're gone, I will he—"

"No!" Polk snipped, severing her words. "Leave him to destiny."

An impatient pause. Kade, "The stars foretell destiny. And if the boy is clever and shrewd, he can change his stars."

"Kade, you can't defy the stars hanging in the sky. You talk nonsense."

A mute silence.

"Then…you had the talk with your benefactor?" she inquired. "Is that what you desire for the boy?"

"It'll put coins in his pockets. Then he can go and do whatever the hell he wants."

"Where is the boy's mother? Who, or rather, *what* is she?"

Eager for his answer Crew had leaned into the canvased tent.

"Dead. She...she died."

"I sense unfathomable energy in him. Not an origin of the human species. Is he?"

There was a grumpy snarl and then the planks of the erected tent creaked. Crew loped into the nearby bushes as Polk bashed open the flaps of the tent. Naked and scratching his chest, which had begun to shrivel due to his disease, he walked into the woods and returned minutes later.

※ ☆ ※

Hanging onto that memory, Crew snorted. He missed Polk. Reopening the armoire, he tossed his bloodied trousers inside, where they vanished. Chimes drew his gaze to a mantel clock on Madam's dresser. Dyke would be expecting him on the ridge within the hour. A tide of anxiety gripped him. Had Aerestol departed as he'd lead him to believe or, was he laying a trap? For him? For Sage? Where did he take Dirge and Darney? *Are they alive?*

Crew walked into the main room, and stationed at the circular table, the oracle was leisurely shuffling a deck of tarot cards, and grilling Sage with questions. "I'm sorry, Madam," he disrupted them. "We haven't time for readings." He took Sage's hand, pulling her to her feet.

"Crew," the oracle said, rising up, "don't get involved with the doctor."

"You know Aerestol?"

"I know *of* him. Polk..." The tarot cards stilled in her hands. "Once you begin working for him, you can't get out."

"You're acquainted then?"

Deviating her gaze from Crew to the cards, she sucked in a breath. "He comes for readings."

"Just readings?" Crew said, sounding fishy. "Polk told you about his dealings with his benefactor."

A self-assured smirk jumped onto her face. "I know many things, Crew. I am the oracle." She leaned forward and splayed the cards on the table. "I see. I hear. I know."

"You are in league with the doctor, aye?"

Her head snapped up. "I promised Polk I'd help you, when the time came. I believe it's in your best interest if you let me."

Sage broke into their tête-à-tête. "You saw us, in the crystal ball, running into the ice castle. You knew it was a trap?"

"I didn't know. Is that where you got that?" She motioned to Crew's injured leg, now covered in a clean pair of trousers.

"Then," Sage said, "you also know it was an illusion that nearly got us killed."

The oracle plinked her fingernails on the table. "Only a master illusionist or a wizard could fabricate such a thing."

"Aye, could be both?" Crew stated.

Crew wondered how much he should say. If he told Sage and Madam everything, it might be detrimental, for all of them. To make Aerestol rely on him and his abilities, he'd worked a couple jobs to gain the bastard's trust. Jobs he wasn't proud of. Crew doubted the man had a trustful bone in his body.

He'd yet to find the exact whereabouts of Aerestol's estate in Wintervine, a territory known for its unforgiving weather and treacherous mountains.

As the delirium had beset Polk, his descriptions became strange and stranger. When Crew struggled to get him to be explicit and reveal where the boobytraps were hidden and how to defuse them, his eyes clouded. He evaded telling Crew the specifics, or, a perturbing thought, Polk wasn't privy to this information.

"Sage! Sage!" Edras burst into the tent, breathing weightily. "Thank the gods you're here."

FIFTEEN
SAGE

"Edras, what's wrong?" Sage said, taking in the campfire stench that had breezed in with her. Edras' light-weight dress was singed, the hem shredded. Her hair, normally pristine, had escaped her bun and was sticking out every which way. Edras ran her fingers under her runny nose, leaving behind a black smudge. "Are you in trouble? What happened?"

Edras emitted a snuffling cry. She wrapped her arms around Sage and squashed her to her chest. "Have you seen Tegan?" she said, her voice breaking.

"No, not yet." Sage pulled away from the embrace. "Tegan was working the mine today."

"Not at this hour." Edras wiped her eyes, leaving behind more ashy residue. "You have to come ho-o-me." The term *home* stuck in her throat. "Now." She took Sage's hand and began hustling them out of Madam Rouges.

Sage jerked back on her hold. "Edras, I'm not ready to leave. Tell me why I have to go home." She cast Crew a quizzable brow. "And why are your fingers covered in soot?" Had her sister been attending to her hearth?

"I...I saw... I..." Edras blanched, lips quivering, and said, "Your...the Steele's cottage is...is gone. Burned to the ground."

Sage cocked her head. "What did you say?" Her sister had been drinking too much mead, even her eyeballs were swimming in their sockets.

"Follow me," Crew said, taking charge. "We can't take a direct route. Someone might be posted, looking for Sage."

"Wait!" Sage accidentally bumped the table with the divination globe as she backtracked into the wall of the tent. Hugging her forearms to her chest, she covered her mouth. "It's true?" she said through her caged fingers. Edras gave a mournful nod and inhaled a sniveling breath. "Where's Mama? Papa? Eadith?"

Edras bit down on her bottom lip, shaking her head as tears washed her cheeks. "I brought Eadith home hours ago. I searched through the..." Her tone was strangled, teeming with apprehension. "I smelled the smoke through the woods. The cottage was smoldering when I got there. I...I found bodies."

"You walked into a burning cottage?" Crew's brow furrowed.

"I had too," she said, weepy, "it was the only way.... I knew Sage was at the Faire. I came...fast as I could..." Sorrow claimed Edras's features. Trembling fingers wiped her tear-filled eyes. "I had to know if she was..."

Her sister's horrific message finally penetrated Sage's brain. Terrified, Sage tore past her sister and Crew. Breaking through the flaps of the oracle's tent, she ran off, blinded by urgency.

Her thrumming heart tightened her chest. Rife with muddling thoughts, she crashed into scads of promenading people. Sage lifted her skirt which provided her ample room to stretch her legs to their fullest. Sprinting, zigzagging, and bumping her way through, notwithstanding affronted folks swearing at her, she reached the gate. The fastest path to their cottage was through the woods.

Sage noticed her sister was tentative to fully explain with Crew and Madam Rouge looking on. Assuming their Doloran heritage was at the forefront of this tragedy. Crew had interceded, fretting that someone might be looking for her. And she knew who—that repulsive doctor had seen her, years ago, he knew where she lived.

Mama. Papa. Little Eadith. Parry. Tegan? They can't be dead. Her screaming thoughts were making her light-headed.

Tears were streaming down her face, feeling them dampening her blouse. Swiping her chin, she blinked, releasing more. She made it to the clearing where her angel tree looked like a shadowy giant with far-reaching tenacles. Not far now.

Neither resting nor slowing, and ignoring the ache in her legs, her slippers scuffed through mulch and twigs. Even the stitch in her side hadn't deterred her. Sage didn't want to believe Edras. She had to see it for herself.

A breeze caressed her face, and with it a tinge of smoke. Snuffling all of it like a hound with a scent, she foraged amid the low-hanging pine boughs, and stopped. Motionless and shocked. The cottage's carcass had crumbled over the darkening land and gray threads of smoke were curling into the ether. A few disjointed timbers were still upright like fingers in the gloom of night.

Trance-like, Sage moved in. The stoned hearth was somewhat intact. Their cottage, burrowed into the rolling knoll, was less than a mile from the village. Not a single person came to help? Hadn't anyone seen or smelled the fire?

A voice in her head said, *Everyone is at the Circus Faire.* Perfect timing for evil to wield its ugly head. Doctor Aerestol? Or Cabal Osfert, retribution for concealing a Doloran?

Sage faltered on the bordering logs, now blackened. She screamed, "Mama! Papa!" In response, one of the vertical logs splintered and timbered inward.

She walked into the charred bowels, through embers and the rank odor of flesh. Instead of disintegrating into hysterics, her temper swelled. Bringing with it wrathful storm clouds filling her to the brim. Unbridling her internal power, burnt logs that had been the supporting walls, what was left of them, rose. She uplifted both arms like she was conducting a symphony. Wooden beams, ashes, fragmented objects, and pieces of her memories eddied into a tornado.

Sage knew what she was doing. Looking for skeletal remnants of her family. Their bodies. None were seen. Was Edras lying? Immersed in probing the particulars, she hadn't detected a presence. An arm hooked her neck, and another arm lassoed her waist causing her to lose focus.

Her back was forcefully thrust against someone and dragged off the cottage foundation. Clawing at a pair of arms, she shrieked, "Get off me! Get off!"

The tornado she'd manipulated began to disperse. Projectiles hurtled downward eliciting a clamorous crashing and splintering.

Regardless of the person crushing her body, her heart shattered. Defeated by the sight, Sage wilted. Whoever it was, he continued to drag her into the nearby bushes, tightening his hold.

She had a slew of grisly images: Mama, Papa, Parry, and Eadith burning, screaming in agony—she couldn't breathe. The world she'd known blurred into fiery ruins, blackening the edges of her vision. Her lungs felt like they were bound in steel, and there wasn't any oxygen to be had. A peculiar calm came over her. Accepting her destiny, her head slumped, squeezing her eyes.

"He said to find you," a voice slithered into her ear. "He didn't say you had to be breathing."

There was a definitive crack of bone, not her bones, and a squeak of pain. Sage's body dropped from his arms. Taking in much needed oxygen, her lungs expanded. Alert, she climbed to her feet, and moved away from the man.

"You filthy abomination," he cussed. "You don't belong here." A rask glowered up at her. A notorious predator. Scaly bodies, a snake-like head and a pronged tongue that lapped out of his mouth. His leg was bent at an abnormal angle, broken. He must have stepped into a rabbit hole or something. *I didn't do it. But, I should have.*

Groping his arms out to seize her, the rask attempted to stand on his one good leg.

Choking on stinging tears, she cried, "Why?" And backed away from his stretching fingers. Moments ago, she'd been willing to succumb. To die. Now—she wanted vengeance. For her family. Sage was a healer, but tonight, she would become an executioner.

Watching his unproductive groveling, a vengeful grin curled the side of her mouth. Exterminating him quickly wasn't good enough for him. She wanted him to suffer, like her family.

"Sage! Sage! Are you okay?" Edras broke through the boughs of conifers and skirted by the fumbling rask. She grasped Sage's shoulders and peered into her eyes. "They're not in there. I took them to my cabin before...before I came looking for you." She hugged Sage, and then turned. "Who are you?" she asked the rask. "You did this?"

"Doloran witches. Both of you," he hissed. "I'll enjoy watching you burn, just like—" His head twisted, and there was a gross snap of his neck. His body collapsed into the weeds.

"Edras, you killed him." Sage swallowed her wrath.

Treading warily toward the rask, Edras stared down at him. Sprawled on his back, his head was facing the ground. "I didn't. I thought it was you."

"We have to find Tegan." Sage couldn't look at the body.

Edras added, "And Eadith."

"I thought... I thought Eadith..." She couldn't say the words and glanced toward the ruins.

Edras pressed her hands to her face, and then raked them through her hair. "Eadith and Tegan weren't here."

Sage's fingers tensed. "It's late. Eadith would have been home, in bed." She glared at the dead man as beads of trepidation worked under her skin. "Somebody must have taken her before—"

"Who?" Edras was quick to intervene.

SIXTEEN
CREW

"Doctor Aerestol, I'm presuming," Crew said, traipsing closer to them. He'd been in the shadows, watching Sage manifest her talents. His gaze went to Sage and then drifted to Edras.

"Who are you?" Edras moved, coming shoulder to shoulder with Sage, as if guarding her from a stalker. "Why did you follow us?"

"Edras, he's okay," Sage enunciated, as if trying to find belief in her words. "This is Crew." Her sister squinted at him. If looks could kill, he'd be dead, just like the rask by his feet. "The boy I told you about."

"Why is he following us. I don't like it." Edras squared her shoulders. "He has to leave." She wagged a cautionary finger at him. "Go back to the Circus where you belong and leave us alone."

"You don't know what you're saying." Sage drew away from her overbearing sister. "Crew saved me from this Doctor Aerestol he mentioned," she clarified, with a prevailing hitch in her throat.

"Noise is coming from down the lane." Crew bent down and anchored his hands underneath the dead rask's arms. "We have to get rid of the body." Effortlessly, he lugged the scaly creature over his shoulder, and tramping toward the cottage, tossed him into the carnage. "Sage, hide him."

Heavy breathing emitted from Sage's sister. He sensed her irate glare burning into him. Whinnying horses and wagon wheels were churning along the lane, drawing near. Sage hastened to manipulate the larger two-by-fours and heaped blackened wood on top of the rask, cinders settled over the body like a pall.

"This way." Edras waved her arm, urging them into the forest.

They crossed the verge into abundant foliage. Sage lagged, looking back. "They sure took their time." Her grumbled undertone circulated in the still of night.

"Apparently," Crew inferred, "a few souls hadn't attended opening night at the Circus and must have seen the flames."

"We don't know for sure who did this." In the dusky dark Edras dragged a wary gaze over Crew. "I'm not ruling out the council. I warned you about them finding out…" her sentence floundered. "Who is this doctor you mentioned?"

"That reminds me, the rask whispered something in my ear. It was hard to understand, 'cause he was squeezing the life out of me." Sage enlightened them. "He was supposed to find me. And said, I didn't have to be breathing."

"Hmph, we can discuss this later. Now isn't the time." Crew added gentle pressure on Sage's back, pressing her to move on. "Where are we going?"

"To my place," Edras answered. She stumbled over a tree root, righting herself.

"Not a good idea." Crew halted and glanced over his shoulder; torchlight shafted between the trees. "People will come looking for you."

"Why would they?"

Sarcasm slipped into his voice, "Because your family's home just burnt to the ground."

"Not my family." her surly tone was off. "And I didn't kill that rask."

"Edras, what a cruel thing to say. The Steeles are your family." Sage turned into a combination of fury and sorrow. Taking off into the woods, her body was swallowed by the darkness.

"Why does she keep doing that?" Crew grumbled and pinned his gaze on Edras. "Lead the way. Hurry."

When Crew and Edras came upon a log cabin, faint sobbing was heard weaving amidst the evergreens. Crew ignored his leg that was on fire, running and gimping on the heels of Edras. He overtook her, and found Sage behind the cabin. Hunkered over her knees, head in her hands. Three burnt skeletons, a gruesome sight, lay in the weeds.

His heart ached for her. But they couldn't dawdle. The villagers or another rask might be tracking them. Her sister sank to her knees and gathered Sage into her arms. Their infectious crying unnerving him, he blinked away the prickle from his own eyes.

"Leave them. We have to move." Crew hadn't meant to sound like an insensitive ogre. "We can't stick around."

Edras wept. "We have to bury them."

"No time." He wiped the sleeve of his shirt across his forehead, ridding sweat dripping into his eyes. "Collect food and essentials from inside. We have to haul ass."

Pushing out of her sister's embrace, Sage stood, facing the corpses of her family. Her body tensing and arms stiffening by her side. Bending her elbows, palms up, she worked her fingers, curling and uncurling them. Crew was and wasn't stunned when shimmering airwaves flittered around her hands. Sage lowered her arms, and then whipped them frontward, simultaneously straightening her fingers, motioning toward the charred skeletons.

An invisible force quaked the ground underneath Crew's feet. He glimpsed Edras. Her mouth hung open, eyes bigger than the moon.

The skeletal bodies exploded into shards of embers and bones. Millions of fragments rose like glittery pixie dust. Whirling together into an orchestrated cyclone. The illuminations developed into silhouettes. Dazzling silhouettes coalesced, holding onto each other, and floating into the heavens, forming a starry constellation.

Sage turned, her cheeks glimmering with spent tears. "I want to know who did this?"

"We will. We will." Edras draped a consoling arm over her sister's shoulder. "You're, umm," tucking Sage into her, she said, "getting stronger. I never—"

"Come on." Crew rushed into the cabin and the girls trailed after him. The diminishing fire in a small hearth gave the interior a dull glow. Edras struck a matchhead, putting the flame to a kerosene lantern.

Crew took quick inventory of the shelves and began tossing supplies on a rectangular table. "Grab what you need for a week's journey. The rest we'll find on the road. Do you have something to put these in?"

"Where we going?" Edras supplied him with canvas sacks. The girls stuffed the sacks with the provisions. "Coin. We need coins."

"Don't worry about that." Crew handled two of the sacks and tossed them over his shoulder. "Let's go." He started out the door.

Once outside, Sage confronted him. "I have to find my brother before we go anywhere."

"Quiet." Edras put a finger to her lips. "People are coming."

"Why are we running away? We didn't do anything wrong. I'm not afraid," Sage said, defiantly. "Alderwood is my home. These are my friends. My neighbors. They're probably worried about us."

"You want to make a wager on that?" Crew quickened his pace, melting into the darkness, and the girls instinctively followed. "I bet an obliging constable is with them. They'll take you in for safekeeping, aye?"

"The boy is right."

Crew was astonished that Sage's sister agreed with him.

Undercover within the dense dark forest, they lingered within sight of Edras' cabin. "Don't make a sound. They might want to search the woods." Crew's voice registered at a low decibel, barely audible. The girls nodded.

SEVENTEEN
SAGE

Sage's reedy intake of breath had harmonized with Edras'. They recognized Constable Erk and the dreaded Cabal, a fierce advocate of eradicating Dolorans.

The king's emissary, Cabal Osfert had been allocated to oversee the council. A ruthless regent, governing Alderwood like his own private kingdom. Villagers were accustomed to bowing and acquiescing to him and stayed clear of his shadow. Misdeeds were treated harshly. Either the gallows for reprehensible crimes or imprisoned in an underground facility to work the mines until their debts were paid.

Holding fiery torches, Constable Erk banged on the cabin door. He handed off his torch to Cabal and walked in. The constable exited rather swiftly. Sage couldn't hear what they were saying as they held their torches aloft, glimpsing the vicinity. The constable wandered to the rear of the cabin and returned shaking his head. They turned to leave just as Sage stepped on a downed sapling. The crunching reverberating in the stagnant night. Crew placed a hand on her shoulder and shook his head, a warning not to move.

Cabal and the constable halted in midstride. Pivoting toward the forest, they squinted, perusing the woods.

Edras tented her hands over her mouth and nose, quashing her nervous breathing. There was further breaking of twigs as something was approaching from the rear. A doe and a baby fawn trod past them and out of the thicket.

The doe and her fawn appeased Cabal and the constable. They shrugged and started back down the rudimentary path.

"Quick thinking. Thanks," Sage whispered after the men were out of range.

"Edras, you can influence animals?" Crew wondered.

Not lingering for her sister to comment, Sage was already venturing farther into a darkening canopy of sycamores. "C'mon. We have to hurry before they get to Tegan."

Edras offered, "He might already have been home and—"

"The mine is closed tomorrow," Sage said, cutting her sister off. "Tegan will make a night of it. He always does." Sage ducked under a branch. "I hear him sneaking in sometimes right before the sun rises." A blithe snort had her rotating to glare at Crew, the gloominess kept his expression veiled. "You think that's funny?"

"Hey, I'm not judging. When Tegan and I worked the Circus," Crew interjected. "He improved my days and my nights. Besides, that hour is standard for the revels in the Court of Hawkswing."

"You've been to revels?"

"Some." His shouldered jerked up. "The king loved the Faire and revels are mandatory."

Displeased by his remark, why did she pine after this boy. She was a mere drop of water in his ocean of admirers. Crew stepped closer, his shadowed expression clearing. Gazing down at her, his eyes darkened into glossy obsidian. He wet his lips, attracting her to the sight. At that instant, she despised herself for evoking his kisses in the angel tree. How his full, soft mouth felt on her skin. Heat stung her cheeks.

Peeling her eyes from his chiseled features, she said, "The Lamb and Kidney isn't far from the mine. If we cut through this section of the woods, we'll find him."

Edras specified, "This night is forbidding. I can't…I can't…." Clearing the maudlin sorrow that had lodged in her throat, she went on, "We needn't break any bones running through the dark forest. Cabal won't know where he is."

Her sister's grief-stricken tone struck a nerve, which she couldn't handle at the moment. Once Sage had literally incinerated the bones of Mama, Papa, and Parry, she'd hardened her heart against the lamenting agony. And clung onto thoughts of Eadith and Tegan who were still out there, somewhere.

"Erk will know where to find him," Sage refuted, and slowed to relieve her cramping legs. "Tegan likes to brag of his run-ins with the constable. And I think the two of them raise a few pints now and then."

"Sounds like they're friends." Crew's long legs kept pace with Sage, as they circumvented trees and waded across streams. "You shouldn't worry about Tegan. It's your younger sister, Eadith, that concerns me."

Sage dug the heels of her slippers into the soil and rotated into him. "What aren't you telling us? If you know something, spit it out." Fury rode severely on her brow. Crew stood his ground, looking down at her.

Edras stooped over and, breathing heavily, stacked her hands on her knees. "Time isn't on our side. We'll discuss this after we get Tegan."

Refusing to acknowledge her sister, Sage glared into Crew's face. "Tell me."

"You said Eadith was home, in bed. She's missing. It makes sense that she was taken. If we—"

"We know that already, you ninny," Sage hurled at him. "Whoever took Eadith might have gotten ahold of Tegan as well."

"Does he have...err," he hesitated, "any *abilities*, like you and your sister?"

"And—like you?" Edras charged, her breathing returning to normal. "You killed the rask, didn't you?" She moved closer to Sage. "We're standing here in the middle of the woods with a murderer."

Crew jumped in. "I'm not—"

"You think you're fooling Sage with your pretty face and easy smile," Edras spouted. "You're concealing secrets. I feel them like I can feel the tips of my fingers."

Even in the dimness, Crew's agitated eyeroll was noticeable. Her sister was distrustful of the villagers and strangers alike because of what and who they were. In her sister's defense, she wasn't exactly incorrect to be suspicious. Sage scarcely knew him.

Their mysterious reconnecting at Madam Rouge's had been nothing short of flabbergasting. Then the perilous, which could have been fatal, incident in the castle. She hadn't yet found a moment to herself to fully ponder the details. *Do I trust Crew?* That doctor knew him, and Crew knew the doctor. A disquieting link. Though—Crew saved her.

"Like you said, we don't have time for this." Her jumbling thoughts were getting the better of her. "We'll find Tegan and then figure out what to do next."

"Know what we haven't considered?" Edras tapped her fisted knuckle on her mouth. "Eadith might not have been taken. Perhaps she got away, flew into the woods."

"She can fly?" Crew drawled.

"Yes. And there's nothing unusual about that. She's only six and probably scared silly."

"That's true. *But...*" Crew moved and examined Edras' backbone. "You and your sister don't have wings."

"A latent inheritance. On our mother's elemental side." Sage repeated her mama's refrain. A refrain well-learned, especially whenever the council or Cabal inquired how Eadith acquired her wings.

"Elemental, aye? Sweet. I have a thought." He itched his eyebrow. "Take a look around for your little sister. If she escaped, she won't come to me. And I'll go to the Lamb and Kidney and get Tegan. Where can we meet?" he flailed his hand that wasn't holding their supplies. "Thoughts anyone?"

"Conniving dribble." Her sister narrowed intimidating eyes at him. "I don't trust you. Why is he here anyhow?" She looked to Sage in pursuit of a logical explanation.

Crew huffed and dropped the two sacks that had been riding his shoulder. He brushed his hands together, as if he were through. "Hey, I can leave."

"You *should* leave," Sage said. "Don't you have a performance tonight?" She peered into the pitch-dark skies, wondering the time. "Good night to show what you can do."

"*Really?* After everything…after…" he clicked his tongue, "I think I missed my performance." Shaking his head, he rolled the edge of his bottom lip into his mouth. "Sage, you saw what happened in the ice castle. The doctor was playing with us. He likes the chase, the games." He hardened his stance. "He has men, bad men. Like the rask. And pays them well. Aerestol will get what he wants."

"And what does this Doctor Aerestol want?" Edras asked, voice nettlesome.

"Sage. He wants Sage."

Several beats passed as Edras and Sage shared a look.

"You work for him, don't you?" Sage frowned, her gaze full of condemnation. How much would he be willing to tell them—if anything at all? And noticed an indecipherable emotion passing through his eyes.

"No." Crew looked grim. "And yes."

"I thought so. I'm not stupid." Sage said. "I remember everything that man said in the castle. Afterwards…I…I'd hoped… Oh shoot." She pressed tense fingers to her brow. "This is terrifying."

Edras raked her eyes over Crew. "This boy could be leading us on a wild goose chase. A trap for that monster he's working for. Sage, let's go— Now." She turned her back on their discussion and headed into the undergrowth. And demonstrated her annoyance by her heavily laden footfalls. Her opinion came across loud and clear by scattering leaves and crunching pinecones underfoot, resonating until her steps faded altogether.

"Edras," Sage hailed. "That monster knows who you are." In the dead of night, silence reigned. No chittering of insects or scurrying of animals, and no sound of her sister.

"Hear that?" Crew's tone broke the quiet.

"No, what?"

"Nothing, that's what. Come on. Hurry."

Crew cautiously perused the woods before nudging her shoulder to get a move on. Together they loped in her sister's wake, but Sage lacked his speed, and lagged behind him. He glimpsed over his shoulder, either to see if she were keeping up with him or searching the woods. Endeavoring to run faster, she wished, while at the oracles with her runed armoire, she'd opted for her breeches, boots, and a bow.

Minutes passed, combing the area. Edras couldn't have gotten far. *Why isn't she answering?* Perhaps her sister had taken a detour to the tavern. There was a drop-off, a ridge that tumbled into Insmead Lake. *She wouldn't go that way, would she?*

"Edras!" Sage hollered. "Where are you?" A hand covered her mouth.

She whiffed balsam and sandalwood—Crew. He'd been leading the way. *How'd he get behind me?* He shoved her sideways into a brushwood of berry bushes and tackled her to the ground.

"Encampment. Four imps around a fire." His mouth, a breath from her head, tickled her ear. "Nasty buggers."

"We can handle a couple puny imps."

"After what I'd seen what you can do at the cabin, perhaps, *you could.*" He released a smart-alecky gurgle. "Did *you* see them?"

"You can torch 'em, right?"

"I'm not into torching innocent imps."

"You just said they're nasty buggers."

"Usually, they are. Shh, keep your voice down." He parted the bushes, scouting the creatures. "Unless they ransacked Edras or cause me grief, I'm not melting them."

"Where can she be?"

"Can she disappear?"

"You mean like that ring you put on my finger?"

"No, I mean—poof!" He made an airy gesture.

Confused, she veered to look at him, and in doing so, her lips brushed the edge of his mouth and cheek. He pulled back, allowing a thread of space between them. Her eyes met his, flashing amber. Her heart stuttered. She remembered those eyes, back when she'd been besotted.

Glad for the cloaking darkness, her cheeks burned. *Crew is a manipulator.* Not a friend, in the sense of the word. "Let go of me," she said, her tone a daring snarl. His expression unreadable, he removed his arms which had been holding her down, but their shoulders still touched as they lay side by side. "Edras *cannot* just disappear. What makes you say that?" His shoulder shifted as he elongated his neck, attempting to spy on the imps.

"You girls aren't fae like you're pretending to be. Aerestol mentioned Dolorans. And I'm not familiar with them. I don't know what a Doloran can and can't do."

"You believed him? That…that scoundrel. How do you know we're not fae?"

"I don't believe much what Aerestol has to say. I just know."

A stiffness worked over her body. "What are you? Not mortal by the vague arc of your ears or the fire you can bend."

"Didn't think a person could detect the irrelevance of my ears." He parted his pitch-black hair where the slight arc of his ear met his finger. "*What am I?* Good question."

"Are you being facetious?" Her burning complexion turned irate, and it festered along the column of her throat.

"I'm a foundling. No clue about my parents, or what they were."

His revelation startled and baffled her. "Now I know you're a liar." *Which means Crew is not fae. Fae can't lie.*

"A lie can be indispensable," he said, "but not this time."

His wayward smirk affected her like a swooning lovebird. She reminded herself, *I'm not a naïve girl of fourteen. He deceived me once, twice, no more.* Harboring thoughts of slapping it off his face, she veered away from him. Hadn't he ultimately confessed, years ago in the angel tree, his principal job for the Circus Faire was to charm and draw people in. A magnetic talent, and he was more than apt to activate it. And today, hadn't he proved himself an expert fire-wrangler? He was a conundrum and a fabricator of lies.

"What about Polk?" She thought she'd caught him like a rabbit in a snare. "*Your father?*"

Crew nested his head, face down, in the circle of his arms.

EIGHTEEN
CREW

One, solitary soul knew how Crew had come to be Polk's son. Dirge. The doctor couldn't hurt Polk; he was already dead. For repressing that information, Dirge had his eyeball sliced out of his head by a madman. Aerestol could be torturing Dirge, interrogating the big kind oaf because of him, desiring facts that not even Crew could supply. He sensed; all would be revealed. Did it matter? Probably not. Though, it bothered him—*What am I? Who am I?*

For attaining the benefactors trust, Crew recently divulged his life story to one other person. And she had been peddling her wares in Finnick Row.

Crew had invited himself into Demelda's modest cottage. And helped himself to a rickety stool by a table that was strewn with garments and paraphernalia. Suspended by rows of coarse twine were bunches of drying lavender, milk thistle, chamomile, ginger, valerian roots, and other medicinal herbs. Whatever was brewing in the kettle in the hearth irritated his nose. "Looks like you're getting ready to leave."

"Dyke sent a telegram. The hiatus is over." She'd been actively sifting through her tableau of bewitched coins, talismans, amulets, and colorful vials filled with unidentifiable potions. Her hair was tied in a knot on top of her head, and she wore a commoner's homespun dress. "The Circus Faire is traveling to Alderwood. Did you get the telegram?"

"We did." He was drawn to a leather-bound tome and its untitled exterior, well-ridged and well-read by the appearance of its creased spine, containing parchment pages. He presumed it was a primeval book, a composition of enchantments.

She'd stopped fidgeting about, and finally met his eyes in earnest.

"Is he…" she pressed her arm between her breasts, shoulders slouching, "Polk…"

"Dead?" The frankness in his voice had drawn her lips into a despondent pout. To assuage her pitiful expression, he offered, "He's hanging on by a thread."

She sighed in relief.

"He introduced me to Doctor Aerestol." The rigidity of her body had given him the answer he'd been seeking. "So, you know him?"

"I know *of* him. Who took you in when you were a kid while Polk went galivanting on a job for his *benefactor*?" Demelda had surprisingly plopped down on Crew's lap, straddling him. Spearing her fingers into his hair, she'd combed it back with callous severity, and eagerly claimed his mouth. She teased his lips, gliding her tongue between them. His body had the audaciousness to answer her lusty invitation.

Nevertheless, he'd been running out of time. Dillydallying with the agile temptress would have to be resumed at a more advantageous date. Steeling himself from her sinister desires, an exponential feat, he played the uninterested lover. When he hadn't reciprocated, she angrily disentangled her fingers from his hair and used his shoulders to thrust herself off him. Before she masked her slighted scorn, her guise told a tale of loneliness.

"I figured you needed to unwind, think of something else besides death and getting yourself killed. I guess not."

Revolving away from him, Demelda busied herself by arranging clothes and articles into a traveling trunk which was stationed on the floor.

Pondering, Crew licked his lips. "I, or rather *we*, Polk and I, have a favor to ask."

"I don't do favors. Polk knows that."

"He told me you'd say that. But, he's hoping, for his final request, you'd comply."

She'd veered back to him. The strands of her hair freed themselves from its lax knot; cascading tangles framed her face. Crew was astonished by her lack of aging. Demelda had never changed in appearance, in fact, she grew lovelier each time they met. The ancient tome had to be beneficial.

She resignedly huffed, and jutting her hip to the side, fixed her hand on it. "What do you want me to do?"

Crew had opened up, telling her *everything*. His abduction from the Foundling Home. His brother, and his mission to find him. And to stop Aerestol with whatever the eff he's doing. To achieve what needed to be done, he had to convince the doctor to trust him, prove his self-worth. He then went on to, presumably, explain what was going to occur once he dropped her in Foundling Square at the designated time.

"My strategy is most likely flawed." He'd trained his sight on her. "You're clever. I've seen what you can do. If all goes accordingly, you won't have a problem." She made a blithe hand gesture when he finished.

"Don't get involved with him," she'd said. "He's bad news. Get yourself killed, or worse."

"What's worse than getting killed?"

She snorted. "*Before* the dying part. I heard stories that'd—"

"Aye, Polk did alright," Crew interrupted. As a boy, he'd eavesdropped on Polk and Dirge after they spent hours getting drunk. They conversed in slurring tones of disposing body parts and how lucky it wasn't them.

"I'm betting that Frankenstein," she had reknotted her hair of tangles on her head, "Aerestol injected cancer into Polk. To see how it would affect a strapping giant."

"Jesus, Demelda." An appalled Crew stood, overturning the stool. "That never crossed my mind." That shocker would remain with him, rallying his aspirations of eliminating that fiend and his experiments.

"It should have." She laid the palms of her hands on his chest. "I'll do it. For Polk. A favor that'll help him sleep for a lifetime." Her hands skimmed downward, then hooked her fingertips over the waistband of his pants. "Did you show Polk the ring?"

"Yes." With her fingers clutching his pants, it was torture.

"Did he put it on?"

"Yes."

"What happened?" she asked, engrossed by what he was going to say.

"Nothing."

"Hmm." She had removed her fingers from his waistband. "You put it on, didn't you?"

"It was as you said. I became invisible and scared Polk half to death." He re-tucked his mussed shirt into his pants. "I was in a gray, ashy dimension, and could still see him lying in the bed. It felt…wrong. I had this feeling, like, I wanted to stay and explore, but Polk was hyperventilating."

"Why didn't the ring work for Polk?" she asked.

Crew put his hands on the table and leaned into them. "Perhaps, because he's too far gone."

"What?"

"Polk has one foot in the grave. The realm of the ring doesn't want him."

"I knew it," Demelda said. "The ring is a passageway into the netherworld."

Crew had mulled over what she inferred. If Mage Marek said it was his birthright, what did that make him?

"When do you need me for this favor?"

"Now," he said.

Despite her bitching for getting roped into a precarious situation, she'd started throwing whatnots into a tapestry bag, amulets, thread, and bone filaments for stirring up a concoction, if the need arose.

He'd flipped open the lid to the leather-bound book. "Are you stuffing this tome into your bag of tricks?"

"It's a grimoire, if you must know. *Very* valuable." In haste, she slammed it shut from his snooping eyes. "Can't take a chance of *asshole* getting ahold of it. I'll hide it."

"Where?"

"Somewhere *you* won't find it."

"You think I'll filch it?" He gave her a winsome smile. "Where's the trust?"

"I trust *no one.*"

They went to Fawke's Livery where he purchased a feisty sorel steed. Riding together they made it into Foundling Square a half-hour earlier than Aerestol's note had specified. "He said I was to leave you here."

"What does he look like?"

"Short. Unimpressive. Ordinary with spectacles." Crew dismounted the sorel, and then grasped Demelda's waist and helped her down. "I doubt he'll come himself. His goons probably have eyes on us already. You know what to do, aye?" An attack of self-loathing cramped his abdomen, feeling like it was full of nails. Putting the witch in jeopardy for his own purposes was a dastardly thing to do.

He detached the tapestry bag from the saddle and handed it to her.

"Hey, pretty boy." She reached up and gripped his chin. "Don't give me those sad puppy-dog eyes. Smile, that's what I love to see."

Demelda had merged with people wandering the cobblestones. Glancing over her shoulder, she said, "See you at the Circus Faire." Her mouth quirked into a snarky grin.

Forever, Crew would remember Demelda's alluring smile. After Madam Rouge gave him the repulsive news, he'd taken a hammering hit to his heart. First Polk and now Demelda.

Sage's voice drew him back from that woeful memory, but not before she'd gotten to her feet. "I'm going in there to ask those nasty imps if they've seen Edras." A boulder impeded her on the left and she was in the course of high stepping over him. Crew caught her by the ankle, she stumbled, eliciting a squeaky sound, and fell. Sage rolled onto her side and sent him a stink face.

"Trying to break my leg," she ground out, and kicked until he detached his fingers. "Let's move it."

A rushed scurrying through the undergrowth had Crew vaulting to his feet.

"Where we's moving to?" said a young imp, leering from behind them, bound in fur and interwoven flora roots.

Concerned for Sage's safety, Crew shielded her. Though, she moved and flanked his side. Snickering she brought her hand to her mouth.

"You had me hiding in the bushes because of this pipsqueak? He's a little boy," she chuckled. "Kinda adorable with those ruby eyes and forked tail."

The imp opened his mouth and lapped a purple tongue over his pointed teeth.

"Aye, adorable dagger horns and fangs too," Crew said, dripping with irony. "Did you happen to see his daddy?"

NINETEEN
SAGE

A husky sniggering had Crew reeling around. And throwing his arm up as if surrendering, he said, "We were just passing by. No need to get your horns bent out of shape."

Recoiling from the sight, Sage's belly tightened.

Extracting a snort, snot sprayed from the imp's gourd-like nose. Conical horns curved over his magenta skull, his height didn't equal Crew's, but his chest, arms, and legs were pure muscle. Interlacing vines and leaves belted his waist, and his hand rested securely on the hilt of a sword.

The boy imp had unfolded bat-like arms. Winging upward, he perched on a tree branch and peered down at them like a vulture.

"Real cute kid," Crew uttered from the corner of his mouth. "We were—"

Sage talked over him. "Did a girl run through here, or near here?" She took a step closer to the adult imp. Although, his tapering ruby eyes were trained on Crew. "She looks like me." Sage upped the tone of her voice attempting to get him to look at her.

Defy the Stars

The creature's gaze left Crew, glanced to the boy, and then resettled on Sage. "What do you want with the female?" he said, startlingly serene.

Sounds like a nice, rational guy, she thought. "You've seen her then?"

The boy imp giggled.

"What do you want with her?"

Imp daddy was procrastinating, playing with words. "She's my sister. Have you seen her or not? She ran through here, minutes ago."

"She ran *away* from you?"

"Hey, *Imp*," she spat like an insult, and fixed her knuckles on her hips. "Where's my sister?"

The daddy imp glanced over his shoulder where moments earlier four imps had surrounded a firepit. Boy and daddy had been keeping them at bay. A flagrant twitch in his cheekbone alerted her to their chicanery. He swiftly drew the sword from his belt. Sage ducked in the nick of time as he hacked it with intent to decapitate.

Fiery sparks stirred over Crew's fingers. He lost his chance of a direct hit when imp boy plunged on top of his head and shoulders. His flare ricocheted off daddy imp's sword. Whether it singed the imp's hands, or he was taken by surprise, he let it go, sending it oscillating into the brush.

Quick on the uptake, Sage scooted into the woods, pursuing the weapon. Frenziedly rummaging in the undergrowth like her life depended on it, which she thought it did, she unearthed the sword from a warren of fleeing gnomes. Clutching the hilt of the sword with both hands, and twirling, she predicted an ambush by a marauding imp. However, all was peaceful, excluding a pop and sputter of kindling from the imp's vacant firepit.

Sage stepped guardedly, slewing her gaze amid the dark apertures. Unhampered, she went toward the berry bushes where they'd been hiding. The imps were nowhere to be seen, and neither was Crew.

Maintaining her guarded stance, she whispered, "*Crew?*" She swiveled toward the shrinking campfire, and back again. Either, the imps had captured and took Crew with them, or they'd violently impaired him. A glacial chill of panic caused an onslaught of gooseflesh. He might be dying. She could save him. Or she was too late, and he lay dead somewhere. Noting the absence of the dreadful creatures, Sage hollered, "Crew!"

An incoherent mumble came nearby.

"Crew, is that you?" Retaining a watchful eye, she ventured further into the copse, intent on heeding the mumbling. An aggressive gruff noise had her turning in the opposite direction. "Oh my gosh."

Trussed to the trunk of a broad tree, Crew vehemently thrashed. Lime-green viny branches twined his body from his head to his ankles. She lanced the imp's sword into the soil and ran to him. Foremost, she pried the vines banding his mouth and eyes. Her hands felt tacky and noticed blood smudging her fingers, but it wasn't her blood.

His features scrunched. "Use the sword."

Retracing her steps, she went for the sword and wrenched it free from the ground. Judging where she'd make progress on the vines, she elevated it over her head.

"Wait—" Crew toned haltingly. "Maybe a bit more to the left."

Sage sidestepped and raised the blade. She put all her weight into her downward stroke, hewing the raw branches, over and over, chopping and slicing. Crew pushed against his restraints. Yet, her headway was daunted by a wrestling vine organism. As soon as she'd cut a significant patch to free him, the vines, like supernatural slithering snakes, wound his body tighter and tighter.

"They're cursed," Crew said, voice thinning from want of oxygen.

Sage backpedaled, wiping sweat from her face. "Burn them."

"I...I can't. They tied my arms behind my back."

"You'd set the bark on fire—"

"And me with it," he finished her sentence.

Permitting her aching arms a reprieve, she lowered the tip of the sword to the ground. She squeezed her eyes, contemplating. "The ring," she said. "Put the ring on."

"I would, if I could," he choked. The vines had managed to reweave across his throat. "It's inside my waistcoat pocket, left side."

"I wish I had a dagger, instead of this sword."

"Sage," he gagged, "I can't…breathe…"

Bending over, Sage collected a handful of her skirt. She made a slit in the fabric and ripped a section off. Wrapping the fabric around the longsword, she could hold it without slicing off her own fingers. Clasping the sword with the safety of the fabric, which increased her control, she positioned the razored point inches from his neck.

"Don't move. Don't breathe," she warned.

"Don't worry, I can't."

With accuracy, she severed the strangulating vines from each side of his throat and pried them off. He wheezily inhaled.

"This might hurt." She repositioned the sword, razored edge up, on his sternum, and wiggled the tip between the bourgeoning vines. "I'm going to make an upward cut. When it's wide enough, I'm putting my hand into your waistcoat for the ring." She met his gaze. "Understand?"

"You might…" the vines covering his chest expanded as he fought for air, "get tangled by them."

"It's the only way. And sorry ahead of time if I stab you." The rim of her mouth curved, a weak imitation of a smile. "Now."

While trying not to puncture his chest, it was a strenuous battle against the reedy vines and against time. Cleaving a niche, large enough to insert her hand, she slipped into his waistcoat.

"Lower," Crew informed her.

"Got it!" Tugging her hand out, she had the ring. "Now, to get it on your finger."

"Cut…by…my hip." Each word, a rasp.

Sage's technique quickened. Wedging her hand behind Crew and grunting from her exertion, she pushed the ring onto one of his fingers.

Crew disappeared.

TWENTY
CREW

Crew collapsed on a hillock of tinder and ashes. He ingested a prolonged breath and instead of fresh air, the bitterness of wherever he'd landed, singed his throat. He knelt and scrubbed at the blood that had been running into his eyes. However his hands came away clean. No blood.

When he'd been tied to the tree, the stabbing pain in his head felt as if it were going to split in two. And gleaning an ounce of oxygen into his constricted lungs had been agony. But now, there was no pain. There was—nothing.

Getting his legs beneath him, the world around him was different. Whenever he'd put on the ring before, he'd been between realms or dimensions, a blurry limbo, which enabled him to see where he came from. Sage was nowhere to be found, nor could he see the breathable woodlands. What was disturbing, he wholly crossed over or transcended into a veritable wasteland. He sensed eyes watching him, and an intuitive growl crawled up his esophagus.

This land was devoid of emerald greens and the chambray skies of Faerie, instead there were hilly patches of grim grays, black, and layers of scudding gray matter.

Dusting ash from his waistcoat, a wink of silver caught his eye. The ring.

Take off the ring!

He touched the trinket rounding his pinkie finger. And feeling like he was snared in the thrall of a siren, he couldn't remove it. An unfathomable sensation had Crew wanting to explore this realm of desolation. Picking his legs through ashes, he began to wander.

A squall harvested a gamut of rubbish as he entered a decimated city. It reminded him of the Unified Territory with its asphalt and concrete avenues lined with high-rising brick and mortar buildings. Cartons of whatnots, cigarette butts, tin cans, sections of newspapers whirled aimlessly.

"Is anybody here?" Crew was being followed. A presence hunted him, and he was its prey. "I know you're following me. Show yourself."

Ahead, an opaque smear went by.

"Who are you, stop!" He ran. "Where'd you go?" His thudding footfalls echoed in the uncharted land. *Where am I?* Trailing after the smear, he turned a corner. The confining buildings were melting, magicked with an oily substance. Thawing goo, black lava, gobbled his boots. Fearful of being drowned in it, his feet slurped as he attempted to make a mad dash.

The oily blackness wasn't wet, it had a density of sorts, immersing his calves. It didn't saturate, but crippled his movements. *The ring. Take it off.* Crew heard it again. A far, far away voice. *"The ring."*

The submerging black lava reached his hips.

Take off the ring!

Eyes were on him. Watching. Judging. Assessing him. "What do you want from me?" he roared. Moving through the cumbersome gunk drained him. He promised himself he wasn't going to perish—not this day.

Crew took a chance and called upon his inner fire. If it were oil, he'd be toast in seconds. A cruel death.

Take off the ring!

Slurping lava reached his chest. He outstretched his arms and unleashed a deluging conflagration.

He suddenly found himself laying on his back. *I blacked out.* He dragged his arm across his face, and the world came into focus. Lush greenery surrounded him. *Am I back in Faerie?* The ring was on his pinkie. Not Faerie. *Where?*

"Very impressive, Crew," said an abrasive voice. "But there's more, much more to you, isn't there?"

He scrambled to his feet. Everything had again transformed, from bleak ashy grays and a black lava metropolis to this: A memorable verdant land. Located on a rolling knoll, it overlooked a low gradient of meadowland. In the near expanse, on a similar rise of land, beneath a drooping willow tree stood a hunchbacked hag in a coarse woven robe, holding a long walking staff, wizard's staff. He couldn't quite make out her facial features.

Pondering dozens of questions to ask, he elected to say, "Who are you?"

She chortled. "*Who are you*—Crew Asgard? But that's not your real name."

Of course, it wasn't because Polk had named him. Whatever was bestowed upon him at birth died with his parents. "I guess you're going to tell me." He turned the ring on his finger, musing if she knew who his parents were. Not attempting to rile the old woman's hackles by making an inadvertent move, he awaited a doomsday setup. Besides the hag, he'd yet to see a living soul. The ether was teeming with magic; he felt it, tasted it, like sizzling sparks. "Who am I?"

"Ahhh, boy, that's a loaded question, ain't it? A young man too humble to utilize the power brewing in your blood. And no lineage to speak of. No guidance to attain what lies within. You were barely out of rompers when you learned a valuable lesson from those sea nymphs, sirens you so loved to watch by the Sea of Tears. Self-taught, you became a spellbinding charmer, an inkling of your power. As a boy, you watched Jero at the circus, a fire wrangler. At Madam Rouges you absorbed the runes of her armoire, and it obeyed your wishes." She banged her staff three times on the ground. "Are you proficient with a blade?"

The old hag was messing with his head, unravelling the tapestry of his past, one thread at a time, and it was and wasn't processing.

"I can hold my own with a dagger." He wondered where this line of questioning was going.

"Swordplay, boy. Swordplay. Watch and learn."

Brandishing steel rapiers, two goblin redcaps sprinted from the western thicket of conifers into the lower meadow, and from the eastern woods, two lumbering orcs.

The competition was unmatched, dominating orcs would indisputably best the redcaps.

Avid sparring of steel against steel clanged across the meadow as the redcaps and orcs clashed. They paired off. Volleying passionate strokes. In an abrupt blow, a redcap propelled his rapier through his opponent's chest. Crew flinched. He hadn't been prepared for the bloodshed. The sole orc left standing befell with a repugnant end, a beheading. Its head rolled through the weeds. When the hag mentioned swordplay, he assumed it meant a practice session, like fencing.

Then there were two. Both redcaps. He'd misjudged them and their wily effectiveness.

The redcaps steered toward the hag, who thumped her staff on the ground again. They nodded, understanding her command, and resumed their dueling stances.

Not again. This isn't going to end well. Crew narrowed his eyes, watching the redcaps footwork, their methods of offense and defense, lunging, feinting. They were of equal caliber. After fifteen minutes of nail-biting warfare, the taller of the pair implemented his blade like a battle-ax. Slewing his rapier and striking his adversary in the shoulder. He prolonged his stroke, slicing through his sternum. The maimed redcap wore an expression of astonishment before he dropped.

The winner of the tournament—Crew's take on the atrocious charade—was a goblin who expressed his victory with an open-mouthed smile of fanged incisors. Doffing his cap, he dredged it into the blood of his two kills, and replaced it onto his head of sweaty, brown hair.

When the rivalry concluded, Crew speculated, *why*? And, what did she have in store for him? An abrupt feeling of lethargy overcame him. He shoved his hands into his hair, the headache he'd faced while tied to the oak tree had returned.

"Crew, show me what you've learned," the hag urged. She stepped out from the overhanging branches of the tree into scanty light. While too far to discern her expression, she pointed her staff toward him.

A glimmering rapier appeared in the weeds by his toes.

"You better pick it up, boy. Griggan is coming to teach you a lesson."

Morbid enthusiasm rang in her voice, she wasn't kidding. The redcap, Griggan, was heading straight for him. As he drew closer, Crew noted telltale scars cutting into his face. An eye-catching weal carved the corner of his mouth that traveled upward, joining his misshapen eye socket. It gave him a macabre demeanor, especially when he cast Crew a fanged grin.

Staving off his undiagnosed weakness, Crew shook out his arms and legs, energizing himself. He had to perform for the old hag. And hoped, she'd stop the rumpus before he lost his head.

"What happened to your face?" Crew's candor caught the goblin off guard, as the corner of his mouth quirked.

"You don't wanna know." Griggan charged him.

Crew didn't have an opportunity to compose himself, or grab his weapon. He dodged the disastrous swish of the goblin's blade, yet it nicked the bone of his jaw. He rolled while jetting his arm out, seizing the rapier from the weeds.

Springing to his feet, he faced his antagonist. *Don't look into his deformed face.* Entrapment. Crew knew that much. Watch the angle of his shoulders, his wrists, the shift of the hilt, his footwork. Steel blades clanked, right to left, low and high, at a discordant velocity. Dodging Griggan's blows, Crew swirled away from another disemboweling hit. The goblin smirked, baring a mouth full of fangs, and sure of his conquest.

The redcap proved himself as an outstanding swordsman, and Crew's defensive strategy waned, along with his strength. If he lowered his sword and surrendered, would Griggan run him through? He didn't want to find out, and the farcical contest continued. Concentrating, sweat drenched his aching body as he shifted positions. Unbearable was the hag's cackling, overshadowing their grunts and groans and singing of steel.

Crew and Griggan's rapiers came together in an intense ascending arc. Razored edges collided, and Crew stepped into the goblin's space. Pressing into him, holding their connected weapons like a buffer between them. Face to face. Griggan's skin rumpled into an ugly sneer. His eyes flicked to meet Crew's. "Griggs, end this," he said, pitching his charmed cadence.

It was the redcap's first mistake, and it would prove to be his last. Growing hot and heated by this madness, Crew invoked a surplus of muscle.

For less than a fractional second, the goblin stilled. Crew slammed his head into Griggs' forehead. The redcap lurched backward. Crew unleashed his reserves, slashing and battering strikes, grounding the goblin. His legs scrabbled in the weeds for purchase, but Crew stomped his foot on the redcap's chest. Staring down his nose at him, his blade pricked Griggan's throat, drawing blood.

"*Smart, boy, you used your inbred talent to addle him. Now, finish him.*"

The hag's monotoned voice spoke in Crew's mind. *She's in my head!*

"I don't kill for sport," he said, and the goblin's yellow eyes tapered.

"You shame Griggan." She scoffed. "By not honoring him with a champion's death."

"He'll have to learn how to live with dishonor then. As I learned how to wield a sword like a champion." Crew threw his blade in the weeds and extended his arm to the goblin.

Griggan's callused and clawed hand clasped his and hopped up. "You aren't what I expected," he said, voice gravelly.

"You were expecting me?" Crew turned toward the hag, but she wasn't there. A second draining wave left him winded. *Take off the ring!* He'd been gone too long. Kneading the pressure from his brow, he tried recalling what Demelda had forewarned him regarding the ring. What was it?

"I've waited centuries for this moment."

Crew spun at the sound of her voice. The hag in all her ungodly glory, a decrepit example of a woman, materialized a mere yard from him. Short in stature, her hunchbacked-frame leaned on the staff for support, and up close, her cat-eyes glared at him. Folds of wrinkles poured down her face, but what drew his sight was a cambered bone piercing the septum of her nose. "I'm too tired to play your games, woman." He fingered the ring on his pinkie.

"No!" Her robed arm shot out, hands gaunt. "I know your ancestry. Intrigued, are you not? I feel it, in the racing of your heart, the flow of your blood."

He left the ring on, turning it.

"Boy—I am your grandmother." Her smile looked painful on her face. "*Many* generations removed." Attempting a snicker, it came out as a wheeze. "I am Queen Esta. Sovereign Ruler of Misbegottens. Souls conceived by the mightiest, indomitable beings of creation. Our kinfolks were feared and revered by everyone, great and small." With each spoken word the hag's stooped vertebrae realigned. Chink by chink, her backbone straightened.

"This is your world, then." Crew took a gander at Griggan, who was trimming his clawed nails with the tip of his sword. "You are a witch, a sorcerer—a *deceiver*? Am I supposed to be impressed, reverent even, to be in your presence? This is my ancestry, my inheritance? Well I think I'll go back to being a grunt in the—"

"You profane, insolent shit." The planes of her face changed, as if a potter's fingers were molding, reshaping her skin. Stretching and tightening it over the bones of her face. The hood slipped off her head, bunching on her shoulders. Bedraggled locks were replenished with a growth of satiny snow-white hair. Her cat eyes flashed him a silvery wink. "Don't trifle with me, *boy*."

The queen's inflection crawled underneath his skin like a nettling parasite.

The transformation was complete. Crew conceded to himself that she must have been magnificent during her reign. Except for what he hadn't detected earlier in her carnelian-colored, wrinkled facade were tattoos. A perceptible crimson mark in the center of her forehead, a crescent moon, and snuggled within the crescent, a pearlescent star. Palpable crescent scars carved her face, beginning from the tips of her eyebrows, and concluding below her cheekbones.

"You are like the oracle. A mystic fae, rife with magic. Seeing the past and prophesying the future." He cocked his head, scrutinizing her. "I admit, you brought back memories. I forgot about the sea nymphs and Jero."

Her succoring staff was no longer imperative, yet she held onto it. "Queen Mab cursed my very body. The woman you see before you is as I once was. Now, I'm a deteriorating hag. Yet, I have breath in my body as Mab rots in her grave." She smiled, a decaying toothy smile; her transformation hadn't extended to her teeth. "Everything I told you is the truth. You absorb certain skills, learning at an astronomical rate."

In an abrupt move, the queen latched onto Crew's hair by the nape of his neck. "Where is it, boy?" She gathered his lengthy locks, tugging his head downward to her level.

"Oww... What the heck are you doing?" Her fingers twined into his hair, yanking his head this way and that.

"Aha! There it is," she said assertively. Behind his right ear, below his hairline, she traced her fingertip; a chill skidded along his shoulder blade.

"What's there?" he asked and brought his hand up to touch what she was so hot and bothered about. "Oh that? It's just a birthmark." He smoothed the slightly raised skin, the mark he'd had forever.

"Not a random birthmark. Quite symbolic, boy." She disentangled her fingers from his hair, and Crew straightened to his full height. "This symbol." She touched her forehead. "A mark of the ill-conceived."

"Does this mean I'm doomed?" He was not fond of her clarification. It had been Polk who'd discovered it when he was a child. A distinctive brown hue. When he'd reached an age of double digits, and for reasons unknown, the mark changed, bleached white. "To find misbegottens, I have to pluck out the roots of their hair?"

"You are a flippant rogue."

He scoffed. "This is your High Court, aye?"

"My *Kingdom* of Despair and Ruins—and my prison." She raised her staff. Griggan became alert, making a trivial bow of his head. "You know of a binding covenant that forbids interspecies relationships? If diverse species mate, it upsets the balance of power."

"Aye. It's well-known."

"That covenant was enacted because of what I'd accomplished. My people grew too resilient. Queen Mab bequeathed my people their name, *Misbegottens*. Means ill-conceived. It was Mab who gathered a multitude of armies; even mortals joined the fray because my people were multiplying. Growing more powerful with each passing decade. My cousin, Mab, annihilated my kingdom, massacring them like scavenging street rats. Then Mab entombed me—here."

"Sounds like an unpromising future for me. Where do I come into the picture?"

"A handful of survivors scattered, but persecuting armies never stopped hunting them. That ring on your finger, I crafted it, eons ago. Whomever puts it on, arrives here. Over the centuries, I've had many visitors."

"It's sorta strange that it came to me, aye?"

Queen Esta and the goblin shared a look. A blush colored his pointy cheeks. "Not so strange."

"It's my eyes that gave me away." Crew reached into his rear pocket. *Where is my cap?*

"The night Mage Marek discovered the ring, thanks to Griggan, he dreamt of a boy, whose compelling eyes change colors." She shrugged. "You have a mystifying incongruity that represents dominant power. Once you put on the ring, I could prognosticate your origin.

"I'm in this prison owing to Mab and her entourage of magicals. *I* can't escape my imprisonment. But others can come and go. Griggan has been a reliable companion and carried that ring on a grueling expedition to locate a blood relative." Flattering the goblin, a twitch found her mouth, which was losing its elasticity. "I'm dying. My cerebral powers are withering with me. You've seen my creations. Disintegrating cities. Charred in ruins. Look at the woodlands."

Crew gazed toward the land that resembled Faerie. A forest of soldiering trees minus their finery, leaving a starkness of gnarled branches, and the fertile meadow had developed waterfilled runnels and muddy holes.

"What am I, really?" he asked, in a combined tone of curiosity and annoyance.

She approached Crew and swiped a finger along his jawbone where the goblin's blade had cut him. She licked her finger.

"Ahh, as I suspected. A misbegotten prodigy. An influential bloodline. A conglomeration of magicals, thriving with power. It's making me giddy," her tongue licked her lips, "*hmm*, this is unforeseen. There is a trace of angel blood in you."

All this foreshadowing was making him queasy and dizzy. Something wasn't right. Yet, he pressed, "You said Crew Asgard wasn't my real name."

"Does it matter? I think not." At a measured pace, her spine crimped out of alignment, stooping her into the hunchbacked hag. "I scry few misbegottens who have sprinkled the territories. Fleeing into mortal lands was their surviving grace, I believe, hiding in plain sight. Humans are easily deceived, asinine beings. You were abandoned, and as a foundling, nobody would become the wiser of your abilities."

He jumped on her narrative. "Are my parents alive?"

"My scrying, like my body, is anemic and fallible. I see bits and pieces of the past, what was and what is to come."

He let that issue rest and focused on the relic rounding his finger. "There is more to this ring than to bring visitors here for your gratification. People carrying it have met with untimely deaths. Somebody wants this ring. Badly." The hag's mouth puckered like a dried-up peach. Either she wasn't going to answer or didn't want to answer him. He endeavored to dig deeper. "Can you tell me anything about a small faction calling themselves Dolorans? I know—"

"Oooohh…" Her gaunt fingers caged her mouth, tittering. "That's what they're calling themselves?"

"You know of them?"

She ousted a breath. "*Know of them*! Boy, it's what you are," she said pridefully. "After their Queen Esta Doloran."

Her proclamation was akin to a blow to the throat, inducing his gag reflex. Realization struck, Sage and he were Dolorans. Like the hag said, *hiding in plain sight*.

"I confess. I am spiteful. Mean-spirited, and an egotistical bitch." Queen Esta's frizzy, gray hair and her deep-rooted wrinkles reappeared. "Before my body decomposes and evaporates into nothingness, I feel the need to compensate for my... um, unethical abuse of power." Girding the robe around her as if chilled, she flipped the hood over her head. "There is a wizard, hell-bent on reshaping a novel breed of misbegottens by siphoning magicals of their congenital gifts. Dabbling in body parts and blood experimentation and..." She rubbed her fingers upon the crescent moon and star on her forehead. "This wizard thinks himself a god. He is a moron compared to me, and he knows this." Said like the true narcissist that she was. "If you have a glimmer of goodness in you, which I tasted, you must put a halt to his splicing and manipulation of chromosomes. Misbegottens had centuries of divine intervention, not procreated in a laboratory."

Crew had a funny feeling regarding her wizard who'd obtained differing labels. A master illusionist. A magician.

Off the cuff, he uttered, "What about my brother?"

Her cat eyes had dulled. "Born defective."

"Defective?"

"The intrinsic nature of intermixing magicals triggered a curse of barren wombs. And why it was essential that I located you." She again leaned on her staff. "Crew," she said his name for the first time, "you are a powerful being. And as such—"

"My brother was kidnaped from the foundling home," he said pushing into her dissertation. "Is he dead?"

"Very much alive. He was born deprived of your talents. *Defective*. But, I fear—"

"He's still my brother."

"Precisely what I'm coming to, if you'll pay attention." She gave an indignant sniffle. "The wizard desires that ring—for a reason. Leggan Dnego has been and *is* my fiercest rival."

Not the person or the name Crew had been expecting. "Leggan is dead."

"Becoming dead is virtuoso; a master can go about his business unobstructed." Her rheumy gaze locked on him. "You know of whom I speak, don't you? He goes by an invented name, such as yourself. Aerestol Paphos."

Yes, the person he'd been imagining came to light. "Polk's benefactor. I will find..." Crew swayed on his feet; the world was turning topsy-turvy. "I...I don't feel so hot. I think I'm going to be sick." His legs weren't cooperating. Failing to support his body, he sunk to the mucky ground, and slumped onto his back.

Crew, where are you? Please, take the ring off!

"Ever since the ring came into your possession, you've entered my realm to disappear from yours. You have your reasons. However, there is a price to pay for time spent." The hag huddled over him, jowls quivering. "You have been living in two realms. Here and there. You've lost a lot of blood. That's why you're not feeling well."

"It's a minor gash." He touched his jaw, caked with clotted blood.

"Heed my parting caveat, too much power creates a chemical imbalance. And you, boy, can inhale it like a heady brew." She leaned over him, her hag face blurring. "The girl is a mystery. I can't read her past nor her future. Whether she'll betray you, be a burden, or an asset. Beware of her." Extending her arm, she wiggled the ring off his pinkie finger.

TWENTY-ONE
CREW

"Sage! Sage! I found him!"

The icepick in his skull returned tenfold. Not only his head. His body screamed in pain as if trampled by a warthog-drawn wagon. He pressed his hands to his temples, hoping to dull the throb. Crew slit one eye. "Where…where…?"

"Sage over here!"

"Shhh…softer, aye, shhh…" Kneading his brow and squinting into the person's face gawking down at him, he said, "I know you." He boosted himself up onto his elbows.

"Don't move." The person held Crew by his shoulder, preventing him from getting up. "Sage, are you coming?"

"I was getting a torch. Here." She handed it off. "Hold it so I can see him."

Crew squeezed his eyes then reopened them, attempting to improve his woolly vision. "I'm back," he sighed, relieved.

"Crew, lay down. Let me take a look at you," Sage ordered.

"As you wish." Pathetically feeble, he couldn't break a smile. It felt like a hammer was whacking against his skull, forcing him backward onto the ground. "Where'd you find your brother?"

"At the Lamb and Kidney."

"Ahh." His eyes shuttered. "He knows then?"

"About our family? Yes."

"Sorry, Tegan."

"Crew," Tegan said, "wish we'd met with a jug of ale instead of this way."

There was a tearing noise. "Tegan, there's a pond just past the red osier tree; douse this with water. Hurry." Before departing, her brother poked the end of the torch into the ground, providing them with insipid light.

Crew peered at her through the slits of his eyelids. She'd kneeled over him, and her hair, branching over her shoulders, caught the light. Possibly due to the heat, she'd thrown propriety to the wind, and had unbuttoned the upper half of her blouse, revealing glistening skin which he'd dreamt of touching. "How long was I gone?"

"I searched most of the day, calling for you, but there wasn't a trace. I had to leave to—"

"It's okay." He discerned the remorse in her tenor. "Your brother comes first. I…" Grimacing, he released a low-keyed drone.

"That's not what I meant. I…I didn't know if you were coming back." She delved her fingers into his hair, marinating in blood. Carefully, she divided the strands from the laceration. "I thought your leg was bad, but this gash on your head is leaking like a sieve."

"A present from that adorable imp. Either from his claws or his knife. I can't believe the kid knocked me out. The next thing I remember, you were calling my name." He lifted his arm to assess the damage, but Sage grasped his hand.

"Don't touch," she snapped. "Infections, once in the bloodstream, are difficult to remedy. Even for me."

"Here," Tegan said, returning with a section of her skirt dripping with water.

Sage wrung it out and applied it to the crown of Crew's head, and then wiped his face. "Tegan, can you bring the light closer? I want to see how deep it is."

"Hey, Crew," Tegan said. "I can see your boney skull."

"Not funny, Tegan," Sage admonished.

Crew managed a snort.

"I can bind it, but it comes past your hairline. It's going to leave a permanent scar."

"It'll make him look mean and folks won't mess with him," Tegan said. "Right, Crew?"

"Aye, perfect." Crew was keeping it together, and he didn't want to pass out like a weakling. "Sage, do it."

"Don't move," she advised. "It might feel like I'm pricking you with pins and needles for a few seconds."

"It'll sting like she's got an embroidery needle in your skull." Tegan chuckled. "That's how it felt when she fixed me."

"Quiet." Sage closed her eyes, concentrating on mending him, and Crew did the same.

When she'd healed his leg from the bullet wound, which seemed like forever ago, that was brutal. But this was far worse. Tegan hadn't lied. If Crew didn't know any better, he'd believe she was sewing with a needle and thread, tugging on his skin to bind it. The sting and bonding procedure went on and on. Scrunching his eyes, he bit down on his molars, stifling his childish whine.

He might have blacked out because he was roused by a cool compress covering his face. She took the cloth off, and veering to the side, twisted it, allowing blood and water to wet the soil. Her features were haggard, deprived of sleep and the heart-wrenching loss of her family. Although, it hadn't detracted her beauty from shining through.

"How do I look?" he said, humor in his voice.

Veiling her lassitude, she turned to him. Her gaze dragged over his face. "Ugly as sin, as you've always been I'm afraid."

Her cheekiness amused him, and pushing off the hard-packed earth, he sat upright. The woods spun in dizzying motion. The sleeves of his once-white button-down were pure filth and bloodstained, along with his fancy waistcoat. His shaky fingers couldn't get a grip on the buttons to relax the strangulating collar, also soaked with sweat and blood. Yanking on the collar, buttons went zinging in the air.

"I'd take it a slow, if I were you." She crouched beside him and took hold of his elbow. "Tegan, come help."

"I don't need your brother. I'm good." With Sage aiding him, he got to his feet. "I'm fine, you can let go." He hadn't meant to sound disrespectful. She removed her arm as if he had leprosy. Tegan was tending a fire, the same camp that the imps had been stationed at the night prior.

Crew brought his hand up to screen his eyes from a shaft of bright sunlight. It had been late twilight when he'd hazarded into Queen Esta's realm.

"We didn't think you were coming back. Tegan and I were getting ready to leave, but he wanted to comb the area again," Sage admitted in a brittle tone. "It's midday. We're going to stay here and rest."

He didn't care to be treated like an invalid, and neither had Polk. "Don't take a break for my benefit," he said, aggrieved. "I don't need to rest. I'm good to go." For his impertinence, he stubbed his toe on a root.

"Your choice. Feel free to leave, but my brother and I have been up all night looking for you. We need sleep." Her shoulders slouched as she left him, and trudged toward the fire.

Why am I being a swaggering cock?

In twenty-four hours, Sage had gone through more anguish and hardship than he'd experienced in a year. The inconvenient stopover at Queen Esta's had his insides tied in barbed wire. Tales of his lineage and her statement of being of misbegotten prodigy and whatnot, he couldn't take seriously. He had to reflect and sort through her silver-tongued monologues.

Crew wrung his hands together. Something was missing. The ring. He dug into the pockets of his trousers and waistcoat. He went down onto his hands and knees, which caused a chain reaction of pain in his head and body. He canvassed the spot where he'd reappeared.

"Are you okay?" Tegan said, noticing Crew pawing the ground. "What are you looking for?"

"The ring. I lost the ring."

Tegan helped hunt for the bewitched relic. "My sister told me about it."

Sage joined the search. "Can't find it anywhere," she said after a thorough sweeping. "Do you remember taking it off?"

He had an image of the hag's grizzled features hovering above him as she'd pried the ring from his finger. *She has it!* "I...I must have lost it when I took it off. Let it go." Tegan anchored his arm around Crew and helped him up. "I'm okay. Thanks." Dusting dirt from his trousers and his hands, he was bothered by a poignant hitch to his heart. Whether he believed her stories or not he'd never see the queen again.

"Eat. Then sleep. I'm bushed," Tegan said when he'd reached the fire. He handed Crew a flat rock with slabs of cooked rabbit, and a large leaf filled with berries and cheese. "Kind of archaic, but we don't have any dinnerware."

Crew hadn't realized how hungry he was and wolfed it down. He licked the juices from his blood encrusted fingers and started in on the berries and cheese. "You snared the rabbit?" he asked Tegan.

"Sage did. The cheese is from the Lamb and Kidney, and the berries Sage picked. Blackberry and raspberry bushes thrive in this section of the woods."

Pushing fingers through her hair, Sage arranged her mane over her shoulder and began braiding it. In the sunlight her features were quite prominent. He admired her delicate bone structure and heart-shaped lips which appealed to him. During his appraisal, her eyes flitted to his face. "Get some sleep," she said, disgruntled.

Neither Sage nor Tegan had mentioned their sister. A complication that needed rectifying. "Edras wasn't at the Lamb and Kidney with Tegan?" She shook her head. "I think the imps subdued her like they did with me and hid her in the dark when we came along. And why they had to distract us."

Crew had been promised a fortune for bringing in Sage; her sister was a bonus. Perhaps Aerestol offered an incentive for her capture. Or more than likely, the self-indulgent imps had been taken by surprise when Edras came upon them. They'd snatched her, figuring to sell her in the underground market. Her attractiveness alone would be sufficient to line their coffers for months. His thoughts increased the irksome throb in his head.

Sage had unraveled her braid, combed through her hair again with trembling fingers, and reworked it. She tied the ends with threads she'd pulled from her skirt and flung it to lay along her back "Thanks for shooting fire at imp daddy's sword," she said in a calm voice, not looking at him. "He wanted my head."

"I can't take credit for that," Crew said. "I was aiming for his chest."

Tegan gave a half-hearted snicker, then turned sober. He pressed the bridge of his nose, and said, "Sage told me everything. About Darney. The ice castle. Some doctor named Aerestol. Your friend, Dirge, and that you're working for this lunatic. He wanted you to snatch my sister and bring her to him. I...I should have been there—home. Instead of..." his tongue stumbled over the words. "Why did this hap... I can't..." He dropped his head into his hands.

Aggravated, Crew picked up a stick and snapped it in half. He hadn't wanted to get Tegan involved. And he owed Sage an explanation. Planning on her cooperation, she was supposed to be his saving grace. That was before that prick, *the benefactor*, threatened them. If her brother blackened his eyes, broke his nose, or trounced him into the ground, so be it. He deserved it.

"It's a long story," Crew said.

"I have time."

Crew chewed on his bottom lip before saying, "Polk worked for Doctor Aerestol, and—"

"Your father?" Tegan leaned forward and fixed his elbows on his knees.

"Polk isn't my father." Crew poked the broken stick into the hard soil. He dug nondescript lines in the dirt while traveling back in time, undertaking a tedious enlightenment. At one point during his narrative, Sage had become fixated on the flames.

He didn't hold back, and becoming emotional, his throat closed up. He cleared the clog and went on. How Polk implored him to join ranks with his benefactor, if not for the money, then to find his brother and save Sage. Mage Marek's demise. A reluctant Demelda who was found dead. Then, the ring.

Tegan gaped at him across the smoldering fire.

Crew unloaded, divulging his secrets, but not Polk's; those weren't his to reveal. The big guy had raised him the best he knew how. The relentless traveling. Never settling down. No lifelong friends or relationships. Just carnies and circus grunts.

It felt like an anvil was lifted from his chest. However, a fragment of that anvil remained because he held onto those hours in the Kingdom of Despair and Ruins.

"You have a brother?" Sage said disbelievingly.

Crew rubbed his pounding head. "I'd appreciate it if you didn't repeat anything I just told you."

"Wait, wait, wait." Tegan said, piqued. "You feckless, ignorant ass! You thought you could *protect* Sage by *bringing* her to Doctor Frankenstein's lair?"

Crew wished Tegan would get it out of his system. Punch him silly, and seriously hurting him for his impudence.

"Eadith might have gotten away," Sage chimed in. "Maybe she woke up smelling smoke and flew off." On second thought, she amended, "I doubt it. She wouldn't leave without looking for Mama and Papa. And— why didn't Mama, Papa, and Parry make it out?" She squeezed her eyes. "I...I think something stopped them."

"What are you saying?" Tegan looked stricken.

"Somebody tied them up, or...or..." Her ragged breathing accelerated.

"Don't say it. I get it." Tegan lowered his chin to his chest.

"I believe they took her, for whatever reason," Sage said. "Maybe to get me to comply with Crew."

Tegan's eyes, full of odium, found Crew. "This is your fault."

I warrant all of his wrath.

In a clipped voice, Sage said, "Now what? Neither the council nor Cabal will do anything to help us. They'll say it was a burning candle left unattended or some such drivel."

Before proposing his suggestion, Crew looked to Sage's brother. Tegan was adrift, immersed in a melancholy halo, wallowing in grief.

"We have to return to the Circus Faire," Crew stipulated. He peered at Tegan, whose cloudy eyes were clearing. "Madam Rouge knows something. We'll need her." He didn't specify *how* they'd entail her services. The cogs in his brain were beginning to rotate, and hoped he was on the right track. And grateful that neither of them asked for clarification because exhaustion washed over him like a tidal wave. "I need a few winks, and then we're off."

TWENTY-TWO
SAGE

The sluggish tones of treefolk stirred them from their restive dreams. They'd slept until the wood in the firepit had turned ashy-white. Observing the location of the midsummer sun, the group had hours before evening descended upon them.

"We passed a lake on our way to the tavern," Crew said. "I'm going for a dip. My bloody hair is sitting on my head like a dang helmet." He demonstrated by shearing fingers into his mop of hair, which had clotted on his head. His eyes pinched, his wound still prevalent.

"That'd be Insmead Lake," Tegan expressed. "I'm coming. Could use a washdown myself. Besides there's nixies in Insmead."

By the sight of her brother's churlish scowl, he'd rouse a water nixie for the lone sake of taking a chomp out of Crew. "Hurry it up," Sage said. Watching them retreat, she noted Crew's slight limp. His bullet wound required further mending, yet her stubborn nature wanted him to experience the twinge.

Quarter of an hour later, wearing palpable frowns, they plodded into camp. Neither of them talking. Crew wiped a thin dribble of blood on his forehead. She should have advised him that submerging underwater with that type of wound might undue some of her handiwork. When he raked back his wet hair, rendering free his face, her heartrate swelled. He could have been sculpted by the gods, with that strong jaw and full mouth now set in a firm line. Those damp luscious lashes and eyes of amber sharpened as he glanced her way, which brought a stroke of heat to her cheeks.

"Here, figured you could use this." Her brother lobbed a sopping chunk of her skirt at her. It wasn't the blood-soaked section she used to bathe Crew with. He must have discovered it in the scrub where she'd left it after cutting Crew from the tree.

She dashed behind thorny bushes. Stripping off her sullied blouse and what was left of her skirt, she sponged her face, neck, and body. She had no choice but to redress in her soiled outfit.

Crew stated it was best to remain unobserved and, her brother agreed. They journeyed along the outer fringes of Alderwood with Sage trailing behind. Since most of her skirt was torn away, thistly brambles all wanted a piece of her bare legs. Noisy revelers and whistleblowing were coming from the village. With folks going and coming home from the Faire, they didn't want to chance getting buttonholed by persons offering commiserating condolences. Sage wasn't ready to deal with that either, not yet.

Tegan seemed to have buried his wrathful hatchet, and not in Crew's skull. Their current standoffish disposition gave her pause to think, pertaining to Crew's hazy commentary.

In her mind, the jury was still convening as far as Crew was concerned. *Do I trust him?* Since their interlude at the oracles, and then through the ensuing days, it had been a storming whirlwind. And, not in a good way. He said Madam Rouge was hiding something, so was Crew. He had an association with Doctor Aerestol, yet, in the castle, there was a falling out of sorts which she couldn't quite grasp. She attempted to cage those frantic notions because Crew had confessed. Told them everything. *Or did he?*

Shrill childish giggling caused Sage to stall and peered through a cluster of conifers. They were passing *Galdoons*, and if her eyes weren't deceiving her, Darney was playing tag with his siblings. She snagged her brother's shirt, halting him. "I saw Darney Galdoon."

"The sprite from the castle?" Crew asked, and peeked between boughs of pines. "Aerestol let him go?"

"I'm going to talk to him." She started toward *Galdoons*, but Tegan held onto her arm.

"I'll go." Tegan lifted a brow at her shoddy appearance. "Stay here."

Sage crouched and Crew saddled up beside her. However, even hunkering down on his knees, he towered over her. Together they watched her brother talking to the sprites, mainly Darney.

Sage hated how Crew made her feel, even after his confession. Heat stemming off his body enveloped her. She couldn't help herself as she breathed him in, decadently exquisite, and hated him more for it. He'd taken advantage of her when she was fourteen, succumbing to his charm and compelling voice. How they'd talked, giggled, and loving his touch. A delicious tingling had the audacity to race through her. She hedged away from him and her feelings. He was her lodestone and she'd make it her priority to demagnetize.

When Fergan came out of *Galdoons*, Crew clutched her arm. Whether it was a stunned reaction on his part or worried what Fergan was going to say to Tegan. His mere touch stirred a wondrous fervor in her belly. She had thoughts of leaning into him, wanting the feel of him around her. Squelching that emotion, she jerked her arm away, putting space between them. He stretched out his fingers and curled them inward, making a fist, and let his arm fall to his side.

Tegan and Fergan's chat ended and the Galdoon children were hustled indoors.

Soon, her brother parted the pine boughs. "Darney doesn't remember anything about an ice castle. He remembers getting lost and said that Sage and a tall guy told him that his father was waiting by the gate."

"What did Fergan say?" Sage asked.

"He wanted to thank you for finding his son and sending him home."

Crew inquired, "Did you notice anything strange about Darney?"

"Strange? Not really. He just went on and on about how much fun he had—Wait! His pupils were enlarged."

"He was glamoured," Crew stressed.

"Sprites cannot be glamoured, can they?" Sage swatted a pesky mosquito.

"Aye, appears so."

Tegan added, "If your doctor is that influential, then there's probably nothing he can't do."

"He's not *my* doctor," Crew derided Tegan. "You think by glamouring a sprite makes Aerestol a supreme wizard?"

"Just saying—"

"You're wrong," Crew declared. He rotated and began walking. "He's getting that power from somewhere."

On the trek to the Circus Faire, a tense silence thickened around them. To break the tension or perhaps to make matters worse, Sage inquired, "Crew, where did you go after I put the ring on your finger? What did you see?" She remembered, after he'd slipped the ring on her finger in the castle, how alarming it was. And having the perception of being in two indistinct realms.

He shrugged.

She couldn't believe he wasn't going to answer. "It looks like you had some trouble, wherever it was." She tapped her own jaw, an indication of his fresh wound.

Looking anywhere but at her, he muttered about a graphic dreamscape, but not furnishing her a direct answer. Again, he was suppressing *something*.

Sounds of the circus dallied through the woody terrain moments before they caught sight of the grandiose tent where the extraordinary events took place. Rather than heading to the gated entrance, Crew ushered them around the periphery.

"This way." Wandering behind the exhibitions, further away from the Faire's pandemonium, Sage figured it was where the carnies bunked. They came upon aisles of ramshackle hovels that had been slap dashed together, and a variety of tents, grand and ordinary.

Crew waved them into an average-sized tent, and with a flick of his fingers, a kerosene lantern glowed to life, dispelling the inner dimness. "My home away from home. It's a bit larger than the other drudges because Polk and I shared this tent. Make yourselves comfortable. There's drinks in the icebox. I'll be right back." He passed through a dividing curtain.

Dissimilar than Madam Rouge's planked flooring, Crew's tent was built on the hard earth. Hay sprinkled the soil, expunging the dampness that secreted from the ground.

Tegan didn't waste a second and headed for the cube-shaped icebox. "Want an ale?" he offered Sage.

"Any juice?"

"Doesn't look like it."

"I'll take an ale then. I'm parched."

"Not a bad setup." Glimpsing around, Tegan pulled out a chair from under a small table and sat. "I like it here."

"Did you stay with Crew when you worked the Faire?" Her brother's throaty reminiscent snigger was and wasn't expected. "Have you no scruples?"

"Hey, give me a break, Sage." He grinned. "Three years ago I was a hormonal fae. And Polk was never here to supervise us. Good times, sis."

"Ugh!" His tawdry response had her imagining all sorts of orgies and revelers parading in and out of the tents. "You give fae a bad name."

Tegan threw his horned head back in booming laughter.

"What's so hilarious?" Crew asked.

Shaking her head, Sage said, "Nothing."

"Here." He dumped a pile of clothes on the table. "Sage, take your pick. See if anything fits. Go in back and try 'em on."

She hadn't budged. "Uhm, where…I…um—"

"Go on, Sage," Tegan insisted. "You can't go around dressed like that."

"They're mine from when I was a kid. If you don't mind wearing boy's pants," Crew said. "I found them in my trunk, tucked underneath at the bottom."

"Oh, man, she's gonna kiss you." Her brother chuckled, and she shot him a sullen frown. "Sage loves wearing pants, don't you? Mama and Papa were always reminding her that she was a girl."

"If I had my bow," she seethed, "you'd be hurting right now." Her comment had her brother chuckling harder. With her temperature rising, hotness erupted beneath her skin. She gathered the clothes and scampered behind the curtain into a tiny annex.

Crew had lit another lantern, hanging from a peg on a two-by-four that supported the tent. Sage placed the clothes on a makeshift cot. His sleeping quarters weren't in disarray as she'd expected. At the foot of the cot was a large trunk and a simple wooden chair stood in the corner where his bloodied shirt and waistcoat lay rumpled.

Sage disrobed and selected a baby-blue, brushed cotton, long-sleeved button-down. A perfect fit for her petite frame and tried to guess how old Crew had been when he'd last worn it. Liking the supple feel, she brought the fabric to her nose and breathed in. She savored the scent of him, aromatic woods, balsam pine, and leather had embedded into the threads. After rolling the cuffs to make a quarter-length sleeve, she then climbed into a pair of pants. The legs bunched around her ankles and were too big in the waist. She chose a different pair of denim breeches. They fit almost perfectly, excluding the loose waist, which she had to keep readjusting so they wouldn't ride down her hips. Tucking in the tails of the shirt, she groaned when she saw her new slippers, stained and coated in soot.

Bending over she tore off the silken bow. "Better," she said to herself, and the breeches slipped past her butt. The waistband was going to be problematic. Every man had suspenders; Papa and her brothers each had two. She stood in front of the traveling trunk, unsure. Snooping into a person's private belongings felt wrong.

"Sage, come on. What's taking so long? This isn't a fashion show." She badly wanted to give her brother a swift kick. Granted he was as fractured as she was. They had contrary methods of dealing with their loss. He grew belligerent by the hour, whereas guilt clutched her innards because she hadn't given Edras or Eadith a moment of her day. Her fortitude came from refusing to believe her sisters were being mistreated in any form, elsewise she'd fall to pieces.

Holding the waistband of Crew's pants, she flung open the flappy curtain. "Do you happen to have suspenders?"

Crew was sitting at the table with her brother, gaping at her, an uncorked bottled brew poised inches from his mouth. She hiked the slack waistband to ride higher on her hips and wondered why he was looking at her as if he'd never seen a girl in pants. His drifting gaze awakened all kinds of feelings.

"Suspenders?" she repeated, and a noticeable blotchiness invaded his cheekbones.

He set down the bottle. "I do." Crew breezed by her and lifted the lid of his trunk. He shoved clothes and whatnot aside and drew out black suspenders.

Rather than hand them over, he went behind her and tugged on the waistband, clicking the clips in place. He brought the suspenders over her shoulders and moved in front of her. She felt awkward, squaring her rigid shoulders.

"This clip is tricky. It broke the last time I used them. I thought I fixed it, but…" His breath fanned her face as he toiled with the suspenders.

His raven-winged hair brushed her forehead, and she drank in his muskiness. Her pulse quickened. And her body temperature heightened. Lightheaded from the hotness emanating from both of them, she readied to thrust him away.

Hearing a click, he took a jerky step back. His gaze lowered, face flushed. Puffing a sharp breath of air, he shook out his hands.

"That should do." His eyes slid to find hers, soaking her in, challenging the aversion she'd built over her heart. "Okay?" He skimmed his hands on his hips.

He is obnoxiously stunning for a boy, she thought. An infallible male specimen which set her teeth on edge. How dare he look at her with those changeable eyes, now rich sapphire, like nightfall in autumn.

"I didn't need your help," she said petulantly, and dropped her gaze from the intensity of his. She gave the suspenders a tug, affording her relief that his, or rather her, pants weren't going to fall to her ankles.

TWENTY-THREE
CREW

Crew swiped his bottled brew from the table and took a long draught before taking a seat. *The girl despises me. I never met a female or a male I couldn't charm*, he thought while scratching his shoulder. Even Aerestol Paphos had evaded meeting his eyes head on. When that goon pointed his Colt to Crew's chest, he thought he was a goner. Lucky for him he was able to snag the doctor's eyes and pitch his voice, a motive for Crew's longevity.

This girl made him feel inadequate. His fingers shook as he'd fixed the clip on the suspenders. All the while longing to glide his hands around her waist. His body experienced a head-to-toe burn, and things he couldn't control got the better of him. If her brother wasn't there, he might have taken a chance, in hopes she wouldn't clobber him. His finger traced the rim of the bottled ale, tarrying until his pulsating blood cooled.

Since tumbling from Queen Esta's, he was preoccupied with getting his head on straight. What had transpired in her kingdom scuttled to the forefront. Both of them were Dolorans. Hence, she could, unknowingly, rebuffed his charm. Three years ago, he mused that she'd charmed him rather than the other way around. It made perfect sense. They were equivalent.

"So now what?" Tegan rested his arms on the table.

"Now," said Crew, "you and Sage return to Alderwood."

Tegan jolted upright. "I'm getting my sisters back from that monster."

"You need me." Sage stood next to her brother, ringing her fingers on the rung of his chair.

"I'd rather not risk it. I go alone." Crew brought the neck of the bottle to his lips and pounded the remaining contents of ale.

"You can't stop me from following you," her brother informed him. "Unless you kill me."

I can stop him. But do I really want to? Tegan had strength and smarts. He'd be an asset for sure.

Sage added her two cents. "I'm on this journey too, whether you like it or not." And folded her arms across her waist.

Seeing Sage in his shirt and pants did something to him. Triggering a slow simmer that was reaching the boiling point whenever he looked at her. Allaying his rising heat, he rolled the cool glass bottle on his forehead, moving it along his cheek and neck.

"Hot in here isn't it?" he said.

"Crew, it's settled." Tegan wiped his brow, flattening his worry. "Fill us in on the details. Where do we find this doctor?"

"I don't know for sure."

"*What*!" Sage gasped. "You must know. There's a reason why you're not telling us."

Crew reclined into the chair, stretching his long legs. "He has an estate in Wintervine and—"

"Wintervine is up north. It'll be a bitch, but we can make it," Tegan encouraged, drumming his fingers on the table.

"Aerestol also has an estate in Quillen."

"Never heard of it." Sage said.

"You never heard of it because it's in the Unified Territory."

Tegan let his head flop backward. "Ack, mortal land?"

"I can get us there, but I'd rather not chance it. I think Wintervine is where we'll find him."

"How can you get us into mortal territory?" Sage wheedled. "There's the toll bridges and we'd need papers and then the Unified Militia."

"Sage, stop already," Tegan reprimanded. "Let him speak." She glowered at her brother, wrinkling her nose.

She was adorable, unlike her opinion regarding the imp boy. "We'll need supplies and a wagon, and my horse is here in the stable. Until we get further north, our best efforts to reach Wintervine is to go by sea."

"Why are we stalling?" Tegan sprang to his feet. "Let's get moving."

"Sounds easy, aye?" Crew put the fix in. "Wintervine is all mountains and deep valleys. It's getting into the winter season there, ice packed and snowy."

"I have coin." For proof, Tegan carted out of his pockets two drawstring bags, jingling the coins. "Today was payday at the mines, and my sleight of hand at the taverns gaming tables was on fire. We'll purchase what we need." His amicable grin reached his eyes.

Crew chafed his hands together. "One more vital statistic. I don't know *where* in Wintervine his estate is."

"May the gods curse you!" Tegan protested and slammed a bag of coins on the table making a racket.

"Why are you lying to us?" Sage's eyes watered. "I heard it from Aerestol's own mouth that you're working for him, or you were. I don't believe you."

"Believe it. I'm not lying. I managed a couple jobs to ingratiate myself to him. Always meeting him or his cronies in Foundling Square. I told you this already."

Sage slapped her hands over her face, growled, and turned away from him.

"I didn't return to the Circus Faire to get Sage into my pants," Crew mocked. "We have an impromptu date with Madam Rouge. The oracle will tell us what we need to know. We just have to wait until the sun sets." He didn't want to be recognized; a tidbit not worth mentioning. After Dyke had promoted him as the Master Fire Wrangler, and drawing an audience to the ridge, he'd been a no-show. Missing his grand debut, Dyke would be spitting bullets.

Crew and Tegan downed another ale and Sage paced. She'd hooked her thumbs on the straps of the suspenders, head down, walking the short breadth of space around the table. She wasn't the sort to parade her emotions on her face. Her thoughts were her own. Though he could cut the tension with a knife.

Night had fallen and the voluble Circus Faire was coming to life. It so happened, the longer the Faire lingered in one place, news had the propensity of traveling to far reaching territories. Attracting miscreants, scallywags, and villains to come and play. Causing those with moral standards to avoid temptations or to excessively engage in them. By the horde of souls and the sights and sounds, it appeared people were quite engaged. Gaslights illumed random avenues, yet creatures liked to be entertained in the darkened shadows. If a person were inclined to bend their ears, they might be able to hear cavorting, throwing caution to the wind, an undercurrent of pleasurable moans, and naughty giggling sifting through the air.

The threesome lurked in the forest behind Madam Rouge's. Crew had and hadn't concocted a plan. Although, he'd bet his balls, the oracle knew more, a lot more in regard to Polk's benefactor.

Tegan was getting antsy, shifting from foot to foot. "What are we waiting for now?"

"Have you seen the crowds congregating outside of her tent?" Crew craned his neck to peer down the gloomy aisle between structures.

"Why don't we go in the back like we did before?" Sage had hunkered down to kneel on one knee, resting her arms on her cocked leg. "Who cares if anyone sees us?"

I care. Typically, grunts like him would be traipsing and working beyond the structures, and most, if not all, would know him. They'd ask questions, alerting him that Dyke was on the warpath for missing his performance. Sliding his gaze to her, she kept rolling and unrolling her bottom lip into her mouth, letting her teeth scrape over it. A vehement shiver chased through him because he remembered how she tasted. Tormentingly sweet, innocent, and malleable. Back in the day, she'd offered herself to him without the formality of pretenses. Aching for her, he'd ended it before totally losing himself.

He had regrets but couldn't change things. Deep down inside he hoped she would forgive him for what happened and for what was about to happen.

"I have an idea," Sage said.

TWENTY-FOUR
SAGE

Sage's sisters' lives were at stake. There wasn't a second to spare. She felt linked to them, experiencing their angst and fear, and their unremitting pleas for help.

Realizing what she had to do, she was reminded of Edras rebuke about hiding their capabilities. She'd said, "Keep it intact for when there's a real crisis."

Edras, it's a crisis.

Sage pushed off the ground, standing tall. She glanced into her brother's face and his skeptical, arching eyebrow. Slinging her gaze to Crew, she said, "Be quick. With this crowd, I won't be able to hold it for long, hopefully time enough to get the oracle's ears and eyes." Crew dipped his head, understanding. He'd witnessed what she could do in the ice castle.

Following her lead, they walked past the threshold of the woods toward the rear of the oracles. Sage faltered, coming to a standstill, doubting herself to stop the continuum of the entire Faire. "I don't think I can... I doubt I can hold this great of..." she wavered. "It's—"

"Don't worry. You can do it," Crew prompted, gazing at her from the corner of his eyes. "I'll help."

"You'll *help*?" She questioned his reliability.

"Do it now," he ordered.

Sage closed her eyes. Envisioning what needed to be done, calling upon her resources. Adrenaline roiled through her veins, faster, intoxicatingly potent, and it was crucial to hold onto it until she couldn't contain the magnitude of its pressure. When the grave intensity filled her body, her fingers flexed outward.

She opened her eyes. It worked. A shroud settled over the Circus. People were poised in mid-step, touting comical and animated expressions, a surreal scene. Turning to Crew, his eyelids were pressed together. His body shuddered, and his strained features softened when he opened his eyes.

She'd sensed his preponderant influence bonding with hers, like weaving intermediaries. "*You*?" she stated, and the side of his mouth quirked. This boy was concealing secrets and it disturbed her.

"Hey, that's incredible." Tegan gave a breathy whistle. "Sage, you gotta teach me that."

Her brother was a sweetheart. Terrifying her was the thought of losing Tegan too. Whatever Crew was plotting it could be far worse than either of them could imagine.

Crew swished his hand. "Let's hurry." He looked around, and then scampered toward the tent with Sage on his heels.

Entering the dusky, private quarters of Madam Rouge, Sage was about to luminate the room when Crew's hand bloomed with flaming light. Her body felt drained, experiencing the aftereffects of delaying time, so it was wiser to rest and restore her energy.

"Wait here," Crew suggested. "I'd rather bring the oracle in here, just in case we can't hold time." He shook his hand, quenching the light.

Tegan snapped his fingers, and the lantern stationed on the bureau flamed to life. "I'm not totally inferior."

His buoyant smile warmed Sage's heart. She reckoned that someone in the Steele family had to have been remarkable in some form. Low fae, while not necessarily adept, were endowed with varied talents. Her eldest brother inherited the magic gene, while poor Parry had struggled. Thinking of Parry, the edges of her heart crumbled.

Tegan made himself at home, diving onto the bed. "Hey, did you notice that healed scar on Crew's neck? It wasn't there three years ago. Did he ever say how he got it?"

"It's hard not to miss. And no, I haven't asked. He seems to be collecting them." Sage swiveled in place and met her reflection in the full-length looking glass. A mass exodus of strands had escaped her braid, and wearing boy's clothes, she resembled a pauper, a street rat. She sneered at herself and knew what Marne would say. "You look scandalous in Crew's clothes." Assiduously unfastening the braid, she worked out the snarls until her hair bore a semblance of unity. She then tucked in Crew's shirt which had the inclination to slither from the loose waistband.

"What's taking him so long?" She strayed from the looking glass toward the divider just as Crew was coming through. A near miss of clunking bodies, he recoiled. She'd taken him by surprise.

"I got rid of her customers and sealed the entrance." Crew's favorable gaze cruised over her long, wavy hair and then cut to Tegan. "We shouldn't be disturbed." He draped back the curtain, shepherding them to the front. "Sage, you can release time now," he said, voice hushed.

For a brief second, she shut her eyes. Her shoulders slouched from the weight she'd been holding and was immediately alleviated. Exhaling her burdensome task and inhaling pungent patchouli, she sauntered into the confines of Madam's divination chamber.

Swathed in an unearthly ambiance, in shades of indigo and black velveteen, twinkling orbs speckled the ceiling. On occasion, the orbs threw sparklers resembling falling stars. *Pixies?*

Nonplussed, Madam was shuffling tarot cards, and a glass globe roosted on a pedestal in the middle of the table.

The oracle's eyes narrowed, finding Sage. "You've changed."

"Um, my skirt was—"

"Not your clothes, deary. A couple days ago, a frivolous girl walked into my tent. The lady standing before me is reeking of sedition."

"How dare you," Sage attacked. "I am neither a rabblerouser or—" The oracle tilted her head backward, hissing glee spilling from her mouth, suspending Sage's spiel.

Crew pulled out a chair, as did Tegan, and plopped down at the table. Sage did what she did best, she paced. Madam's black and flaxen mane had been twisted into a chignon, though wisps of loose hair lined her shoulders. And what she hadn't perceived on their prior intrusion was that Madam Rouge had classic pointed ears. *She is fae.* Sheer colorful robes ensconced her body, and on her wrist was a bracelet with tiny bells that tinkled as she shuffled the deck of cards.

"What can I do for you today, boys and girls?" the oracle said, precociously. "Let me deal the cards, see what lies in the future."

"We didn't come to have our fortunes read." Crew overlapped his arms on the table.

His reply hadn't deterred the oracle's shuffling, possibly the deed mollified her nerves. "What I just experienced," she said, "was the world coming to a halt before my eyes; I'd say you have a lot of explaining."

Why doesn't Crew speak up? What's he waiting for? Sage walloped her hands on the table, causing the crystal globe to jitter. "Stop playing us. You know why we're here."

"I see." Madam stretched her neck. "You need my help."

"You know Aerestol Paphos. Quite well, I imagine," Crew uttered.

"I already told you." She thumped the cards on the table, a show of animosity, a flush tinging her cheekbones. "Yes. I know him. He comes for readings and—"

Crew interrupted, "Where does he live in Wintervine?"

"I…I…" Nervous fingers swept into the sides of her hair. "He…he doesn't allow uninvited guests."

Sage took a seat and leaned into the edge of the table. "You know where his estate is? You've been there?"

"You don't know what you're asking of me." She spread the tarot cards in front of her. "It'd be detrimental to my health and livelihood if I—"

"I don't care about your health." Sage's hands trembled into fists. "He killed my parents and my brother and took my sisters."

"And we're going after him," Tegan growled.

TWENTY-FIVE
CREW

"Sage, your tragedy rips out my heart. Please forgive me if I sounded callous. I can't believe Doctor Aerestol would be involved in your families' deaths. He keeps a low profile for a good reason, owing to dealings with an underground market. I'm not a fan of…um… his *methods*." She brushed the backside of her fingers across her mouth. "I admit, under duress, I've traveled with Dyke to Wintervine. Aerestol supplies the Circus with suitable hirelings and he…he is a superstitious man. And persists on having me read for him."

The oracle was convincing. Crew sensed truth to her words. Truth of omission more like. "Madam, what can you tell me about his character?"

She hooked her fingers together and propped her hands across her midsection. "I told you. He is brilliant—and immoral."

"You misunderstand my question. Is he mortal?" Queen Esta had unveiled Aerestol Paphos for who he really was. Would Madam forfeit her knowledge?

With her hands coupled, she smoothed her left thumb over the knuckles of her right hand. "He is a phenomenal wizard. In my lifetime, I haven't come across anyone like him."

Aha! Not a lie. "Long ago, the benefactor traded his name for another. To hide from the depravity of his sins, aye?"

Her breath caught on a snag. "You're too young to know. No one knows. No one." Knitting her eyebrows, her face twisted. "Who told you? Not Polk?"

In a measure move, he shook his head. "Tell me. Confirm what I already know."

The edges of the oracles mouth hardened. Browsing over her tarot cards, she selected seven from the splayed deck. "Aerestol has several estates." Attentive to rearranging her face-downed picks, her solutions were chosen by a turn of a card.

Crew had to be careful not to push her over the brink by demanding she say Aerestol's given name, Leggan Dnegos, and losing her altogether. As with the utmost extraordinary performers at the Circus Faire, their egoistical heads weighed heavily upon their shoulders. And Madam Rouge was the headliner, the bigwig, and the grunts working behind the scenes all knew it. Dyke was known as an ass-kisser when it came to her and her outlandish demands. Shipping in lobster and ordering the crew to go hunting for grouse and quail to whet the mystic's appetite, elsewise she'd refuse to perform. Her clairvoyancy act in the main pavilion reaped a profitable sum and expanded Dyke's greedy pockets.

"Madam." Crew set his sight on her. "Forgive my rudeness." Capturing her eyes, he said, "I once overheard you talking with Polk that you wanted to help me?" Her pupils inflated. "Regarding my destiny, aye? You can assist me now, simply by locating Aerestol Paphos." Pinning her with his gaze, not blinking, his charmed voice ensnared her. "It's within our grasp. But we need you. You can save many lives. You'll be a hero." Flattering her as he did might entice her vainness. From the margin of his vision, it appeared Sage was preparing to voice her opinion. He sprang his fingers off the surface of the table, and she swallowed whatever had crossed her mind.

The membranes of his eyes were dry, but he'd lose her if he blinked. "What say you?" Wielding his weapon, a cadence like a twining lariat, he persuaded the oracle to submit and to concur with his request. Blinking and rinsing his dry eyes, he lounged into his seat.

Coming out of a stupor, Madam blinked and smoothed her brow. "Aerestol's palatial estate is difficult to breach," she supplied, voice tentative.

Crew slanted a look at Tegan and Sage. Sage's mouth pressed into a firm line. He hadn't been certain his charm would sway the oracle. Her prevailing power was supposedly surpassed by no other. Even after her reply, he realized, it might have been staged. His heart hammered in cautionary beats. The woman might guide them on a wild goose chase into a frozen tundra where they'd meet death. Yet, if she were willing and able, he'd take whatever she offered. To keep Sage safe and to find his brother and rid magicals of a treacherous monster.

"Let's imagine," she spoke with her hand, swirling airily, "you don't die trying to approach his estate. What do you propose will happen once you come face to face with him?"

"We'll burn him alive like he burned our parents!" Tegan hopped in, teeth gritting.

Madam fluttered her eyelashes and sucked in the sides of her cheeks. "That might be tricky. Did you not hear me mention, *Aerestol is a wizard*? Not your typical mage that you are acquainted. He can do great things. Terrible things, but great."

"What happens once we find him isn't any concern of yours," Sage voiced. "Crew has a br—"

"We need a map," Crew charged in. "Something to guide us. Land markers. I've been informed the wizard has boobytraps in place."

"Polk told you," she stated, not a question, and plinked her nails on the table. "You won't need a map. I'm coming with you."

A muscle in Crew's jaw ticked. There was something fishy going on. He made a tactical move. "Dyke won't allow you to leave during the peak of the Faire."

"I can take care of Dyke." She wore an amiable smile and lowered her gaze to the tarot cards. The seven she'd dragged out during their discussion, she flipped over, one by one. "By the reading of these very intriguing cards, you will need me."

Cunningly, she was drawing them into her web. Crew didn't want to look and have a premonition hanging over his head. *Fate is a mean fucker.* A smirk slipped onto his face, and he thought it should have been Polk's epitaph.

"I'm riding into Foundling to charter a launch. It'll be faster by sea." Crew rose.

"It will be," the oracle rearranged the seven cards. "Bring coin for transportation. There's a livery near the port in Wintervine."

"We're leaving through your private quarters," Crew said, "and we'll be acquiring a few items from your armoire."

"I expected no less." In a deliberate rhythmic tempo, the oracle tapped her finger on the Death card and next to it the Magician, purposely drawing their gazes. And then the Hanged Man. The Strength card. Ace of Swords. The Chariot.

She said, "Get a good night's sleep; you're going to need it." Madam gathered the cards into the stack. "If you weren't going to Foundling tonight, I'd say stay so we can collaborate. Aerestol's *boobytraps*, need to be addressed."

Offering a look to Sage and Tegan, he prompted, "This is vital. We better stay." Groans ensued as they plopped down into their seats.

Madam Rouge sent them a conciliatory wink. And donning a superior mask of authority, she pinched the indigo cloth that covered the divination globe. "Gather round, kiddos." In a theatrical fanfare, she whipped it off. The room blackened, and the glass globe shimmered, dragging their eyes to the main attraction.

Crew squinted, adapting to the luster. It seemed involuntary as he peered through the globes aura to encounter Sage's intent brow. The brilliance arresting upon her beauty, and a thudding started in his chest. As if she sensed his attraction, her eyes darted, linking onto him. His pulse increased until she diverted her gaze toward the globe.

Why did she affect him like a hormonal boy? Crew had the pleasure of women; they brazenly sought him out. Three years ago, he'd hungered for all of Sage as she would have been an easy conquest. She was too young, and he wasn't a salacious rake. What threw him off his axis since their dalliance in that tree, she'd split open his heart and had crawled in. Somehow, she became a part of him, and ever since, he'd been trying to forget her. His life wasn't fit for any girl. To get her out of his system, he'd been tempted to have his way with her. Currently, if he tried anything, Sage would carve out his heart with a spoon.

Madam Rouge flattened the palms of her hands on the table, spreading her fingers. Shutting her eyes, her mouth formed an O. The crystalized innards of the globe roiled, faster and faster, like whisking starlight. Shady depths of images began to take shape. The oracle sloped over the table and discharged a breezy breath over its glassy circumference.

The oracle said, "There it is. Wintervine."

"It looks like a blizzard." Tegan closed in, his breath fogging the glass.

"Move back and concentrate." Madam extended her arms, palms facing the globe and crisscrossed her hands. "See it?"

"There's a mountain," Sage confirmed. "Is that...that it?"

The oracle confirmed, "The doctor had the mansion built into the side of the mountain, for a reason."

"To prevent interlopers from breaching his compound," Crew retorted. "Which means, we can only come in from the front."

"Problematic, if we're planning on sneaking in undetected." Tegan added.

"It looks familiar." Sage tapered her eyes. "Like…like the—"

"The ice castle," Crew said.

Sage leaned in. "Am I seeing things, or is it also made of ice?"

"The walls are two feet thick, but you'd never know it was made of ice from the inside. It's warm and…" Madam's mouth puckered. "Aerestol likes to brag about his wizardry and this mansion is one of his creations."

Crew immediately wondered if his fiery talent would be stymied in the mansion as it had been in the Circus' ice castle.

"Look closer," the oracle advised. The image zoomed in, like she'd adjusted the sight of a telescope. "There are guards stationed at key central zones. At the front doors. Both sides of the mansion. And if we move back," the image ascended a bit, "there's a security booth further down the winding path that leads to the house."

"We can't scale a mountain. Or can we?" Crew stroked the bottom rim of his mouth. "There is a dusting of snow. Can you move the image to view it on all sides and from above?"

"Is this real time, what we're seeing here?" Tegan expressed.

"It is," Madam replied. "And that region is capricious when it comes to the weather. The wintry season is just beginning. One day there's a dusting and the next, the clouds drop five feet of snow on that mountain."

For someone who made it sound like her visits were infrequent, the oracle had plenty of information concerning the wizard's estate. Crew didn't trust her, but she was invaluable for this mission.

"What about the boobytraps." Sage looked to the oracle. "Are they outside or inside? From this aerial view, I don't see anything out of the ordinary. Will the security guards let us pass if we—"

"No." Madam Rouge said succinctly.

"Well then," Sage said snootily, "how did you and Dyke get in?"

The oracle released a disdainful breath. "We were expected. Aerestol's men know us."

Sage slumped her chin to her chest and propped a balled fist over her mouth.

"See the bridge? Aerestol is in residence," Madam indicated, pointing her finger. "You have to cross it to get to the mansion. It's enchanted. If you aren't on Aerestol's guest list, or merely a pathetic person on a climbing expedition, it will break apart. Whoever is on that bridge will fall to their death in the ravine."

Tegan cocked an eyebrow, casting Crew a sidelong glance. "Why is the bridge proof that he's home?"

"Because it wouldn't be there. When he's traveling, he removes any temptation for nomadic creatures to wander onto his estate."

"Is there another way around it?" Crew inquired, optimistic. "Perhaps going around the ravine, find another spot to travel over?"

The oracle shrugged. "I wouldn't know. It's desolate up there, and if the weather turns, it will get dicey."

Encased in a tension-filled hush, Sage had a faraway gaze. He didn't have long to speculate what was strumming in that brain of hers.

"For some reason, Doctor Aerestol wants me," Sage began, "Madam Rouge, bring me to him. Tell him we're coming. That will get us through."

A tight grin played on the oracle's face. "That will work."

"Absolutely not!" Tegan sprang off his chair and, pancaking his hands on the table, leaned into them. "Are you out of your mind? The guy is a whack-job."

"We can't take that chance," Crew jumped in. Sage chewed on the inside of her cheek and peered at him through thinning eyelids. "We'll think of something else."

Sage clutched the edge of the table, her gaze leveling Crew. "We got this, don't we?"

Her steadfast attitude felt like a weighty mantle that was riddled with holes. He comprehended what she was implying. Between them, if the oracle were part of their team, they'd have the influence and power to divide and conquer.

"The girl made a bold proclamation." Madam bowed her head at Sage. "Sounds like she's a lady who can handle herself. I think it's a logical approach to get into his mansion without getting ourselves injured or killed. Aerestol has a carriage made exclusively for us. It's in the livery behind the harbormaster. It has a hidden compartment where he stashes—"

"Bodies," Crew murmured. "Why bother hiding them?" Madam Rouge extracted a breath, and flopped her head forward, as if their conversation had turned tedious. "Paphos is the main contributor in the slave market, aye? He abducts magicals and sells them for profit to affluent mortals. I've seen them, as servants laboring in prosperous manors in the Unified Territory. What I can't wrap my head around, is why they don't take flight?"

In a melodramatic manner, the oracle said, "I've heard the rumors too. Have you ever considered the plausibility that those creatures leave willingly? An escape from these lands. The Unified Territory is abounding with amenities." Sighting those around her divination globe, she spread her arms. "Can we, *pleeeaasee* concentrate on why *you* want to invade the wizard's domain? I agreed to get you into Wintervine, but I am not going to start a revolution to—"

"Why are you helping us?" Tegan spat. "The truth."

Wetting her lips, she returned, "I have my reasons, which I won't relay to you brigands."

"We're not thieves." Sage responded, balancing on the edge of her seat.

"Ahh, but you are. Think about it. I am fae and can't lie."

"Aye, fae can't lie; they sneak around the truth," Crew amended. "It's getting late. We need to rest and be on the road before daybreak. We'll meet at the livery and have plenty of time to resume our strategy. Then—"

Offensive swearing filtered through the tents sealed entrance. "Kade! Kade! Are you sick? You better be dying for not taking customers on the biggest night of the Faire! Where the hell are you? Open up!"

TWENTY-SIX
SAGE

"It's Dyke. He can't find you here." The oracle looked toward Crew and threw the indigo cloth over the crystal ball. "Ever since you were a no-show performance on the ridge, he's been in moody."

"We'll leave through the back." Crew rose as did Sage and Tegan.

She wagged her wrist, hurrying them along. "I'll be there in the morning."

Sage pushed through the curtain divider just as Dyke barged in. Crew went directly to the armoire, and Tegan toward the egress.

"Dyke, I deserve a break." Madam Rouge crooned. "I've been working overtime and I hit a brain glitch. My readings are off…and I'm—"

"Kade, we sold out of tickets for your performance on Thursday," Dyke said, querulously. "I don't give a rats ass if your brain is malfunctioning. Fake it for all I care. First Polk's kid gives me the slip, and then Dirge hasn't made an appearance. I had to hire locals to get things moving along. You know how much I hate doing that."

"Calm down, Dyke. Calm down."

Sage turned and tiptoed away from the curtain. Her brother's eyeballs were bulging out of his head, wildly signaling for them to flee. Not daunted, Crew swung open the armoire and pulled out a fine-looking bow and quiver and handed them to her.

Examining her newly acquired weapon, she whispered, "There's only three arrows."

"You need more?" He collected the arrows and withdrew them from the quiver. Three more arrows quickly materialized. "It's an endless quiver of arrows."

"Oooo. Nice."

He swung back to the armoire and retrieved a wide belt with an attached sword and a sheathed dagger. Lastly a pistol, Crew turned it in his hands, seemingly appraising it, and then inserted the pistol into his rear pocket.

"Tegan," his whisper was almost inaudible, "preference?"

Tegan waggled his head. "Mallet or axe."

Crew reached into the armoire and produced a pickaxe. A suitable weapon for her brother, who worked the mines.

Kade and Dyke's argumentative voices had moderately softened, yet Crew wasn't ready to leave. Closing his eyes, he appeared to be mediating. Again, he opened the door to the armoire and lugged out fur coats, gloves, boots, socks, and a paper bag. All the while lobbing the items on the bed.

Sage brushed her hand over one of the snowy-white pelts. "Polar bear?" The pelt mutated beneath her fingers to mahogany brown. "What the...?"

"Chameleon pelts. Camouflage for blending in."

He positioned a hushing finger to his mouth, and looking to Tegan, twitched his head to get a move on. Her brother wasted no time in stockpiling as much as he could carry. Sage and Crew took the remainder. Their departure swift, as they merged into the refuge of the woods.

Eluding mishaps and entering Crew's tent, the memory of the past hour bled into Sage's brain. A swift shiver tweaked her shoulders. She'd offered herself as a sacrificial lamb and was determined not to dwell on what could go wrong. Was it absurd to feel noble, gallant even?

"Sage, what the hell were you thinking?" Her brother chucked his load on the ground and turned on her. Fisting his hands into his hair, aggravation and frustration clenching his teeth. "I don't want the oracle taking you into that mansion alone."

She disentangled herself from the bow and laid the quiver on the small table. "I won't be alone. You'll be there, silly. Both of you." She swiveled toward Crew, but he wasn't looking at her. He also laid the belted sword on the table. Her sense of nobility spiraled.

Crew went to the icebox, which was only stocked with ale, and lobbed a bottle to her brother and then offered her one. She declined with a shake of her head. Uncorking his bottle, he glugged and then wiped his mouth.

"There's sandwiches, berries, and nuts in the paper bag." Crew's voice was raspier than normal. "I figured the oracle owed us. So her armoire provided for our journey. Tegan, we'll need your coin for the sailing craft. I plan on hiring someone for the long haul and pay for the oracle's carriage and incidentals. Dyke owes me wages, but I can't go to him now."

"You got it." Her brother nodded and took a slug of brew. Somewhere amid their vexing day and nightfall, Tegan and Crew had sought absolution through bottled ale. "We all should invest in one of those armoires. Instead of sandwiches and berries, you should have conjured roasted boar with all the fixings."

Crew winched his bottle like a salute, beaming with a full-fledged smile. It took Sage's breath away. She detested how, not merely his looks, but his mere presence affected her. A sublime angel came to mind, which he wasn't. Yet his raspy voice and teasing smile weakened her knees, not to mention his dark hair that had the penchant of feathering into his intoxicating eyes. She pivoted on the spot and walked out.

She was beat, downtrodden. In body, mind, and soul. She'd caged her parents, and Parry into the nether region of her brain. Bolting them securely in steel along with a treasure trove of memories. Locking them away enabled her to walk, talk, and think. The same went for Edras and Eadith. Except, they were alive. That was a fact. She sensed them and their beating hearts. Losing focus was not an option. Or else, she'd be good for nothing. She'd dissolve into a gazillion pieces of misery. An unmitigated, blubbering puddle.

Longing for fresh air, there was none to be had. Besides the humid dankness, the atmosphere was replete with discordant cicadas and a hooting owl. In the distance, people and creatures were nosily roaming behind the tents. Turning her sight upward, she gazed into the starless sky and the moon clouded in mist.

"You have to sleep."

Startled, she twisted. Crew stood behind her. "I will."

"Come on back. You shouldn't be here, alone."

"I'm not alone. You and Tegan are within spitting range." The rim of his upper lip pulled. "And I'm not a wimp. I can handle myself." Cloaked in shadows, it was difficult to read him.

"Sage," her name coming from his lips was sweeter than honey, "this isn't how…" Crew left his words hanging, and took a timid step. "I am sorry. For everything." A nerve ticked in his jaw, now blanketed with nubby whiskers.

He was close enough that she had to look up at him. "Don't try that charming voice on me." A mild grunt came from him.

"I didn't. I wasn't." Two-handedly, he forced back hair that dangled in his face. Ambiguous tension banded between them. "We started off wrong. I'd like to make it right."

Sage had a thing for him, a thing that had slipped into her bloodstream years ago like a contagion. She didn't know if love had been building ever since that night in the angel tree, or fickle infatuation. Inhaling his musky scent, she longed to fall into his strong arms and give her worries to him. Let him take her away from the nightmare she was living and convince her everything would pan out. They'd rescue Edras and Eadith and his brother. But she knew what his was; A charming manipulator of men and women and, again, hardened herself against him.

"What are you going to do?" she uttered, reining her temper. "Turn back time? Like, three years?"

To eradicate the burn behind her eyes, her mood turned foul. "This is all your fault. If the Circus Faire hadn't returned to Alderwood, none of this would have happened."

"I didn't know they were setting up here until it was too late."

She stoked the hurt she was inflicting. "Can you reincarnate my parents, my brother? Can you assure me that my sisters are unharmed and we will find them?"

He rammed his hands into his pockets and looked down, scuffing his foot on the grass. "No," he uttered, drooping his shoulders.

"I want you to promise me something."

His head perked up. "Anything."

"When this is over, promise me—you will never come back to Alderwood. *Ever again.*" He inhaled a hissing breath. If they managed to survive this predicament unscathed, he would leave, like he did before. He'd leave her wanting, breaking her heart, letting her life essence drain into the ground like a forever weeping willow.

Crew stiffened. Several breaths passed until he articulated, "That's really what you want?"

No! I want you to stay with me—always! "I...I think it—" Before saying another syllable, his hands slipped out of his pockets and cupped her face.

"Don't say it." He leaned in and kissed her. His hands smoothed into the sides of her hair, and he moved in closer.

She brought her hands to his shoulders, intending to thrust him off. Instead, she wrapped her arms around his neck, burying her fingers into his downy hair. His tongue traced her mouth and a carnival of sensations skittered over her skin. He was chipping away at her hardened resolve and she parted her lips, taking him in.

The tips of Crew's fingers scored down her spine, the desired result had her arching her body into his chest. He kissed the curve below her bottom lip and moved to her temple and then pressed his full, soft mouth to her forehead. He positioned his hands on her shoulders and stepped back, building room between them. "I promise."

TWENTY-SEVEN
CREW

Crew's eyelids slit, seeing blackness. He'd passed out during the night while sitting at the table. Unrolling his spine and pitching back into the chair, he yawned. His stomach growled, queasy from plenty of ale and lack of food. After speaking with Sage, he'd drowned himself in the honey brew, finishing off the provisions. Getting to his feet, he stretched out the kinks in his arms and legs. A blanketed lump on the ground moved, Tegan. They'd insisted his sister take the room with Crew's cot. That suggestion had set off fireworks of bickering. Sage refused to be treated like a lame powder puff. So, Crew squatted and shoveled up a handful of hay that littered the ground. Crafting three equal pieces, he broke one in half. Whoever drew the shortest piece got the cot. Sage.

Going to the flap of the tent, he ventured outside and estimated, it was four in the morning by the muted navy and grays marbling the sky. Yesterday's mugginess had been curtailed, and he filled his lungs with the fragrant woodsy odor.

Standing on the exact spot where he'd promised Sage never to return to Alderwood, his heart did a weird stuttering. In her attempts to chastise him, she looked considerably vulnerable.

His yearning to kiss her had consumed him, and it might cost him a knuckled fist or a knee jerking groin crunch. Not caring, whatever the consequences, he went for it. He anticipated her resistance but, instead, she melted and surrendered to him. She tasted like sugary-ripened blackberries with a hint of hazelnuts.

Grinding the heels of his hands into his eyes, he buried the unforgettable moment in his heart. Tegan was pushing out of the flap, he nodded and grumbled, striding past Crew, and headed into the woods. They hadn't a minute to spare, especially if they'd welcome a shower in the crew's improvised stalls.

After her shower, Sage inquired, "Is that magic?" She continued buffing her wet hair with a towel. "The falling water, I mean."

"It could be. If someone wanted to stand there all day. But Dyke would never allow it. Magic is best expended elsewhere." Crew sat on the chair and leaned over his legs to pull on a woolen sock. "Grunts dig deep until we reach a pocket of water."

Out of the blue, she said, "You shaved."

Crew smoothed a hand over his face, surprised she'd noticed or cared. "Good or bad?"

"Doesn't matter what I think." Somewhat surly, she spun away.

It did. To him.

Crew recalled that Dyke was a late sleeper due to his evenings in the Brew house and at the gaming tables. After their bout of refreshing showers, Crew directed Tegan and Sage along the winding avenues. Believe it or not, at that hour, before the sun broke the horizon, few drifting souls gave them queer glances as they carried furs and boots, or at Tegan with a pickaxe reposing on his shoulder.

Crew escorted them into the Gingerbread House. The circulating aroma of honey cakes, muffins, and pastries had his mouth watering. On display were plates of churned sweetened butter, elderberry, and gooseberry jam.

Weary-eyed brownies were huddled in a corner booth, and in an adjoining booth, inebriated, saggy-eyed sluaghs had jam glopping around their mouths.

"Thank the gods," Tegan wailed. "I'm famished."

They'd roped their fur coats together, and Crew deposited them on the floor before taking a seat. Sage had trashed her slippers, preferring to wear the boots. And resembling a hunter with the bow's cord strung diagonally across her chest, she placed the quiver near the furs before removing the bow. She combed hands underneath her damp hair and splayed the strands over her shoulders to dry. Ever since their unprecedented kiss, she'd been shunning him. He had yet to meet her eyes.

"We have a half hour before we have to be on the road." Crew eyed Sage, who looked anywhere but at him. Her olive-toned skin shined, and her flushed cheeks complimented her beauty, if that were possible. He removed his cap and hooked it on the spire of his chair, and like Sage, roughed his hands into his damp hair. "While were eating, we'll have them pack an extra basket to go," he said as an addendum.

Sated with bloated bellies, they trekked to the livery to bridle Fries, Crew's horse, and to meet Madam Rouge. "Foundling is roughly an hour's ride from here. I dislike doling out coin for a carriage when we have other options."

"What other options?" Tegan asked. His wet hair had dried into scads of curls around the horns on his forehead, prettifying them.

"You are fae, are you not?" Crew's glib comment elicited a chortle from Tegan.

An entertaining grin sat on Sage's face. "Not inferior, remember."

"Yeah." Tegan rolled his warm toffee eyes. He propped his pickaxe on the wooden frontage of the livery stable and walked toward a swamp. He returned holding a huge bullfrog in his hand. "Here's your ride, Sage. Let's see what you can do." Her brother crouched and put the bullfrog near her booted feet. "Come on then."

"It was supposed to be *your* ride." She knelt and picked up the bullfrog and gazed into his rounded, black eyes. "You ready for this?" The frog croaked, ballooning the skin of his throat. "I'll take that as an affirmative." She gently placed him before her and stood. Spreading her hand over the bullfrog, they watched it grow. Her hand tweaked as if pulling on the reins of a horse. "That'll do until we reach Foundling."

"Nifty. Where did you learn to do that?" Crew took it all in.

"Edras taught me how to enlarge and reduce things. Easy peasy. Minor magic."

Tegan's brow skewed, and glimpsed around before saying, "You told me that it's not magic, per se."

"It is and it isn't. Our power is bred into our very souls. Hiding what lies within is simpler when magic sparks the ether on a daily basis. If Edras or I cast a morsel of our energy here and there, no one is the wiser." Sage patted the slimy amphibian, and Crew felt she was giving him a tutorial regarding her genetics. "I was a baby when Edras brought me here, neither of us knows our true history. If our parents had survived…" Her words clenched, clearing her throat she rubbed fingers under her nose. Crew figured she was thinking of the Steele family.

Crew would have to come to terms with his Doloran heritage. What perturbed him, he didn't quite grasp the disparity between a Doloran and fae. Both species have magic or as Sage said, power. There would come a day when he'd divulge everything to Sage in regard to Queen Esta. Deeming her misbegottens had been spawned from generations of formidable magicals, making them superlative beings or some such nonsense.

Crew asked Tegan, "What are you riding?"

Sage's brother sauntered into the stable, a minute passed before he reappeared leading a harnessed warthog. "I spotted him when you were hitching up Fries. Only cost eighteen coppers."

"Coin we could have spent on a decent boat." Sage shook her head. "It'll stink sailing in a two-by-four with our knees knocking together."

Tegan's brash smile gave way. "You're right. I'll return her and catch another bullfrog."

"Keep your ride, Tegan." Crew flicked a dismissive hand. "You still have plenty of coin, aye? We'll figure something out." He pivoted toward the Circus Faire with all its attractions and scoured the vicinity for signs of the oracle.

With the rising sun, the washed-out, gloomy shades were beginning to sharpen. He'd endeavored to be in Foundling sooner than later. Waiting upon her highness was more irritating than a magpie pecking his head. To voyage across the sea, they'd require a full day and a half of light. Even Fries picked up on his stress, blustering and bobbing her mighty head.

"Where's Madam Rouge?" Sage sidled next to Crew and perused the avenue with him. "Maybe she changed her mind."

"I think not." He didn't expound, but presumed the mystic was plotting. However, deprived of her valued information, they might have spent a frustrating month or more trying to locate Aerestol's estate. A precious loss of time for Eadith and Edras.

He had to give credit to Polk. If it weren't for his warnings, trespassing through the wizard's domain could, and still might, mean certain death. More reasoning the oracle was essential, providing the ins and outs of the conjured traps.

A gawky stick of a boy, rubbing his eyes, shambled from the mouth of the livery. "Sorry, I fell asleep. Is your name Crew?" The boy's groggy gaze went between Tegan and Crew.

"I'm Crew."

The boy didn't cover his jaw-distorting yawn. "Madam Rouge said she'd meet you in Foundling."

"That answers that," said Tegan. "Let's hightail it outta here."

"Hey, you want a harness for the frog?" the boy asked Sage. "That'd be great, thanks."

Trotting into Foundling beneath an overcast sky, cool breezes swept off the sea, bringing with it salty water and fish. He reined in Fries and dismounted. "I'm making a quick stop." He looped the reins over a hitching post and headed into the Mercantile.

After the long ride, Sage and Tegan alighted from their mounts and stretched their shoulders and legs.

Disparate from rural Alderwood, Foundling abutted the waterfront, making it a thriving township. The main thoroughfare consisted of the Mercantile, the Foundling Orphanage, a blacksmith, bakery, modiste shop, bootery, the marketplace pavilion, and the largest and grandest building was the Gypsy Brewery and Hotel. Foundling was a trading port with the Unified Territory and where magicals and mortals could be seen socializing.

At that hour just after dawn, dozens of vendors lined the roads setting up their wares to lure mortals to drop their coins for remedies. It would be a day of pandering to unsuspecting travelers. Cures for all types of maladies, and talismans, amulets galore for whatever their hearts desired. The bestselling items were magic potions. Promising romance, love, beauty, marriage, fertility, and sterility. There was a slew of bogus remedies, however, the fae knew where to purchase what ailed them.

Minimal traffic of pedestrians dotted the walkways, mainly horse-drawn carts making their morning deliveries. By mid-morning until late afternoon, pockets of people would be clogging the avenues.

Toting a brown paper bag, Crew sauntered from the Mercantile. His boots clunked on the planked walkway and down the step into the dirt road. "I'll be right back."

Whenever he came into Foundling, he paid a visit to the children in the Foundling Orphanage. He held scant memories of the place. Excluding a sketchy one, where a teenage boy's warbling had made his skin crawl. The whimpering came from the whipping shack where bad girls and boys went for punishment. Crew, a naïve and curious child, opened the door to witness the boy, a faun, his pants gathered around his cloven feet, and the headmaster standing by his backside. The ogre, headmaster, turned on Crew with fire in his eyes. "Get the fuck out or you'll be next!"

Polk had killed the ogre and his partner when he liberated Crew from the orphanage. Three years ago, when the Circus Faire was in Alderwood, Polk and Crew paid an overdue visit into Foundling. Spying that the shack was still standing, they lingered until midnight. Crew wanted the whole of Foundling to perceive the flames, and utilizing his energy, he ignited the night.

A smile had its way on Crew's face as he manipulated the locked gate, and walked in. The gated and fenced property was intended to restrict the children from leaving, but it didn't. Orphans wandered Foundling unhampered. The older children did hard labor in the shops or down at the docks, which provided the orphanage with living necessities. Many were accosted and hijacked onto voyaging ships as deckhands, heading for various territories.

Crew had scarcely taken a step into the yard when the front entrance popped open. Children tumbled outside in their nightgowns and romped around him. A child's shrill voice outrivaled the others. "I saw you from the window!" He knelt to their level and ruffled a few heads of untidy hair. Opening the brown paper bag, he doled out licorice sticks, sugary candies, and nuts. He waved goodbye and recrossed to where Sage and Tegan were waiting.

"Hey, man, you have a heart," Tegan quipped.

"Yeah, who knew?" A smirk slipped into Sage's face.

Fries whinnied as Crew mounted the horse. "I come when I'm able. C'mon, we're behind schedule."

"I wonder if Madam Rouge is here?" Sage straddled her frog and winced. Crew felt sorry for her. The jockeying amphibian must have been brutal. Before leaving Alderwood, he'd considered asking if she'd ride with him, but figured she'd scoff in his face.

The town was in the midst of awakening, whereas the docks were a hive of activity. Crew rode straight toward the Livery. After unloading the sparse necessities, he nuzzled Fries, petting her neck and flanks, then paid to board the horse until his return. "Don't sell her, and keep her well-fed. If any incidentals crop up," he said pitching his voice at the stableboy, "I'll pay when I get back. Do you hear me?" The stableboy's eyes had been fixed on Crew as he dumbly nodded.

Meanwhile, Sage had reverted the bullfrog to its former size and Tegan handed the warthog to the stableboy as well.

Crew headed for the harbormaster's building in hopes of securing an adequate boat. He dug his hand into his pants' pocket and clinked his dwindling coins. "Hey, Tegan, before bartering for a boat, how much money are you willing to spare for our voyage? Then I'll know what I can haggle with."

"The armoire provided most of our gear," Tegan said. "I'm estimating about two-fifty to three-hundred."

"Great. That should get us—"

"You who! You whoooo!" Madam Rouge's distinguishable voice hailed them.

TWENTY-EIGHT
SAGE

Madam Rouge looked more mortal than fae with her bouffant hairstyle and black velvet toque bonnet with ostrich feathers, a herringbone traveling jacket, gloves, and matching skirt that pranced around her fashionable laced-up boots that were *clump-clacking* toward them on the wooden boardwalk. "We're ready to up-anchor," she said, spiritedly. "Or is it anchors aweigh? I think that's how they say it."

Wearing suspenders, boy clothes, and boots, Sage self-consciously fingered her lengthy braid, the lone part of her that implied she was a girl.

"Up what anchor?" Crew asked. "We haven't seen the harbormaster yet."

The oracle peered at Tegan as a knot formed between her eyebrows. "What's with the pickaxe? We're sailing not mining."

"It might come in handy." Her brother twirled the handle of the axe that was propped on his shoulder.

"Come on. Come on. Follow me." Madam motioned a floppy wrist like she was fanning herself and pirouetted on the heels of her boots. "This way."

"Hmmph." Crew flung the roped furs over his broad shoulder and rounded his fingers on the strap of his duffle that hung over his opposite shoulder.

Sage's eyes had a mind of their own, gauging how his woolen pants hugged his legs, tucked into knee-high boots. And noting his trivial limp, the bullet wound hadn't mended. Indeed, looking like a pirate with his belted sheathed sword riding low on his hips. He'd overlain his flannel shirt with a snug woven waistcoat, accentuating his narrow waist and hips. Crew had also supplied Tegan and Sage with woolen pants, shirts, and socks from his trunk of incidentals. They'd dressed for inclement weather, and if it weren't for the cool nip in the air, she'd be sweating through her clothes.

"I took the liberty of hiring three seafaring men." Madam walked at a brisk pace along the boardwalk.

Crew inquired, "Three? Why so many?" Either the oracle hadn't heard him amid the cacophony of squawking seagulls winging overhead and the reverberations of the drudges on the wharfs or she was ignoring him.

Arriving on the hectic pier, stinking of fish and salt water, boats were delivering vats of fresh catches, and an irregular line of fishing vessels could be seen on the calm sea. A large trader was moored further down on the western side of the harbor where men were unloading cargo.

"Here we are." The oracle halted by a sailing craft, rigged with two masts. "Let's get your things stowed below deck."

"We can't afford to pay for this," Sage expressed, gawking at the boat. "Is this a pirate ship?"

"Amply put, but no. This is one of Aerestol's vessels. He'd made renovations. It's been moored here collecting barnacles, so I figured why not borrow it. He calls it Caravel, whatever that means." Madam Rouge started toward the gangplank. "I have generously provided for our expedition to Wintervine. The seas in the north can be menacing, and drowning isn't in my cup of tea leaves and I prefer it that way."

"Three men plus Tegan and me, that's not sufficient hands on deck. I was thinking a small sloop or boat," Crew protested. "Tegan and I could man that, and I was going to hire another man to guard—"

"Hey, you forgot me. I can haul and rig a sail," Sage carped. A total fib. She'd never been on a ship, but she darn well wasn't a weakling. Rather than shrink beneath Crew's inflexible glare, she breathed in fortitude. "Show me and I will do it."

He lifted an indulgent arching brow, and silver flecks flashed in his eyes.

In a huff, Madam outspread her arms. "It's done. I wasn't about to endanger my life in some tiny dinghy thingy." She repositioned the bonnet on her head and marched up the gangplank and onto the boat.

Crew was in a hurry to set sail. It required all hands on deck, and Tegan's muscles to raise the canvas sails and whoever the oracle had hired. They dropped the furs, pickaxe, and their baggage on the deck. It riled Sage that it was her chore to lug it below. Clutching the roped furs, she literally dragged them down the ladder into the farthest region on the ship, out of the way of someone tripping over them.

She stood erect and inspected their quarters. A low ceiling with intermittent wooden beams throughout, and bordering the hull, wrought-iron enclosures like jail cells. Going toward the cells, a quiver scuttled across the nape of her neck. She jiggled one of the wrought-iron doors, locked. Suddenly an image appeared behind the bars. A teenager. Fae, with tears snaking down his dark face. Reacting to the boy's panicky fear, she bit down on her lip. Letting go of the bars, the ghostly image dispersed like mist in the wind.

Spinning away, she pressed her eyes to eliminate the manifestation. Sage drew in a tremulous breath and slowly exhaled, quelling her palpitating heart. These sights always disturbed her. Seldom experiencing them, but here, her psyche was awakened in an overflow of emotions that were rooted into the ship.

Visions, though uncommon, jumped out at her when she least expected them.

These inexplicable visions began the day she'd wandered into a graveyard, buried with a miscellany of creatures. Most spirits were at peace, the fight was over. It was people kneeling above them, watering graves with their tears that roused spirits. Poignant emotions that strangled Sage by the throat as she beheld diaphanous forms slinking from their tombs to console their loved ones.

She squeezed her eyes while moving from the cells and found herself enmeshed in a ropy hammock that had been slung from the rafters, and others suspended nearby. By the stern, a door stood ajar. She took for granted that was where she'd be sleeping, not in the fraying hammocks. Her body shimmied, purging ghosts walking through her, and then went toward the room.

A bulky carpetbag laid on a desk which had been bolted to the floor, and two more traveling carpetbags were deposited on a portside berth. Madam Rouge had claimed her bunk. This was probably the captain's cabin where he charted maps and held his meetings, doubling as his lodgings. Two inlaid berths resided on either side of the room, and Sage disengaged her bow and quiver and placed them on the starboard side bunk.

Underneath her feet she felt the ship lurch. Sounds of groaning and creaking wood had her looking up. Light shafted between the slatted planks above, the quarterdeck. It must have been Crew's boots standing at the helm.

There were three windows that gave out to a watery horizon. They were already moving out to sea as the bilge plowed through turquoise waters, creating foamy waves. The undulations activated a precarious roil of her belly.

Slogging back to the main deck, she took the pickaxe below and leaned it against the wall. Lastly, she climbed to the deck and snagged the basket of food from the Gingerbread House and a duffle that Crew had lent her. Since everything she'd owned was burned in the fire, he'd opened his traveling trunk and told her to take whatever she wanted. After stashing her meager belongings in the cabin, she stumbled from the sway of the boat. She'd have to acquire sea legs, and fast, or else she'd be good for nothing.

Breathing in the fusty odor, she sneezed. The outer appearance may have been renovated, but the interior had samplings of weathered wood and slight rot and mold from water dripping through the cracks. Holding onto the handrail, she ascended the narrow ladder, and stopped.

In the galley, a man was slicing vegetables, and sitting at a corner table, the oracle was sipping steaming tea. She must've engaged a cook and was lazily reading her tea leaves while everyone else was hard at work. Sage returned to the cabin and seized the basket of food and then squeezed into the claustrophobic galley. Her boots crinkled on sheets of tin. "What's this for?"

"Don't want to burn down ship," the chef said in a stilted accent. Next to the wall were barrels of coal, necessary for firing the stove. There was a smattering of scorched marks on the tin where the cook had unlatched the stove's access to add coal.

Sage set the basket on the table. "We bought breads and cakes from the Gingerbread."

"Oh, yummy." Madam Rouge removed the cotton napkin that covered the food. "The Gingerbread House has the finest cakes in the world. The baker adds a pinch of magic to her ingredients." Madam's cultured timbre reminded Sage of her sister's voice, and her constant harping on Doloran tenets. "You have to savor the magic. It's like a reviving tonic."

"This morning was the first time I had the pleasure of eating at the Gingerbread House," Sage expressed.

"Ah, their pastries and biscuits are splendid. Nobody can eat just one." The oracle withdrew a glazed honeybun. "My favorite." Taking a liberal bite, she then passed her fingers across her lips.

"We've set sail," Sage said, more so than asked. The man glanced up from his cutting board and gave her a squinty-eyed nod. There was something different about him which she couldn't put her finger on. Appearance wise, he resembled fae, but her senses told her otherwise. The oracle was intent on swirling her teacup. "Madam Rouge, what are your leaves telling you?"

While holding the honeybun in one hand, she sloshed the tea in her cup. "I'll let you know when I'm finished. This is Boris, by the way. An excellent cook. His brothers, Petryk and Heinrik have been sailing the seas for years. Isn't that right, Boris?"

The chef grunted a reply. His complexion was comparable to the potato peels on the cutting board.

"They were born in the elven territory of Yugovanya, and Boris has been Dyke's private chef for years." The oracle held her cup aloft as if saluting the man.

"Elven magic superior to faery cakes." Kissing the tips of his fingers, and in his heavy accent, he said, "Mmmah! Superb." He was rather tall and wiry, a button nose, rosy cheeks, and a low-slung ponytail. He made quick work of a potato, adding peels to the pile.

Sage questioned, "Won't Dyke be upset?"

Supping her tea, Madam wiped a pinkie finger along the rim of her lip. "We made an even exchange. Of course, when our trip is at its end, Boris will return to the Faire."

"Care to join me for a cuppa?"

"Thank you, but no."

Madam went in for another bite and, speaking around the gooey muffin, said, "Tell Crew to see me. We have more to discuss."

Sage took her leave of the oracle and Boris. Stepping onto the main deck, she found Crew on the quarterdeck at the helm. And Tegan was by the prow looking green and gazing up at Heinrik who was on the yardarm of the foremast. Neither

Tegan nor she had ever been out to sea, and Sage was experiencing a bout of the queasies too. She hoped she hid her seasickness better than her brother.

On the top sail of the mainmast, Petryk was knotting or reinforcing the canvas to the mastheads. *Or whatever the crew does.* Intrigued, she keenly studied their every movement, the pulleys, knotting and positioning of the ropes, and rigging. Sweat glistened on their pinched faces as they toiled. Her brother brushed her shoulder with his, joining her. Neither of them spoke as they watched the men.

"It's even harder than it looks," Tegan said. "Crew and I helped hoist the sails, and the rigging is complicated. There was a rip in the upper sail, and Petryk is fixing it now or the whole canvas might tear from the yardarm and be lost. Exhausting."

Her brother flipped his hands over and frowned. His palms, previously callused from laboring in the mines, were now red and abraded from pulling on the ropes. He left her side to aid Heinrik, who was having a problem with a jammed pulley.

Filling her lungs with sea air, she perused the rippling water and the rambling landscape off the starboard side. If the ship stayed its course, she could probably swim to shore. With the oracle's talk of drowning, that thought gave her a boost of self-confidence.

She moseyed toward the quarterdeck and ascended the steps. The sway of the boat threw her equilibrium off, and grabbing the rail, she steadied herself. Feeling balanced, she turned, taking in the vessel. Sage gasped at the magnificence of the leeward billowing sails, and overhead, the sun had yet to reach its peak. Swathes of blushing pinks and white painted the sky. Strands of hair whipped about her head, and she attempted to pin them behind her ears, only to have them come loose again.

Noticing the boat traversing farther from the sighted land, she said, "Why are we going so far out to sea?"

"We don't want to get snagged on the coral reefs or rocks. We have to get into deeper water for the long haul."

Surrounded by boundless water and the occasional plinking of pulleys and grinding of the yardarms to catch the wind, time inched by. Sage made use of her day by observing Petryk, Heinrik, and Crew operating Caravel. As an eager apprentice, she absorbed all there was to learn.

Tegan and her labored side by side with the brothers and Crew. She heave-hoed the ropes through the pulleys shifting the yardarms, and when the rigging jammed, or a sail required mending, she'd carefully scaled the lines. Once, she'd bungled her footing. Her leg fell through the line and became suspended upside down in midair until Petryk helped her down. Climbing the pegs of the mainmast was more to her liking and finding a place in the riggings to rest and scan the splendor. Her legs had eventually adjusted to the length and width of the lines. Heinrik said, "You spider monkey, no?"

Minutes turned to hours and her arm and legs cried. Nonetheless she was accomplishing tasks she'd never dreamed of, obeying Petryk and Heinrik by dragging the lines to the mainmast and the foremast. She palmed the hot skin of her face and suffered the sting of a sunburn. Boris had supplied them with several jugs, and the crew had been partaking in the cool water. In the large flagon was ale. Earlier she'd seen Crew splashing water on top of his head, and then shaking his hair like a wet dog. With the inclination of sponging the hard-earned sweat from her face and neck, she rounded her fingers on the handle.

"Here, let me." Crew yanked a cloth from his rear pants' pocket. Taking the jug from her hands, he poured water, soaking the cloth. "You might want to slather your face with ointment tonight." Rather than wringing out the excess water, he brought the cloth to her forehead.

She laid her hand over his. "I can do it."

"Let me," he said, voice soothing. "You helped me, remember?"

She let her arm fall, and closing her eyes leaned her head back, luxuriating in the coolness. He was gentle. Not scrubbing her sunburned skin, but applying the cloth like a compress on the contours of her face. He allowed the water to stream over her chin, bathing her neck, leaking into her shirt, and cooling her body. Anticipating inclement weather, the day's heat had surprised them all. Earlier, Crew and the men had castoff their shirts, and Sage had the gratification of watching them work.

He tentatively moved her head forward and swabbed the cloth on the curve of her neck and beneath her braid. "Feel better?"

"Yes. Thanks." Upon opening her eyes, it was his defined chest satisfying her sight. To be honest, since leaving Foundling, her eyes had been glued on him. Appreciating his muscles cording across his shoulders, back, and arms as he heaved the ropes. Sweat was trickling down his chest, over his flat stomach and into the waistband of his pants that were riding low on his hips. It took disciplined willpower to combat an impulse to glide her hands over him.

Crew said, "I have to relieve Petryk." He sloshed additional water on the cloth and walked away mopping his face, neck, and chest. He jumped the two steps onto the quarterdeck, becoming the helmsman once again.

"Hey, there's an island over there." Tegan motioned to a rocky landmass and headed to the poop deck. "Are those mermaids? They're waving."

Inquisitive, Sage joined them.

Crew let loose a chuckle. "Ignore them. Or I'll have to tie you to the mast. They're sirens."

"Really?" Sage stepped to the portside and held onto the rail. "I've never seen them in person."

Tegan's mouth drooped. "They're singing. It's…it's…"

"Aye. Luring and seductive. Spellbinding is what it is." Crew turned the wheel a notch. "They'll get under your skin if you let them. I hope the brothers aren't taking the sirens' bait. If they've seafaring men like the oracle said, they'll look the other way." Heinrik and Petryk had left their duties and surreptitiously ambled to the prow. "Sage, take your brother below before he jumps ship."

"Look—" Tegan shouted, reaching his arms as if hankering to touch one of them. "They're diving in the water, coming to see me."

"Sage!" Crew entreated.

"I'm trying. Come on, Tegan," Sage complained, towing on her brother's arm. "He won't budge." Tegan leaned further, watching the agile sirens swimming toward the boat. He lifted his leg, hooking it on the railing. "Crew, he's going to jump. I can't—"

"Take the wheel," Crew ordered. "Just hold it steady."

Not until Crew clamped her brother around his waist did she let him go. She sped to the ship's helm. Spellbound, Tegan resisted, arms and legs flailing as Crew manhandled him, going below deck.

A siren climbed the ship's outer hull and propped herself onto the ledge of the deck. Her extremely long brownish-red hair look like eels squiggling over her body. Pretty, not exceptional, and unashamedly naked. A sight that would drive boys and men somewhat ravenous.

"Go away." Sage balked; she didn't need the distraction. A laidback Crew made navigating the boat look easy. It wasn't. Clutching the spokes of the wheel, holding it against the resistance of the churning waters, her arms burned.

The craft listed eastward. Exerting herself, she put her weight into steering starboard.

"Where's Crew?" The siren's voice had a lyrical cadence that pulled Sage's eyes to her.

Unfortunately, her hands clamping the wheel deviated along with her head. "Darnnit." Endeavoring to right her error, she sighed when Crew strolled onto the main deck. "I think we went too far out. Sorry."

"Crewww," lilted the brunette beauty, "it's been toooo loong."

Crew's engaging smile threw Sage. *Does he know her?*

Was it her imagination or did Crew have equivalent lyrical pitches like the siren? "Hey, um, are you going to relieve me here?" She tried getting his attention, but he'd stilled within a yard of the helm. *Is she seducing him like my brother?* "Crew?"

Oh, no! If he jumps—

"Geia, we're sailing into Wintervine. How's the seawaters in the north?" He shouldered up to Sage and took a negligible step behind her. If she inclined a fractional inch, she'd be pressed against him. Finding herself wrapped in body heat, it was both marvelous and unsettling. Instead of commandeering the helm, he rounded his fingers over hers, and gradually made the correction. There was a shift of his shoulders and his chin rested above her head.

"A storm is coming." Geia gathered her wet hair and tossed it over her shoulders, exposing herself. Staring naughtily into Sage's eyes, her mouth twisted.

Sage pretended to concentrate on her course-plotting skills. Crew's fingers tightened around hers, whether from the sirens disabling pull or troubled about the storm.

"Thanks." His tone placid, as if seeing a naked siren was an average day for him. Geia blew him a kiss and dove into the water. "We can't outrun a storm. We'll have a layover at Port Havelsgard."

"How far is that?"

"The wind is in our favor. Should make Havelsgard sometime before dawn, if all goes well, unless we get bogged down in the storm. I can take the wheel, but you should know how to steer the ship." His hands detached from hers.

"Why?" Sage sidestepped for him to takeover. His bodily warmth disbanded as cool sea breezes slammed into her. "You plan on diving in after Geia?" He barked a laugh. She approved of the sun alighting on his upturned face and, lacking his cap, his ebony hair glistened. He passed his fingers across his brow, untangling strands of hair that were sticking to his eyelashes. "So the siren doesn't affect you like my brother?"

"Not exactly." He veered to catch her eyes. "There is a pull, but it's simple for me to resist. I'm assuming Tegan never faced a siren. The initial encounter can be debilitating to say the least. Many boats and men have died or gone astray because of bewitching sirens."

Sage let this sink in while witnessing the irises of his eyes changing. Starry sapphire to golden umber. His fluctuating color wasn't ordinary, yet again, he wasn't ordinary. She went to the railing and the endless sea. Mercifully, her belly had calmed so it wouldn't be a mortifying voyage of vomiting over the stern.

She revolved back to Crew but remained by the rail. "How did you learn to navigate a boat this size?"

Skirting his gaze past her, he stared beyond the riggings, and then reached into his waistcoat, removing a compass. "Polk, Dirge, and I voyaged the Sea of Tears quite a bit," he spoke while examining his navigation tool and then returned it into his waistcoat. "And we sailed across with the Faire, but Dyke prefers to travel around the sea. At night, Polk taught me how to chart a course by the stars and constellations. I catch on pretty quick and, I think you do too."

He wasn't looking at her when he gave her an offhanded compliment.

"I traveled in huge clipper ships with the Circus. I was mainly a drudge but learned a lot. Petryk and Heinrik over there," he jerked his chin, "seem to be managing the sails well enough though."

For the pure sake of conversing with him, Sage queried, "Tell me what it's like in the Unified Territory."

"What do you want to know?"

Crew conversed with her, but his eyes were somewhere faraway.

"I heard they have modern conveyances and cities with buildings that reach the sky."

"In the cities the walkways are crowded with people coming and going into stores lining cobblestoned streets. The skyscrapers—"

"*Skyscrapers?*"

"Towering buildings."

"Oh." She tried picturing it. "I heard they have motorized contraptions?"

"It's an invention they haven't perfected, as far as I know. Automobiles, that's what they're calling them. A carriage with four rubber-like wheels, and a crank. A person cranks-up the motor to get it running. Most people still use horse-drawn carriages like Faery. And like Faery territories, there is an abundance of wilderness. It all looks the same."

Sage hugged her arms around herself, colder breezes were gaining momentum. "Did you see any fae there?"

"Are you, in a roundabout way, asking about the slave trade?"

"I guess I am. I thought since the accords, magicals can't cross or live in the Unified Territory and vice versa unless they have authorization."

"Yes and no." His answer vague. "Mortals can't detect glamoured fae living among them. But somehow, someway, a well-paid snitch unearths them. Then the militia is called in. The slave trade is highly profitable. The upper crust of society has servants and lots of them are magicals."

"How come the militia don't take them?"

"They are bought and licensed by their owners as property," he said, glimpsing her. "What I can't wrap my brain around, is why magicals don't revolt. It's like they're powerless. I tried talking to a few, but they get skittish and scared. Though, some are content."

A hush fell over them. Standing in silent solitude, the wind fluttered the canvas sails, and the sea sluiced the hull of the boat. For seventeen going on eighteen years, she'd lived in her own little world in Alderwood. Protected and carefree with the Steele's, yet her life had radically changed. Her future speculations were bleak, especially if she didn't find her sisters.

Discussing the slave trade steered her thoughts to Polk and Dirge, and what they must have done for Doctor Aerestol. The cells below deck gave her the creeps, and an indication of the doctor's nefarious deeds. Crew had clarified some things, but he was still holding back. Whatever it was, it was bad.

She asked, "Do you think Dirge is alive?"

"Depends."

"*Depends?*"

"If Aerestol is going to use him against me."

TWENTY-NINE
CREW

Tegan had been a rollicking nuisance to pry away from Geia, and the siren was aware she'd hooked a whopper. Crew was one second short of clocking Tegan's lights out as he wrestled him into the cabin. When Crew came up from below, Sage was manning the helm, and he wanted to kiss the tension from her face. Although, it was fleeting thought because after he'd kissed her outside of his tent, she'd been reserved and downright unapproachable. But when Geia hit his sight, Sage's gritting teeth might have been earmarked for her, not him. When the siren evacuated the premises, Sage relaxed and actually chatted rather than growled.

Now, his eyes trailed Sage as she went down the ladder to check on her brother.

Crew withdrew Polk's telescope, which he'd inherited, from his pants' pocket. The cerulean sky touched the deepening sea in the eastern horizon. Sluing the monocular due north, full-bellied clouds were stirring like a toxic brew. Rain was in the air and the wind was picking up. They were approaching one hell of a ride.

"Hey, Petryk," he called to the seafaring guy the oracle had hired. "Can you handle the wheel?" Petryk was rotating the pulley and after securing the aft sail, he shambled toward Crew. "Can you handle the helm?" Reckoning he better ask before handing the boat over to a novice. Petryk gave him a toothless grin and jerked his striped hat over his brow.

"I do jus' fine," he said in a coarse accent.

Crew shook out his cramping arms and hands. Before Sage went below, she mentioned Madam Rouge wanted to speak with him. His twenty winks would have to wait. Descending the quarterdeck, he teetered at the top of the ladder just as Sage, with her bow in hand and quiver looped over her shoulder, and her brother were in the process of climbing up.

"You first." He moved over for them, and inhaled Sage's passing lemony-orange scent. She might have indulged in a cake from the Gingerbread. "What's with the bow?"

"I haven't been hunting in a while. Thought I should practice."

"How's that going to work? We're at sea."

"I'll figure something out." Sounding buoyant, her mouth turned up.

His gaze toured the length of her body, from her vibrant eyes, to how the suspenders shaped around her curves, and shirt tails, loosely tucked into her pants and knee-high boots. The harmless girl in the angel tree had transformed into a tenacious, strong-willed woman. He sighed and swiveled to her brother. "Tegan, keep an eye on Heinrik and Petryk. And make sure your sister doesn't put an arrow through them."

Tegan tsked a chuckle. Then sobering, he said, "Hey, sorry for being such an ass."

"No problem. You're not the first and won't be the last to fall into the sirens' call."

The swish of a soaring arrow flew by, piercing the mainmast. Then another and another and another. Her accuracy astounded him, firing arrow after arrow between the rigging.

"She always was a good shot," Tegan said with pride. "When I went to the mines, Papa took Sage hunting."

From the start, he hadn't wanted her with them, worried she'd become a liability. But now, Crew felt an ounce of appeasement. He turned and went down the ladder and into the galley, stopping short of bumping into the oracle. "You wanted to see me?"

"I was going to rest for a while." She glanced at the cook. Boris was busy spooning carrots into a kettle. "Come to my cabin." Winking both eyes, she canted her head for him to follow. Widening the door to the captain's cabin, she plumped down on the bunk. "You can sit here." She patted the blanket next to her.

Crew ducked under the door lintel. "Umm, I'm good." He preferred to brace himself against the wall and folded his arms.

Madam plucked the hatpin from her velvet chapeau, embellished with an ostrich feather, and set it on the bunk. She fluffed her hair, knitting strands into her bouffant. "I sent my raven before we left, informing Aerestol that I have a surprise for him."

"You didn't mention Sage's name?"

"No. But he'll allow the carriage to pass over the bridge." She coiled a loose hank of hair on her finger. "You and Tegan *cannot* be seen at the livery in Wintervine because Aerestol will have a driver waiting for us. We'll have to retrieve you farther up the road. Let me think…" She rubbed her eyelids. "About a mile from the harbor there is a hamlet called Bear Hollow. And a local market or is it a trading post? Umm, I can't recall the name, but you can meet us there."

"Either way, we're screwed." He wiped down his face. "Won't the driver be suspicious when he sees us tagging along?"

"I thought of that. We will dock at Port Havelsgard, and where you and Tegan will get off. Rent horses or do…" she rolled her eyes, "*whatever*. Havelsgard to Bear Hollow is less than a two-hour ride. Sage and I will sail on to Wintervine."

It bothered him that he was unfamiliar with the territory and had to rely on the oracle. The Circus Faire never journeyed into Wintervine for a reason. The land and the weather were harsh and unpredictable. "We should've hashed this out before we left."

"As I recall, you and Sage were in a hurry, so there wasn't time. *And* if this doesn't bode well for you, I can't be implicated in your mess." She scoffed. "*After* we arrive at his estate. How are you and Tegan going to get inside?"

Pensively, Crew brought his thumb to his mouth and flicked his nail on his teeth. "We'll sneak out of the carriage and go to the side of his mansion and break in through one of the windows."

As if boredom set in, her head bobbed side to side. "That's what I thought you'd say. And not going to happen."

"What do you have in mind then?"

"After we debark, the groom or more than likely one of the guards will bring the carriage into the stables. They'll unharness the horses, brush them down, and put them in a stall. Once that is completed, I believe the guard will return to his post, but I have no idea what the groom does. You'll have to be stealth."

"Okay, then we can find a window and break in?"

"No." She swept wrinkles from her skirt and then laid her hands on her lap. "I haven't been there in months. Aerestol might have made changes to his alarm system. He trusts no one. If you break or try to jimmy up a window, you'll get a spritz of flounder."

"A fish?"

"It'll scramble your brain. You won't be able to walk or talk."

"Sounds like an intoxication hex." He propped his booted foot behind him on the wall. "Can it be dispelled?"

She hiked up one shoulder. "You could practice dispelling it?"

"What makes you think I can do that?"

Her mouth tipped into a know-it-all smirk. "You have the power—inside you."

"Hmmm." Madam Rouge and Queen Esta had a lot in common. *I'm not convinced I'm a prodigy with infinite capabilities.* Nonsense. "What if we walked in through the front door, aye?"

"The guards will nab you."

"Maybe, maybe not. When you get a chance, unlatch the door. I'll do the rest."

Her chest expanded drawing in a reflective breath. "I'll have to disable the alarm."

"Isn't it under one of the wizard's spells?"

"I'll see what I can do."

"Aye, and I can try dispelling flounder."

She placed her finger over her puckering mouth. "After you get in, don't look into any of the mirrors. You'll get pulled in and entombed forever. Not all of them are cursed. He cautions me when I get there."

"Aerestol is a genius and insidious rolled into one," Crew declared. He shrugged off the wall and loomed over her. "Tell me Madame Rouge, why are you doing this—helping us? Are you leading us into a trap? A trap premeditated by Frankenstein himself?" Her cheeks reddened.

"I…um… I scratch your back and you scratch mine."

"What the hell does that mean?"

"It's not a trap. I swear." She thwacked a balled fist to her chest. "Aerestol has a son. A boy who needs rescuing from his demented father. I require your expertise in getting him out of there."

"A son?" Crew chased a hand through his hair, tousling it. "You want us to kidnap his son?"

"You and Sage wanted my help to find her sisters—touché." She bent over her knees and began untying the laces of her boots. "Now, if you don't mind, I'm going to rest before dinner is served."

She thinks this is a pleasure cruise? "If we take his son, he'll hunt us down, break every bone in our bodies, and then he'll torture us." The ship swayed and Crew steadied himself on the wall.

She tugged her boot off and straightened to catch his gaze. "Crew, you're not obtuse. We both know where this will end."

Waging an eye war with the oracle, he didn't blink until he saw his death.

THIRTY
SAGE

"Divine, Boris, just divine." Madam Rouge smacked her lips. "What do you call this delectable cuisine?"

"Venison stew," Boris drawled, unimpressed. "Every day dish."

"Ahhh...with a dash of magic, no doubt." The oracles remark sparked a sideways grin and a twinkle in the chef's eyes.

Residing in the cramped quarter of the kitchen galley, Sage finished the last bite of stew and placed the bowl on the slim counter. "I'll send your brothers down to eat." A gurgled grump emanated from Boris. "It was delicious," she complimented, and his stiff countenance softened.

On the deck, her brother and Crew were perched on barrels spooning into their bowls. Petryk was toiling with the foremast, and Heinrik the helm.

Walking toward Heinrik, she said, "I'll take over. Boris has dinner waiting for you and your brother."

"Tank you, miss." His accented words were hoarser and thicker than his brothers.

"Call me Sage." Heinrik bobbled his shorn head of vermillion hair, unlike Boris' with his long ponytail. The brothers were tall like Crew but thin as rails. Crew had told her, "They reek of magic," which explained how they were able to manipulate the sails.

While dining with Madam Rouge and the chef, it was revealed that Petryk and Heinrik were twins. Satisfying Sage's curiosity since she hadn't been able to tell them apart. Boris was the elder, and as he related, "Superior to his younger brothers."

Throughout the day, the auspicious wind had bloated their sails, propelling the ship forward, making progress toward Wintervine. With the sun on a downward slope, the sails had slackened. Tegan wandered toward the helm, with Crew limping behind him, both sets of eyes on the sky. A wall of darkness lay ahead, and every so often, lightning lit up the clouds with remote rumbling of thunder.

"There's no wind," she said as if they hadn't noticed.

"The calm before the storm." Crew scratched the thickening black stubble on his jaw. "We'll be hitting it soon."

"If it's fast-moving, maybe we should consider dropping the anchor and let it pass over? But hey, what do I know." Tegan lifted his arms and shoulders, a sign of uncertainty. "Feel the warm air clashing with the icy cold?"

Crew withdrew a telescope from his rear pocket and brought it to his eye. "If we were sailing a sloop, I'd get my ass in gear and head toward land. But this ship might be able to withstand the wind and waves." He slipped his hand into his waistcoat and extracted his compass. "We're on course. Get the brothers up here, Boris too. Start battening down everything. If it's as violent as it appears, we'll lose it overboard."

"What do you want me to do?" Sage asked.

"Hold tight for now."

Sage held tight, observing the flurry of activity off the quarterdeck. Even the oracle made an appearance, her herringbone jacket slung over her arm. She strolled through the commotion and joined Sage at the helm.

"My, don't you look like the pirate now." She eyed Sage's boots. Sage had stolen Crew's fashion statement and tucked her pants into her knee-high boots. "The worm has turned," she said like a precursor to danger.

"What worm?"

Madam tutted. "It's an adage. Like, red sky in morn sailors be warned. Red sky at night sailors delight."

"What does the worm turning mean?"

"That things have changed direction. In this case the weather." Her bouffant had deflated, flopping like a mop on her head. "I had hoped we'd avoid unpromising weather."

"What did you see in your tea leaves?"

The oracle hesitated. Her eyes narrowing as she perused the forthcoming storm. A severe crimp drew her brow. "I saw death."

Sage stiffened. A harbinger that tumbled in her heart like a jagged rock. Her brother, Crew, Henrik, Petryk, and Boris, who would be taken? Please, not Tegan. Not Crew.

"Your predictions could be misleading, can they not?"

"Misleading? Depends on how you see it," she said, and slid her arms into the sleeves of her jacket. "I see what I see. And I tell it like I see it. I've been doing readings for hundreds and hundreds of people. I have a following, hailing me as the greatest mystic they have ever seen. Raving that everything I predicted had come to pass. Can my predictions change or develop into a differing outcome—it is feasible. After people listen to my prognostications, they might attempt to change the outcome. Occasionally a person's future is hazy, and I receive contradictory readings. A sign that their destiny is contingent on the gods. And when the gods get involved, it gets complex, and who am I to interfere? Nevertheless, I believe once a person's destiny is determined, they can't outrun it."

The oracle's message hadn't assuaged Sage. With the thought of death stalking Caravel, a shiver began in her shoulders, colonizing throughout her body. She watched the men assembling on the main deck. Crew was saying something.

"We're dead in the water," Crew declared, and looked to the twins. "If we crap here like driftwood, the waves might bring us down or crash the hull into the coral reefs. You two have been riding these waters for years, what say you?"

The brothers swapped glances. Petryk replied, "We go fast and hard, angling into storm." The brothers nodded, confirming what he said.

Heinrik contributed, "We see how bad wind in storm, maybe furl and stow main sails. Keep jib sail."

"Good thinking," Crew agreed. "We go into the storm running on full power. Hit it head on and then angle in."

"Sounds like a plan," Tegan interjected. "But there's no wind. How can we get the ship moving?"

Crew turned from her brother and captured Sage's eyes. "Minor magic."

Targeting the foremast, the elven brother's and Tegan pooled their magic. Meanwhile, Crew and Sage conspired, spurring a cyclonic intensity into the sails.

"Try avoiding the spar. With the storm ahead of us, we don't want to crack the mast," Crew pressed. "Aim for the sails."

Yelping cheers cut through the air as swollen sails began moving the ship.

"More!" Crew hollered. "More speed!"

By combining their energy and inflating the sails, Caravel plunged ahead. Faster, increasing velocity and heading straight for a murky wall.

The bowsprit lanced through a blackened barrier of sleet and rain, merging into a glacial atmosphere. An ear-deafening torrent hammered the sails into submission, and pelleting rain riddled the decks. Water crashed against the starboard hull, pitching it sideways. Howling winds battered the sails, looking like wings of a tenuous dove in distress.

Crew cupped his hands on either side of his mouth and screamed. "Now! Stow the foremast sails. Sage, to the helm."

"You're stronger to hold the wheel. I'll work the sails."

He swiped at the rainwater pelting his face. "Do as I say!" His teeth clenched on the words. Unceremoniously, he linked his arm through hers and rushed them to the quarterdeck. Crew seized the juddering spokes and planting the soles of his wet boots on the deck, he put his weight into the wheel. Angling the rudder, elsewise the crashing waves might capsize them.

"Aren't you furling the main sails?" Sage yelled. Crew bent down and lugged coiled rope that he had prepared next to the helm. Hastily, he secured it around her waist and then trussed it to the wheel. "What are you doing?"

"Don't want you going overboard." He yanked the knot, making sure it was taut.

"What if the ship sinks?"

In pirate manner, he guffawed, not a merry sound. "Then you have something to hold onto, aye."

Lightning shattered the sky and thunder roared.

"If you can't control it, I'll tie it off." He took Sage's arms and positioned her hands on the spokes. "Hold it steady, right here. Use your talent." He let go, giving it up to her. "Got it?" Water was spilling over her body as he pushed back a curtain of hair that had adhered onto her face. Leaving his palms against her cheeks, he said, "Can you do this?"

Her arms shook from the force of the jittering rudder. "I...I..."

"You're stronger than you think." Crew pressed his wet mouth to hers. Spooling away from her, he leapt onto the main deck.

The tempest raged, listing the ship like a tin can in the water. It felt like an eternity as gusts stormed the sails, boisterously flapping in the downpour. Sage squinted into sheets of rain, wondering if the ship was going to break apart. The wheel was attempting to get the better of her. She had to concentrate, guiding her energy to manage the helm, abilities she never imagined were achievable. Crew had faith in her, but why?

Veined lightning careened into the water. Seconds passed before explosive thunder vibrated the ship, jolting Sage's shoulders. Another lightning show serrated across the darkened sky, and she saw Crew on the upper yardarm. Heaving and hauling the ropes, furling the top sail. A cresting wave splashed over the deck, swaying Caravel portside. A barrel loosened from its ties and rolled over the deck; a deluge of seawater swallowed it whole. The vertical mastheads fluctuated like an out-of-sync metronome. Blinking amidst bucketing rain, an upsurge of water drenched the masts, and Crew was hanging in the air.

Sage screamed. The rigging had twisted around his arms and waist, and his body was swinging in the wind. He struggled to scale the ropes. A rigorous, slow process. He straightened his legs, attempting to connect with the yardarm. Hurling wind dipped Caravel starboard, flinging him outward; the sea was trying to claim him. And the oracle's premonition of death cut into Sage's heart.

Treacherous waters flooded the decks, tossing the ship side to side, and Crew was still suspended by the lines. The twins were making haste to the upper sails and Boris was footing the pegs of the mainmast. The men were within reach as Crew's boot rooted into a section of the rigging. With assistance, he inched onto the yardarm.

Sage ousted a breath of relief.

Tegan had been fighting with a pulley and the rope when a torrential wave took his legs out from under him. He flopped onto his backside and body surfed toward the ledge.

"Tegan!"

THIRTY-ONE
CREW

Crew had been smart enough to tie himself to the yardarm. He hadn't anticipated the body-clobbering storm that threw him off his perch. Stinging rain blinded him as he fought to grip his fingers on the slippery ropes. With each swagger of the ship, he set his sights for the yardarm. His endurance was waning and steeled himself from self-pitying thoughts. Whenever the ship lurched starboard, he utilized his forward momentum, striving to clamp onto the arm. Exerting his inner strength, he wedged the toes of his boots under the rigging and held on.

Boris and the twins had reached him, and together, they labored on stowing the upper mast.

Amid the turbulence, he heard a snippet of Sage's voice. Her arm was extended, frantically waving toward the main deck. *She'll lose control of the wheel.* That's when he noticed Tegan off the portside of the ship, his arms embracing the balustrades. *He can't hold that for long.*

Crew patted Boris' back and gestured toward Tegan. The chef nodded, waving Crew to help him. "We got dis. Go."

Crew did the unthinkable. He dove off the yardarm and prayed he'd be able to snatch the ratlines. Lightning lit the shroud. Descending fast, he stretched his arms and fell into the lines. Tumbling, clawing for purchase, he seized the ropes.

"Tegan! Hang on!" He scrambled down. Fixing his gaze on Sage's brother, only his fingers were now clutching the rail. Crew plunged, outstretching his arms. Body blading over the deck, Tegan's fingers were slipping, falling overboard.

"No! No—Noooo!" Sage shrieked.

Crew surfed and dangled over the ledge, catching Tegan's wet hand. "Don't give up. Give me your other arm!" There was a thread of lightning and remote booming. The storm was receding. "Tegan, I can't get a grip. Help me out!"

It was like trying to hold onto a greased pig as he fought to clamp Tegan's other flailing arm. "C'mon, man." Endeavoring to tow him up, Crew's grunting turned into a scream. "Tegan!" Suddenly the world stilled. The curling waves. The ship. Drops of rain—froze. Sage.

"I can't hold it!" she hollered.

The suspension of time enabled him to grasp both of Tegan's hands, heaving him onto the deck. As abruptly as the world froze, the scene burst into pandemonium. Sage's head drooped to her chest; she'd overexerted herself.

Tegan shut his eyes against the water masking his face. He'd sustained a nasty cut on his forehead. "I'm not dead?" Propping himself up, he wiped down his face.

"You will be soon enough." Goodhumoredly, Crew cuffed him on his shoulder. "Go help Sage at the helm. It looks like we're through the worst of it."

"You think?" Blood trickled, smearing his eyebrows.

"The rains are letting up and the wind is simmering down." Crew clasped Tegan's hand and pulled him to his feet. "Get to your sister."

The ship fitfully rocked beneath Crew's feet and hoped what he told Tegan was true. They made it through the storm without any casualties. He heard Tegan addressing his sister, and her gaze found him standing on the deck. Crew two-handedly raked his sodden, ropey locks from his face and turned to inspect the boat.

Trembling like a leaf, Sage had been dismissed of her duties and went below. She'd get some shuteye. The rain subsided to a miffing drizzle, making them cold and miserable. Crew darted to the crew's quarters and changed out of his saturated clothes and donned his woolens and shrugged into his coat. He fished in his duffle and found his cap. He hadn't worn it for good reason, afraid of it drowning in the sea.

Foreboding clouds rolled onward toward the eastern shores of the Sea of Tears, allowing a smidgen of twilight to peek through. Crew checked his compass, they'd veered into an easterly direction, shadowing the storm as if it desired another hell ride. Judging by the stars, they were behind schedule. Not bad, considering. They would make up the time, weather willing.

There was a decent headwind, and the crew was suffering from fatigue, cold and drenched in their garments. After dropping the sails, an arduous chore, the twins, and Boris had an expedient reprieve and were now folded in their hammocks.

"Tegan, get some sleep," Crew said, steering the wheel a fraction westward, righting their misadventures.

"I'm okay." He yawned for the gajillionth time.

His yawning contagious, Crew covered his mouth. "You're making me groggy. You can help by getting a few hours' rest and then relieving me."

"Sure?" His voice lifted, mouth slanting.

"Get out of here."

"Thanks again, Crew."

"For what?"

Tegan gave Crew's shoulder two indebted whacks and went below.

Hours of periodic slush mixed with rain dampened the decks, and Crew. A dark night of the soul, filling his head with images and reflections. *Demelda is dead because of me.* The description of her mangled body still had the affinity to twist his guts into mincemeat. *Who else will die?*

"You have to be in league with the devil. Learn how he thinks, acts, and then you can outsmart the bastard," a saying of Polk's that had Crew reluctantly accepting Aerestol's proposition. His intentions had been pure of heart, to save Sage and his brother.

After their encounter with Aerestol in the ice castle, events catapulted into warp speed. The wizard had upped his game. Brutalizing Dirge, and then sending a rask, a mercenary, to the Steele's cottage. Aerestol Paphos aka Leggan Dnego: Evil incarnate.

The ring. He hadn't given it much thought since Queen Esta pried it from his finger. Was it possible— did the wizard crave that relic more than anything—more than Sage?

Each blink of Crew's eyes lasted a bit longer than the last. He had to shake off his drowsiness. He tied off the wheel and removing his wet cap smacked it on the rail, ridding the slush. Roughing fingers into his hair and combing it away from his face, he crammed his cap back on, and then stretched his body. Bending over he massaged the blasted twinge in his thigh. On the outside of his leg, there was a mean-looking divot where the bullet had gone through. Troublesome was the underlying ache.

Crew meandered along the deck, chuffing into his hands, and chafing them together for warmth. He wasn't a natural deckhand, he ruminated while scrutinizing the masts, just a circus grunt. But for some uncanny reasoning, he knew how to do things, like trimming the sails as they headed into port.

Queen Esta is right. Remembering the sea voyages with the Faire, he'd been engrossed, studying the mechanisms. *I absorb things.* Like propelling wind into the sails, as did Sage. Anyone would think it magic, though he never uttered an incantation or performed tricky signals. His power and energy came from within.

This evening, he'd thanked the gods, they made it out of the storm in one piece. If anyone had gone overboard, Crew would've blamed himself.

Twice around the perimeter of the ship, the frosty blood in his veins had thawed to moderate warmth. Clouds choking the skies had all but dissipated, unveiling a velvety sky strewn with stars. He always counted on the constellations. Steady and constant.

Trekking by the mainmast, he stilled. Sage was folded in on herself on the step of the quarterdeck. As he neared, the thudding of his boots caused her to unfold her body.

Sage said, "The snoring woke me up."

He resisted laughter by rolling in his lips. "The guys were dead on their feet."

"Yeah, but I'm talking about Madam Rouge." He snickered. "Thought I'd get some air."

"The farther north we travel, the colder it's getting." As if his words chilled her, she raised the collar of her fur coat.

"Aren't you chilly just wearing that?"

Pocketing his hands he walked closer. "I was too lazy to untie the bundle of furs," he admitted. Earlier, he'd hung two kerosene lanterns on rusty hooks, which were now swaying in harmony with the motion of the ship, shedding dismal light. Her unbraided mane had dried into wavy tendrils dangling to her waist, and in the dusk took on the hue of a new copper coin. The rosiness tinging her cheeks and the tip of her nose added to his attraction.

"What's that you're standing on?" She gestured to a trapdoor with a screw pin for a line to go through to hoist it open.

"This," he prodded the large screw with the toe of his boot. "It's the cargo hold. If this is Aerestol's vessel like the oracle said, then you wouldn't want to go down there." Her brow rumpled as a shadow passed through her eyes.

"You're still limping."

"Am I?" Not one to broadcast his pain, he hadn't hid it well enough.

"If you'll let me, I can heal it."

"You did that already, aye?"

Resting her hands on her lap, she wove her fingers into the pelt of the coat. "If you remember, there wasn't ample time to fully mend it. I merely slapped a bandage on it. Sit down," she palmed the step next to her, and stood, "let's see if I can dull the pain."

Frankly, he'd merited his own inflictions. Although, refusing her healing talents wasn't logical. Especially when lives were at stake. Once they arrived at Aerestol's he couldn't falter due to his leg. Conceding, he lowered to the exact spot where Sage had been sitting. The wood still holding her warmth, and he extended his bad leg.

"Show me where the bullet entered?"

He indicated where on his woolen pants. "Here." Sage moved in and knelt. Angling over his leg, he drank in the scent of her hair seasoned with salt water. Her hand skimmed his thigh, igniting a diverse type of throbbing. He hissed.

"Sorry. This will be painful."

She has no idea.

Sage's voice softened. "I have to reopen the wound in order to regenerate the damaged muscles and tendons."

She found the wound, the divot that lay underneath the wool of his pants. Tenderly, her finger traced the weal. Before proceeding, her gaze raised to meet his. An indecipherable flash passed between them. A flash that jumpstarted his heart. She slowly blinked and lowered her gaze, breaking whatever bond they formed.

She splayed her fingers above his thigh, the lids of her eyes shuttered. While she immersed herself in the healing process, he took the opportunity to dwell on her sunburned face that had morphed into an incredible bronzed umber, her nose and cheeks dusted with freckles. She was oblivious of her allure, which knocked his socks off.

Her hair had fallen forward, veiling her beauty from him, and his fingers itched to touch and drape it back. His appraisals were rudely crushed by spiking pain. He clutched the sides of his leg to stop from shaking. Sage hadn't moved her hands, nor had she dug her nails into him. Yet it felt like icepicks, jabbing into his bones. Radiating pain had him biting down on his molars. Jaggedly breathing, he leaned backward, buoying himself up on his elbows.

The healing of his cracked skull was bad, but this was excruciating. He had to think of something, anything to stop himself from moaning like a sissy. Squeezing his eyes, he went back in time, to the angel tree with Sage. Every day after she'd left the Faire, he followed her. She wore innocence like an immaculate glove, and she'd intrigued him. How any creature could be that callow was beyond him because his life had been anything but wholesome. It was Sage, who initiated that first kiss. A kiss he'd never forgotten.

When the Circus Faire had picked up stakes and moved on, he promised himself never to return because he wanted her more than the air he breathed. And deep down, he knew, he'd make her life miserable.

While he'd been reminiscing, enduring her healing ministrations, he'd flattened himself on the quarterdeck. He didn't know when the intense ache had abated, not until her hair tickled his cheek.

"The scar on your forehead looks good. No infection." Cracking open his eyelids, her breath warmed his face. She outlined the scar leading into his hairline, a faint touch that aroused him. She'd made space, her hips kissing his, and was leaning over him.

"Do you have any headaches?"

"No headaches." She went from feeling the scar on his head to fingering the welt below his earlobe on his neck.

"I've been wondering where you got this scar. Two inches lower and—" Crew rounded his hand over hers and lowered it to lay on his chest.

In a hushed voice, he said, "How's my leg?"

"You tell me?"

"I don't want to move."

Her eyebrows pulled. "Why, afraid it'll hurt?"

"That's not the reason." Cranking up on his elbow, he claimed her lips.

At first, her body was like a wooden plank, then pliable dough, she relaxed. Crew buried his fingers into her hair and pulled her against his chest. She exhaled a fervent sigh and parted her lips. Their tongues composed an impassioned dance while he parted the front of her fur coat and dipped his arms into the heat. Embracing her, he rolled them over. Hungering to explore her feminine curves, his hand ventured underneath her flannel shirt. She didn't protest, yielding to him. A faint moan winded through her lips, which urged him on.

"I come back when you done," drawled a thick voice.

Crew bolted off Sage and faced Petryk. "Ahem...I was waiting for somebody to relieve me. Err, take the helm." He grabbed Sage's hand, aiding her to her feet. She snugged herself into her fur coat. "Keep her steady. She's on course and should be in port in a few hours." With hands entwined they started for the ladder.

THIRTY-TWO
SAGE

Sage squinted. A dull shine spilled through the windows, easing the shadows into the corners. Remiss to unearth herself from the balminess of the fur coat, her thoughts strayed to last night. She'd lain awake for hours, so it seemed, it was after Crew disentangled their fingers, and mumbled, "Night," ditching her by the cabin door. He'd trudged to a hammock and sunk in. What did she expect? Not to be left alone and blindsided by their make-out session. A kiss, a hug, or even a comforting hand squeeze would have been nice.

When she finally drifted off, it was with visions of Crew.

She mused how difficult, if not downright impossible it was to resist him. Even now her skin tingled, torquing hot, fantasizing his touch, his hands setting her skin on fire, and felt a ghost of them still. Skimming fingers across her mouth, face, and neck, touching the memory of his kisses, she sighed. He'd ignited an inferno she couldn't quite extinguish. If Petryk hadn't interrupted, how far would she have willingly let him take her. She shuddered. With that face of his, he could fool an angel. From what he'd related to Tegan and her, about the jobs he did for Aerestol and his part in Demelda's demise, she figured he was *exactly* like Polk. A cajoling carnie. Sleight of tongue and practiced in the art of deception.

Whiffling from across the cabin scattered her memories. Rolling to the side of the bunk, she winged open the lapels of her coat, flapping vigorously to cool herself, and then removed it altogether. Giving the oracle a transitory glimpse, drool trickled from her, and smacking her lips, the snoring stopped.

Sage grazed her fingernails into her salty hair, running through the lengthy mane while listening to the creaking, moaning, and groaning of Caravel, sounding like an old woman who'd outlived her time.

Attracted to the swelling light, Sage ventured toward the windows. The storm had caused damage to a casement, cracking the edges of the glass. Gazing out, she was struck by the canopy of shades, cerise and interlacing azure to break the day.

There was hubbub above the slatted planks to the quarterdeck. Before going topside, Sage detoured into the galley to douse her hands in water, scrubbing her face and rinsing her mouth. Scrounging through Boris' tin of herbs, she plucked the leaves from a spearmint stalk and chewed them.

Caravel's sudden listing and grating thump had her catching herself on the wall. She rushed back to the cabin to grab her coat and repack her duffle. "Good morning," she said to the oracle, head deep in her carpetbag.

"We've docked at Port Havelsgard," Madam stated. "Leave your things."

"I thought we were only going into Port Havelsgard if we couldn't beat the storm? Aren't the seawaters safe enough to voyage into Wintervine?"

"*We* are sailing on to Wintervine. Your brother and Crew are debarking here. Boris and his brothers are heading to the harbormaster to procure two deckhands for the ship."

"But…but why aren't Tegan and Crew coming with us?"

"I already spoke to Crew," she said, voice sidling toward annoyance. "It's best if they meet us on the road to Wintervine."

"He didn't mention it." That riled her more than Marne bragging about her hoity-toity clothes from Hawkswing and her dainty wings. On the deck last night, it had been his chance to fill her in on the specifics, but he kept it to himself. Slipping into an impartial voice, she asked, "Why the change of plans?"

"My dear, girl, there wasn't any change of plans. The less people who know about our subterfuge, the better." She rummaged through her carpetbag. "Ahah!" Madam yanked out a brush and started in on her hair. "When we dock at Wintervine, do me a favor, don't say your brother's or Crew's name." She pantomimed zipping her lips. "Not one syllable. Aerestol has eyes and ears everywhere. Get the gist?"

Sage loathed being treated like a moron. Volunteering as the guinea pig to get them inside the wizard's estate was redeeming. Though, not foolproof. It could backfire. She'd do anything to find Eadith and Edras. Neither Tegan nor Sage had brought up the subject of Crew's determination to find his brother as per his request. The invasion of the estate was supposed to be a team effort, and they *all* should have been included in whatever Crew and the oracle were hatching.

Sage seized her coat and marched from the cabin. Passing the galley, she caught an inviting waft of percolating coffee. Boris nodded a good morning, and then she climbed the ladder to the main deck. The harbor of Havelsgard was small compared to Foundling. Sloops, fishing and row boats, and an enormous merchant vessel, perhaps, delivering indispensable provisions for the winter season, were anchored within the inlet.

From her vantage point, Havelsgard resembled Alderwood, excluding the harbor. The village dwelt within a low valley, hugged by a mountainous region of woodlands. A surfeit of conifers and stark trees were in the end stage of shedding their leaves. Logged cottages and a few buildings constructed with the accustomed stone and mortar reminded Sage of home.

An overhanging sign weathered and faded, on one of the buildings, read *Inkling's Pub*. Probably the busiest hub in

Havelsgard. There wasn't any snow to be had, although she sensed it, cooling her skin. She shouldered her coat.

Caravel had been moored, and she sighted her brother and Crew on the docks, both in fur pelts, girded in leather. Duffle bags were slung over their shoulders, and Tegan gripped the pickaxe by the handle with the head balancing on the ground. She spied the twins coming around the corner of a two-story, stone-and-mortar building with a man, a husky orc. Crew veered toward them. They must have been delaying until they were assured Caravel had plenty of deckhands.

How did I sleep through this? Were they going to leave without saying a word, or apprise her of their plans? A maddening streak went through her.

Trooping off the gangplank in a huff, she hurried toward them. "Hey! Why aren't you sailing the rest of the way with us?" Her breath misted in front of her face, and she breezed through it.

"This is Sage Steele and Madam Rouge is on the ship. Your two passengers," Crew introduced her to the orc. The orc twitched his nose. "I was telling him we lost the sail to the jib in the storm. What's your name again?"

"Balak," the orc said, a voice like a sonorous gong. Cloaked in moose hide and belted in buckskin, a leather harness crossed his chest with a sheathed longsword riding his back, the hilt seen over his right shoulder.

Crew turned to Heinrik. "Weren't you going to replace my brother and I with two deckhands?"

His brother? The twins are going along with this?

Heinrik shrugged. "Balak was the only one willing."

"Folk don't go to Wintervine," Balak said, his words clouded and blew away. "They call it land of the forsaken."

From the corners of their eyes, Heinrik and Petryk traded glances.

Tegan's brow furrowed. "Why's that?"

Balak's dark eyes wandered over Sage. "Are you visiting the doctor?" His question was directed to her and acted like her brother hadn't spoken.

Crew hadn't provided her with the pieces of the game. She looked to him for support and in response he cast her a moot eyebrow lift. Infuriated, her lips pressed together into a hard line. Squaring her shoulders, and winging it, she said, "Madam Rouge is an acquaintance of the doctors, and we're paying him a social visit."

"You don't look sick," Balak expressed, and again, examined the length of her body.

"I'm not."

"Balak," Crew regained the orc's interest. There was a tenseness in Crew's inflexible posture and his compressing jaw. "Is there a livery stable where we can rent horses?" No one would suspect the bitter bite of his pitching tone. Sage did.

The orc stretched his arm. "Up that road, make a right past Inkling's. Then go left."

"Let's downhaul the sails," Petryk intervened, and dipped his head to Crew, his goodbye. "Time to shove off." The twins led Balak down the wharf to Caravel.

"What's going on?" she inquired, confusion and anger in her tone.

Crew's eyes drilled into the retreating orc. "Ask the oracle." He clasped the strap of his duffle and turned away.

"Tegan?"

Crew swirled back to her. "Don't say our names. Didn't Madam tell you?" His eyes piercing, incisive, making her lower her gaze. "There isn't time; they're hoisting the anchor. Get going. Ask the oracle."

Like a chastised child, she moped. Madam *had* told her not to say their names, but she assumed in Wintervine, not here. Regardless of Crew's reproach, her brother wrapped his arms around her.

"I love you, kid!" Tegan pecked her on the head. "If anybody sees us hugging and asks, tell them we had a brief fling on the ship." He chuckled; it was a dismal drone.

"That's sick."

"I know. But…I hate leaving you alone like this," he said, indecisively. "We will find Eadith and Edras. And promise me—don't take any chances."

She stared at her handsome brother, so strong-willed and good hearted. "I won't—if you don't." Their gazes united, she wondered if he was thinking what she was thinking. They were playing a game of chance. A dangerous game that could get them killed.

Feeling scorned for being left out of the loop, Sage rotated toward the ship. Her boots thumped on the dock, then she stopped, and turned back. From under Crew's snug cap, inky strands of hair fluttered on a breeze. As if he'd sensed her, he looked over his shoulder, catching her eyes. He lifted his chin and turned to the road ahead. That slight inverted nod consumed her. What did it mean? *Be careful. You got this. I'm sorry.* Or it meant nothing.

As soon as Caravel cast-off, the oracle hustled her into their cabin.

"I should tell you what to expect once we reach Wintervine," Madam said. "Aerestol will have a carriage waiting for us and a driver. But we must delay, make an excuse to give Crew and Tegan sufficient time to ride from Havelsgard. I believe there is an Inn near the harbor that has decent food. Maybe we can stall the driver by getting something to eat."

"How far is Havelsgard from Wintervine?"

"An hour or two. Depends on the weather." The oracle unbuttoned her jacket and slipped it off her shoulders. "Once were on the road, I'll ask the driver to stop at Bear Hollow. There's a trading post, and I'll make an excuse of needing a necessity."

"Why?"

"There, Crew and Tegan will steal into the coach behind the carriage. Then we'll continue on."

Sage's finicky nerves, strumming under her skin, would be appeased until she was reunited with her brother and sisters. Haunting her was Crew. How those eyes of his stared down at her last night on the quarterdeck, before he took her breath away.

"Sage, you look green around the gills. What's bothering you?"

Sage nervously flicked her thumbs on her fingers, and then rose from her bunk. "Before the storm hit us, you saw death in your tea leaves." She balanced her backend on the edge of the captain's desk. "The leaves were wrong." Her brother should have fallen overboard and drowned, but she'd tampered with time.

"I saw death." The oracle crammed her shoes into her carpetbag and extracted one boot and then hunted for its mate. "Interference," she glimpsed Sage from beneath a judgmental brow, "can modify premonitions."

Someone told her what I did? "What's your prediction now?" she plinked her fingernails on the desk. "Have you seen what's going to happen next?"

"You better prepare yourself because nothing has changed." The oracle sat on her bunk and wedged her foot into her boot. "Death and dying takes precedence every time."

Sage scraped her hands into her hair.

"You never remove those earbobs?" Madam inquired.

She'd forgotten about the trinkets. "These were the last things my father made before he died." Browsing her fingers over the copper, she visualized Papa, sloped over his workbench fashioning the earbobs.

"They are irreplaceable then." A tribute from the oracle.

For the last leg of the voyage Sage's objective was to keep busy. She paced the decks, assisting the crew. During a lull, she found herself standing on the cargo hold and heard screams furling from below. Trapped ghosts and haunted souls crying and screaming for release.

Heart-clutching panic seized her; she covered her ears. It didn't help. Nausea ripped through her stomach, and dashing to the rail, she retched. Wiping a hand across her mouth, she stared, saddened, at the trapdoor to the hold.

Madam approached her after Caravel was anchored. "Boris will be going with us."

"Why?"

"As a treat for Aerestol, to relish his fine cuisine. Balak and the twins will remain on the ship or partake in what Wintervine has to offer."

"There isn't much to be had," Sage alleged, by the looks of the secluded village.

The anchorage consisted of four docking berths, all vacant excluding Caravel. A building buckled the wharf, and she presumed it was where the harbormaster resided. Across the way, a sign fluctuated in the breeze: *Snowy Pines Tavern and Lodging*. An elongated two-story structure with a sturdy stoned exterior. Three chimneys stood on the roof, exuding pewter smoke. Neighboring the tavern was the livery stable with a placard saying *Snowy Pines*. It appeared the owners of the tavern also operated the stables, which made sense.

Trailing the twins, who were toting the oracle's baggage, Sage carried her duffle with her bow and quiver riding her shoulder. Scant snow dusted the hardpacked ground, which was speckled with patches of frost, and it crackled beneath their booted feet.

Balak swaggered by, not even a farewell passed his lips, and headed into the tavern. Madam Rouge was decked out in her ostrich-plumed hat, and had layered her herringbone ensemble with a heavyweight, wool coat that swept the ground. She stood on the wharf like a prima donna, chin upraised, scanning the surroundings, searching for someone.

Three dwarves funneling through the doorway of the *Snowy Pines Tavern* came rushing toward them. The dwarf in the lead greeted them with a red, windblown face, russet mustache and beard that laid over his buckskin coat, and rather than buttons, it was toggled with fangs. "Madam Rouge, I presume. I am Harthorn, at your service." He bowed as if she were a reigning queen. "And may I introduce, Svel and Crispin." Harthorn tucked the oracle's bags under each armpit and also seized the handle of the carpetbag. His strength compensated for his stature. "This way, the carriage is at your disposal. Unless you'd prefer to satisfy your thirst in the tavern before we get on the road?"

"I am rather parched," said the oracle, ringing her fingers at the base of her neck. "I hear they make a hearty gruel that warms a body."

Wide-eyed delight spilled into the ruddy-faced dwarf. "The best in these parts," he said, congenially.

Madam threw Sage a conspiratorial wink, as she was affording Crew and Tegan traveling time. The boys were an hour behind them, lacking any problems. A dwarf filched the straps of Sage's duffle from her fingers. His squat legs scurried toward four bridled palomino horses who were harnessed to a black-enamel carriage. A series of white swatches tarnished its surface, either from salt that sprinkled the air or the frost. Coupled to the carriage was a smaller coach similar to a peddler's caravan.

"I be judge of gruel you speak of," Boris said, fixing a beaver hat on his head. Outfitted in a fleece of furs from head to toe, he handed off his box of herbs and baggage to a third dwarf, Crispin. Youthful and free of blemish, his sparse mustache and beard had yet to mature.

While the dwarves stowed their baggage, their party entered *Snowy Pines Tavern.* Similar to walking into an oven, the heat rapidly thawed the chill that had grown over Sage's bones. She noted four men in the farthest corner, and as she strode in the oracle's wake, their eyes stalked her.

Madam was drawn to the inviting hearth, choosing to plop onto a chair bordering the blazing flames. Sage joined her, hooking her coat over the chair. Boris and his brothers elected to belly up to a pinewood bar next to Balak.

The *Pines* was a no-frills establishment, excluding three elk hides, which had been tacked to the stoned walls, otherwise the tavern was devoid of trimmings. A crude stoned interior and exterior were protection against the weather, along with scarred and bruised hardwood floors. On the side of the pine bar was a narrow hallway that led to the scullery and on the opposite side of the inn, a staircase for overnight lodgers. The barkeep, a pudgy troll with a bulbous nose and craggy features, chortled at something Balak said.

Minutes later the door flung open, admitting a frosty draft. The dwarves scuttled in and went toward a table that had already been supplied with plates of food and green glass bottles. It was obvious their dining had been disrupted when Caravel moored at the dock.

"See those men in the corner?" Sage said to the oracle. "They keep staring at us."

"They're mortals." The straight-backed oracle removed her gloves by pulling on one finger at a time, and then laid them on the table. "Wintervine is at the northern tip of the sea, and it's divided."

"We're on magical land, right?" Sage scrubbed her nose, allaying the persistent downdraft excreting smoke, fogging the tavern.

"Yes. But the tolls are lax. Plus, the magical wards are at their weakest due to the unreliable weather. The king's regent, or whomever governs Wintervine, doesn't like to travel this far north to reinforce the wards. To crossover the expanse of land would mean braving the mountains. Only a fool would take such a chance."

"How can you tell they're mortals?"

"They're simple to read. And the man with oily, brown hair has rounded ears."

"Why are they here?" Sage's back was to them, but she felt their eyes on her.

Madam licked her dry lips, and then brushed the rim of her mouth. "Perhaps it's the only tavern within miles *or* they simply like the food."

A perfect clandestine location for the wizard's slave trade, Sage thought.

"Something is amiss," the oracle's murmur was barely discernible.

Sage leaned in, and copying Madam's low tone, said, "What makes you say that?"

"I feel it—here." As if besieged with heartburn, she ground a balled fist to her chest. "Aerestol usually sends Quen to the shore. A dreadful rask. Today, we get these… these silly dwarves."

"Oh, I don't know," Sage threw a smile in the direction of Crispin. "I like them."

Withing the hour, the wheels of the carriage were trundling along rocky roads, causing Madam Rouge and Sage to bounce like joggling jumping beans. The steaming porridge and biscuits she'd devoured at *Snowy Pines* caused mayhem in her stomach.

"How far is the estate?" Sage inquired, staring out the window at gridlocking foliage.

"Honey, it's a bumpy ride, roughly an hour. Once we pass Bear Hollow, we begin an upward jaunt into the mountain."

Boris sat across from them, snoring. The joggling had rocked him to sleep. Eyes closed, head waggling.

"You told Harthorn we needed to stop in Bear Hollow, didn't you?"

The oracle released a winded tsk. "Of course, I did."

"We just passed a sign that said we were in Bear Hollow."

"I explicitly told him to stop." Madam braced her hand on the jostling carriage and hammered the roof. "Stop in Bear Hollow. Stop!"

"Let me." Sage scooted on the cushioned seat to the other side of the carriage. Careful not to fall out, she tried opening the door. "I can't budge it. Are we locked in?"

The oracle jiggled the other latch. "They locked us in. I can't believe it."

"Hey, stop the carriage," Sage screeched. "We need to stop!"

Someone was pounding the roof from above, and then an upside-down Crispin was peeking at them. "Doctor said not to delay for any reason."

"But…but…" Sage had to think. "I…I feel sick. We have to stop."

Crispin narrowed his eyes. "You're not sick." His head went up and disappeared. The roof creaked; he must have settled back down.

Sage frowned. "What are we going to do?"

"I kick out door." The noise had awakened Boris. "You jump. But if carriage don't stop, someone get very hurt, maybe break bones."

Madam Rouge dumped herself onto the cushioned bench, mouth bunching into a knot. "Never mind. The boys will figure something out."

Sage sank to her seat. Crossing her arms like a breastplate she nestled her chin into the nook of her hands.

THIRTY-THREE
CREW

"Explain it to me again." Tegan nudged his mount, urging the horse up the gradient. "You don't trust the oracle?"

Crew removed his cap, ran his arm across his brow, and then shoved his hair over the crown of his head. "I don't like the odds, is all." He put his cap back on. "We'll figure a way to cross the bridge."

"It made sense to hide in the coach."

"Not to me. There is a guard they have to get by. I didn't want to be trapped in that cubicle with no way out."

"Aren't you a fire wrangler?" he said, sardonically. "You could have blasted them."

Crew huffed. "That'd set off a chain reaction. Warning the entire compound of our arrival."

The hoof of Tegan's horse struck a tree root, jarring him forward. His horse, Clemson, righted himself and Tegan settled back into the saddle. "Off roading at this elevation is going to get us killed anyway. No sane person would build a mansion on this mountain."

"Who said Paphos was sane?" Crew reined his horse to the left, avoiding a clump of thorn bushes. "It can't be much farther."

They stayed clear of the winding mountainous road, riding alongside it, undercover in the forest. Although, the ascent was becoming problematic because the foliage had been thinning and the last thing they needed was to be seen by the guards.

"I wonder if Sage and Madam Rouge are there yet?" Tegan adjusted his pack.

"They should be."

"This is going to sound heartless, but I try not to think of my parents and my brother because I'll lose it. I've been focused on my sisters, and now Sage. Who knows what that monster will do to her?"

"Using Sage as bait was my lone prospect of locating my brother. But now—I don't like it. Rubs me raw." Crew had been desperate, formulating a strategy to find his brother and somehow keep Sage from falling into the hands of Aerestol's goons. That was prior to the ice castle and the succeeding chaos. "Paphos, Dyke, and the oracle are in bed together. The only thing that gives me a grain of hope, Madam Rouge asked for a favor."

"She asked you to do something for her?"

"She agreed to help us on one condition, if I can get Aerestol's son away from him."

"Like, kidnap the kid?"

"She said Aerestol is demented and concerned for the boy."

"This is getting complicated." Tegan's horse snorted and bobbed his head. "Clemson agrees with me."

Crew didn't have the heart to tell him—it was more than complicated. The Frankenstein doctor could have experimented on his sisters. They might be dead or sold into the slave market— just like his brother.

"It's getting dark and fog is rolling in," Tegan grumbled. "And it's beginning to snow. Can you believe this crap?" He raised his gloved hand, catching flakes.

"Perfect weather for this job." A cold gust of air stung Crew's cheeks. He delved into his coat pocket and withdrew his gloves.

"Hey, lower your voice, and keep your ears and eyes open. Paphos might have men patrolling the area."

Tegan clucked his tongue, pressing Clemson up the slope. "What's this doctor hiding that he built a mansion into the side of a mountain, and has guards keeping people at bay?"

Queen Esta had provided few details. Aerestol Paphos, a phony name for Leggan Dnegos. That was a fact. A ruthless wizard motivated by power and greed. His goal, to create a master race. What Crew couldn't conceive was the *how*? Paphos was also neck deep in the slave trade, a highly lucrative venture. In the Unified Territory, he'd seen creatures as indentured servants, and others who worked the Circus. None of them had ever slipped a word regarding the doctor.

"There it is." Crew pulled back on the reins and his horse pawed the ground.

"Holy shit! It really is built into the mountain." Tegan pressed Clemson to flank Crew's mount. "See the bridge?"

"Yep, and the guard house." Crew rubbed his gloved hands together. "I spot a guard on the bridge. Don't know if there's a second guy in the house."

"How we going to get past him?"

"We're not," Crew said tersely. "There's only one way." Tegan's brow pulled. "What did you expect? To ride in there like a knight in shining armor and the wizard was going to roll over and let us destroy him?"

"*Magic*?" The leather saddle squeaked as Tegan shifted. "I might be able to scramble his noggin, but it won't last long. It'll give us time to get over the bridge."

"The whole concept is to get inside without alerting the guards. We can't take that chance. Especially with your sister's lives at stake."

Sucking in his lips, Tegan nodded.

Crew rounded his leg over the horse, dismounting. "We'll tie the horses here. Follow my lead."

Furtively scooting behind craggy formations, Crew and Tegan hunkered down behind a rocky elevation. Crew peeked over the crest, and then lowered. "The guard house is tiny. I only see the one walking back and forth on the bridge."

Tegan unfolded his body and glanced over the crest. Sinking back down, he warily whispered, "What the hell is that?"

Crew pressed his spine into the rock. "*Minotaur.*"

"That thing is a beast. Worse than a beast. I've never seen anything like it. How are we going to take it down?"

Crew dropped his chin into his hand, covering his mouth. His main concern was the noise factor. It had to be done quick and without making a sound. "We get him to walk this way. Then you'll scramble his brain. And I'll take him from behind. Can you bind his tongue too?"

"Uh, I can try. But…but what makes you think you can take that thing from behind? It'll tear you limb from limb before—"

"You got my back, right?" Hearing his snarky retort Tegan snorted. "Got any better ideas?"

Tegan kneaded the skin beneath the horns on his forehead. "How are we going to get him to come this way? If he sees me—"

"No—don't let him see you." Crew searched the ground. Shoveling pebbles into his gloved hands, he poured them into Tegan's. "Throw one over there," he said pointing to a thicket of evergreens. "Space them out. Make him curious, but don't show yourself. If he sees you, he'll call for reinforcements. When he reaches the pines, do your magic thing, and don't forget to bind his tongue."

"What if it doesn't work?" Tegan asked. "What if it all goes to hell?"

Crew's lips flattened against his teeth. He'd been flying by the seat of his pants and taking Tegan and his sister with him. After the oracle had divulged where the doctor's estate was, he'd intended on leaving Sage and her brother behind. He alone would make the journey and devise a ludicrous plan to eliminate Aerestol Paphos. If it all went south and got himself killed, so be it. But now, he had numerous lives to consider.

"If all goes to hell—" Crew squinted, shaking his head, "Then, I'll see you in hell."

THIRTY-FOUR
SAGE

Observing Aerestol's ice castle in the oracle's crystal ball hadn't compared to witnessing it in person. A palatial structure fabricated into the mountainside was a sight to behold. The facade wasn't smooth or even, it mimicked the edifice of the mountain, jagged, full of ridges and grooves.

Attached to the archway was a cedar door, lacking a knob or a handle, and the lone part of the exterior that hadn't been formed of ice. Two gaslights showered the engraved runes that scrolled the archway of the rock-hard ice. Sage wasn't fluent in runology. These symbols were not identical to the armoire in the oracle's tent. Yet, she sensed their importance. A defense against interlopers. Beware to the uninvited who chanced to enter. She poked her finger into one of the runes and traced the ornamental swirl, which uncannily brightened.

Madam and Boris stood on the concrete, frozen entryway, and the door creaked open. They crossed the threshold, screening Sage behind them. Harthorn, Svel, and Crispin rushed in and deposited their luggage on the marbleized floor.

"Madam Rouge, how nice to see you again," a young male's voice, "my father said you were bringing a surprise. Is Boris going to cook for us?"

Boris clunked his booted heels together and, removing his beaver hat, bowed his head. "My pleasure, Master James."

"James, where is your father?" the oracle said, voice sophisticated.

"He is working at the moment. But asked me to settle you into your rooms. He'll meet you in the parlor within the hour. I will show Boris to the kitchen."

"Um, James," Madam shoulders tensed beneath her traveling coat. "Boris is not your father's surprise. He was very attracted to meeting this young lady." That was Sage's cue to step out from behind Boris and the oracle, revealing herself. In the custom of making introductions, the oracle waved her arm toward her. "This is Sa—"

"Yes, I know," James said, wearing a smug grin. "Sage. My father has spoken of you."

This is Aerestol's son? His height and bearing and strong jaw, struck a vague likeness to Crew. Along with the manner in which he cocked his head, his almond-shaped eyes, and full lips. He twitched his shoulder, and a tic found his eye, uncomfortable with her scrutiny. *James is Crew's brother.* She was sure of it. Except for the hair, unlike Crew's coal black, his was akin to bleached-cornsilk. It was the glimmer in his starburst pupils that disturbed her.

Sage stated, "Then, your father knows that I'm here." It didn't entail tea readings, tarot cards, or a crystal ball to feel the entrapment. Quicker than humanly possible, she snatched her bow and nocked an arrow, aiming for James' chest. The oracle and Boris gasped, shocked by her untoward execution.

"I've come for my sisters," she threatened.

Claret specks blazed in James eyes. Dipping his chin, he glowered at her under a daunting brow. His lips moved, enigmatic words, an incantation.

A gut-wrenching spasm knocked Sage to her knees. Unintentionally, her nocked arrow twanged off her bow, impaling James' leg. His jaw clenched, grimacing. Sage's discomfort swelled taking her breath. Wheezing, she doubled over.

"Madam, my father… will indeed… be quite… surprised." Pain laced James' voice. Heavy footfalls surrounded Sage. The quiver and bow were ripped from her. "Take her to the laboratory."

Rough hands anchored beneath her armpits and lugged her along a hallway. She tried curling her knees to her chest to curb the spasmatic twinges. Hopeless. She was hopeless.

THIRTY-FIVE
CREW

When the minotaur made his about-face on the bridge toward the mansion, Crew made his move. Hunching over, staying in the shadows, he scrambled to the thicket of evergreens. Vigilant of the mulch and twigs, his boot regrettably crunched a brittle pinecone. The noise amplifying like an alarm.

The minotaur spun in place, and stilled. His sizeable skull with chilling horns swiveled ever so slowly, probing the vicinity. Would the beast think it was a passing squirrel or deer? The minotaur's hand rested on the hilt of a sword that hung from his girded waist. He galumphed off the bridge and stopped by the guardhouse, peering amid snowflakes into the deepening darkness.

Crew, on his hands and knees, crept to the border of the pines. If the minotaur scouted out the thicket, he'd be waiting and ready. He glided the dagger from his belt. The beast hadn't budged from the confines of the guardhouse. A pebble hit a pine bough and tumbled to the ground. Tegan began his luring technique.

The minotaur's head jerked in the direction of the sound but hadn't initiated forward movement. Minutes passed when a second pebble pinged the nearby ground. The beast wasn't taking the bait. Crew picked up a section of a decaying log. He threw it into the mulch; it rolled, imitating a person hiking through the leaves.

Posed in a stalwart stance, the guard unsheathed his sword. Crew hunkered down.

Guarded and watchful, the minotaur lumbered from the protection of the guardhouse and into the shadows. He paused on a flat plane of rock. Clouds of vapor ejected from his nostrils as his antlers shifted with each turn of his head. Tegan flung a rock that landed in the midst of the evergreens. The beast stepped down from the flat plane, judiciously approaching. Crew snared a wink of silver, dangling by a chain on the minotaur's neck— a whistle. If he lifted it to his mouth, they were doomed.

Now Tegan, hurl your magic.

The minotaur stumbled. His head tilted to his shoulder as if the antlers were too weighty to uphold. Tegan had befuddled the beast. Was he able to bind his tongue? The beast staggered into the boughs of a pine tree and twirled around. When his slitty bull eyes caught sight of Crew, he clumsily charged, raising his sword.

"Hey…" Tegan rushed into the fringe brandishing his axe like a lumberjack. The minotaur backpedaled, fetching the whistle to his mouth. Crew ran and vaulted onto the beast's back and hooked his arm around his expansive shoulders. There was a humming shrill just as Crew dragged his dagger across the minotaur's throat, slicing his jugular. The bleating beast wobbled. And Crew jumped off before the minotaur collapsed.

Crew raced from the thicket with Tegan in his wake. "I thought you could bind his tongue?"

"I did," Tegan said, panting. "I guess you don't need your tongue to blow a whistle."

"Hmph, there goes our incognito plan of sneaking in."

"He knows we're here, doesn't he?"

"Aerestol would have to be deaf and dumb not to know."

They paused at the guardhouse, shielding themselves from the sentinels on the opposite side of the bridge. "Oh fuck. Hear that?" Crew said, breathing heavy.

"Another whistle?"

"Yes and no. Cracking ice. The goddamn bridge is caving. We have to get across, now."

Crew readied to dash ahead just as Tegan grabbed his arm, jerking him around to face him. "We'll get cut down the minute we get to the other side."

"Maybe. Maybe not. It's the only path to your sisters." Crew yanked his arm free from his grasp. "Come down swinging with that pickaxe of yours. Let's go."

"We might not make it across."

"I'll take my chances. Tegan, you can come, or you can go." Digging into his pocket, Crew clutched the Derringer, an exact replica of Polk's, hoping one shot might startle the creatures from an all-out barrage. As if it mattered, he uttered Polk and Dirge's mantra, "No snitches. One bullet." He slid out his sword. With pistol in one hand and sword in the other, he was prepared for battle. Crew ran toward the bridge.

A solid channel of ice, framed by wooden supports that were interwoven with rope. A yard of thickness, fifteen feet in diameter, and thirty lengths from one margin of the creviced ravine to the other. Wide ranging for caravans of slavers to pass over.

Crew's boot touch downed on the frozen surface, activating a strident snap. A recent memory caught him by the throat, of Sage and him fleeing the ice castle at the Faire. It felt as if the earth had quaked, eliciting a tense jittering below the configuration of the bridge. The vibrations intensified, triggering a jagged crack stemming the dimension. Hastening, he watched his footing, or else he just might be plummeting into the ravine. Random gaping fissures splintered its denseness. The upheaval causing Crew to slip and almost fall, but he saved himself by seizing the ropey supports. The bridge was dismantling, chunk by shattering chunks, falling into the dark chasm.

Tegan sprinted by, hurdling the fractures. In unison, they leapt over the precipice onto the rock-hard ground. The ice bridge was gone, all that remained were the wooden rails which was suspended over the crevice.

Two rasks wielding rapiers and another swinging a spiked mace were coming for them. Crew aimed his Derringer and pulled the trigger. The bullet slammed into the rask's head, producing a gory cavity. He toppled.

Having practiced reloading while on the ship, he put a cap on the tube, poured black powder, and rammed the ball into the barrel. Crew then swiveled and dodged a rask's lashing mace. A spike sliced the fibers of his coat cutting into his arm. Leveling his pistol, his shot misfired, grazing the rask's shoulder, not enough to take him down. The rask's lips curled over rotting teeth as he switched the mace to his other hand. Crew retreated and dropped the unmanageable pistol into the accruing snow.

Tegan was dealing with an orc and a troll. In an aslant sweep, he swung his pickaxe and spliced the troll's temple, shaving his skull. The orc didn't hesitate and went in for the kill, exerting his sword and nicking Tegan's neck. The orc had him twirling and dodging his steel. Tegan's axe sheared his lower quadrant, although, it hadn't hindered the storming orc. Tegan was under siege.

Crew should have known better than to take his sights off his assailant as the mace-hurling rask rushed him. Feinting the flogging mace, he anticipated the rask's next volley. Rather than duck and withdraw, he charged, ramming the rask in his midsection. The creature flew backwards into the snow.

Swiftly, Crew slipped out his dagger and flit his blade toward the orc who had Tegan boxed in. Latching his energy onto the dagger, it sliced the air, gaining impetus. Rocketing, and avoiding Tegan, it split the orc's face in two, splattering gore. Tegan gave Crew a flimsy salute and swiped at the blood dripping down his neck.

Taken off guard, a spike slashed Crew's cheek. His weapon flew from his hand and noticed his blood peppering the snow. Before he had a chance to counteract, the rask stood above him, triumph decorated his scaly features. Suddenly, the rask's body jolted. Sticking out of his chest was an incisive blade.

Sidewinding, Crew hopped to his feet. "Griggs?" He gawked at the goblin from Queen Esta's kingdom. Shadows occupied his scarred face, giving him a sinister countenance. "What are you doing here?"

"That's the thanks I get for saving your ass?" He wrenched his steel from the rask's backbone and the creature crumpled.

Crew picked up his cap and searched for his sword. Wintervine became oddly tranquil as flakes disguised the blood and dead creatures with its immaculate snow.

"Who's this?" Tegan shouted, loping toward them.

"Griggan Carbunkle," the redcap bowed. "Queen Esta's humble servant."

Confusion touched Tegan's brow. "What happened to your face?"

"You don't wanna know." Crew beat Griggs to the punchline.

The goblin dispensed a throaty jangle. He then held out his hand. "The queen requests your attendance." Blossoming his fingers, he revealed the ring.

"I don't have time for the queen. Sage, her sisters—"

"She begs for a minute of your time, that's all. It's a matter of survival—Yours. You must go to her."

"I… I can't. After—"

"She's dying." A crease deepened between the goblin's eyes. "Go, before it's too late. I will fight side by side with your friend."

Tentative, Crew reached for the ring. "If this is a hoax, I will—"

"I know. I know." Griggs flapped his arm. "You'll hunt me down and—"

"Disembowel you, showing no mercy," Crew growled.

The goblin's snort prompted pluming fog to wreathe his head.

Crew positioned the ring on the tip of his finger. As he was wedging it on when a stampede of crunching snow and guttural snarling had him turning toward the stables or was it quarters for the guards. A preview of rasks, bumbling trolls, orcs, and dwarves were joining the fray. Everything vanished and found himself standing next to a bedframe.

He hadn't a minute to waste. Feeling where the ring fit tightly on his finger, a skeletal hand clamped onto him, deterring him from tugging it off.

"Give me a moment, Crew." Queen Esta coughed. "*Pleeease.*"

It was like revisiting Polk's dying bedside. Haggard, sallow skin stretched over her bones; the queen looked more dead than alive. Toothless, her lips caved into her mouth. "You will *all* die if you don't heed me." Her bedchamber was comprised of withering flora, crispy tree branches, and decay, all dying with the queen.

"They'll get slaughtered if I don't go back." He was astonished by her endurance as she continued clutching his hand.

"Griggan can handle things until you return. I made sure of it. You've been of little help to your cause, by not developing what has been inbred in you."

"How dare you—"

"My pensieve." Her head turned, and Crew followed her trajectory. A round disc was filled with a silvery substance. "Scrying, since I first found you." Her mouth spread, taking in a harried breath. "My kingdom needs a monarch. A king will be crowned before I breathe my last."

"Woman, stop with the cryptic message. Spit it out."

"Again, you prove to be an insolent shit." Her head laid in a nest of her spindly, gray hair. "I like your spunk."

She let go of Crew. Bringing her hands together, she tried prying a burnished ring from her finger. "Help me." Deficient of stamina, she merely lifted her fingers. "Take it."

Queen Esta hadn't any meat on her bones, and it effortlessly popped off. "Another ring?"

"That simple ring will save countless lives."

THIRTY-SIX
SAGE

Sage moaned. It felt like somebody took a hammer to her skull. A repercussion of overindulging in Mama's hard apple cider, she thought. Disoriented, she blinked, cleansing the haze. This wasn't her cozy cottage. *Where am I?* Iron bars surrounded her; she'd been caged like an animal.

She remembered. Crew's brother—James. He cast an incantation to incapacitate her. The spasms he'd inflicted had frittered into a subtle ache in her abdomen. This was the boy Crew had journeyed to find. *James doesn't need rescuing.* If only she could warn Crew and Tegan. Madam Rouge was a lying traitor. She'd been playing them from the beginning. What was in it for her? Money. Power. Prestige.

She'd been stripped of her fur coat, and frostiness wrapped her body. She shivered. Irons shackled her arms behind her back and her ankles. Moreover, there was a constricting weight of an iron collar strapping her throat. She scooched upright and braced herself on the wrought-iron bars. Doctor Aerestol had certified her as a Doloran, not fae, why then all the fuss with the clamping of irons. Fae abhors cold iron because it dilutes their magic. Apparently, Aerestol wasn't taking any chances.

Striving to ease her discomfort there was none to be had, the cold bars leached into her bones. The room held no warmth whatsoever. She drew her legs up to her chest and leaned into them.

My sisters! Jerking her head off her kneecaps, she was in one of several cages that spanned the walls. After thoroughly eyeing each cell, Edras and Eadith weren't here. *Where are they?* Her hopes and heart disintegrated like the ashes of Papa, Mama, and Parry. Stifling pricking tears, she squeezed her eyelids and again, nuzzled her head between her kneecaps and cried. All was for naught.

Pull yourself together. This isn't finished.

Breathing in determination mixed with vengeance, she inspected the enclosures a second time. A few empty but most were occupied. Creatures, known and unknown to her.

"My name is Vale. What's yours?" said a meek voice.

She peered over her knees to a girl with doe eyes, ears, legs, with a soulful expression; a vacant cage separated them. "I'm Sage."

"You're fae?"

"Um...."

"Your ears."

Sage's earbobs must have parted through her hair. "Err... yes." She wasn't fae, and the habit of lying tumbled easily off her tongue. As a child, Mama's numerous scoldings for telling falsehoods came to mind. She'd say, "Fae can't lie. You cannot be caught in a web of deceit." It had become a prompt that her parents would drill into her. She'd learned that while fae couldn't lie, they had the propensity to weave words around a lie.

"You have magic then? Can you shapeshift like high fae or fly? Do you have wings?" Vale's doe eyes were swimming with curiosity.

There were other creatures caged in the spacious room, craning their heads toward her. The majority were fae, and like her, chained in irons, which resulted in waylaying their magical prowess. One fae kept her head down and was braiding a teal mane that was arrayed over her shoulder. Not one braid, but dozens. There was a sprite, fluttering pixies, and a woodland nymph, young and advanced in age. She opted neither to disclose nor speak unless it was a means to an end.

"Oh, I do so hope you're not high fae or extremely magical." Vale's maudlin uttering touched Sage. "The doctor will take it from you, like he did to my friend. Fae don't last long here; he takes them first."

"How can he take their magic?"

Her shoulders hiked up the column of her neck, shaking her head. "They took him into another room. I heard his screams. It must be very painful, stripping fae of their magic. They brought him back and he lay in a cage for days. I thought he was dead. When he finally moved and woke up, he'd changed."

"Changed? In what way?"

"It's hard to explain." Vale wasn't bound and chained like Sage, and the girl laid her cheek on the palm of her hand. "His appearance hadn't altered. More like drained of color like he'd been bled dry. It was the browbeaten, defeated look in his eyes that was heartbreaking. And he wouldn't talk about it, like he was ashamed, or maybe he couldn't."

"Where is he now?"

"I don't know. The doctor's minions took him away. Like I said, fae come and are gone within days."

Sage leaned her head back, plunking into the bars. "How long have you been here?"

"It feels like forever; time goes slow here. Four, five days, I think."

"I'm looking for my sisters." She raised her voice an octave, reaching all those imprisoned. "They might have been here. Eadith is only six, a little thing with a head of curls. And Edras, she looks a lot like me."

"I've been here the longest," said the nymph, her fingers rounding the bars of her cage and peering between them. "There was a young one, but she had green hair and they took her away. Though, I didn't hear any screaming." The nymph's fingers worried over her lips, her eyes skittering to the other occupied cages. "That's what usually happens, screaming."

The four imprisoned fae, like herself, fettered in irons, trembled.

"I haven't seen anyone resembling you."

Sage came for her sisters. Never supposing they'd be lost forever. She met Vale's pitiful gaze. "You're not magical then?" she said, voice tremulous.

Vale gave a negative nod. "He takes my blood." She pulled up the sleeve of her shirt, and the downy fur on her arm didn't hide the wide-ranging bruises. "Don't ask, because I don't know what he does with it."

"He takes my blood too," said the lovely nymph. She kept combing her fingers through her mossy, emerald hair. "Shhh… someone's coming."

Footfalls were coming closer. Two rasks marched in and went to a caged fae. "Are you ready for your appointment with the doctor?" said the rask with a reptilian slur.

"Nooo—Noooo!" shrieked the woman. The rask keyed the bolt and flung open the barred door. The two of them reached in, grabbing her arms, and thrust her onto the floor. The rask's forked tongue flicked in and out of his mouth, cackling. The other booted her away from the barred enclosure. The woman was sobbing hysterically.

Fae held onto their beauty; nonetheless, observable fine lines and wrinkles were prevalent on those well advanced in years. And this woman showed signs of her longevity.

"What are you doing to her," Sage called. Managing to crawl to her knees, she angled her body onto the bars to see. "Let her go! You're hurting her!" On its own accord, or so it appeared, the barred door to the cage started to move, shearing the rask's forehead and slammed shut.

Both rasks hacked their beady, black eyes to her. In haste, they gripped the woman by her arms and dragged her out.

I have to get out of here.

By means of her talent, she occupied herself by freeing her wrists from the manacles. She concentrated on turning her skin buttery. The bones took effort, making them malleable. Due to the restraint, she was forced to dislocate her thumbs. It hurt terribly and smothered her squeal of pain by biting down on her knee. Little by little, she wedged the shackle off one wrist and then the other. Afterward she focused on mending her thumbs.

Maintaining the ruse of being handcuffed, she fastened her arms behind her. She breathed deeply. Had anyone heard her struggle? All the captives were curled into tight body balls, squashing eyelids, hands covering their ears.

Muted voices neared, one very identifiable from the ice castle. The Frankenstein doctor.

Sage heard pinging of instruments or some kind of equipment, and then, "Ready." James' voice, clear and distinct. She put her ear to the gaps between the bars as undertoned utterances came from the adjoining room. "Waiting for you… must…timely manner." A word here and there, but she couldn't register the person speaking nor did the sentence make sense.

A faint toggling of switches was heard, and then an unexpected onslaught of static energy. A peculiar sting hummed over Sage's skin, spiking the hair on her arms.

Venting from the nearby room—the screaming started. Terrified yowling like she'd never heard before, a heinousness that folded the limbs of Sage's body, stopping her heart from beating. She plugged her ears but couldn't thwart the petrifying screams. Those in cages were rocking in despair, keening filled the ether and Sage joined in the dirge.

The screaming stopped. No noise. No movement.

They exchanged panicky glances. Commotion came from the adjacent room, and then a rask schlepped in carrying the woman. Her arms and legs joggling lifelessly as he spread her body on a metal table. And on the wall above the table, what looked like, were tools of a surgeon. Saws, big and small. A hatchet, drill, knives, lots of knives.

"This one was half dead already. Got what he could outta her," the rask said, blasé and callous.

"What is he going to do to her?"

The rask's mouth pulled, but not into a grin, more like a foul hole in his face. He took in the range of enclosures, as if he were performing and they were his spectators. "See these?" He strode to the pegboard, directing their gazes to the saws and scalpels. "Each of these handy-dandy tools will carve up the old bitch. The doctor likes to dabble, see what makes magicals tic."

Appalled, Sage's breath came in deep, short increments. Gritting her teeth, she couldn't, and didn't want to crush her building fury. "You worm-infested dung pile!" she bellowed. The rask's snake-like face turned ugly, crimping his lips, and lashing its tongue. "We killed one of your buddies in Alderwood, twisted and snapped his slimy neck. And then threw his body into the burning trash where it belonged."

The rask came at her. Sage backed off, as he used his boot to kick the bars of the cell. "I know who you are—a freak of nature. I'll take immense pleasure watching you squirm, just like your sister."

"My sister?" Sage's stomach dropped to her knees.

"Yeah, that redheaded bitch eased my sore eyes, if you know what I mean." His forked tongue lapped around his mouth. "Hostility festered in that one."

She was *almost* afraid to ask. "Where is she?"

Sniggering, he said, "Can't say. Maybe..." his mouth gathered, and he tapped his finger on the nub of his chin, "the doctor twisted and snapped her neck and threw her in the garbage."

Wrathful pestilence crawled into the marrow of her bones, wanting nothing more than to kill this repulsive being. She grasped the iron bars and pulled herself up. Standing level with the rask, her eyes burned like hot pokers, flaring into him.

"What are you doing to me?" The rask's chin dipped to his heaving chest. "Stop it," he slurred breathily.

Sage stretched her arm through the bars, extending her fingers, reaching for his heart. Focusing on his rapid heartbeats, she carved deeper, breaking his ribs. He screamed. Her fingers confined his beating organ like a cage.

"I…I…" puffing for oxygen, the rask juddered, "breathe…"

Squeezing his heart, tighter and tighter. Until the beating stopped. Like popping a balloon, it burst.

The rask dropped dead.

THIRTY-SEVEN
CREW

Crew reappeared within a yard of Tegan and Grigg's.
"Your disappearing act is getting old," Tegan squawked, steeped in blood and gore. He swung his pickaxe, decapitating a dwarf. Its head rolled into the carnage that had turned the white snow red. The stretched tight atmosphere reeked of blood and sweat.

Crew found himself in a strongly knit pod where Griggs and Tegan were fighting back-to-back. A mange of creatures corralling them in, a blitzkrieg on all fronts.

Griggs grunted. "You saw her?"

"Yes."

"It is done then." Grigg's evaded a rioting ogre wielding a mallet. "Crew, time for you to finish this."

Crew gulped a profound breath. Shuttering his eyes, diffusing the cries of creatures begging for help as their appendages lay about them. The yelping, swearing profanities, the sound of steel upon steel, shuffling of boots in icy snow. He concentrated.

Like dousing a flaming matchhead in kerosene, the blood in his veins ignited. His body transformed into a sweltering tempest; it had to be unleashed or else undergo internal organ damage. Opening his eyes and stretching his arms, he let it go. A blaze erupted from his hands. Shooting fiery lassoes, interlocking their enemies. An inferno of screeching creatures detonated on impact, while others arbitrarily ran, fanning their flaming bodies.

Burning flesh tainted the air, Crew rubbed the stench from his nose, frowning at the sight before him.

"Hey, why'd you keep that trick under wraps?" Tegan said. "Could have used it an hour ago."

"Aye, it's a ghastly way to go."

"Yeah, but faster than suffering and bleeding to death without arms and legs."

"I thought I was showing mercy."

"By not frying them?"

"Are you boys going to stand here jabbering like nitwits or should we finish this?" Griggan drove his blade into its sheath and jogged toward the main entrance of the mansion.

"After having each other's backs while you were vacationing," Tegan said to Crew, "he calls me a nitwit." Sprinting and leaping over bodies, they caught up to the feisty goblin.

Tegan said, "It's odd, isn't it? This place is made of ice and it has a wooden door."

"No handle to get in either." Griggs fixed his clawed hands on his hips.

Crew pushed to the front. He smoothed his hand on the inlaid runes scrolling the archway of the wooden door. "It won't let us in. We're not invited."

"Then we knock it down." Standing off to the side of Crew, Tegan elevated his pickaxe and hacked into the wood.

"No—" Crew barked. "Stop!" The axe inexplicably disappeared into the wooden door, towing Tegan in with it. "Let go. Tegan, let it go!"

Tegan was up to his armpits. "It won't let me."

"Pull him out." Griggs dropped to his knees and wrapped his arms around Tegan's legs.

Crew banded his arms around Tegan's waist, and gasped, "Pull harder."

"I'm trying," Griggs said. "The door is sucking him in."

"Burn it," Tegan garbled, Half of his head had melded into the door, and his one eyeball was locked Crew.

"What if it burns you?"

"Do it," Griggs said. "We're losing him either way."

One-handedly, Crew entangled his fingers into Tegan's coat, refusing to let him go. Targeting the upper half of the wooden door, fire shot from his hand. Implementing his fingers like a torch, he worked over the door lintels separating it from the runed archway. The door timbered inward and Tegan's body eased out of the wood.

Crew outstretched his arm, aiding Tegan to his feet. "Thought we lost you."

"Me too," he said, picking a sliver from his lip. "Have you ever gnawed on wood?"

"Can't say that I have."

Griggs gave Tegan a good back thumping. "Glad you made it, kid."

Lit sconces suffused the foyer of the crystalized structure, winking on tall reflective looking glasses. Ascending before them was the grand staircase, a representation of the ice castle, on a much larger scale. "It's too quiet." Crew stepped in, wary of a boobytrap.

Madam Rough shambled from a lofty archway. "I didn't think you were going to make it." Her expression strained as she wrung her hands. "Get out of the foyer. The walls are enclosed with mirrors."

"So?" Tegan swerved toward his reflection and became mesmerized.

Crew sent a volley of sparks into the glass. Instead of shattering, the sparks went through the mirrored glass as if it were liquid mercury. As though throwing a stone into water, it rippled and then hardened into its reflective frame. Tegan blinked and shook his head.

"Nobody look at them," Crew advised. "You'll get sucked in just like the door."

Griggs cuffed Tegan on the shoulder. "Kid, you don't learn, do ya?"

The oracle waved her hand, "In here."

Awestruck by the exterior of the icy mansion, a person would believe the interior to be harsh and cold. They walked into a cozy room with a crackling fire in a stoned hearth, a plush rug, two overstuffed sofas, a recliner, and an oblong, low-lying table. Ornate framed paintings decorated the walls and in the corner stood a grand piano.

"Where's Sage?" Crew was quick to ask.

The oracle paced in front of the fire, still wringing her hands, shoulders slouched. "They took her as soon as we came through the door."

"Took her where?" Tegan rumbled.

"His laboratory is below, where he conducts his experiments." They turned to leave, but Madam Rouge snagged Crew's arm. "You promised me."

He scowled. "Madam, you know this isn't going to end well."

"His son is a good boy." Her eyes glistened with unshed tears. "He shouldn't have to pay for his father's sins. Aerestol changed him."

"Changed him?" Tegan asked. "Literally or figuratively?"

"Both." She passed a hand over her distraught expression. "James was a sweet boy, full of joy and happiness. Aerestol took it all away from him."

"What are you saying?" Crew said, voice a low snarl. "What are we dealing with that you forgot to mention?"

As if her legs couldn't support her, the oracle flopped down on the sofa. "Aerestol has achieved success in extracting magic from fae and elves. And experiments with creatures of the wild, hoping to...to..."

"Create an invincible race of people?" Crew disrupted her thoughts. "A supreme race to rule them all? And Aerestol Paphos will be their king."

Wearing remorse in the wrinkles of her brow, the oracle sunk her head into her hands. "His son was a disappointment to him." She went on, "James showed no signs of becoming a grand wizard like his father. And Aerestol has been working to correct James' flaws."

"The guy is experimenting on his own son?" Tegan spat. "He's—"

An outbreak of pounding boots vibrated in the hallway. The redcap drew his sword as dwarves filed in. Griggs hurdled the sofa and came down swinging. The wooden door had unarmed Tegan of his pickaxe, but he was able to hex the dwarve's feet. A few of them bungled their footing, weeble-wobbling like drunken sailors.

Swamping dwarves grinded to a slow halt. Fixed with combative expressions, their movements dawdling. Griggs and Tegan retreated toward the hearth, abreast of Crew.

"What kind of deviltry is this?" said Griggs.

Crew bent his elbow and tweaked his fist sideways. The necks of each dwarf abnormally twisted cracking bones nauseating. The dwarves fell like timbering logs.

"My deviltry." Crew exhaled, feeling hot and overwhelmed. "I'm not proud of killing defenseless people."

"Defenseless! Are you kidding me?" Tegan said. "Another trick you hid from us. You can stop time like my sister."

"I haven't perfected it like Sage. I'm learning."

Madam Rouge dragged her gaze over Crew's face as if seeing him for the first time. Objective wonder tapered her eyes, augmenting her pleated brow.

"This is going to be easier than I thought." Tegan twitched his arm in a prelude of victory. "Let's do this, find my sisters and—"

"He won't be able to sustain that power for long." Griggs, Tegan, and Crew kinked their heads to the voice addressing them from beneath the archway.

The oracle greeted the newcomer, "James."

THIRTY-EIGHT
SAGE

What have I done? Sage dropped to her knees, dazed, staring at the rask. She was a healer, not a murderer. Closing her eyes, she rested her forehead on the bars. Extreme fatigue ate away her resilience. *Edras? Is she...* Taking in a deep breath, it barely revived her.

"Well, well, well. What have we here?"

Sage had seen the doctor once. In the ice Castle he'd worn a classy bespoke suit, which stunk of wealth. Currently, a bloodstained surgeon's smock with a vest and button-down shirt underneath. Sauntering in, he pushed his spectacles up the bridge of his nose and then prodded his foot into the rask's ribcage.

"You did this?" he asked, peering through his lenses. She expected him to spew reprisals, show signs of aggression, not a gloating message. "I am impressed, my dear."

"Where's my sisters?"

"You must know, Eadith was merely a means to an end." He girded and knotted the ties of his smock around his waist. "It was unfortunate your family got in the way."

"Where is she?" Wrath filling her again.

"You swindled me that night at the Circus Faire. Crew gave you a ring, didn't he? That's how you escaped. You don't have it now because I'd sense it. Do you know where it is?" He yanked on the collar of his shirt as if it was choking him.

"Go to hell!"

"You first, my sweet thing." His smile askew like a sneering sphinx. "Where is Crew? Did he die in the castle?"

He doesn't know? The oracle didn't tell him. Deploring his snootiness and mustering strength, she managed to stand on weak legs. Rather than furnish him with information, she repeated, "Where are my sisters?"

He moved his fingers, a conjuring magician, and the iron collar strapping her neck unhinged. She pulled it off and let it clang to the floor. "Apparently, iron doesn't deter your magic like the fae. What *does* foil a Doloran's power?" he inquired, angling his head.

"Did you hurt Edras? Where are they?"

He advanced within a yard of her cage. "My dear, you are a repetitious parrot." Rebellion and fury condensed the air, pressing her to act. "Tit for tat. You give me what I want. I give *you* what you want."

"What do you want from me!" Shrieking the words around gnashing teeth, she attempted to govern her power. As if he'd been lingering patiently for her to break, his look of supremacy cut Sage to the quick. Putting him in the crosshairs of her sight, she let go an incising barb.

His eyes widened. Whipping his arm sideways, he redirected her energy. Ricocheting the incising barb into a caged fae. The fae gagged, eyeballs rolled in her sockets and crumpled.

Sage's worst nightmare. Killing an innocent.

She was thrown backward as his rebuttal was swift. Her skull whacking against the bars. Seeing stars, she compressed her hand on the back of her head. Blood bubbled between her fingers.

Men trooped in, and minus a key, the door squealed open.

"Take her." Aerestol stood aside until his guards had her secured, and then they hauled her out.

She was brought into a cavernous section of the mountain, and she was instantly enmeshed in haunting, spine-chilling screams. Not hers, but hundreds of souls the wizard had harmed and butchered. She gagged down bile that was creeping up her throat. They backed her onto a slanted stave with a circular crank on its frame.

Everything came to a standstill when a rask marched in. In a military-type uniform, with a hunter-green beret on his flat head, he represented himself as the leader of Aerestol's sentinels. He kept swiping at a seeping gash on his face as he conversed with the doctor.

She strained to interpret their low undertones while being jostled by the guards attending to her. They banded leather straps around her wrists and her ankles, buckling her down. Lastly, they belted her neck to the slat. She felt like Mama's taffy being stretched and pulled to her limits. It irked her that she hadn't the pep to rebel and hoped for a speedy rejuvenation.

Examining her whereabouts, it looked like a scientific lab. Electrical components with lots of wires, gadgets, thermometers, odd units, and metal thingamajigs.

"Go get him. I want him in here. Now," the doctor commanded. The guard nodded and revolved on the heels of his boots; his footfalls bounced on the walls as he went toward a contracted hallway.

"Bring her up," Aerestol's voice sounded behind her. A guard gripped the crankshaft attached to the side of the stave. Oscillating the cogged wheel, the table she was bound to gradually reclined. "Enough." He leaned over her and swept the hair that had been sticking to her perspiring face. "Keep your eyes open. I wouldn't want you to miss this."

"Is this what you did to my sisters?" She spat into his revolting face. "We don't have fae magic. You know that."

Using the sleeve of his smock, he wiped spittle from his cheek. He arched an analytical finger, motioning in sweeping circles over her. "Ah-hah, your genetic gifts are all in here. In your body and mind. And I am going to take them. All of it. They'll be nothing left except a vacant husk." He scoffed, pleased with his analogy "Do you know what the best part of our performance will be?"

Sage stared, not at the predatory doctor, but at the domed ceiling. Her breathing shallow with beliefs of vitalizing her energy and engaged in untangling taut nerves.

"My dear, you don't want to take a guess?" His fingers rounded her forearm and squeezed her tender skin. "Your brother and Crew will be joining us."

THIRTY-NINE
CREW

Inspecting the fallen dwarves, James stepped into the parlor, his gait unbalanced. "They're not all bad." Sadness pinched his brow. "They follow orders. My father sent them. They weren't going to hurt you."

"They weren't going to hurt us, aye, like the party we had outside?" Crew said, ridicule coating his words. "I am skeptical of your allegation." Had the boy been expecting company or did he always dress like royalty? Tailored in the height of fashion, a high-collared, white shirt accessorized by a silk cravat, black velour waistcoat detailed in threads of gold, red, and silver, and black velour lapels on his fitted, maroon frock coat. Judging him to be an inch or two shorter than Crew, and, unlike his muscular build, James was scrawny beneath his refined attire. Whether it was the gaslights shedding insufficient light or because the boy had blond hair, his complexion was gravely pale.

James slid his fingers into the pocket of his frock, hooking his thumb over the cuff. "What are you looking at?"

"Your eyes," Crew said bluntly. The boy, perturbed by his examination, shifted his shoulders and his feet. "The pupil—"

"You mean *this* eye?" He pointed to his own left eye. "It isn't *my* eye."

A breathy sob broke from Madam Rouge. "Poor boy." Stationed on the sofa, she sought Crew's receptiveness. "There's more. Tell them, James."

"Madam, you overstep propriety." James frowned, hardening his mouth. His gaze deviated from the oracle back to Crew. "You are here for Sage, I assume."

Tegan burst in, "My other sisters as well. Edras and Eadith."

I don't like this. Too easy. They didn't just go through a maelstrom to have tea and crumpets with Paphos and his kid. A toxic brew was afoot. Crew had been biting at the bit to ask about his own brother. Yet again, something felt off.

He'd struck a deal with Madam Rouge, and she'd done her part, getting them to Wintervine. Not solely advising them on the doctor's location, but making the journey, no doubt, for her own intents and purposes. She had a bleeding heart for the boy. A boy he was supposed to abduct or, rather, rescue from his own father. He didn't care a fig about her reasons.

The doctor, ascribed as an almighty wizard, was a prodigious prick of a father. A father who'd pluck out his own kid's eyeball and replace it with another. The oracle said there was more. Evidently, Aerestol didn't have any qualms in experimenting on his own son. *His son?* No, not his son!

"Your father won't be pleased that you're helping us."

James' stoic features changed with a lopsided grin. "What makes you think I'm helping you?"

From Crew's periphery, he noticed a muscle jumping in Tegan's jaw. Crew's arm darted, blocking Tegan from beating the shit out of the boy. "Not now," he hushed in a cautionary manner.

"This way. She's in the laboratory." James turned and with his unbalanced gait left the parlor.

From the side of his mouth, Tegan uttered, "You know this is an ambush."

"Probably." Crew tugged the rim of his cap over his forehead. "Stay alert and don't do anything stupid."

"Like what?"

"Like getting yourself killed."

"I'll try not to."

Crew turned to the redcap. "Griggs, this isn't your party."

Griggs doffed his putrefying hat, blood soaked from their previous melee, and raked his hand into his hair. "If you don't mind me tagging along, I kinda like this soiree." He smirked, exposing tangible fangs.

Crew gave a crisp nod and headed out of the parlor behind Madam Rouge.

Passing the grand staircase, they veered left toward dual doors that were yawning open. Merging into the mouth of a stairwell, not frozen, but hewed rock, they were going into the mountainside. Their footfalls reverberated off rocky bulwarks while making a gradual descent that levelled into a passageway. Gaslights were attached along the channel, amplifying the eeriness, and ghostly shadows followed. Jagged formations, slight crevices, and rivulets of water enhanced the dankness.

Sliding steel resonated, as Crew and Griggs pulled swords from their sheathes.

"No guards," Griggs murmured. "I don't like it."

"Aye, maybe Aerestol doesn't need guards."

"Why is that?" said a wide-eyed Tegan, and Crew cast him a wry look. "Oh yeah. He's a wizard. Crew, you all powered up?"

Crew countered, "Are you?"

Tegan stood a little taller. "I want to butcher the bastard, limb from limb, and feed his entrails to the pigs."

"Good," Crew said. "Keep that anger."

Moving past closed metal doors, howling and loud banging had them trading glances.

Entering a commodious fortification, Madam Rouge said, "*Aerestol?*"

Crew zeroed in on Sage, bound to wooden stave, and puncturing her arms were rubber-like tubing. Wire receptors were fixed onto various parts of her body. A tin contraption had been molded to her head with additional lines interconnected to complex-looking equipment. She'd been gagged and blindfolded, and was struggling with her restraints.

"Sage!" Tegan bolted. "What have you done to her."

"Tegan, don't. Stop!" Crew attempted to grab hold of him, but he slipped through his fingers.

Aerestol swooped his arm upward, and Tegan flew off his feet. Jetting into the air, his body whacked the rock. Limply, he descended, hitting the ground, blood smattering his face.

Quick to disarm the redcap, Aerestol cast a destructive spell. Griggs raised his sword like a protective shield, recoiling the wizard's spell off the blade. It detonated into the rock, vibrating the mountain.

Smothered screams derived from behind Sage's gag.

Fireballs danced on Crew's palms. However, he was unsure of unleashing them because Aerestol was effectively leaning near Sage. She'd get burned in the crossfire. *Where is James?*

He'd been distracted by Tegan's and Grigg's row with the wizard and hadn't seen James move. But there he was, sprawled out on a wooden table contingent to Sage. Having disrobed, wearing just his trousers. His frock coat, vest, cravat, and shirt were in a muddle on the ground. Seemingly detached from the altercations, he'd applied the wire receptors to his arms, throat, and chest. Madam Rouge, a short distance from Crew, wore a multifaceted expression. Riveted to James, a tear tripped over her eyelid. She pressed her fingers to her mouth, holding onto a perceptive snuffle.

"Crew," Aerestol sneered. "I know you have it."

Crew caught Griggs' caveat, a subtle negative nod. When Queen Esta gave Crew the second ring, she'd forewarned, "Do not offer it without a fight. Aerestol is no fool."

"Let her go," Crew said. "You don't need her."

"She's my first Doloran. I will tap all she has to offer." His face, molded in granite, wouldn't be dissuaded.

"Edras—" Tegan rasped, coming cognizant. "What did you do to her?"

"Ahhh, yes. Desirable, though an adverse Doloran. Morg has her. When Kade sent me the message of an impending surprise. It was James who saw your ship crossing the sea with Sage aboard. We knew you were coming. Just like James saw Morg and Edras."

Crew intervened, "Who's Morg?"

"The imp who bested you and Sage in the forest."

"How does James know?" Tegan was staggering to his legs, gripping his head.

"Demelda didn't tell you?" The wizard's heartless grin tossed Crew's stomach. "Mage Marek donated his eyes for my research." He peered toward his son. "The grafting of one eye didn't take, but we had success with the other. He now has the sight. Don't you boy?"

"Then he can see this coming." Crew unleashed a fireball. A searing meteor targeted the boy. James crossed his hands above his face, palms outward. As the fireball closed in, he sprang his arms forward. Boomeranging the meteor back to Crew. Crew snagged the fireball, absorbing the flames into his body. Narrowing his gaze, he mused, the boy's wan appearance was deceptive.

Sensing a twinkling of magic, Tegan had unmasked his sister and the gag popped out of her mouth.

"Don't kill James," she croaked, thrashing her body. "He—" Aerestol slapped his hand over her mouth and, stooping, whispered in her ear. Afterward, her chest pumped, up and down, agitatedly hissing between her teeth. Whatever he said had silenced her.

The wizard made some sort of signal with his fingers. There was a squeal of metal, and then a slothful thwack and scraping coming from the passageway. Not taking his sight off Aerestol,

Crew retreated a few paces to gauge what horror the wizard had in store for them. Griggs took a fencer's stance, prepared to attack.

Tegan was closest to the passageway, he flinched, face blanching.

A seven-foot, emaciated troll came into view.

"*Dirge?*" Gawking at the man who'd been like another father to him, Crew couldn't believe his eyes. Jackalope antlers sprouted from his cranium, head slack from the burden, and his pants were unraveling strips of cloth. Uneven, bumpy flesh masked the socket where Aerestol carved out his eye. Sighting all the cuts and gashes on his bare chest, it looked like a pare knife had a heyday, and festering with diseased cankers. His movements lethargic and clumsy because his right leg had been amputated below the knee, replaced with a dragon's claw.

"Dirge. I'm sorry. Dirge." Tears sprang into Crew's eyes and rolled down his cheeks. He spun to Paphos. "You son of a bitch. What kind a fucking monster are you!"

An implacable smirk peeled over Aerestol. "I demand loyalty. Polk and Dirge knew the penalty for betraying me. Isn't that right, Crew?" He made a point of holding onto Sage's arm. "I took you on because Polk never defied me. He raved about his *son*, your street smarts. That you'd give your allegiance to me. But, you are not his *son*, are you?"

Dirge had yet to lay his eye on Crew.

Incensed, striving to rein in his temper before he did something stupid that'd get them all killed, Crew prompted, "What did Dirge say?"

"James," the wizard kept his eyes on Crew, "what did you get out of the troll when you were sawing off his leg."

As if bored James replied, "He didn't snitch."

Feverish adrenaline heightened Crew's rage. He couldn't contain it. For crimes committed against Dirge, he turned on James.

James gasped and started pawing his hands along his throat. Crew considered crushing the boy's windpipe, a negligible twist would suffice. James' eyeballs protruded, his pasty features blooming cherry-apple red.

"Crew, stop. Don't do—" Sage hollered. But the wizard again put an end to her pleas by covering her mouth.

James gurgled, foam dribbling over his lips.

"Stop it!" Madam Rouge roared. "Aerestol is sewing division. He's clever. Playing you boys against each other. Crew, he's a sadist. You know the House of Games at the Faire. That's his choice of entertainment. Aerestol is writing his own performance. Don't do this!"

Crew, filled with revulsion and a drive for revenge, had an insurmountable task to squelch his power. Unexpectedly, the oracle was standing in front of him blocking his sight. An offshoot of his energy slammed into her. Madam's head flung backward, and she emitted an airy gasp. Crew rushed and scooped her into his arms before she fell. Appearing dazed and wonky, she attempted to wrench herself from him.

Chortling echoed throughout the cavernous mountain. The wizard ordered, "Dirge, kill him now."

Crew let go of the oracle and turned toward the troll, bumbling closer to him. Dirge's dragon claw scraped the solid ground, leaving rutted impressions. "Dirge, you don't have to listen to your benefactor anymore. I'm getting you out of here." The troll's shadow eclipsed Crew. "I don't want to hurt you."

Dirge's eye met Crew's beseeching scrutiny, and in that second, Crew saw a void. The doctor destroyed him. What remained was an automaton that obeyed its master. Yet, Crew couldn't kill him.

Tegan had conjured a spell, guiding it toward Dirge's legs. Crew had seen it coming and jaunted backwards or else be mashed into mincemeat. The troll toppled, catching himself on his hands and knees. Griggan swiftly scaled the troll's backbone. He clenched his sword with both hands. Elevating it, he was primed to plunge into Dirge's spine. His eyes sought Crew, seeking a nod of consent. His minor hesitation cost him.

A harpoon of ice skewered Griggs in the chest. The spike driven threw the redcap, pinioning his body to the mountain wall. His beleaguered gaze locked on Crew, wheezing his final gasps of air.

"Noooo—!" Crew cried.

Traumatized, Crew's open-mouthed inhalations turned risky, blurring his vision. Squeezing his eyes, the sight of Griggs' body had embedded into his brain. The wizard's throaty sniggering exacerbated his frenzy. Crew was desperate, wanting to torch the doctor just to watch his skin melting to the bone, and his hellacious screams wouldn't bring Crew pleasure or bring Griggs back, but…

Deterring his thought of vengeance was Dirge, scrabbling to get his legs under him. A magical glimmer was frisking around the troll's fingers. Polk's old Derringer materialized, and Dirge gripped it in his hand.

"Kill him!" Aerestol commanded. "Shoot him. Now!"

Dirge aimed the pistol at Crew, and said, "No snitches. One bullet." In an unprecedented maneuver, Dirge inserted the pistol's barrel into his mouth and pulled the trigger.

FORTY
CREW

A creeping pool of blood was forming around Dirge shoulders, where his head once was. Horrified, Crew swiped brain chunks from his face and neck, cleaning the gooey matter on his coat.

Remembering the assignment, he dug his hand into his pocket making sure Queen Esta's ring was still there. Sage's shouting brought him back to reality. "Crew—Tegan."

Crew pivoted to the juxtaposed tables. The tubes inserted into Sage's arm was siphoning her blood. Pursuing its snaking lines, it was being transfused into James. The wizard was in the background, turning knobs and toggling switches on his convoluted contrivance.

An eruption of sparks shot out of the machine, spurring a bristling sensation through Crew's body.

Sage's spine arched off the wooden stave. Experiencing her bone-chilling screams, Crew shuddered. Her brother, Tegan took action, casting magic. Alas, his spells were useless. Aerestol had erected a failsafe bubble around them. Tegan bolted toward the wizard. He managed to survive until he was catapulted off his feet, again, skyrocketing headfirst into the craggy mountaintop.

Crew jet out his arm, palm forward like catching a baseball, and latched onto him before his skull was shattered. He lowered an unresponsive Tegan to the ground.

Crew started toward Aerestol, but the oracle grabbed him. "Get off!" he scorned, yanking his arm free.

"Don't hurt James," she implored, grappling with his arm. "Aerestol uses the boy like a pincushion. Experimenting on him because he proved to be powerless after he'd stolen him from the orphanage. He's innocent," she whined. "You promised."

"*Where* did he get him?"

"From the Foundling Orphanage. I thought you knew."

"I didn't."

"James is—" Her lips separated in midsentence, looking like a human statue.

"Sage!" Crew dashed to the table. Paphos was also immobilized, a perplexing scowl shaping his features.

Crew tore out the rubbery tubes, sprinkling blood everywhere, and then removed the electrodes and the tin cap from her head. Hurrying to unbuckle the leather straps, he cradled her into his arms.

"Can't… hold…" Shuttering her eyes, her head slumped to his chest.

Her stationary continuum dissolved. Crackling electricity again ignited. Madam Rouge blinked, confounded. James had also detached himself from the constricting tubes and wires. In haste, Crew went and laid Sage next to her brother.

Wheeling about, he returned to bedlam, and was feeling shit out of luck because they hadn't accomplished a damn thing.

However, he might have found his brother. And raised by a pernicious fiend.

The doctor clacked a switch, quelling the prickling static, and swerved to face him. "Tell me," Aerestol said through barred teeth. "Who are you?"

"*Me?*" Crew placed a hand on his chest. "I'm just a grunt who works for the Circus."

The wizard's nostrils flared. "For years, I've seen you work the Faire. There was nothing *special* about you."

"That's me. Nothing special."

"I never sensed magic in you. And then—"

"I can't do magic."

He scoffed. "Then what do you call it, boy?"

"Queen Esta is very convincing, aye. Said I'm…umm… something called a misbegotten prodigy." Crew was laying it on rather thick. And it was working because the wizard's eyes widened to the tenth degree.

In an awed and breathy voice, Aerestol said, "You have it?" His gaze darted directly to the pocket where Crew had stashed the ring.

Madam Rouge stepped into his eyesight with a fully clothed James beside her. "You've seen the queen?" she inquired, disbelief ringing in her tone.

"Aye, seen her, talked to her. She had a lot to say."

"Kade," the doctor said. "What did you see happening today?"

She brushed a finger across the seam of her lips. "Death and dying." To verify her soothsaying, she cut her gaze to Dirge, Griggs, Sage, and Tegan, and fastened her sights on Crew. "Who are you, *really*?"

"Enough stalling." Aerestol stomped closer, madness in his eyes. Shrugging out of his smock, he let it drop, and buttoned his high-collared shirt and righted his jacquard waistcoat. "If you don't hand over that damn ring, I'll kill both of them," pinpointing Sage and Tegan, "right now, where they lay," he intoned with such venom that Crew flinched.

"Are you positive you want to meet the queen?"

"Dammit, boy! None of you are getting out of here alive. My men are infiltrating the grounds as we speak. Give me the ring and I might reconsider my options of bleeding your girlfriend, her brother, and you, dry."

Crew figured he'd somehow summoned his minions. "Just a warning. You killed the queen's reliable companion." Veering toward Griggs, he winced. "She's not going to be happy."

"Do you think I care about her feelings?"

"Aye." Enhancing his performance, he grudgingly reached into his pocket for the ring. A chance of survival. Clipped between his finger and thumb, he held it up. "Call off your men and you can have it."

His nose crinkled as if sensing something foul. "I agree. James, you know what to do." The boy nodded. "Give the ring to Kade first."

That wasn't a confirmation that he'd let them live, and gambling with people's lives embittered him.

Crew deposited the ring on the oracle's palm. She curled her fingers around it, and then closed her eyes. Her body erratically twitched, and a furrow embedded between her eyebrows.

"Crew speaks the truth," the oracle said. "The ring derives from Queen Esta."

Jubilant glee developed on Aerestol's face. He plucked the ring from Kade's hand, ecstatically staring down at it. "I've waited a lifetime for an audience with the queen."

Hearing movement from behind, Crew looked over his shoulder and snared Sage's forlorn eyes. *Her sisters?*

"Before you visit the queen, tell me, where are Edras and Eadith. Sage's sisters."

Crew's wish would not be granted, the wizard barked, "If this is a damn magic trick, I will make each and every one of you wish you were never born." He forced the ring onto his finger, and evaporated.

Crew moved a shushing finger to his lips. From his own experience, once the ring was in place, the wearer could be hovering between two dimensions. Here and there.

Minutes passed. "I fulfilled my promise." He turned to the oracle. "Take James, Sage, and Tegan out of here."

"Where are you going?" Madam Rouge asked.

Crew headed to Griggs, where he'd perished, bayoneted to the mountainside. Picking up his blood-encrusted cap and his sword where it had flown from his hands. He drove the blade into the sheath that belted the redcap's waist. Applying a smidgen of his power, it was an elementary feat to withdraw the harpooning spike. Griggs' body collapsed over Crew's shoulder. He shoved the hat into his belt. "I won't be gone long. Just get them out of here." He stuffed his hand into his other pocket of his pants and extracted another ring.

"*Crew?*" Sage called.

"I'll be back." Clamping his arm around Griggs', he slid the ring onto his finger.

FORTY-ONE
SAGE

"I'm fine," Tegan said, swatting his sister's arms. "Just had the wind knocked out of me."

"You weren't breathing. I thought you were dead." Sage aided him to his feet, and Tegan braced himself on the mountain wall. "Be careful. You have a broken rib. I tried mending it, but..." Her brother massaged his sternum.

"Madam Rouge! Madam Rouge!" Boris sprinted into the chamber, carrying Sage's bow and quiver. Spying the body of the massive troll he skidded to a halt. "A new kind of species?"

"No," James said, calmly, like the past hours hadn't affected him. "One of my father's experiments."

"Where is your father?" Tegan scanned the chamber and the wall where Griggs' body had been impaled. "And where is Crew and Griggs?"

Grim lines imbued the oracles features, along with a nervous twitch. "Crew had two rings. He gave one to Aerestol and poof. Disappeared. Crew took the goblin and put on the other ring."

"I've been trying to get down here, but even my hexes couldn't break the impenetrable seal." Boris quivered, face splotchy. "I've been laying siege upstairs. Creatures I've never seen in my life are trying to get in."

"The wards my father established must have been tampered with. Incantations aren't my forte," James disclosed, dejection written in his expressive gaze.

Boris went to Sage, proffering her bow and quiver. "You're going to need this. Come with me." He waved his arm, directing them toward the passage.

Sage arranged the bow on and shoulder but didn't follow Boris.

"James, wait," Sage said. He stilled but didn't turn. "Tell me— where are my sisters? You are not your father's son. You are better than him." James didn't budge or make a sound. "Please."

James hung his head, his voice hollow in the passageway. "Meet me by the stairs." And then continued on.

"Let's go." Tegan pressed a hand to his chest. "I can't believe Crew. He left us with this mess."

"He said he'd be back." She sighted her brother's aggravation. "I'm not condoning what he did. He had his reasons."

"Yeah, like when we searched all day and all night in the woods for him. Those imps were long gone with Edras. We might have caught up to them if it weren't for Crew."

Sage rubbed the ache happening in her temples. "Crew was the driving force that got us here." Her brother shut his eyes, and frustratingly tapped the back of his head on the wall.

"We haven't found Edras or Eadith." In a gesture of defeat, he dropped his head into his hands. Speaking through tense fingers, he said, "We're living in a nightmare, and it's not over."

"C'mon." Sage sprinted into the far room toward the cages. She seized a ring of keys from the peg board. "We're getting everyone out." Skittish cries escalated as she inserted key after key into a bolted lock, trying to find the right one. "Tegan, can you do something here?"

"Patiently waiting for you to ask, sis." Door after wrought-iron door squealed open, liberating captives. "Sage, this should have been a no-brainer for you."

"I'm bottled up. Can't think straight, let alone concentrate."

Vale looked relieved to see Sage. "I thought you were dead."

"Not yet."

"Now what should we do?" Vale asked.

"Go back to your villages. Your homes. But be aware, danger is lurking outside."

Tegan filched accouterments from the peg board, a chisel, a serrated saw, and slipped a scalpel into the pocket of his coat. When they came upon the dual doors to the main level of the mansion, Sage nocked an arrow on her bow. The noise of breaking glass was followed by boisterous singing, and then a firm thwack.

"Some sap just got skunked," Tegan said.

"Skunked?"

"One of the wizard's boobytraps, an intoxication spell. Crew said it'll scramble a person's brain, and you won't be able to walk or talk."

"Apparently a person can sing." Watchful for what was skulking in the foyer, Sage whispered, "At least it's not an all-out war in here."

Coming to the grand staircase, Sage's heart tumbled. James wasn't in sight.

"Somebody was able to get the door back on." Tegan crept across the marbleized floor. "Sage, in here." He pointed the scalpel toward the parlor.

The lanky chef walked toward them, arresting underneath the archway. "We're reestablishing the wards. Madam is in the library. We have to go room to room. It would be far easier and quicker if we could get outside. The wards would be restored in minutes."

"How many are out there?" Tegan questioned.

"I can't tell. They're hiding in the dark. I downed two mallusks. Watch out for them. They have poisonous quills."

"Oh, great." Tegan grumped. "Any more good news?"

Sage lowered her bow. "The mountain protects the mansion from the rear. That leaves three sides. I noticed a third-story balcony when we arrived. That's where we'll be, protecting you and the oracle. Wait five minutes until we can get in place."

"Boris, find Madam Rouge and get outside and get those wards up," Tegan said, and swiveled to the staircase. "Let's do it."

Plush carpeted stairs deadened their footfalls as they ascended to the second story. "Over there." Sage indicated a spiraling staircase, similar to the ice castle at the Faire.

Climbing the spiraling stairs, they walked onto the third story landing where gas lamps were easing the gloom into the corners. "Do you think it's odd that the lamps are lit?" Tegan said.

Sage was wondering the same thing. "In here." She went through a doorway into a dark room. Turpentine and paint fumes permeated the air, and stacks of canvas boards, a palette, brushes, and an easel occupied the room. "Somebody likes to paint," she stated. "The balcony."

Sage couldn't open the balcony door, frozen shut.

"Let me," her brother offered.

"I got this." Determination fortified her voice. She chafed her hands together and sparks ignited. Spreading her fingers, she deiced the doors mechanism. "Hah, I did it."

"Something Crew taught you?"

"In a way."

Stationing themselves on the balcony, Sage spied a rask sneaking by the side of the stable. Drawing the cord of her bow, she steadied herself with a calming breath, and let it fly. The rask jolted, the arrow punctured his throat.

"Good shot." Tegan praised.

"I was aiming for his heart."

"Still a great shot." Tegan leaned over the balustrade. "Cool watchtower, eh?"

Sage's teeth chattered.

"Geez, where's your coat?" Tegan unbelted his fur and slung it over her.

"Keep it." She pushed it off, but her brother dragged it back around her.

"I'm used to the cold, working the mines in the winter."

Sage spotted the oracle and Boris exiting the mansion. "Here they come." Becoming alert, Sage and Tegan surveyed the premises. "With this blanket of snow, we can see them coming."

"There—" Tegan released a hex, blasting a troll into a tree. "Awesome. I wasn't sure my magic would go the distance."

"You're selling yourself short, brother."

"They're making a head-on assault. Luckily the snow is slowing them down." Tegan cast spell after spell, though his magic hadn't the clout to reach the bridge. "There's the mallusks."

"They're flinging quills at them." Sage's arrow stabbed a mallusk in the shoulder. She sailed another, shaving the side of his head. "Madam and Boris are moving toward the door."

"They must be done getting the wards up. Let's get out of the cold."

"I thought you were used to the cold?" she joked, handing her brother his coat, and less stressed with the erected shields.

"Not these sub-zero temps." Tegan draped his fur across his shoulders. "Now what?"

"At least Crew found his brother," Sage said, voice dismal.

Tegan stalled and turned to face her. "He did? Don't tell me." He rolled his eyes. "*James?*"

She nodded.

"Cripes. Probably not what he expected."

The suspenders that had been keeping Sage's pants from riding down her hips popped off her shoulder. She tugged it in place. It felt like a lifetime ago when Crew had fixed the clip.

Her face had been hotter than Mama's frying pan. "Before we leave, we're going to find our sisters. Turn this place inside out. I'll start up here. Go to the second level and search every room."

She was watching her brother cruising down the spiral staircase when someone tapped her on her shoulder.

Jumping out of her skin, she whirled around. "James. You scared me."

FORTY-TWO
CREW

Crew materialized in the queen's chambers. Expecting to see her suffering, on her deathbed, instead, she was wrapped in an embrace, with Paphos, kissing him.

It was evident, Aerestol and the queen shared a history. *Long-lost lovers perhaps?*

Besides the disbelief of their coupling embrace, astounding him was the casement window that framed their forms. The high-towered window overlooked lush woodlands and tributaries of sparkling waters.

The wizard, downright taken by the queen, hadn't seen Crew appear. And a revitalized Queen Esta was again an exalted beauty. She drew away from Aerestol. "Crew." Her fragile voice belied her youthful manifestation. "Thank you for bringing Griggan home." Indeed, she knew. Crew spotted the pensieve with its mirrored liquid in the corner. "Lay him here." She indicated the bed with mussed blankets.

"How did you get here?" said the wizard, eyes razor-sharp. "What's going on?" His gaze departed from Crew and lashed to the queen.

"Leggan," she called him by his actual name, "if we are going through with this, then we need a witness. I summoned him here." The queen clung to the bedpost and winked. Whatever power she'd been utilizing, it began to wane. He read it on her woeful brow, the crescent moon and pearlescent star markings on her forehead were dulling. Her chamber that had been permeated in verdant greenery, perfumed honeysuckle, wisteria, and cloaked in flowering morning glories, was all a sham. The bountiful veneer was withering like the queen. Denuding silky petals drifted from their vines like flakes of snow.

Crew respectfully laid the redcap on the bed. He withdrew Griggs' blade from its sheath and, folding his arms across his chest, fit the hilt into his hands. Next, he adjusted the goblin's crusty, blood-soaked cap on his head. In a strangled tone, Crew said, "Sleep well, my good and faithful friend."

Having a witness, as Esta declared, was reweaving the truth. Fae didn't join themselves in holy matrimony like mortals. Crowning a monarch, especially in the High Courts, comprised of pomp, courtiers, and nightly revels. However, the wizard seemed content to get on with the show.

Aerestol, Leggan, the wizard, the doctor didn't have a clue.

When the queen fabricated the second ring, an innovative trinket, she'd ensconced an amalgam to bind Leggan, and the incantations had depleted what little breath remained in her. And when the time came, she'd clarified that Crew was indispensable. She would be in need of his energy. The queen made him swear an oath, to return after the wizard put it on.

Obviously, she'd rallied to conjure the scene before him.

"Come here." Esta motioned to the wizard. "Stand before me."

Aerestol paused by an oval-looking glass that was implanted into the trunk of a tree. He preened, examining his reflection. Sauntering around the bedposts, arms extended, he said, "My Queen." She didn't extend him the courtesy of holding his hands.

"Leggan has accepted my proposal of becoming my king, a monarch to rule my kingdom," she said to Crew. "We have an understanding, to be subservient to one another till death do us part."

After the phrase, till death do us part, Leggan chuckled. "My Queen, we will share everything for millenniums to come. Together, by uniting our magic, our kingdom will stretch far and wide. Creating a legacy we will trounce mortal lands, taking what should have been ours. Enslaving mortals as they have enslaved us."

Queen Esta's mouth quirked. "Show me the ring." Leggan held out his arm, a glint touched upon the ring. The queen chanted, moving her hand over his. "With this ring, you are tied to me and to my kingdom."

Crew sent forth his energy, uniting with the queen's. Sensing her debilitating condition, he amplified his power, sustaining the failing queen.

Flittering, translucent ribbons emerged from the silver trinket, twining Leggan's hand, his wrist, his arm. Esta continued, "Ribbons of honor, loyalty, and fidelity binding you to this kingdom." Myriads of ribbons obeying the queen's incantations were interlocking Leggan's body, leaving no part of him exposed. "I call upon the gods to sanctify this accord." She paused, drawing a breath. "Leggan, you are now spellbound. My Kingdom of Despair and Ruins has accepted their new king. King Leggan Dnegos."

The translucent, woven ribbons faded.

Queen Esta nodded, pleased with the outcome. Her shoulders feebly stooped, her vigor forsaking her. Using the bedpost like a crutch, she moved to the vacant side of the bed and lowered next to Grigg's, who looked serene in death.

"Dearest Esta, I beg of you to show me your kingdom and its prestigious fiefdom." Aerestol's sanctimonious smirk latched onto Crew. "As monarch, I impose my first edict. Decreeing, the name and person of Crew Asgard be forever banned."

"You might not wish to impose such an edict." Queen Esta's voice thinned like honey in water. "I enacted the same decree with my cousin, Mab. And I lost my chance for redemption and exoneration."

The wizard's head swished toward the queen. "Esta, are you ill?"

The queen's beauty was rapidly diminishing. Her snow-white hair mutated into layers of spindly gray, and the markings on her forehead, the crescent moon and star, warped into grooved wrinkles. The wretched hag had returned.

"What is this charade," Aerestol crowed. "Before you croak, Esta, you are coming to Wintervine. You *will* impart your wisdom to me." Rushing over to her, he clutched her arm and tried lugging her from the bed.

Crew shoved him away. "Let her die in peace."

"Crew, I wish we had more time. I could teach you so much." She attempted to smile and failed miserably. "I hope by helping you, the gods will be lenient with me. I triggered anarchy amongst the Courts and the creatures. I was an unforgiving queen, full of brutal power. I created an ill-conceived progeny." Her snicker, a gasping cough.

"Aye, misbegottens." He knelt beside the bed.

"I had the flair to shape-shift, before…" her voice ebbing in and out, "a lynx." Her hand groped across the bed, rounding her fingers on Griggs' arm. "Taking my companion with me." Queen Esta's cat eyes dilated and glazed.

The queen and Griggs' body decomposed, flesh and bones disintegrated into white ash. A mysterious wind whipped about the chamber, vanquishing the ashes.

"We went through these theatrics for nothing," the wizard seethed, throwing his arms up. "Why waste my time? So your little friends can make a getaway while I was being detained? Well guess what, *boy*?" he said contemptuously. "James knows what to do. And they're not going anywhere."

Crew stood his ground. "Well guess what, *King Leggan*, you're not going anywhere either." Crew held aloft his ringed hand, catching Aerestol's eyes. Crew slipped off the relic and left the wizard to rot in his kingdom.

FORTY-THREE
CREW

Crew reappeared into the cavernous mountain, deserted by the looks of it. He unbelted his coat and rammed the ring into the inner pocket of his vest for safekeeping. Why? He didn't know. Maybe for memory sake. Doubting he'd ever have use or need of it again.

Leggan Dnegos aka Aerestol Paphos' slave trade and his sadistic experiments had been terminated. Heading into the far room, making sure not a creature was stirring, he saw Sage's fur coat. Snatching it, he sped along the passageway that led into the mansion.

"Crew—" Tegan barked, coming down the grand staircase. "You're back."

Boris and Madam Rouge rushed out from the parlor. Anxiety whittling their expressions as they shifted, glancing behind him.

Crew said, "Are you expecting somebody else?"

"Where is he?" Madam asked, clasping her hands.

"He's never coming back." Crew lobbed Sage's coat over the newel post of the staircase.

Tegan clapped a hand on Crew's back. "You killed him?"

"Just desserts. I say." Boris bobbed his head.

"He's not dead. He's alive."

"What?" The oracle recoiled, breathing heavy. "He'll destroy me. He'll destroy all of us." Ripe with trepidation, she whined and passed a hand over her forehead. "Why didn't you kill him?"

Looking from face to fretful face, Crew witnessed the fear one man could inspire. "By killing him, he'd get off easy. Aerestol has to suffer. Serving a life sentence, imprisoned for the crimes he's committed will drive him mad. Aye, a punishment well deserved."

Their overwrought expressions subtlety softened.

"Imprisoned? Where?" Boris inquired.

"In another realm. In the Kingdom of Despair and Ruins."

"He'll get out," the oracle alleged. "I know Aerestol. He's relentless."

"It's not possible. Believe me."

"What makes you so sure?" Tegan added his voice.

"It's a long story." Crew removed his cap, and brushed fingers into his mane of unruly hair. "I'll tell you on the journey home." His gaze skipped over them. "Where's Sage?"

Tegan peered up the staircase. "She was right behind me."

A howling screech resonated from somewhere above them.

Crew raced up the stairs with Tegan a breath away. Landing on the second story, Sage was stepping off the spiraling staircase.

"Tegan!" Eadith squealed, her arms hugging Sage's neck. She spread her wings and glided into her brother's arms. "I missed you so much."

Behind Sage, James approached.

"She's been here the whole time." Sage's glorious smile was for James alone. "He kept her safe, away from his father."

"Let's all go downstairs." Crew scowled, not trusting the boy after what he did to Dirge. "James can explain himself."

Gathered in the parlor, each of them showed signs of fatigue, drained of energy. Crew noticed that somebody had disposed of the dead bodies. From the archway Boris said, "I cook dinner long time ago. I warm up. We eat. We sleep."

"Aye," Crew acceded. "There's a couple hours before daybreak. We need rest before getting on the road."

"I can't wait to leave this place," Madam Rouge said through her yawning.

Settled into the overstuffed sofa, little Eadith had fallen asleep in Tegan's arms. He kissed her forehead, and rested his head on the back of the cushion.

"James," Crew paced the room, his arms braced behind him, "explain how you helped Eadith."

"I heard what you did to my father." James evaded the question. Sequestered from the group, and sitting by the window, he sloped forward bracketing his elbows on his legs. "I…I can't say I blame you. He…he wasn't a good person. Um, it was—"

"He tortured him," the oracle interjected. "The poor boy has never known kindness. Aerestol kept him alive for one purpose, using him like a lab rat."

"I didn't cut off Dirge's leg, if that's what you're thinking," James supplied. "My father said that to upset you. He likes—liked head games."

Sage broke in, "Tell him how you saved Eadith."

Sage sat next to Tegan. Her eyes never left Eadith until she turned and focused on James and smiled. A weary smile, yet radiant. For the first time since arriving at the mansion, Crew couldn't take his eyes off her. Surviving through pain and heartache, there hadn't been a moment of reprieve. And now she acted as though his brother were the hero of her story.

"Rasks brought Eadith to the house when my father was gone on…on business." Crew imagined what kind of adulterated business Doctor Frankenstein had been on. "I hid her in the tower, afraid of what he had planned for her." James talked down to the floor, fiddling with his fingers.

At least the boy was self-effacing. "Aerestol hired them," Crew said and walked behind the sofa. "I can't say for certain if his thugs were hired to kill the Steele's and kidnap Eadith, or since they couldn't find Sage, they took the next best thing. Her little sister. With a prize like that, didn't they ask your father for payment?" Crew turned to James, eyes tapering.

"Umm. They...um, had an accident."

In soft tone, so not to wake Eadith, Tegan said, "You killed them?"

"They fell into the ravine when the bridge gave out." James unrolled his spine, and inclined into the chair. His crestfallen gaze pinned on Sage, longing for her absolution. "My father returned home sooner than expected. I kept Eadith hidden. It's rare when he remains here for long periods of time unless he's in his laboratory. I was waiting for him to leave, go off on one of his trips. I told Eadith I'd bring her home, to Alderwood."

Silence dropped into the room.

Crew sank into the recliner, stress gradually leaching out of his body. The hearths fire and splintering embers took center stage. A comforting sound, warming bones and mind. Each of them resting, mulling over private thoughts while imbibing a bouquet of Boris' spicey cuisine.

Madam Rouge, her tone docile, ruined the solitude. "James, would you be willing to work with the Circus Faire? You could stay with me during the Faire's hiatus, or at least find lodging preferably more temperate than Wintervine."

Three drowsy pairs of eyes strayed from the oracle to James. Crew hadn't given the boy, his brother, much consideration as to his living arrangements. He had zilch to offer. Since Polk's death he'd been on the run, vicariously living Polk's life under false pretenses. He had done what he set out to do: finding his long-lost brother and saving Sage from a demented doctor. The topper, Eadith was safe, thanks to James, although, failed to find Edras.

James hemmed and hawed, lifting his shoulders, staring at each of them in turn. "I...I think I would like that. I... Crew, I'd like to get to know, um, my...my brother."

Intaking a breath, Sage said, "You overheard Tegan and I talking upstairs?" James gave her an evasive head tilt. "Because as soon as my brother left, you poked me on the shoulder. I wondered if you'd heard us." An apology rang out of Sage's gaze toward Crew.

"That's impossible." Madam hopped to her feet; her bouffant hairdo had plunged into disarray. "James' brother was murdered, buried at the Foundling Orphanage. I saw the body with my own eyes."

Crew held his tongue. Maybe it was better to let them believe him to be dead. He'd been a loner. He didn't need a younger brother messing with his routine. Queen Esta had explained who he was. What he was. Let it go at that.

"Crew, tell her," Tegan prompted. Crew rolled his lips in and out of his mouth. "We didn't go through hell and back for nothing. *Tell her.*"

As an alternative of telling her what he knew, Crew said, "You're the great oracle. What do you see?"

Madam fastened her knuckles on her hips. "I can't read you, boy. I never could." She scoffed, setting her sights on him. "I'd been aware of Polk's association with Aerestol, calling him his benefactor. And when he showed up with a kid, I never believed his story. When I saw your eyes, I was intrigued." She let her arms fall to her side and stepped closer to him.

Crew pushed himself back into the recliner, her examination disconcerting.

"They reminded me of *someone*." A speculative, deep crease formed between her eyebrows. "Over twenty years ago, I met a young man— like you." Her slitty eyes widened. Shaking her head and bringing a closed fist to her mouth, she talked into her hand, the words muddled. "Something stopped me from seeing it."

Crew dunked his chin to his chest, allowing his long, black hair to spill over his forehead, cloaking his features.

"My sister was only sixteen when she ran away with a boy. A boy with eyes like yours, being hunted by patrolling guards of the High Court." She blinked, rinsing watery eyes. "James, you are a spitting image of my sister, Kia." Slinging her gaze back to Crew, she said, "And you are his son. Balen."

She twisted away and went toward the hearth. Hugging herself, she appeared mesmerized by frolicking flames. Crew and James locked eyes, warring with one another, until James lowered his gaze.

"Kia came to me under the dark of night. Dying of consumption." Madam spoke into the mouth of the hearth, the past unfolding. "A bundled baby in her arms and holding the hand of a child. King Vectors army finally caught up to Balen and assassinated him. My sister fled, not for her life, but for their children. It's forbidden for creatures to mate with other species. We all know who and what I'm talking about." She remained stagnant. "After she'd succumbed, I left her children on the porch of the Foundling Orphanage. Where no one would know what they were."

"When did you tell Aerestol?" Sage presumed.

Madam turned from the hearth, revealing her misery. Overflowing tears streamed down her cheeks. "It is my guilt to bear. My biggest regret." She dabbed dripping tears from her chin. "Kia shouldn't have come back, leaving me with…" she paused and pressed fingers to her nose, attempting to compose herself. "I wasn't in a good place after my sister passed. When Aerestol came for a reading, he saw the children. I broke down, telling him about Kia and Balen. He was kind and consoling. It was his idea to leave them at the orphanage. Years later, I discovered he'd known Balen. A man with extraordinary powers."

FORTY-FOUR
SAGE

Throughout the hours of restless slumber, Sage was plagued by harrowing screams and sobbing spirits. Grinding the heels of her hands to her eyes, she flattened the burden from her brow and went to the window. The incredible winter wonderland's lackadaisical snowflakes continued to bury the bloody massacre below. Her second-story room overlooked the stables and beyond, the treacherous ravine, minus the bridge.

There was a knock on the door. The young dwarf, Crispin, stood in the hall tendering a ceramic pitcher of water. It was a startling reunion because numerous dwarves, and sentries for the wizard, had been slain.

"Boris thought you might like to wash before you get on the road." Filled with appreciation she took his offering. "I know what you're thinking." His rosy cheeks shined, and a smattering of flimsy whiskers dotted his youthful face. "Me and my cousins, Harthorn and Svel, were lackies for the wizard, tis all. Not part of his legion of sentinels."

She took his explanation with a grain of salt. "Thanks for the water." Using her hip to close the door, Crispin blocked its path with the toe of his boot.

"Ahem, I'm supposed to tell you the carriage is packed and ready to go. Crew said to," he quoted with his fingers, "get a move on."

"Did he now?" she said smartly. "Tell him to hold his horses."

Twenty minutes later, they mobilized on the snowy mountain peering upward at the frozen structure. "We are in agreement," Crew stated, his words fogging. "Our plan was to destroy the Frankenstein doctor. End the savagery of suffering souls who endured here. Put them to rest for all eternity. Sage, we have the power to do this." She gave him an embolden nod of consent. "Ready?"

Crew glided his hand into hers, lacing their fingers. Uniting their dynamic energy, they raised their arms. An intensity, unlike Sage had ever experienced, surged through her.

"Hold your sights, concentrate on the mansion," Crew uttered. "I'm with you." A volcanic force vibrated the mountain. "Ste-e-e-ady."

Huge portions of the façade cracked. Saw-toothed veins stemmed from the uppermost tower to the ground. There was an ear-shattering explosion, pulverizing and imploding Aerestol's mansion.

Not delaying until the ice had settled, Crew and Sage mounted their horses, which they'd taken from the stables before setting free the livestock.

"Hyah!" Spurring their mounts toward the ravine, the four-horse carriage and its passengers waited for them.

Embarking from the enclosed carriage, Tegan, Madam Rouge, Boris, James, and little Eadith assembled on the ravine's precipice.

"The wizard has no authority or influence here," Crew said. "We will make a bridge to pass over."

A league of misfits had bonded in harmony, and by linking their mystical talents, they created, section by section, a new, sturdier bridge. Together, they were a composite of tenacious willpower, fortitude, and faith.

Sage gnawed on a fingernail as Crew slowly headed across the bridge, giving it a thorough inspection from end to end. He procrastinated every once in a while to check something, and then went on. Beneath the band of his cap, his damp hair curled at the tips. He must have ducked his head into a bucket of water to wash it, something she wished she'd thought of before they'd left. She flipped the hood of her coat up to cover herself. He hadn't shaved since they'd gotten off Caravel and his scruff had grown into an established mustache and beard. It made him appear older, and disturbingly, more roguish and handsome.

"Get down from there," Crew ordered Crispin, who sat on the bench manning the reins of the horses. "I'm taking the team across. Make sure it holds." While the dwarf clambered down, Crew went to the lead horse. Petting his flank and his neck, he held the horse's muzzle over his shoulder.

What had he whispered into the horse's ear? Her brother joined Crew and rounded his fingers onto the harness of the second lead horse.

"I'm doing this alone," Crew said to Tegan.

"We'll cross together."

"No. We won't." Crew gave a curt shake of his head. "You now have a family to provide for, to protect." Tegan glimpsed Sage, holding Eadith's hand. "I'm pretty sure the bridge is sound, but I can't take that chance. If it goes down, it's up to you to figure another way down this damn mountain. Tegan, I'm counting on you."

"You have a family now too."

"James doesn't need me."

I need you! Implored Sage's inner voice. She'd depended on him, throughout this dreadful escapade, she came to trust him.

She'd been conflicted after the incident at the ice castle, and then contending with grievous emotions after the loss of her family. Enduring through their daily dilemma's, she found herself battling her exacerbating desire for Crew. She'd been forging her heart in galvanized steel because she assumed, if they'd survived, he'd merely leave again. He was a main attraction with the Circus Faire, journeying to territories far and wide. Thinking of his imminent departure, her heart ached.

Tegan lumbered toward Sage and held onto Eadith's other hand.

Crew guided the team of horses to the brink of the bridge. He didn't rush them. Petting the lead horse's muzzle, using his soothing, pitching tone, he urged them onward. The bay jerked its head, neighed, and led the team forward.

Clomping hooves touched down on the bridge, next came the rotating wheels of the carriage. Halfway across, there was a strident snap and a pop. Crew brought the team to a halt. The rope upholding the side railing had snapped. It looked like a pendulum breezing into the steep precipice of the ravine.

Go! Go!

Shepherding the lead horse, he took tentative steps. Once they were safely across, Sage released a pent-up sigh of relief.

FORTY-FIVE
CREW

"You should've traded places with Tegan," Crew said to Sage. Their horses trotted behind the carriage with Crispin on the bench, driving the team. She pushed back the furry hood of her coat, allowing her hair to prance over her shoulders. Exiting the sheltering grove of trees into a clearing, rays of sunshine set her locks on fire. "It's bitterly cold up here."

"Maybe I'll trade places with him later." Her glowing cheeks and darkened, olive-toned skin enhanced the violet hues of her eyes. "I need to flush the stench of the past few days from my lungs. It's good to feel alive again."

Reining his horse through the accumulation of drifting snow, he'd been pondering Sage's future, not his. "Have you given any thoughts about Edras?"

"That's all I've been thinking about." Flakes of snow adhered to Sage's eyelashes. "Edras taught me everything I know. I always thought she was stronger than me. Why can't she escape from Morg? And why didn't Aerestol take Edras from him?" She wiped at the flakes thawing into her eyes.

"Good questions."

"What are you going to do when we get back to Alderwood?" she inquired. Crew let her question simmer because he hadn't a clue. "Are you going to stay with the Circus Faire, or maybe reapply to the university in the Unified Territory?"

"I haven't had a moment to consider my options." Answering honestly, though, he'd pondered the concept of making Alderwood his permanent residence. Without Polk, he'd rather live in the magical territories than with mortals. Anyway, it was where he truly belonged.

"You'd be a main attraction, a fire wrangler."

"Aye. That's if Dyke will take me back. With the oracle and I absent at the height of the Faire, he'll be a cantankerous grouch because of coin that could have been had."

Perusing the downhill-sloping mountainside with its terrain cloaked in snow, Crew pulled back on the reins. "Whoa." Stalling on a flat plateau, the carriage rolled along the manmade channel. Sage joined him. Side by side, their mounts nickered, bobbing regal heads and muzzles expelling mists of air.

"James showed me his leg," she said for no particular reason. "He barely balked when I hit it with an arrow."

"Can you heal it?"

"It's withered, hardly any muscle left. He'll lose it soon."

"I asked, can you heal it?" Crew stated.

She turned her dazzling eyes on him. "*You* can heal it. You have the power, same as me."

It had been a while since they'd been alone. And she wasn't snarling, ready to scratch his eyes out of his head. He took his time, scrutinizing and admiring her striking beauty. "Sage, can you turn your head and lift up your hair?"

"Why?"

"Amuse me, please."

Swerving away from him on the saddle, she gathered her hair and pulled it up, exposing the base of her neck. Crew brushed the tip of his finger across the faint mark of a crescent moon and star. He felt a tremor going through her.

"What's there?"

"Look." He removed his cap and forked fingers into the hair behind his ear, showing her the similar mark. "We both have it."

"Edras has it too. I thought it was a birth mark, nothing more."

"We have a lot in common. Perhaps I can fill in the blanks of your Doloran progeny where Edras couldn't."

"Huh?" Her eyes rounded.

"Your Papa engraved a crescent moon and a star on those earbobs of yours. He must have known."

She touched the tips of her ears where astonishingly, the quaint jewelry had remained intact with the aid of Papa's magic. "Tell me more."

"It'll make interesting dialogue for our journey." He leaned toward her and she met him in the middle. Their lips coming together in a heart-rendering kiss. An emotional kiss of loss, death, pain and sorrow. And most of all hope. Hope for new beginnings. New adventures. New love. Crew glided his fingers around her neck, yearning for more. And Sage clutched his arm, holding onto him.

As they parted, he said, "I know where I'm going when we get back."

"Where?"

"To Finnick Row. Demelda had a cottage there. She hid an ancient tome, a grimoire inscribed with incantations. It would be disastrous if it fell into the wrong hands."

"Maybe it'll lead us to Edras."

"Sounds like a plan." Crew smiled and leaned in for another kiss.

ACKNOWLEDGEMENTS

Thank you, God, for everything

I spent years creating Defy the Stars, and it's changed quite a bit from that first draft. I assume most writers can relate to the endless revisions and editing, those moments working on a single sentence or paragraph, rewriting and/or rephrasing it. When I felt I was on the right track, I had fun writing the whimsical aspects of the enchanted Circus Faire and the diverse inhabitants.

I'd like to thank my beta readers, Noelle Manzella and Nicole Falkner. They helped by putting me on the right track when my writing had gone astray.

Melissa Levine of Red Pen Editing worked her own magic, polishing and tightening this project. Thank you, Melissa.

A Great Big Thank You to Melissa Stevens of The Illustrated Author and Design Services! Melissa has outdone herself on this Freaking Magnificent Cover! I'm so, so in Love with it! And the interior is Absolutely Freaking Amazing too!

My heart goes out to all those who have supported me over the years. My family, friends, and my readers, and those wonderful people who took the time to post reviews.

www.ingramcontent.com/pod-product-compliance
Lightning Source LLC
LaVergne TN
LVHW042252070526
838201LV00106B/303/J